Tobacco Sticks

William Elliott Hazelgrove

Pantonne Press, Inc.
329 West 18th Street
Chicago, Illinois 60616

OTHER PANTONNE PRESS BOOKS BY
WILLIAM ELLIOT HAZELGROVE
Ripples

Tobacco Sticks
A Pantonne Press Book
Pantonne Press, Inc.
329 W. 18th St.
Chicago, IL 60616

For information:
Pantonne Press, Inc., 329 W. 18th Street, Chicago, Illinois, 60616

Library of Congress Card Catalog Number: 94--061347

ISBN 0-9630052-8-6

All of the events and characters depicted in this book are fictional.

Printed in the United States of America.

To Kitty

"I suppose that poetry is a Northern man's dream of the South."

—F. Scott Fitzgerald
The Last of the Belles

Tobacco Sticks

PROLOGUE

There is a scrapbook. The paper has turned to a rich sepia and crumbles when it is moved. The pages are a thin and delicate cardboard and the newspaper articles have faded along with the pictures that have no gloss and look hopelessly grainy. The scrapbook has that reassuring smell of old books. It smells of permanence, of the way things used to be. These people did not record their movements as we do today in so many magnetic impulses on so many tapes. Their history came down to a brown box in a basement that has been closed for many years. The newspaper articles seem quaint and innocent by today's standards. There were actually rules of engagement and even adversaries were allowed dignity. The snapshots show people in various moments of immortality: at the beach, dressed for dinner, sitting on a wide Southern porch. They are of a time when this country was still of the small-town, the community we had only to fit into and nestle our lives. We, after all, are not a people of big cities, but really a small town people who react to the carnage of the day with that sensibility. But now there are the tiny sprinkles of brown pulp on the carpet as I put the scrapbook back. I kneel down and pick them out of the short rough and go to the back door. It is cold and dark and the November wind shows no mercy. I sprinkle the confetti to the Chicago night and watch the pieces ride the wind, and I see, even now, after all these years, the wind blows toward the South.

1

The sky and the land were gray-cold and went together in the distance. The field rows were tipped with frost and slaves worked in the seed beds and put the tobacco in the cold, black dirt. They worked on their knees, covering the mounds with manure, then broke branches over the ground against the frost. The planter watched from his horse and could see their breath go into the ground. It was twelve days after Christmas and the best time for planting.

The summer my brother came home from the war was so hot they had to repave the soft tar of Hermitage Street twice. I remember watching the crews, their white t-shirts glowing in the July night with the gravel smoke dancing white under a low moon. It was the last war summer and we had received a telegram saying Lucas had been wounded. First we thought he had been shot in the leg, then it became the foot.

And even then I didn't believe he was coming home. The war was a twelve-year-old's imagination and men disappeared magically the way they appeared. The war had been carried on in newspapers and through the radio, but Richmond was still a Southern town that when not called upon to act as a city, fell back asleep on the rolling hills of Virginia. But Lucas brought the war home and that was the beginning of everything.

My family had sailed from England 200 years before to escape the confines of that island along with the other adventurers, entrepreneurs, missionaries, and criminals. I think after the long voyage we must have had enough adventure, because we settled along the James River and didn't bother moving till we were forced to. We were tobacco growers and enjoyed the spoils of the slave economy so much we donated a sergeant to an artillery unit in the Revolution, then produced a commodore for the Confederate Navy. Reconstruction came and the land went for taxes.

The family migrated to Richmond and there were rumors of a saloon, followed by a blacksmiths, a wholesale grocery, and then it gets cloudy till my father, Burke Hartwell, legitimized the whole migration by taking up law.

Richmond was a busy city in 1945. The war years vitalized the town along with the rest of the country, but the radio was still something of a marvel, people traveled mostly by train, and doors were still left unlocked.

There were no strangers in 1945. Nobody moved from our neighborhood. People called each other by their first names and walked between houses, staying for lunch, then dinner, and not going home till the heat of the day had long passed into the night. Nothing had really changed for us. The war produced rubber drives, tin drives, bond drives, and lots of impassioned speeches, but the day-to-day slowed time of Richmond remained unchanged.

But here was Lucas. He looked thinner, less color, and walked with a cane.

"Hey Lucas!" I yelled, running toward him as he bumped down the sidewalk.

He smiled darkly, his eyes crinkling.

"How you been, boy?"

I ran up and hugged him with the rough Army material scraping my cheek. He leaned on his cane.

"Brought something for you."

He reached into his belt and pulled out a soft green Army hat with a bar on the front.

"I can have this?"

"I don't need it anymore."

I took the narrow V-shaped hat and it promptly slid down on my forehead and stayed just above my eyes. It smelled like burlap in a trunk.

"Now you're in the army, Lee," Lucas nodded, keeping his one foot just above the ground.

"Thanks!"

Jimmy and Clay ran up behind me.

"You two sure are a lot taller than I remember."

Jimmy stared at his foot and pointed.

"That where you got shot?"

Lucas looked down, nodding slowly.

"Yep, right in the arch."

Jimmy's dark eyes grew.

"We'll catch up later, Lee," he said, beginning to hobble off. "—better go see Daddy and Mother."

"Got lots of new books for you, Lucas," I hollered after him.

"Good," he called back. "Think I'm going to be doing a lot of reading."

I stared at the foot he favored as he went down the sidewalk.

"You coming or not?"

Jimmy's face bunched up under his dark crew-cut. I pulled the hat down on my head and ran back across the close-clipped grass to the side yard. Our house was a white clapboard, three-story structure with a horseshoe driveway that pushed the house back from the road. Six white columns marched across the front porch in six even spaces, the front lawn running a half acre to the road with the backyard rolling out a full two acres to a line of trees. We called it Buckeye and to this day I'm not exactly sure where the name came from, except that somewhere on my mother's side of the family there was a summer place rumored to be called by that name.

Clay and Jimmy ran into the backyard between white sheets heavy with moisture.

"Get away from there! I don't want them sheets coming down, Lee!"

Addie's face shined in the gloom. She stood in the back doorway

9

with her hands on her hips, her gray uniform melting into the shadows until only the white sleeves were visible.

"You all go on and play in the woods—don't have no time to fool with you!"

I ran from Addie's voice, passing between the clean sheets, breathing a faint perfume of soap. Jimmy and Clay huddled between the two lines.

"Addie gone?"

"She is," I grunted.

Jimmy straightened up, peering over the line. He ducked back down.

"Let's go to the tree house."

Clay pushed his glasses up on his nose, his hair less blond against the sheets.

"Think Addie thought I was you, Lee."

"She knew it was me," I said, walking toward the woods.

Clay shook his head.

"Seemed mad as hell!"

"'Cause of y'all—"

"She wasn't that mad," Jimmy said, walking ahead with a weed dangling from his mouth.

"*You* won't catch hell at dinner."

The crickets breathed around us and dragonflies swerved and darted around the honeysuckle bordering the yard. I wiped my forehead, minding the poison ivy along the edge of the grass, slipping between bushes onto the dirt path snaking into the woods. We followed the brown line to a large oak with boards climbing to a leaning box of plywood in the cradle of the tree.

I climbed the boards with the bark running close to my face and the tree ants disappearing into holes, grabbing the rough angled boards hand over hand till I pushed up against a piece of plywood and was inside the sawdust-smelling box. Clay and Jimmy pulled themselves up and we placed the piece of plywood back over the opening. I reached into a knothole and pulled out a dirty, crumpled pack of Wing cigarettes.

The slanting sun filtered through the hanging smoke and greenery in the slow pulse of another day where smoking in the tree house had become a ritual of the summer. Jimmy lived down the street and Clay was across from Buckeye, our universe bounded behind by the woods that camouflaged all our activities—smoking being the main one.

I watched Jimmy puff his cigarette red.

"You inhaling?"

"Course I am."

Jimmy took a deep pull on the cigarette, his eyes watering and his face becoming darker before giving forth the smoke, cigarette, and spit, then beating the dusty floor of the tree house for air. I turned and watched the smoke glide out, the drone of cicadas winding up and then slowly back down.

"Want to go on down to the graveyard?"

Clay stared into the cavernous woods, the light nestled in the treetops reflecting on his glasses.

"Don't know, Lee, getting dark—"

"Ah, come on...." Jimmy croaked, looking for lost dignity. "You ain't chicken, are you?"

"Yes!"

Jimmy stood up and shook his head.

"Let's go, Lee."

"I'll go too," Clay cursed, standing up.

"Maybe old man Hillman will be there."

Clay stared at him.

"Why would he be there?"

Jimmy shrugged.

"Never know."

The Hillmans owned the property that bordered ours and no one was sure where their property began and Buckeye ended, but the line was deep in the woods so no one really cared either. The Hillmans were the wealthiest family in Richmond and probably all of Virginia. The Hillman steel mills had become bigger during the war years and blackened the skyline of Richmond with smoke during the day and roared through the night. Long ago we had discovered the Hillman burial ground lay in what we considered "our woods."

The path shrunk to a line of horizon light on the forest floor. We moved into the dense part of the woods and it became darker. Leaves

11

brushed us with the early damp of nightfall. Greedy vines and plants snaked up trees in the low parts of the woods. A crow flapped out from a tree, dark and majestic. I saw the sharp points of iron jutting against the leaves as the small cemetery took form from the forest. Vines had woven around the black iron so thickly the gravestones were hidden.

I came to the entrance and paused. The gate was already open. I peered through to the mossy blue headstones and didn't move. Jimmy bumped me from behind.

"Hey, what—"

"Quiet!

We pressed against the vines on the fence.

"She's beautiful!" Clay whispered next to me, clinging to the iron rods.

The apparition moved past us, her hair and dress shimmering in the gloom. The mossy dinginess of the stones took fire as she knelt and placed a cluster of red and yellow flowers in front of a headstone. She removed wet leaves from the top of the white marble.

"Who's she?" Jimmy whispered.

"—think she's Mr. Hillman's daughter."

A voice floated through the wet air and was lost, then came clear as she knelt in front of the grave.

"I brought you chrysanthemums, Mother—you can look at them whenever you want now."

Her voice went away with a rustling in the trees, then came back with the stillness. She seemed to crumple, her head down in her hand, then her crying was flowing across the dead air like current.

"Her mother must have died," Clay whispered.

"Last summer, ya dope," Jimmy whispered back. "Our yardman Roy says she was murdered!"

Clay turned.

"How Roy know that?"

"She was sick," I said, remembering Mrs. Hillman's sudden death the summer before.

I shifted my position, stepping on Clay's foot. He yelped and the small head turned suddenly to us. I didn't move, smelling earth and chlorophyll in the damp ivy. Her eyes flickered, heaven glistening on

12

her cheeks, then she turned back to the grave and picked up a red flower. She kissed it with a small sound, then placed it on the grave. We pressed ourselves low in the grass and vines as her footsteps faded into the forest.

"Damn! Was that something!" Jimmy exclaimed, a queer expression on his face.

Clay rolled over on the ground and looked up at the sky.

"She kissed that flower!"

"I'm going to get it," Jimmy declared, going toward the gate.

I jumped in front of him.

"Leave it."

"Why? We came down to go to the grave—"

"We shouldn't go in there."

Jimmy snorted loudly.

"I'm going!"

I looked around at the gloom descending.

"It's getting too dark—I'm going back to the tree house."

"Me too," Clay said quickly, moving for the path.

"You guys going to wait?"

"Nope," I shouted back.

"You guys ... Ah, *shit!*"

I heard his heavy footsteps behind.

"How'd your brother get shot in the foot?"

I leaned back against the plywood wall of the tree house, sucking on my damp Wing, watching the ember devour paper. I glanced at Clay and shrugged, talking through a mouthful of smoke.

"Don't know—guess some German shot him."

"My daddy says he's lucky to come home. Most of the time they have to go back to war."

I glanced lazily at Jimmy, knowing he only had sisters and felt compelled to assert his knowledge of men and war.

"It's 'cause he'd always limp that he came back," I said.

Clay's eyebrows disappeared into his hair.

"I wonder if he'll get a Silver Star like Scotty's?"

Jimmy glanced at me, rolling his eyes. Scotty was Clay's older brother who had been killed the year before. Lucas and Scotty joined the service at the same time and were together on the day he was killed. After that, Lucas quit writing letters, then came the telegram saying he had been wounded. A few months later, Clay brought Scotty back from the dead.

"Don't think he'll get a Silver Star, maybe a Purple Heart."

"Purple Heart is good," Clay nodded.

"I think so," I said, flicking ash on my shorts, rubbing it off and trying to determine if the seeing eyes of an adult could detect the gray streak.

Jimmy yawned and held his cigarette in front of him.

"Timmy Boster's dad says guys who don't want to fight shoot themselves in the foot." He paused, looking at me. "Then they get to come home."

I looked up from my shorts and stared at him.

"Shoot themselves on purpose?"

Jimmy nodded.

I tried to imagine placing a gun to my own foot and pulling the trigger, then I saw Lucas doing it and jumped to my feet. I yanked Jimmy up by his dirty shirt.

"Saying Lucas shot himself?"

He opened his eyes wide.

"No, but Timmy's dad said some guys shoot themselves in the foot...."

"And?"

Jimmy's mouth puckered like it was full of water.

"—and Lucas was wounded in the foot and maybe he wanted to come home—"

I let go of his shirt and slammed my fist into his fat stomach. I stood over him as he coughed on the dusty wooden floor.

"You're kicked out, Jimmy Mason!"

I threw the board from the entrance and climbed down the tree, marching indignantly out of the woods into the sun of the backyard. I stomped across the yard, considering going back to punch him again, cutting through the garden.

14

"Whoa there!"

Two black wrinkled eyes beneath a straw hat were level with mine. Nelson stood on his knees between the rows of corn and tomatoes.

"Where you going in such a hurry? You just about run over me!"

"Getting away from my friends!"

I looked back at the woods.

"Gittin' away from your friends?"

"Away from one of them at least," I grumbled, plopping down in the grass.

Nelson pulled off his hat and mopped his head with the rag he kept in his pocket. His white t-shirt clung to his back and chest between his suspenders.

"Why you doing that?"

"'Cause he's not a friend ... friends don't call other friends' brothers cowards."

Nelson turned and leaned back on his legs.

"Who callin' your brother a coward?"

"Jimmy Mason."

Nelson pushed his lips out and moved his head.

"Lucas just got wounded."

I kicked a weed back into a pile of dead vines and watched a grasshopper pop across the cut grass.

"I know—that's why I punched him," I said, trying to touch the grasshopper with a blade of grass.

Nelson leaned back down and his chewed, floppy straw hat moved from side to side.

"Don't know nobody call him that."

Nelson stood and moved down the row of brown corn stalks to the tomato vines on the white lattices. He touched different tomatoes, squeezing some, taking the bad ones off the vine. I laid back in the grass, watching cotton tinged with gold move slowly over Buckeye. I sat up and stared at Nelson.

"You ever heard of anyone shooting themselves so they didn't have to go to war?"

He stopped at a vine and bent over.

"No sir—can't say I has."

I picked up a fat blade of grass and put it between my thumbs, blowing hard. The blade squeaked loudly.

"Lee, you know that hurts these old ears."

I dropped the grass and looked at him again.

"You ever heard of someone shooting themselves so they can come home?"

"No, can't say I has." Nelson was down on his knees in the corn again. "Jimmy say that?"

"Yes he did, the son of a bitch!"

I enjoyed the way I could cuss around Nelson.

"Don't sound right to me." He opened a stalk and broke off a white husk-covered piece of corn. "You want some of this corn, Lee?"

"Sure."

Nelson walked over, pulling off the husk and silk. He broke it in half and handed me a piece. I bit into the corn and tasted the tough, sweet kernels.

Nelson sat down next to me.

"Corn ought to be just right come fall."

"Tastes good now."

Nelson shook his head slowly, his eyes on the tawny stalks.

"No sir, not till the fall."

2

*The planter rode through the trees down to the seed beds.
The tobacco was small from his horse, then the leaves were
dollar size in his hand. He felt the dirt in his fingers. The
wind was sweet with tobacco and new grass as he looked up
to the sky, the land spreading around him with distant field
rows waiting for the tobacco seedlings. He swung up above
the earth and clopped away looking for rain.*

The electric kitchen clock buzzed against the wall and the faucet's leaky washer measured the time left till dinner with a tinny drop on the enamel sink. The sun glanced in through the window in a single molting glare. I pushed Lucas's Army hat back on my head, eyeing the red-topped jar of oatmeal cookies. The swinging kitchen door opened and Addie lumbered in.

"What you doing in here, Lee?"

The cabinet dishes shook as she went to the stove.

"You just a mess! You been out in the dirt or somethin'—don't have no time to be messin' with you now."

She picked up a cleaver by a cutting block, arranging the pieces of chicken.

"How come we're having fried chicken again? Just had it day 'fore yesterday," I grumbled.

Addie's large purple birthmark below her neck shook as she hacked the chicken.

17

"'Cause Lucas home."

The chicken made a dull, fleshy sound when the knife hit it.

"Sure am hungry."

"That's good, 'cause we havin' yams too," Addie said, picking up the blood-rimmed pieces and carrying them to the sink.

She turned on the faucet with her wide back to me and I looked at the jar of oatmeal cookies on the counter again.

"Biscuits too?" I asked, slipping toward the jar.

"Course we havin' biscuits—don't we always have 'em at dinner? This is one damn small chicken."

I watched the loose flesh of Addie's arm wiggle as she placed the pieces next to her on a towel, then lifted the lid of the jar and snatched a cookie.

"If I was you, I take my hand out of that cookie jar 'fore I take the cleaver and cut it off."

I kept the cookie in my hand, staring at Addie, trying to figure how she saw me.

"Ain't no girls going to talk to a boy with one hand."

I let the cookie go. She turned, wiping her hands on her apron.

"You know better than to eat close to dinner."

"I'm hungry!"

"Boys always hungry," she said, going into the pantry. "You get yourself one cookie an' then go get cleaned up," she called out.

I grabbed a cookie as she came out of the pantry with a burlap sack of potatoes.

"You better eat your dinner all I got to say."

The screen door slammed shut and Fanny came in with the sun behind her. Her light skin was darker in the half light of the kitchen. She moved slowly like a cat with her brown eyes keen and alert. She nodded to me and then Addie saw her.

"About time you got here—I got lots of work!"

Fanny was Addie's brother's daughter. He died when she was young and Fanny's mother had run off to New Orleans. Addie had taken Fanny into the house where she lived with her sister, Mary, on the colored side of town. When Addie started living at Buckeye, Fanny stayed in the house with Addie's sister.

"You start peelin' them potatoes in the pantry," Addie said, stopping long enough to rest her hands on her hips. "We got a lot of cookin' to do with the Masons comin'."

I stared at Addie.

"Masons coming to dinner?"

"Ain't that what I just said? I have to keep repeatin' myself to you, Lee. Now get on an' clean yourself up!"

I got off the stool and touched the Army hat on my head. Addie walked through the swinging door into the dining room.

"How you put up with that Addie, Lee?" Fanny asked, dumping the sack of potatoes on the table, her tight, washed-out pink shirt pulled open at the top. "You getting to be such a handsome boy now." She looked at me again. "You blushing!"

I shrugged.

"Naw—sunburn from working with Nelson."

Her eyes narrowed.

"You been working with that old Tom?"

"He's not so old."

Fanny shook her head.

"Seem pretty old to me. He thinks I talk too much—too smart for a colored woman." She paused. "He don't understand a young colored woman of today and thinks we should all be Uncle Tommin' fools like him," she said, holding the peeling knife. She smiled, moving her hips like she was dancing and leaned her head down over the potatoes, her straightened hair against her cheek. "Nelson just don't understand that I is going places." Fanny peeled a potato, the tawny muscles of her forearms rippling. "Things is different now."

The door swung open.

"*Lee!* Get up to that bathroom 'fore I take you up there myself! And Fanny, I told you to get peelin' them spuds!"

I started up the back stairs.

"And clean up that pigpen, boy!"

The tinkling keys of the piano were somewhere below the spiraling banister that descended two flights and flowed down into the hall

19

breaking between a living room on the right and a dining room on the left. In the living room—besides the piano, radio, and fireplace—was Burke's study. The open door to his office shaded the room with the faint scent of tobacco and a wall of plaques and degrees.

More than once I'd sat in the black swivel chair behind the wide mahogany desk, taking the fountain pen out of the gold holder engraved *"Burke Andrew Hartwell"* and began writing on a pad with my head slightly bent, the shelf clock ticking, the sepia light of the brass lamp touching my hand, passing order onto the world the way I had seen my father do a hundred times.

The playing started again as I walked into the dusky living room. Burke was seated at the piano and Jimmy's father was just behind. They crashed into another rendition of the song my father had written just after Pearl Harbor. Burke could only play chords and after many titles it was deemed "The Chord Song."

"Olivia? They ever going to tire of that song Burke wrote?"

Mother turned on the couch and looked at the piano.

"When they quit drinking, then it might stop sounding good to them." Mother's steel-blue eyes flickered with light from the windows. "God knows no one else will sing it."

She turned and straightened her back, reaching behind. Her hair had turned prematurely gray and she always swore it happened the day Scotty was killed, but it was white before that.

"I think my kidneys are acting up again."

Mrs. Mason looked at Mother intently. She was a big woman and her flowered print dress filled the armchair.

"Have you been taking the hot baths like Dr. Williams said?"

Mother smiled.

"First I thought it was indigestion, you know what a bad stomach I've always had. Dr. Williams says I don't have an ulcer, but I must!"

"You worry too much, Olivia—you will worry yourself into the grave," Jimmy's mother declared. "I don't wonder all your ailments are just worries!"

Mother looked up.

"Lee—Why don't you see if Addie is ready?"

I crossed the room as my father and Big Jeb left the piano for the kitchen. I followed them across the hallway into the warm kitchen. Burke went to the pantry and came out carrying a bottle of tea-colored whiskey. He lined up seven fruit jars on the center table.

"Dinner almost ready?"

Addie wiped the back of her hand across her forehead.

"Can't you wait—"

"*Mother* wants to know!"

Addie turned back to the stove, scraping a spoon against a pot of mashed potatoes.

"'Bout ready."

Big Jeb put tap water into two of the fruit jars while Burke put water and ice in the other two and filled the remaining jars with whiskey.

"One for you here, Addie."

Big Jeb raised his whiskey with the kitchen light shining on his forehead. He was one of those men who could carry his weight in a way that made him seem large rather than overweight.

"Salute."

Burke raised his fruit jar.

"To the boys overseas."

Big Jeb nodded.

"To the boys."

The jars went up in toast and they sipped the spigot water, shot the whiskey, and followed with the ice water. Burke refilled the fruit jars again and took the bottle back into the pantry. Addie picked hers up off the counter and tossed it down. Big Jeb laughed.

"Addie, you like the taste of bourbon?"

"Ain't bad," she said back by the stove. "You all just drinkin' too many things for me."

"Ever since prohibition we've drank that way and I don't know if we'll ever stop—bootleg whiskey was nasty stuff."

Burke came out of the pantry.

"We almost ready, Addie?"

"Just about."

"Lee—why don't you go get your grandmother."

I ran up the narrow back steps and crossed the second floor landing to the third floor.

"Come in!"

I opened the door to the stuffy smell of old furniture and medicine. Mimaw's white hair glowed in the shrouded light next to her bed; the large steel needles moving in small circles above a knitted shawl. She put the needles down on the bed.

"Well! I thought everyone was going to let me starve up here!"

Mimaw lived on the third floor and rarely descended except for dinners or to talk on the telephone to her sister who lived in Georgia. They would talk once a month and cry about something very sad for hours. Then they wouldn't talk for another month and when they did they would cry for hours again.

I helped her out of the bed and she put on one of her many shawls. We started down the steps.

"What's for dinner, Lee?"

"Fried chicken."

She stopped and stomped her foot.

"She *knows* I don't like fried chicken and here we are having it again!"

"'Cause of Lucas coming home."

The points of light faded from her eyes.

"Well, then, why didn't you say so?"

"I did—"

"Speak up, boy! If Lucas wants fried chicken, then that's alright with me. I guess a war hero deserves fried chicken—though I have never heard of anyone getting shot in the foot."

We reached the second landing.

"There's the war hero!"

Lucas walked out of his bedroom with his hair slicked dark and a crisp new shirt and khaki pants. He moved slowly with his cane.

"Maybe I should help *you* down the steps!"

Lucas grinned, moving awkwardly, the cane swinging from his arm.

"I'm alright."

"Boy, couldn't you think of anywhere else to get shot? Don't put your foot up—give them Germans an arm or a leg—I can't tell my friends you got shot in the *foot*—although most of my friends are dead."

Lucas nodded.

"I'll work on that."

"That's alright honey, it's good to have you home. When are you going to come up and read to me?"

"Maybe I'll get up there tomorrow."

"Well I hope so, boy. One time you'll come up and I'll just be dead and gone in that bed, so you better make it soon!"

We reached the bottom of the stairs and crossed into the dining room.

"We're having your favorite, Mother," Burke said, holding out her chair.

"Don't trifle with me, Burke. I know we're having fried chicken," she said, sitting down stiffly.

The dining table had the leaves and was covered with a white tablecloth. The chandelier tinkled with a soft wind that waved the curtains in the open French windows. Evening light speckled the room from the crystal overhead.

I sat down next to Mimaw across from Jimmy's father and mother and Lucas. Nobody said anything and I began to relax. Burke sat down at the head of the table with the cracked oil painting of my great-grandfather behind him in full uniform, one hand tucked in his dress vest, steely eyes piercing the lambent shadows. To the right of my father was an empty chair. My oldest brother Burkie had been sent by the Air Force to Canada. His chair stayed empty even when guests came. It had been the same with Lucas.

The swinging door opened and Addie wheeled in a painted metal cart trailing steam. She clunked a plate of chicken on the table in front of Burke, then followed with a bowl of mashed potatoes, gravy, corn, yams, string beans, and fruit salad. Addie padded around the table, shaking the crystal in the buffet and muttering to herself as she spooned food onto plates. Burke bowed his head.

"Father, bless us for what we are about to receive and for keeping us all safe and bringing home our family members. Amen."

23

The door swung open again and Addie returned with a streaming silver water pitcher. She set it down hard on the table and water darkened the white tablecloth. Everything went along fine till my sister began talking about the latest letter from her husband, Jim. After the war started Sally had moved back home from their apartment.

"—and he said he hopes he will get a leave soon or be transferred home—now that the war is over in Europe."

There was a silence.

"Jim wounded yet?"

Sally smiled at Mimaw.

"No, Mother Hartwell."

"In the leg you say?"

Sally paused the way people do for children.

"I say he's not been wounded."

"Why didn't you just say that!"

"Mother, that's what Sally just said."

"I heard what she said, Burke! I'm not *deaf*, you know—not yet, anyway."

Sally looked down at her plate with the silver crucifix falling from her shirt neck.

"I just thought he might have been wounded," Mimaw grumbled.

"No—he hasn't been, and I'm sure God will bring him home safe and sound—"

Mimaw snorted.

"God—"

"Sally still going to church every Sunday for all of us?" Big Jeb asked, winking at Burke.

"Every Sunday."

Addie brought in some more biscuits, but the plate caught on the edge of the table and fell to the floor.

"*Shit!* Spirits is messin' with me tonight!"

She bent down heavily, her knees making the floorboards groan. Mother stared down the table as Addie grunted up to one knee, then lifted herself the rest of the way. She turned and went back through the door with the biscuits. Mother's blue eyes bore down as a dish crashed in the kitchen.

"Lee Hartwell, take that hat off at dinner!"

I pulled the hat into in my lap.

Big Jeb's chair creaked.

"What's this I hear about you beating my boy?"

I looked at him sideways, my heart thumping into my ribs. I had almost forgotten about the afternoon. Big Jeb's eyes were twinkling, but it didn't help.

"Seems to me, you got the best of it," he said in his rumbling laugh, turning to the table. "Jimmy came home holding his stomach and I don't think he wants to tangle with Lee anymore!"

"Did you hit Jimmy?"

Big Jeb laughed again.

"Leave him alone, Olivia—boys fight all the time."

"Not this boy! Why did you hit Jimmy, Lee?"

I kept my eyes on my food and felt hot.

"Lee Hartwell...."

I let out a loud breath of defeat.

"Jimmy said ... he said some people shoot their foot to get out of the war."

The table was quiet and I could hear a dog far down the street barking in the late light of day. I looked up at the flicking yellow flames and saw Lucas's dark eyes, then his chair scraped the floor.

"If y'all will excuse me," he mumbled.

Burke began to get up.

"Son, nobody here—"

"I'm just going for some air, Daddy," he said, his voice going away with the stumping of his cane.

The screen door slammed. Burke slowly sat back down.

I was sitting on the porch swing after dinner when my father walked out.

"Walk with me to go feed the chickens," he said, tilting his head.

During the war we had started raising chickens. We kept them in the barn and Nelson fed them most of the time, but Burke would occasionally walk down and spread the corn feed in the pens. We also had

25

two goats that I had gotten as a present the Christmas before. It had started out as a practical joke between my father and Jimmy's father, but somehow the goats had never left and then Burke gave them to me on Christmas on the condition I shovel out the dung.

The worn path through the backyard was a line against the gray grass. Burke stopped and lit a Viceroy, cupping the match against his gray suit—the gold pocket watch chain on his vest glinting the night-fall. His pressed white shirt glowed unnaturally and made his bow tie darker. He adjusted his glasses and we started walking again. The tobacco floated white behind us and the dew was on my feet as we walked toward the red barn hunching under the woods.

"Lee, you're going to hear things about your brother...." He paused and his steps slowed. "Some of those things might not be too flattering. I don't know what happened over there—and I really don't care. He's back and that's all that matters—you understand?"

"Yes, sir."

"Just remember that he's your brother and needs our support."

We reached the end of the yard and stopped outside the barn. Burke paused, looking out to the lawn, his cigarette glowing brilliant then soft. The woods rustled and lived with the close insect life. I could smell the rough scent of hay in the barn.

"Lots of fireflies tonight," he murmured, putting a hand in his pocket. "Lee ... you might consider discussion before you resort to hitting someone next time." He finished his cigarette, stubbing it out with his shoe. "Friendships can only endure so many punches in the stomach."

I nodded sheepishly.

"Yes sir."

"Come on," he said, putting his hand on my shoulder. "I think we have some mighty hungry chickens on our hands."

3

Warm rain fell on the fields and forest hills and spattered in the mud doorways of the slave cabins. They went to the seed beds and knelt in the mud while the planter watched from his black horse. The tobacco plants were carried to the soft fields. Slave children walked the rows with mud over their feet and put the tobacco in the small planting hills. An older slave planted the dirt around the stem carefully with his face close to the earth. The foreman walked the rows and re-planted many of the seedlings. The covered lanterns were brought out when night came.

The war ended as mysteriously as it started. Burkie came through the door with his duffel bag over his shoulder, striding with his khaki uniform tight on his football thighs and pulling at the elbows. His size twelve service shoes cracked across the floorboards as he went right for the icebox and upended a bottle of milk. He winked at me and pulled out all the food he could lay his hands on while he told stories about the service, people, adventures, all the time winking and grinning, methodically eating four sandwiches, and then a chocolate cake. Burkie's laughter hollered through the house and it sounded like horses when he came down the steps. After he finished his feast and made Addie and Mother laugh till they cried, he promptly went into the living room, stretched out on the couch with his feet hanging off the end, and fell asleep with his mouth open. He snored majestically for the rest of the afternoon.

The first thing I noticed about Burkie was he kept his uniform on. Lucas's uniform disappeared the day he came home and I never saw it again. Lucas had been a ghost, staying in his room and venturing out mostly at night. But Burkie took possession of Buckeye and left food, the sports pages, clothes, shoes, and socks behind him. Addie chased around after him, suggesting Burkie go find another war to fight so she didn't have to work as hard. But everyone was glad he was home.

That night he took his seat to the right of Burke and told more war stories. They weren't exactly war stories—more like fishing stories. Burkie had been stationed in Canada and apparently there had been lots of time to go fishing. Addie made sure his plate was kept full till he held his hands up that he couldn't eat anymore. He slumped in the chair with his long legs stretched out to the side and drank his coffee. Burkie had my father's eyes, the color of the sky on a perfect day, and he could make them twinkle when he laughed. People said he was just like Burke.

Mimaw pointed her bony finger at him.

"Did you get wounded?"

"No, ma'am, sorry about that."

"You didn't get shot in the foot, did you?"

Burkie laughed.

"No, ma'am—these dogs are whole," he said, nodding to his shiny service shoes.

Lucas smiled darkly across the table. He had never told any stories when he came back—never talked at all about the war. Lucas and I had a secret kinship before the war. He would pass books on to me and explain why *Tom Sawyer* was a great book and *Moby Dick* was the best fantasy ever written. But now Lucas didn't say much and passed the summer by staying in his room and going out nights to the Supper Club Bar. Burke said he was going to go to college, but I thought this was more his idea than Lucas's.

28

"Don't worry about me, Mimaw—I wouldn't let anyone shoot me," he said with a big wink. "The Germans and the Japs would have had to get up pretty early to catch this ol' boy."

He laughed again and everyone smiled.

"'Specially since there weren't any in Canada," Lucas said so quietly I wasn't sure he even said it.

Burkie was still smiling, but the corners of his mouth had tightened. "What's that?"

Lucas paused, then spoke slowly.

"I said, the Germans and the Japs wouldn't shoot you, because there weren't any in Canada."

I could hear a lawn mower down the street in the silence. Sally leaned into the candlelight, her pale eyes snapping.

"I don't think that's a very chivalrous thing to say to your older brother."

Lucas shrugged and leaned back, then Burkie set his cup down on the saucer loudly.

"Lucas is right," he said, becoming solemn. He looked at everyone, his mouth a tight line. "There weren't any Germans or Japs around." He took a deep breath, then a smile lit across his face. "They don't fish!"

Everyone laughed and Lucas even smiled, but it wasn't a good smile. Burkie launched into another story about restoring an old fishing boat and I never even saw Lucas leave the table.

A week later Jimmy and Clay slept over on the sleeping porch. Mother's pink and red roses flowered the night breeze outside the dark screens. June bugs and crickets chirped a rhythmic breathing and beetles pinged the yellow bug light on the front porch as we talked in low voices. We fell asleep sometime around midnight with the cold metal scent of rain in the air.

It was an hour later that the world cracked open and I sat up as the dark flashed white.

"Some storm, huh?" Jimmy said, looking out at the rainy night.

"Yeah."

The rain drummed on the roof and sizzled in the trees. A flash blinked to a tremendous crack and I heard steps on the front porch. I turned as Lucas stumped toward us with the porch light behind him. He had been coming home late and spending the nights on the couch most of the summer. I had forgotten to tell him we would be on the porch.

He opened the screen door and stopped, the light glistening off his flat hair.

"—y'all doing in my bed?"

He leaned on his cane darkly, the antiseptic smell of hard liquor wafting over on the breeze.

"Forgot to tell you we were sleeping out here," I said quickly.

The world turned into a film negative and a tree somewhere was split in two. Lucas turned and observed the storm as if for the first time. He walked forward, bumping into a wicker table with a lamp on it. He fumbled around and turned on the light. His clothes hung heavily, his eyes glinting and bloodshot. The lightning cracked again.

"A storm," he grumbled, taking two steps and stopping. Lucas waved his hand at the rain, dropping his cane with a clatter on the wood floor. He reeled around. "Always need rain, boys. Don't ever forget that." He shook his finger at us, then kicked the cane skidding across the floor.

Lucas stumbled across the porch to a table along the wall. The phonograph case shook as he bumped into the table, jerking around, wild-eyed.

"Y'all want to hear some music?"

He swung back around and picked up an album from a stack of records next to the phonograph. I heard an explosion far off that rolled like a wave hitting the shore. The rain misted across the yellow light.

Lucas bent over with his shirttail hanging out of his pants like a wet rag. He leaned further into the phonograph, holding the record with his elbows out. The needle rumbled and fell off. Lucas picked up the needle and plopped it down again. Big band music cut through the wet night.

Lucas straightened up with a savage grin on his face.

"Now—*there's* some music!"

He stared at the phonograph for a long moment, then bumped into

30

a hanging paper light that looked like a large orange. He switched it on.

"Lee—turn off that damn light over there. Too damn light out here."

I clicked off the light on the table and the porch was bathed in orange. Lucas stared at the light, raising a hand unsteadily, pausing, then pushing the light. The orange globe swung back and forth as he stumbled from the light back to the phonograph. He picked up a stack of records and reared back with his legs apart.

"Ya'll ever seen a record drop and not break?"

Lucas raised his eyebrows, pulling out one record like a magician. A rolling thunderhead shook the house and the hammering on the roof was faster. He set the other records down next to him.

"—one little miscalculation and the record will break," he said, standing in the amber light, carefully holding the record edges with his fingertips.

He leaned over the album intently, pausing as the music stopped, then let go. The record cracked into three jagged pieces on the floor. He stared at the pieces, then held up a finger.

"I know what it was! There has to be a slight twisting motion when you release it."

He pulled another record out of its sleeve. Again he leaned over the floor like a bombardier intent on a precise drop. When the record hit the floor it split in half. Lucas stared down at the record and raised his finger again.

"*Ah ha!* I understand—you have to give the record a downward motion to compensate for the falling."

The big band music was blaring again and a light went on behind the double doors.

"Now watch this, boys, three is a charm."

Methodically he aimed again, his shoulders rose with breath and the record floated down to the floor. There was the familiar crack and the scattering pieces. The double doors pulled back as the screens lit with white fire. My father and Burkie came out in their robes. Lucas snapped his wet shoes together and saluted smartly.

"Private Hartwell conducting an experiment, sir," he said cradling his next record.

31

"At ease, private," Burke nodded, looking at the black glass on the floor.

Lucas swung his arm down.

"—just showing Lee and the boys here how to drop a record without breaking it, sir."

He bent down again over the record and I thought Burke was going to stop him, but he waited till Lucas smashed another one. Burkie stepped in front of my father, bigger in the orange light with his bare feet smacking on the wet floor.

"Lucas, put down that album—those are my band records!"

He tilted his head away, saluting again.

"Must continue on with my mission."

Lucas started to line up again.

"Let's go to bed, son," Burke said, taking hold of his arm.

Lucas broke his grip and hobbled away, wincing as weight came down on his bad foot. He limped to the other side of the porch into the shadows. I looked for his cane on the floor. He saluted again, standing on one foot.

"No, sir! Have to do it ... told these boys I would."

He clutched the album to his chest and hobbled to the other side of the porch. Burkie came across the porch and Lucas hunched over the album by the screen.

"Lucas—*put the goddamn album down!*"

He turned away as Burkie grabbed for the album.

"Daddy, you aren't going to let him keep breaking the records!"

My father held up his hand. His eyes had dark circles and looked curiously naked without his glasses. He walked between them and I wished someone would pick up the phonograph needle grinding on the inside of the record. Jimmy and Clay watched wide-eyed and quiet in their sleeping bags. Burke rubbed his eyes and pulled his red-checked robe tight. He touched Lucas's arm.

"Alright, son, let's try and drop that record."

Lucas stared at him suspiciously, but brought the record out from his chest. They went to the middle of the porch and Burke pushed the broken pieces away with his slipper.

"Keep it flat, son," he said, huddling with Lucas over the record like a couple of football players. "Keep it perfectly flat and let go with both your hands together."

He put his hands on Lucas's to steady them. The rain receded to a steady purr and the world became strangely quiet as we watched. Burke tilted his head up.

"Ready?"

Lucas nodded and my father's hands stayed on his as the record went out from under them, passing through the orange space as a black phantom. It fell flat on the floor and smacked loudly. I could only stare. It was one perfect piece. Burkie shook his head and walked back into the house.

Lucas snapped his wet shoes together.

"Mission accomplished, sir!"

Burke stood in front of him with his hands in his robe pockets. Lucas was rigid with his hand to his brow, water streaming down his face. Burke slowly took out his right hand and touched two fingers to his brow.

The rain had slowed.

4

*The tobacco ripened all through the summer. The planter
and his slaves went to the fields early and stayed till dusk.
Each plant had to be weeded and the tobacco hills hoed
many times. Slaves walked in the hot dirt that made it hard
to breathe. They moved down the rows with long, weathered
sticks and propped the veined leaves toward the sun. The
tobacco sticks became shiny from the hand.*

The Indian heat effectively ignored September and Buckeye still
didn't cool down till past midnight. The summer had slipped
away and we found ourselves in the seventh grade of Guienna
Park Junior High. Jim Fitch had come back from the service and was
over at the house practically every night for dinner. Sally was always
looking at his uniform and touching his shoulder or resting her hand on
his. Jim was as big as Burkie with wavy brown hair starting to grow
back from his G.I. haircut. His blue eyes watered a lot when he laughed.

He was over the night I first heard about the election. I was concentrating on a bowl of orange sherbet sinking into soup. Lucas hadn't
come home for dinner and his chair stayed empty about half the time
now. Addie had just taken a tray to Mimaw's room when Mother spoke
of the election.

34

"—and there's a good chance Burke will manage the senator's campaign in Richmond."

Jim nodded slowly.

"Who's running against Senator Herrin, sir?"

My father finished lighting a cigarette.

"Eugene Trenton."

"They always run!"

He looked at me and exhaled slowly.

"That's true—Mr. Trenton did run against the senator in the last two primaries."

"And got massacred both times," Burkie scoffed.

Jim turned back to my father.

"He's going to run again?"

"He's just a glutton for punishment," Burkie said, pushing his cleaned plate away. "Nobody in the last fifteen years been able to beat Herrin."

"The Republicans don't have a candidate?"

"Not since Reconstruction," Burke said, one elbow resting on the back of his chair. "The Republicans always run somebody, but the Democratic majority in Virginia has made the primary the election."

"I think Trenton just runs to see his name in print," Burkie laughed.

Burke tipped his Viceroy.

"This election might be different."

Mother clinked her spoon against her coffee cup, then set it carefully on her napkin.

"Why is that?"

"Eugene Trenton has the support of the unions this time," he said evenly. "And the AFL wants Senator Herrin out of Congress. The senator has voted against the unions a number of times and supported the president's decision to run the mines and railroads with federal troops during the strike."

"You've always supported Senator Herrin, Mr. Hartwell?"

"Shoot!" Burkie grinned, nodding to Jim. "Daddy's always been a Democrat and a Herrin man."

My father paused, moving his finger on the edge of his cup.

"I have supported Senator Herrin, but I'm not against labor." He paused again, his face darker. "I don't believe in outside influences coming into Virginia and dictating policy. The senator has always seemed to put Virginia first and that's where my heart is."

"You'll be managing the campaign here in Richmond, sir?"

"Richmond is pivotal to the election—I would be honored if the senator asked me to run the campaign here." He brought his cigarette forward stubbing it dead. "But no one's asked."

"Honored! After all you and the firm have done for that man!" Mother's pale eyes were bright. "He better ask you or I'm going to talk to him!"

Burke smiled down.

"Well, we'll see."

I didn't have much interest in what newspapers printed, but one of the classes of the seventh grade was "current events" and we had to pick a story and follow it. The election seemed as good as any and I started with two headlines: "TRENTON HAS GOOD CHANCE IN AUGUST ELECTION" and "TRENTON HITS HERRIN ON LABOR ISSUES." I cut out two more articles the next day and showed Burke the beginning of my scrapbook in his den. He took the book from me and looked at it carefully on his desk.

"How long will this class project last?"

I shrugged.

"Just another couple of weeks—then we're going to study the stock market."

He leaned back in his swivel chair and rested his hands on the arms. The wall plaques were white squares of evening light. I stared at the Roman lettering for President of the State Bar and being Virginia's Elector in the last Presidential election.

"I'll tell you what," he said, closing the book and handing it back to me. "From here on I will give you a dime for every article you cut out about the election."

"For how long?"

Something of a smile glimmered in his eyes.

"Till the end of the election."

36

A dime for every article—I would have coffee cans brimming with dimes by the time of the election next August.

"Yes, sir. I'll do it!"

"And I'm willing to make it retroactive," he added, reaching into his pocket. "How many articles do you have there?"

"Four."

He pulled out some change and counted four dimes into my palm. I held the coins in my hand.

"Thanks, Daddy!"

"One more thing, Lee—"

He pushed back his suit coat and slipped his right hand into his trouser pocket.

"I saw that you cut out the article about Senator Herrin speaking at the courthouse. I'm going there next Saturday and you might find it interesting."

"I'll go," I nodded quickly.

"Fine. We'll leave early Saturday morning."

The hub of city justice was old, 126 years old to be exact, and sat in the middle of town on top of a hill. It was a long red brick house with white colonial windows protruding from the roof. People were gathered in the shade of an oak that had been split in two by a Yankee shell during the Civil War.

"Looks like it's about to start," Burke observed as we pulled up.

I noticed a lot of new cars parked around the courthouse. Some of the cars were black with American flags waving from both sides of the hood. A man walked to the top of the stairs and turned around under the portico. A spot of sun made the top of his bald head white as he held his hands up for quiet.

"It gives me great pleasure to introduce the man y'all have come to hear speak today—Senator Herrin!"

I clapped with the people around us. A stout man with a wide smile mounted the steps and waved. The clapping and cheering increased. The senator pointed to people and waved. He had his coat off and a red tie whipped up against his shirt as he waved everyone down to just coughing, a clap, then nothing.

"Well, I can't say that my first speech of the campaign is not to a friendly crowd!" He drawled in a voice like the country people. "It is a beautiful day for oratory—as long as it's mine and not my misinformed opponents."

He showed his teeth and looked at the men on the steps as if they were in on a joke.

"Friends, I don't have to tell you what this election is about," he said, his voice booming like the radio. "Unions, with the great power they have, cannot continue to exercise that power in conflict with the public interest!"

The clapping caught fire again, dying like a wave.

"My opponent, Mr. Eugene Trenton, is supported by the AFL Political Action Committee! The very committee that wants to see my demise!"

He was leaning forward, anchored with his hands on his hips. I thought he looked like he might spit.

"I have evidence that Mr. Trenton is receiving full financial backing from labor organizations and they will do their best to place him as their pawn in the Senate of the United States!"

He leaned back and looked over the crowd.

"My position is clear! I will do nothing to injure the legitimate rights of the laboring man!" He swept his hand over the people. "But— if re-elected—I intend to use my influence, as I have done in the past, to correct the conditions which are responsible for the situation now confronting us!" Clapping rippled across the crowd, growing stronger. "No threats or personal vilification by dictator labor leaders will turn me from my purpose!"

The clapping was like fast rain.

"I have been asked on occasion if I favor the use of troops in strike situations. My answer is a resounding *yes!*"

The avalanche of voices and hands came down, but now the senator wasn't waiting. His fist hammered into his palm.

"I never want to see another Black Thursday where the trains of this great country are virtually shut down!"

I looked up to see if the leaves were fluttering from the outpouring of voices. Many people had their hands up over their heads. The storm slowed and there was a single voice as loud as the senator's.

"Senator! How do you respond to the charge that you voted against pay increases for the G.I.s during the war?"

I turned to the voice with other people. At the back of the crowd was a man with PRESS clipped to his hat. Senator Herrin smiled like a teacher.

"Well, son, in this campaign you will hear a lot of things about me that will be spread by the labor-backed machine of my opponent, Mr. Trenton! Of course I have *always* voted for pay increases for the boys ... The fighting man of this country deserves the highest compensation!"

The crowd drowned the man out for a moment. The PRESS hat bobbed from my view.

"Senator, isn't it true that you voted against the Social Security Act of 1935 and the Fair Labor Standards Act of 1938?"

Senator Herrin spoke to the bald man next to him, then turned back and pointed down at the man.

"Son, you go tell your labor bosses that their plan to disrupt my speech didn't work!"

A rumbling tide swelled up around me and clapping broke out in patches. The senator kept his finger out and his face was dark. "And tell them next time to come themselves! And I will *confront* them on the issues!"

Again a thunderclap of support deafened me. I jumped up, trying to see the PRESS hat. Senator Herrin shouted, the veins on the sides of his forehead standing out and his finger stabbing the man.

"THAT'S RIGHT! GO TELL YOUR LABOR AGITATOR BOSSES THAT THE PLAN DIDN'T WORK! *THAT MY SPEECH WENT ON!*"

The crowd-storm broke with clapping and shouts. I spent the rest of the speech looking for the man with the PRESS hat. The senator spoke for another twenty minutes about the budget of the state, then turned to the split oak tree where slatted crates of dark apples and light brown jugs kept a checked tablecloth from flapping away.

"Now—I want everyone to have some apples and drink some of the fresh cider that has come straight from my orchards!"

Burke squeezed my shoulder.

"Let's get some cider, Lee."

We passed through the men in suits into the deep shade of the tree. A breeze stirred the leaves over us and I could see the senator's red tie and hear his guffaw.

"These are some of the best apples in the state," Burke said, looking at the shiny fruit spilling out of the crates on the table.

"Senator Herrin grows them?"

Burke nodded, cupping his cigarette against the wind.

"He has the largest orchards in the state and sends crates to his allies and enemies alike."

Senator Herrin was stomping his foot and laughing again over the shoulder of a broad-shouldered man with his back toward us. The man turned like a wall and there was a fast thump in my chest as the luminous girl from the Hillman cemetery took form. The man turned and blocked my view, then there were voices over my head and Burke was talking to someone. I rubbed my hands dry.

"Come on, Lee, I'll introduce you to the senator."

The senator held out his hand and smiled.

"Well! Mr. Burke Hartwell, how are you, sir?"

"How are you, Senator? This is my son, Lee."

The senator kept smiling and his face was rounded close up.

"How you, Lee?"

He extended his hand, a gold cufflink glinting the sun beyond.

"Fine," I said, hearing a voice like one of Jimmy's sisters.

The senator laughed and stomped his foot in the dust.

"That voice is a real attention-getter—maybe I should use that when I start my speeches!"

The men around the senator laughed.

"Burke, I believe you know Buddy—"

"Burke and I are neighbors," Mr. Hillman rumbled in a deep voice.

They shook hands over me and I felt warm knowing the girl from the graveyard was nearby.

"Buddy, you remember my youngest son, Lee."

I watched my hand disappear into his. His eyes burned like two dark lanterns up on a mountain and his thick neck barely moved.

40

"I'd introduce you to my daughter, Lee, but she just left for home."

My skin cooled with the wind gusting dust circles under the tree. Mr. Hillman turned to my father.

"When is your first campaign meeting, Burke?"

"When the senator asks me to run his campaign."

Mr. Hillman snorted his disapproval.

"He will, don't worry about that."

Burke smiled tightly.

"The senator is someone we need, Burke. I'll give my guards orders to shoot before I let one of those organizers into my mills. They'll ruin American business. Hell, they want to give jobs to all the nigras!" He shook his head. "We can't afford to lose this election."

"I'm sure the senator will be re-elected, Buddy."

Mr. Hillman nodded absently, circling the gathering with his eyes and coming around to me.

"Lee, you and your father come on over next weekend. I have a closet full of suits that I don't wear anymore and you can try on the ones you like."

"Lee has plenty of clothes," my father said easily.

Mr. Hillman's eyebrows went up.

"I found some good suits for Burkie, didn't I?"

I looked down and there was dust on my father's wingtips. Usually they were mirror perfect.

"Everyone can use more clothes, Burke. Y'all come on over for dinner and Lee can take a run through my closets—he can wear them when he gets older."

Burkie had come back with lots of suits. He had come up on the porch wearing one and saying one day he was going to be president of a company like Richmond Steel.

"Make it Sunday for dinner. I'll get Anna to cook us some ribs and we can discuss the campaign. Could you see your way clear to some ribs on Sunday, Lee?"

I opened my mouth, then looked at Burke.

"Fine, fine. We'll see y'all then on Sunday," he said, clapping my father on the shoulder and walking off.

Burke winked at me, dropping his cigarette into the dust.

41

"Lord, it's a beautiful day!"

Senator Herrin had walked around the checkered table and stood with his hands on his hips, squinting out from the shade to where Mr. Hillman was talking to some men.

"Buddy Hillman is a good man," he nodded, glancing at Burke. "Biggest contributor in this election and I'll need every penny with these unions ... that heckler was sent by the unions, you can be sure of that." Senator Herrin's eyes darkened. He turned suddenly. "Your firm represents Richmond Steel doesn't it, Burke?"

"Yes, sir."

The senator smiled widely.

"Well, good! Y'all have worked together before." He put his hand on my father's shoulder. "I want my *campaign manager* to be able to work with my biggest supporter!"

Burke smiled.

"I'll do my best, Senator."

He laughed and clapped my father on the back.

"I have no doubt of that."

5

*The male slaves were naked to the waist in the hot part of
the summer. They worked spread out in the knee-high
tobacco, swinging the machetes side to side with the tobacco
tops falling behind. The planter watched the steel flash
between the green rows and knew the tobacco wouldn't
flower. The life would go into the leaves and make the
tobacco better. The slashing machetes were like singing
wind.*

Addie got me out of bed early on Sunday and made sure I had
scrubbed behind my ears and cleaned my fingernails. There
was a memorial service for Scotty's friends who were away
during the war. His body wasn't back and no one knew if it would ever
come, but a headstone was going to be put in the Nettleton plot.

"You has to be extra clean—don't want nobody sayin' you is dirty
at the funeral," Addie grumbled, handing me a new bar of soap in the
hallway.

"Open your mouth and let me smell your breath."

I breathed—her eyes lighting up.

"You is the most lying boy I ever known! Get yourself in the bathroom and brush them teeth!"

I turned to walk away and she grabbed the back of my coat, tug-
ging it down.

43

"An' I told you don't sit on your coat. Boys is such a damn nuisance," she said, turning back to the mirror in the hallway, smiling at the lacy French hat. "I think I going to win the hat rally with this hat your mother gave me."

I walked out with the toothbrush in my mouth. Addie's eyes rolled from the mirror.

"What you doing? Get back in there an' finish your business!"

I rinsed my mouth and wiped it on a towel, then walked back into the hallway and stared at Addie's hat.

"Church having a hat rally?"

"They is," she said, smiling with her false teeth in for church.

I cocked my head, looking at the delicate hat balanced on top of Addie's large head.

"I's going to get sanctified today and want to look my best."

Addie got sanctified when she felt "sinnin'" was getting the best of her. Then there was no drinking or swearing and a lot of humming till the next time she felt the need for a shot or a good healthy cuss.

"Thought you got sanctified last week, Addie."

Her teeth disappeared as she turned from the mirror.

"Get on, boy, an' wait for your mother downstairs!"

I walked down the hallway to the stairs and looked back. Addie was standing in the mirror again, adjusting her hat in the morning light.

The trees swayed with the low roar of cool morning air. Pyrocantha vines had climbed the porch railing long ago and sent spiraling tendrils up the white columns. I pushed up the porch swing and closed my eyes, listening to a hinge squeaking on the top. The honeysuckle just below the porch was in the air and there was the blond-haired girl kneeling in front of the mossy grave with steam rising around her.

The screen door banged and I opened my eyes. Lucas hobbled onto the porch and stopped by the banister. I slowed the swing down with my foot and stared at him. He stood looking out at the bright morning.

"Hey, Lucas—"

"Yeah," he said not turning.

I hesitated.

"What's it like to be shot?"

Lucas squinted against the light for a long moment.

"Like a hot needle," he said finally.

I nodded, moving again, looking beyond him at the trees bursting into autumn.

"Scotty was lucky—it was instant for him."

I jammed my foot down and the swing stopped. Lucas just stood against the white column like someone standing before a fire. Burke had told me never to bring up Scotty to Lucas and this was the first time he had spoken about him.

"—pretty quick," I ventured.

Lucas snapped his fingers.

"Like that."

"Thought the papers said he was wounded and that he—"

"What do the goddamn papers know!" Lucas's black eyes pinned me to the swing. "They only say what people want to hear."

The front door opened.

"There you are, Lee Hartwell!" Mother walked onto the porch in her light blue Sunday dress. "Don't dally, boy—we have to pick up your father and Sally before we go to the cemetery."

I jumped off the swing. The screen door popped open again and Burkie hurried out in his uniform. I followed my brothers to the car.

We turned into the narrow roads and steep hills of Hollywood cemetery, passing under the eclipsing oaks and shady dogwoods. Gray tombstones with faint indentations fluttered by the window, then a tall stone pyramid that was the common grave of 18,000 Confederate soldiers. Cars lined the sides of the road and Burke parked behind the last one.

A crowd had gathered at one of the plots under a tree. Burkie shook hands with his friends. I envied them being able to stand around in the smart light brown khaki with glinting medals and shiny brimmed officer hats shadowing their eyes. Everyone knew they were in the war. Lucas stood behind Burkie and didn't look at anybody.

"Hartwell!"

Lucas turned around to the voice behind us.

"I was wondering when you would get back," he said, grinning as they clasped hands.

I always thought Terry Bowers was what a person in college should look like—tanned, blond hair, a perfect smile. He was over at Buckeye all the time before the war. Terry's father had left when he was a baby and his mother was sick—sick with alcohol, Lucas said. There were gifts for Terry under the Christmas tree and Burke had given him his first bicycle. Lucas and Terry were best friends and had even planned on going to the same college before the war split them up.

"Thought you went AWOL," Lucas said, smirking.

"I did—but when you're an officer you're allowed to do that—heard you were hit in the foot."

Lucas jabbed his cane into the soft ground.

"Yeah."

Terry grinned.

"Didn't make you any uglier."

"Who's this good-looking young man? Couldn't be Terry Bowers?"

Terry's back straightened as he shook my father's hand.

"How are you, Mr. Hartwell?"

"I'm fine—we've been waiting for you to come back and get this boy out of the house," Burke said, winking at him and Lucas.

"I intend to drag him out, sir—he's looking pale."

"The Air Force treated you well?"

Terry lifted his hat and fitted it on the back of his head.

"Yes, sir. I didn't wreck too many of their planes."

Burke smiled.

"I'm sure we'll be seeing you around Buckeye."

"You can bet on that, sir," Terry nodded.

"Why don't you come over after the service? Did you tell him, Lucas, we're having a dinner—"

"Didn't get the chance to yet, Daddy."

Burke held up his hands, stepping back.

"I'll let you two catch up."

"Nice seeing you again Mr. Hartwell."

Terry stared after him.

"Your father seems well."

Lucas stabbed the ground again with his cane.

"Daddy's always well."

People had gathered around the area squared off with white cement dividers. A marble stone shaped like a small house was at the top of the plot and sparkled with the name "NETTLETON" in sharp-edged letters. Two cement steps entered the plot where the earth raised from the road on a gentle curve. There was only one stone and the letters were dark in the high sun.

PFC. Scott Andrew Nettleton II
Born January 5, 1920
Killed in Action Cologne Germany August 12, 1944
Someday We'll Understand

Reverend Dobbs stood by the headstone holding a Bible.

"I would like to thank everyone for coming out today in memory of Scotty Nettleton," he said. "It is a sad occasion that brings us together, but let us rejoice in the fact that he is with God and has gone the way of all men who believe in Him."

There were some murmurs of "Amen" in the crowd and someone blew their nose. He tilted his head.

"Scotty laid his life down for his country so that those here might live in freedom. He and many other young men gave their precious lives—so we may carry on—in their memory. Scotty was a sweet boy by nature and had achieved much in his young life...."

"Go farther, you guys," Scotty called down the backyard. The ball shot from his shoulder, black in the twilight, and landed between us. We were still running after the bouncing ball when Scotty was next to us. "Can't y'all catch?" He slipped by us and scooped up the football and we grabbed at his torn sweatshirt. He fell to the ground and we

47

were on top of him. "No piling on," he said, jumping up again and sitting down in the cool grass. We jumped on his stomach and he just laughed, pushing his blond hair up off his forehead and shaking his head. "Y'all are dirty players!"

"What can we say about the death of a young man?" Reverend Dobbs looked around. "We can't bring him back...."

Jimmy leaned over, his breath hot in my ear.

"Look right across from us."

I looked into the people.

"To the right! To the right...."

I froze, a blood heat prickling my skin. There was the girl from the graveyard.

Jimmy nudged me.

"Lee ... Lee, bow your head!"

I bowed my head for what seemed a very long prayer. There was finally an "Amen," and when I looked up the girl in white was gone again.

There was a small reception at Buckeye. The late summer breeze flapped through the hallway, twirling the long curtains and pushing the drapes against the windows in the living room. The sugary smell of a ham baking floated out from the kitchen over the gleaming silver and white china on the dining room table.

Jimmy and I stood in the hallway as people started to arrive.

"See that girl from the Hillman graveyard?"

I shrugged.

"You did too—I saw you looking at her."

"Don't think that was her."

Jimmy's mouth dropped open.

"It was her!"

"Don't know."

"Course it was!"

I looked away, feeling the strange heat again.

"Maybe—"

"I say it was her." Jimmy turned. "Oh no, here comes my sister."

A chubby blond girl came from the living room carrying a glass of wine. Laura was the oldest of the Mason sisters. She was also the largest.

"Hello *boys*," she drawled loudly. "Why don't y'all have a Coke?" She flicked her curls and sipped wine. "It's tough for little boys like y'all at these grown-up affairs."

"You aren't so old, Laura, you—"

"You're looking more grown up every day, Lee Hartwell," she said, turning to me.

She stuck her tongue out at Jimmy, sipping her wine again in front of him.

"See y'all later," she said, looking down her tilted-up nose. "I think I'll get some more wine."

She bounced back into the living room.

"Just once I'd like to tell her where to get off," Jimmy muttered, looking after her.

We eventually walked into the living room. Burkie was telling a story by the fireplace and people were gathered around the piano.

"Lee, Jimmy, y'all come over here and sing with us."

Big Jeb was standing next to my father. He motioned us over as a glass shattered behind me and I turned to see Burkie pin Lucas against the fireplace. Lucas's face was red and veins bulged on his neck as he struggled to get free of Burkie's grip on his coat. My father was suddenly between them.

"Burkie, let go!"

"He can't talk that way about Scotty!"

"Let him go, Burkie!"

He released his grip and Lucas pulled down his coat and shirt, his face a deeper red.

"Now, what happened?"

"I was just reading what the paper wrote about Scotty getting the Silver Star and he says the paper just prints lies and called Scotty a coward!" Burkie pointed at him. *"He's* the coward!"

Lucas bolted across the room.

"Lucas!"

He hobbled into the hallway and out to the porch. Burkie watched as my father walked across the hall after him, then he slowly sat down on the couch and stared at something on the coffee table. I picked up the newspaper and saw a picture of Scotty in his uniform and a short article.

SILVER STAR FOR RICHMONDER

Scott Nettleton was awarded the Silver Star posthumously for bravery. Private Nettleton, acting as scout and forward observer for a battalion intelligence section, was pinned down by an artillery barrage while returning to friendly lines with captured documents. He was buried in his foxhole for thirty minutes by a near hit. When dug out by rescuers he refused to be sent to the rear for medical treatment. As he continued on to his forward command group with valuable documents, a second shell killed him instantly.

I left the living room and walked up the steps holding the paper. I pulled out my scrapbook, but ended up lying down on my bed with the article and picture of Scotty laying next to me. I saw Lucas snap his fingers again in the Sunday morning light. The evening flowed in through my window and softened life again. I shut my eyes and felt sleepy. Someone snapped their fingers and I was gone.

6

*The late September sun slanted across the rows as the
planter walked the field of brown-gold tobacco. He picked a
leaf and crushed it between his fingers, then kneeled and
touched the earth. He thought of white frost and dead leaves,
but of not-yet-ripe tobacco too. The tobacco would be cut
soon, but not too soon or too late—just soon. Then it would
be right.*

I pasted two more articles from the Sunday paper in my scrapbook
and showed the clippings to Burke. He held out the dimes and I left
him with the scrapbook in his study. The coins jingled in my pocket
as I passed through the kitchen to go meet Jimmy in the tree house.
The electric fan whined on the kitchen table. I glanced around and
opened the icebox. The dining room door swung in.

"*Lee!*" Addie advanced toward me. "Get your hand out of that icebox—you has drank enough soda today!"

"I only had one bottle—"

"An' that is enough, now put that bottle back!"

I let the bottle go and shut the icebox. Burkie laughed behind her
in the doorway.

"You know Addie has the ears of an elephant, Lee."

Addie went to the stove and opened a pot.

"Now come on, Addie, tell me where I can find those wine bottles. Katy and I are going for a picnic today."

Katy Dealy had been Scotty's fiancee and had appeared at the memorial service after being away for over a year. There had been rumors she was in a hospital, visiting relatives, or in an insane asylum. But now she was back and had come by Buckeye the week after the service. Burkie started taking her out and said she had been with relatives in South Carolina for the past year.

"Don't be messin' with me, Burkie. I got too much to do to worry about your wine," Addie grumbled, moving the trash can from the corner to the front of the stove.

Burkie scratched his cheek slowly.

"Addie, I know before I left for the service I had twenty bottles of wine down there in the cellar. There's only two of those bottles now. I just want to know what happened to the other eighteen."

He came off the doorway and picked an apple from the table in the middle of the kitchen. Burkie took a bite, chewing loudly.

"I knows nothin' 'bout it," Addie said, shaking her head and filling the pot in the sink.

"Come on, Addie."

She turned off the water, hoisted up the pot, and carried it back to the stove. Addie positioned the fan to blow on her as she pulled a potato from the burlap sack at her feet. She began peeling with a paring knife.

"Alright now, I tell the truth," she said, not moving her eyes from her hands. "Those wine bottles just started explodin', Burkie, an' there ain't nothin' I could do. I was down there one day and one of them bottles just blow up!"

Burkie flipped his apple core into the trash under Addie and slipped his hands in his pockets.

"Exploded, huh?"

"Yes sir—I said to myself—Burkie ain't goin' to have no wine bottles left when he come back from the war. I just keep cleanin' them up and they just keep explodin'," she continued, flipping another spud around in her hand.

Burkie's eyes narrowed.

"How those bottles going to explode?"

Addie's brow came down and her lips pushed out. She dropped a potato on the table.

"Well ... now I—"

"It's true, Burkie!" Addie's eyes darted over. "Heard those bottles pop myself."

He stared at me closely as I held my hands out.

"Jimmy and I were sitting up here and heard something and it sounded like someone broke a bottle in the cellar. We ran down and glass was everywhere and the whole cellar stunk with wine!"

Addie plopped another potato in the water.

"Wasn't going to tell you, Burkie," she said, nodding, "'cause I said to myself that Burkie ain't goin' to believe me." She looked down at the potatoes. "Burkie's wine just blowin' all up an' he off at the war with no one to stop it."

He took his hands out of his pockets and stood up from the door frame.

"I'm going down and have a look at those bottles myself," he said to Addie, then to me. "Because I know about you two."

"You do that, Burkie," Addie nodded. "An' be careful one don't explode on you."

Burkie looked at her with his tongue rolling on the inside of his cheek and then we heard his hard shoes piano down the stairs into the basement. Addie looked toward the cellar door, then dropped the potato and I had the bottle in my hand and she was already back to her pot.

"Thanks, Addie."

"Uh huh," she murmured.

I ran through the hot breath of clover toward the blue-hazed trees along the back of the lawn. The woods closed and the dirt path was cool and slippery. I turned a corner and there was the leaning wood box in the fork of the oak. Jimmy's head popped out as I reached the bottom of the tree.

"That a soda, Lee?"

"Yep."

"Come you didn't bring one for us?"

"Had to fight Addie just to get this one," I said, climbing the badly nailed boards, holding the bottle in the crook of my arm.

I pushed myself up through the plywood floor and there was a girl sitting Indian style. It was Jackie Tramling. She was from the neighborhood, several years older, and rumored to take off her clothes and run naked in the woods. Her brown hair was the color of the woods, her lips a deep red, her eyes dark and sooty.

She nodded to me, chewing on a pink wad of gum. I knocked the wood dust off my shorts, then sat down across from her. Jimmy leaned over and put his hand to my ear.

"Jackie said if we show her our fort she would show us her *tits.*"

I looked at Jackie and held out my Coke.

"Sip of my pop?"

"Why thank you."

She put the bottle to her lips, slendering her throat up and down.

"You can keep it."

She smiled with the bottle in her pink nails and looked around.

"Y'all have a nice place up here."

She crossed her tan legs, a black and white saddle shoe bobbing in time with her gum.

"Built it last summer," Jimmy said, hitting the plywood like he had just finished it.

Jackie upended the bottle again. Jimmy slumped down and looked between his knees.

"Can we see your tits?"

Jackie gazed out into the trees.

"Be partial to a cigarette if y'all have any."

"Have some old Wings," I said.

"Do you? That would be grand!"

"How about seeing your tits?"

"Get her the cigarettes, Jimmy."

He reached into the corner between the boards and the tree and pulled out the pack. I handed a fairly straight one to Jackie and lit it on the third match. She inhaled deeply.

"Thank you."

She blew the smoke out coolly through her nose and mouth. I lit my cigarette with Jimmy. He breathed in deeply, his cigarette shrinking. I was impressed.

"Ahhhh," he said, then his eyes watered, his cheeks ballooned, then detonated.

He exploded into a terrific hacking fit and crawled on his hands and knees, coughing like someone who'd just thrown up. He collapsed, holding his ribs and drooling on the floor.

"Jimmy don't smoke?"

"Not an inhaler," I said, stubbing out his cigarette.

Jackie held her blue-trailing cigarette on top of her knee.

"That's the way I was when I first started."

"Ohhh...."

Jimmy turned over, tears leaking back into his bristly hair.

"Well, since y'all have been so hospitable," Jackie said, tipping the ash off her cigarette onto the floor, "let's go for a run in the woods naked."

Jimmy sat up, holding his stomach, his eyes burning. Jackie put the bottle down and stood with her white blouse pulling tight.

"What do y'all say?"

"We'll go," Jimmy said hoarsely.

Jackie climbed down the tree and we followed her into the woods away from the trail and reached the tall pines where the light was hard and the copper needles cushioned our feet. The pines blocked the sun with light falling in sharp spots on the large pine cones scattered every few feet.

"This looks good," Jackie said.

Jimmy looked at me like he was going to start coughing again. Jackie started unbuttoning her shirt. Neither of us had seen a naked girl before except for the black and white pictures I found in Burkie's room under his bed. Jackie laid her shirt in the rusty needles, folding the small sleeves in. There was the tan line above the white bra I had seen when Sally's door was open and she was putting on earrings. But this bra rose up to two smooth bosoms. Jackie moved behind a pine with sap hardened on the sides.

"Aren't y'all going to take off your clothes?"

Jackie peered around the tree with her eyes reflecting like an animal in shadow. I pulled my shirt off and dropped my shorts. Jimmy followed. There was movement behind the glazed tree and her shorts and underwear were next to the trunk.

"Y'all ready?"

Jimmy's eyes turned to marbles as I jerked my underwear to my feet. His caught on his ankles. We stood with our hands on our hips and our shorts, shirts, and underwear in a heap. I turned to the tree.

"Ready."

Jackie let out a scream that was high in the trees and I turned to a flash of flying hair, bosoms, and white skin running into the dark pines. The woods screamed again and she was a pale figure getting smaller in the shadows. I yelled and started running through the tall trees with air streaming cool on my skin and the curved body flicking in and out of shadows ahead.

I dodged between the oozing trees, my feet on the pine needles and wind tingling cool then warm with the turpentine smell in my nose. I turned the corner around a group of trees and didn't see Jackie anymore. I slowed down and stopped, hearing my breathing among the dark, spiky trees.

"Lee—"

Jackie's voice was ahead in a group of pines forming a circle. Her white body came from the shadows of the tree and the pounding came back with the heat. Jackie walked slowly out of the trees and into a clearing in front of a patch of sun.

"Don't know where Jimmy is," I said, hearing myself.

"Maybe he's lost."

The cool slicked my sides and my legs were trembling. Jackie stepped into the light with her bosoms making shadows beneath and a dark shadow between curves of thighs.

"Seen a naked girl before, Lee?"

"—sure ... lots," I squeaked.

She stared at me with her standing bosoms like the pictures under Burkie's bed. Her wide smile and red-lipped teeth were close.

"Like to touch?"

I shrugged, nodded.

"—sure."

"I don't usually let boys touch me."

I walked forward hearing the needles, but not feeling myself walking. The pines had taken sound away. Her hooded eyes were glass as I reached out.

"LEE!"

"AHHH!"

I jerked my hand back and grabbed it with my other. Jimmy's fat white body came huffing out from the trees. Jackie was gone.

"Where'd you go?" He panted with his hands on his knees. "Jackie here?"

I ignored him, looking into the pines where she had disappeared.

"Aren't done running naked, are we?"

"Guess so!"

I began walking back toward our clothes. Jimmy shook his head.

"*Damn!* I was just beginning to like it—did you see that Jackie? She was something! She really has some tits!"

We made our way through the pines back to where we had left our shorts. I retraced our steps, but the tall trees all looked the same. We walked through the woods for twenty minutes, weaving one way and back the other, then ending up where we started.

"Where's our clothes?"

I shook my head.

"How should I know! Everything looks the same ... shit!"

I began to walk off again.

"I gotta go to the bathroom."

"Then go," I called back, still walking.

"I'm going over by those trees."

I didn't bother to turn around and went to where the green trees began.

"You better learn...."

I flattened down into the second growth, smelling the black dirt. The voices were close.

"—White folks don't want no smart-talkin' colored woman...."

It was the heavy old voice of Nelson.

"—don't want to be someone's yard nigger."

Fanny's tawny skin and Nelson's deep color passed not five feet in front of me. They were walking from the Hillmans'. Nelson helped out in Mr. Hillman's gardens and Fanny cleaned the silver service twice a week.

"Ain't no secret, Fanny, you been sleepin' with white men."

They were so close I held my breath.

"... don't need some old nigger to tell me what I can do. If folks got a mind to talk I can't be bothered. Bunch of old Uncle Tommin' niggers who's just jealous. If people want to talk, I can't stop them—"

"—when you talk like that, you sound just like your daddy. An' if you ain't careful, you going to end up like him too!"

Fanny's polka dot scarf floated through the greenery. She had on the gray uniform Addie wore.

"... least he wasn't some old Uncle Tom—"

The leaf crushing moved away.

"—an' it was just his thinkin' that way that killed him."

"—had his dignity ... More than I can say for a lot of folks round here...."

I stood up from the ground and could see them again.

"... dignity right up till when they took him...."

Nelson's grizzled head passed through sunlight and he was mopping his face with his white handkerchief. I moved lower to the ground.

"You is goin' to be one troubled person. White man's world is what we live in, Fanny, an' you better learn. Otherwise you goin' to have a troubled life."

I was moving when Fanny screamed. I peered through the leaves and Fanny's hand was on her eyes and Nelson was staring with his mouth open.

"Jimmy!"

I looked past Nelson and there was Jimmy bent forward in front of them with his hands between his legs. Fanny kept her hand over her eyes and Jimmy stared at Nelson dumbly with streaks of red on his cheeks.

"You seen Lee?" He gasped out.

Nelson's head moved.

"Jimmy—don't think you should be runnin' around with no clothes on."

He jumped off the path behind a tree, keeping his hands below his stomach.

"—just looking for Lee," he said, his sides sticking out both sides of the skinny tree. "Seen him, Nelson?"

Nelson's head moved again.

"No sir—Haven't seen him since this morning ... but I tell him you lookin' for him."

"Thanks."

Jimmy crouched down and ran to a bigger tree, then just ran with his fleshy buttocks bouncing into the forest. They were walking again with Nelson's heavy laughter and Fanny's shrieking in the trees. She smacked her hands together. I heard her voice high in the branches long after they were gone.

"White boys, runnin' naked in the woods!"

7

The rough-handled machetes glinted down the rows. The short days were coming and the row shadows were long when the cutting stopped. The slaves walked by dusk-wet tobacco piles on the edge of the fields. They ate in their cabins still smelling the cut tobacco. Later at night their arms swung the machete with the steel holding the sun. Then they woke and went back to the fields.

D addy, what happened to Fanny's father?"
Burke squinted down the Sunday evening road.
"Why do you ask?"
I shrugged, watching the trees rush by the car window.
"Just wondering I guess. Was he killed?"
He took a deep breath and rubbed his eye under his glasses.
"He was murdered."
"They catch the people who did it?"
My father tilted his head, driving with his arm on the car door, twilight flickering behind.
"I don't think anyone was ever convicted. They found him out in the country."
"How did—"

"He was lynched."

Burke looked down the road for a long moment; the tire rhythm in the quiet.

"It is the only lynching I know of in Virginia."

I nodded and heard Nelson's old voice in the woods.

"You going to end up just like your daddy...."

We turned into a driveway, a narrowing gray path slipping up the long hill till it blotted in front of a white mansion. I looked at the wide lawns running from the car in every direction as we drove toward the clouds. The house grew till it was over us.

"Here we are," Burke said, pulling into the circle drive.

The car doors and our footsteps had no sound against the mansion. I turned and could see downtown Richmond in the distance. It looked like the mansion was higher than the state capital building. Burke put his hand on my shoulder as we started up the steps to the white columns. It reminded me of the buildings we had visited in Washington. The double front doors had brass knockers shaped like lions' heads. My father pressed the doorbell and there was a chiming deep inside.

The doors swung open to a hobbled man in a bow tie and white coat.

"Why hello, Mistah Hartwell, Mistah Hillman expectin' you."

"Thank you, Peter."

Burke handed him his hat.

"This is my son, Lee."

"Why hello, Lee!" He put out a curled leather hand that was muscle-strong. "Mistah Hartwell—he look like you with hair!" Peter cackled, shaking his head. "I let Mistah Hillman know y'all here."

He walked down the hall with his shoes clicking on the white marble floor. A red stairway and curved gold banister floated down from the second floor into the foyer.

"It's quite a house," Burke murmured behind me.

Footsteps came down the hallway and Mr. Hillman walked up in a dark sport coat and white shirt. Black hair peeked out where his neck bulged from his loosened collar. He shook my father's hand, then put his hands in his pocket, chinking coins.

"I'm glad y'all could come out. I have a raft of suits for Lee to try on."

I had almost forgotten about the suits.

"Boys always need clothes," he said to Burke. "I tell you what, Lee, you try on some of these old suits and if you don't want any, that's fine with me. But some day when you're old enough, you'll be glad you had the suits."

My father smiled tightly.

"I'll get us a drink Lee, how about a soda," he said, leading us down the dark hallway he had come from. "Just had some people over and I drank too much damn coffee ... need a drink to calm down."

The hallway opened to a kitchen and then a pine den that was buttery and warm. I sat down next to my father on the couch.

"Peter, get us a couple of bourbons and Lee a soda."

"Yes sir," he nodded.

Mr. Hillman sat in a high-backed upholstered chair and picked up a pipe from a round table.

"Good old servant. Been with the family since I was a baby," he said, sucking flame from a lighter, sending up short, blue puffs.

Behind him were plaques, degrees, awards, photographs of Mr. Hillman shaking hands with presidents and congressmen. I recognized Senator Herrin in several pictures. I looked down and there was a fireplace and on the hearth was an engraved slab of iron.

"You looking at my steel, Lee," Mr. Hillman nodded. "That's part of the first steel ingot forged by my grandfather. I keep it there to remember where all this came from."

He stoked his pipe with a match. Peter came back into the room with his footsteps ahead of him on the hard floor. I picked up my soda from the tray and sipped the fizzy Coke.

"I be in the kitchen, Mistah Hillman."

I listened to the uneven tap of his shoes fading to a faint echo till Mr. Hillman gaveled his glass down on the table.

"Senator asked you to run the campaign yet, Burke?"

"Not officially."

"He will," he nodded. "The senator needs to carry Richmond with a strong return. Trenton is making this labor issue so big that we need someone not associated with labor or industry who can get the support of the people." He stabbed the chewed end of his pipe toward us. "You can get that support."

"That's a big ticket," Burke said, but he didn't seem to hear him.

"The unions are going to make a lot of trouble trying to stir up the workingman in this state." He held the pipe down. "They even got some man down in the colored section handing out leaflets trying to get the nigras to join the union!" He pointed with the pipe again, his forehead glistening and his legs apart on both sides of a footstool. "I had to chase them from my steel mills before and by God I'll do it again! I pay a decent wage and the men are thankful to get it." His neck swelled out of his open collar. "No union will *ever* get into my mills."

Burke lifted his drink and brought it down slowly to the arm of the couch.

"I don't think you have to worry."

Mr. Hillman tapped the ashes out of his pipe into a brass ashtray. I tried to remember some of the articles I had cut out lately. *"HERRIN TERMS SELF: TOP MAN ON AFL'S SENATORIAL PURGE LIST"* and *"TRENTON SAYS HERRIN ONLY FOR THE BIG CORPORATIONS"* were the only two I could think of. There were footsteps coming down the hallway. They were lighter and quicker than Peter's. The steps came into the room with the heavy thudding in my chest.

"Careen, this is Burke Hartwell and his son, Lee."

I was up with my father and into the two blue eyes regarding me curiously. She smiled and I saw freckles. They were on her nose, a fine collection just above the bridge. And she had pants on. I found myself as she became real and even the hammer in my chest took pause.

"Nice to meet you," she said in a voice like water flowing over smooth rocks.

"Hartwells live in the house behind us ... you go to Guienna Park Junior High, don't you, Lee?"

"Yes sir."

"Careen is starting there tomorrow. She's been traveling and is getting a late start. Maybe you can show her the ropes," he said, winking.

... ever seen a girl naked before, Lee?

"Yes sir."

"Daddy!"

"You'll need some friends at that damn public school and I know Lee is a gentleman."

... want to touch me, Lee?

"Yes sir!"

"Daddy ... *please!*"

Mr. Hillman held up his hands.

"Alright, forget I said anything."

He grinned at us, shaking his head.

Careen turned and took her hands off her hips.

"It was nice meeting y'all."

"Nice meeting you, Careen," Burke said over me while I nodded dumbly.

Her quick steps faded back into the hall gloom and I hastened after her and pushed her into a room and—

"You ready to try on some suits, Lee?"

I jumped up.

"Yes sir!"

My father looked at me oddly, but I couldn't help it.

"We have a little time before dinner," he said to Burke. "He could just look and see if he likes any."

"No harm in looking," my father said to me.

"Yes sir!"

His eyes narrowed again and I knew he was trying to decipher what had happened to his son in the short span of a half hour. We went upstairs to a large bedroom with a walk-in closet. Mr. Hillman held the closet door open and motioned me in.

"These are suits I wore when I was younger, Lee. Pick whatever ones you want."

I walked in with the suits brushing the old smell on me, walking past gray, blue, pin-striped and brown suits, then back through again. I came out of the closet and Mr. Hillman and my father rolled up the sleeves and pants. I hoped not a damn one of them would fit, but they said three would be fine after some age and alteration.

The tobacco was cut and taken to barns near the fields to cure. The barns were fifty feet tall and built of red-painted wood. Slaves climbed up into the darkness with the heavy tobacco and hung it on the rafters. Soon all the barns were full and the doors were left open for the air to move through. The tobacco hung in the attic warmth and the dusty floor became sticky with resin.

W e had the first chill of fall in the last week of October and Addie pulled out my blue jacket from a box in the attic marked "WINTER CLOTHES." I was on the porch swing with my coat on, enjoying the snap of cold air that smelled like burning wood, when Addie's fleshy arm pushed the door open.

"There you is, Lee! I was callin' you to come on in and wash up—everyone already sittin' down. And go get Miz Mimaw."

I got off the swing and followed her in. There was an extra chair at the dining table.

"Who—"

"Lucas havin' a lady friend," Addie hollered back disappearing into the kitchen.

Lucas was bringing a girl to dinner. Katy Dealy had been at dinner at least twice a week and Burkie always told stories and made her feel at home. They would sit out on the sleeping porch till late in the evening. Katy's voice had woke me on the swing the week before.

"Burkie, don't—"

"Nobody is around, Katy."

There was the cricket quiet and the porch light was off. The moon glowed between the columns. There was a bump on the floor, some clothes rustled, and the springs of the old couch groaned. I swung my feet down and stood, groggy with sleep, peering into the dark.

"Burkie—*someone's there!*"

Burkie's shirt was up in the half-light through the screens.

"—Lee," he said breathing fast.

Then Katy sat up next to him, smoothing her dress.

"Hello Lee," she said in a normal way, but her hair was sprung and wild against the screens.

I washed my hands in the second floor bathroom with my jacket still on and the cold on my cheeks. I ran up the steps to get Mimaw and when we came down everyone was already seated for dinner. Lucas had on a clean white shirt and a razor part in his hair. Addie bustled in and set a basket of rolls on the table. The doorbell chimed.

"You can bring the food in, Addie," Burke said, going to the door with Lucas.

"Set up in that chair, Burkie! You know your mother don't want you leanin' back an' breakin' her antiques!"

"That's right, Burkie," Mother said, stubbing her cigarette in an ashtray. "I didn't buy hundred-year-old chairs to have them broken now."

Burkie grinned and let his chair down slowly. Sally leaned in to the table.

"I didn't know Lucas was dating anyone."

"Maybe that's where he's been going at night. Better than going to a bar," Burkie scoffed, leaning on his elbows.

"I observe no one has lit on you for studying in Daly's pool hall," Mother said, smoothing her napkin.

"Daly's?"

"And from what Eddie's mother has told me, you ought to be running out of your G.I. pay soon with all the money you've been losing to him."

Burkie shook his head.

"I'm studying plenty. These old college courses aren't so hard."
Mother slid the silver-rimmed ashtray to the side.

"I've heard that before."

"I don't think I have ever met any of Lucas's girlfriends," Sally
said, running a hand through her thick curly hair.

Her eyes flitted around the table and came back to Jim next to her.
He had been living with his family while he and Sally looked for a
house. Sally talked about Jim starting college and becoming a lawyer,
but Jim said he was going to work for a while first. He had been over at
Buckeye a couple of times in a tight suit with his pants high on his
ankles and his forehead wet from walking around. He looked funny,
but he said he was going to find a job and put on the tight suit every
day.

Footsteps came into the hallway and there was a pretty, dark-haired
woman in the half-light.

"This is Miss Bonnie Randall," Lucas said, leaning on his cane
next to her.

She smiled like a movie star with perfect teeth and brown shim-
mery hair flowing out from a part. She had on a cream-colored dress
with shoes that matched. Everything about her was modern and new.
Burkie leaned back in his chair.

"Do you go by Miss Bonnie or Miss Randall?"

"Most people just call me Bunny," she said, holding a small purse
to her side.

Lucas introduced everyone, then seated her at the table. She smelled
of perfume the way Mother did before she went out. The door swung
open and Addie came in with the cart and began dishing food.

"—I work at the bank in town and go to school for journalism,"
she explained later.

"Oh, a writer! Lucas didn't say anything about bringing a writer to
dinner," Burke said, winking. "Do you want to work at a newspaper?"

"I plan to work at a newspaper, but eventually I would like to work
overseas."

Sally cleared her throat with her pale eyes in the candles.

"How long have you wanted to be a journalist?"

Bunny smiled.

"Ever since I was a little girl."

"That's an interesting ambition for a woman," she said, picking a crumb off the table and putting it on her plate.

I should have told Bunny to get up and run because I knew that tone of Sally's. It was the whip drawing back.

"I'm sure there are woman correspondents, Sally," Jim said next to her.

Sally fixed him with a look, then picked another crumb from the table.

"*I* certainly don't know of any."

There was the clinking silverware and the candles flickered.

"Never heard of any woman doing that kind of thing either," Burkie said, licking sherbet from his spoon. "I'd think it would be too dangerous."

Bunny kept her eyes on her plate, but her smooth cheeks now had two red spots of color. She looked up and faced Burkie and Sally and her voice only wavered twice.

"It seems to me, during the war, women took over the jobs that men left behind and did them very well."

Burkie snorted.

"Like Rosy the Riveter?"

Bunny fingered her wine glass.

"No—like Eleanor Roosevelt or Amelia Earhart."

Sally's eyes snapped and I saw her readying the whip again.

"I think it's admirable to want to be something. Lord knows running a house isn't the end all."

Burkie and Sally stared at Mother and Jim was smiling behind his hands. Mother leaned toward her.

"Do you live in Richmond, Bunny?"

"I live over on Grace Street with my grandmother. My parents passed away when I was young."

"Mrs. Hartwell and I lived on Grace Street when we were first married," Burke said.

"And it was much easier to take care of than this circus house," Mother nodded.

"Now, I want to know how you two met," my father said leaning back in his chair.

Bunny smiled and looked at Lucas.

"Well, actually, Lucas tried to sell me some knives."

"He tried to sell you *knives*?"

Lucas shifted in his chair.

"I didn't have a chance to tell you, Daddy. I picked up a night job ... think I'm gonna take a break from school," he said quickly.

Burke pursed his lips with the candles flickering in his glasses.

"We could find a different college for you, Lucas—"

"It's not the school," he said looking at his plate. "I just don't want to go right now."

Burke coughed and smiled quickly.

"We can discuss it later ... Bunny, can I get you some more corn or something?"

"Oh, no sir, Mister Hartwell, I'm fine," she said, smiling again, more beautiful in the candlelight.

I watched her the rest of the dinner and sure didn't blame Lucas for quitting school.

I had been going down to the Hillman graveyard and the other side of the woods in the hope of seeing Careen. But it wasn't until the Hillmans had a barbecue on Halloween day that we met again.

She came through the haze of barbecue smoke like we were old friends.

"Hello Lee, nice to see you again."

"—Careen," I said, dry-mouthed with her blue-green eyes making my face red.

"I'm glad you came to the barbecue."

"Me too!" I shouted.

Careen just smiled, then turned to the barbecue ovens that looked like small houses with chimneys. She turned her nose up and looked at me.

"Would you like to go up to the house for a plate of fried chicken, Lee?"

"... you don't like barbecue?"

She wrinkled her nose at the belching chimney houses.

"You can stay if you like. I was just going to eat some chicken—"

"That's fine!" I shouted again. "Don't care for chicken, either—I mean barbecue! I mean I like barbecue! But I like chicken and barbecue...." I trailed off and gave up.

She smiled with spreading light.

"Let's go have some chicken, then."

"Let's!"

I followed her in the relief of something to do.

"Don't you want it heated, Miz Careen?" Anna asked, her dark brow furrowed in the kitchen light.

We were sitting in the tiled kitchen at a small table. Careen shook her head.

"No. Do you, Lee?"

I looked at the plate of cold chicken on the table.

"No ma'am! Like it cold!"

Anna reached up to a rack and hung a pan against the autumn light with a thin scar on her cheek taking form.

"Mistah Hillman don't like company not havin' good meals," she said to herself more than us.

"But Lee likes cold chicken."

"I do!" I swore. "I *love* cold chicken!"

I stuffed nearly a whole piece in my mouth then to prove it. I was wound up like a clock and I wished the alarm would go off or something so I could relax. Careen winked at me and I didn't taste the chicken or feel it going down my throat. I ate with Careen and she even licked the grease off her fingers.

We went out on the front porch later. Downtown Richmond was in the distance and the barbecue gathering looked small on the wide, evening-colored lawns. Careen turned with the light in her hair.

"Would you like to see mother's grave, Lee?"

"Sure," I said, thinking of the flower from so long ago.

The food had slowed me down and I felt more like myself as we started down the hill to the line of trees fiery in the dying sun. The early darkness was down between the trunks with the twilight playing in the high branches. I followed Careen on the trail passing raised underbrush smelling of damp wood and moss. The trail veered to the right and there were the jutting black spikes. Careen squeaked open the gate. We moved into a patch of cool air as I slipped off my jacket.

"Here," I said, draping the coat over her small shoulders.

She held the edges of the jacket.

"Aren't you going to be cold?"

I shrugged, slipping my hands in my pockets.

"... don't get cold easily."

Careen pulled the coat around her more.

"Thank you, but let me know if you get cold."

"Sure."

HILLMAN hovered on a glowing marble slab in a long rectangle in the center of the cemetery. Crying trails ran from the letters to the ground. On the right were smaller stones with the names stained dark. To the left was a newer headstone.

"This is Mother's," she whispered, kneeling down and brushing away leaves.

Careen Hillman
1901-1944
Beloved wife of Buddy Hillman

"I've come down here every week to put flowers on her grave and talk to her," she said softly. "I even write letters and leave them here."

The trees rustled above us and leaves scraped against the iron fence.

"I can't really remember much about the day she died," Careen said, still facing the stone. "It's all such a blur when I think about it. I just remember she was sick suddenly and then she died." Her hand floated through the near dark and touched the smooth marble. "Right after it happened Daddy sent me abroad. I was kind of sick and didn't even go to the funeral. I didn't go back to school for six months."

"You really going to Guienna Junior High?"

Careen turned around with her eyes flickering the light beyond.

"I just started in the eighth grade."

71

That was why I hadn't seen her. She was a year older.

"Oh," I nodded, looking at the name on the white marble and wanting to change the subject. "What was your mother like?"

Careen bowed her head, moving some grass with her loafer.

"She was a painter. Maybe you saw some of her paintings? There are some in the house."

She was standing so close I could hear her breathe.

"But most of them are still in her studio behind—"

Shivers went over me.

"You're cold, Lee! Here, take back your jacket."

"No I'm not—you can keep it. Tell me more about your mother."

I started rubbing my arms and she paused, but I told her I was just scratching.

"She had a wonderful library and read to me all the time. She even wrote poetry."

I nodded, shivering involuntarily again.

"You *are* cold! Either take your jacket or we'll go back to the house."

"—fine," I chattered.

"Let's go," she said taking my arm.

We started through the forest and I began talking about Lucas.

"What do you think made him change?"

"Guess the war. Used to talk all the time—even made up a play once together." I paused. "He did give me his Army hat, though." I kept my eyes on the black line of the path. "He and my older brother Burkie don't really get along and my sister hates him too ... only person I ever see her be nice to is Burkie. But he has a girlfriend now so maybe he'll be happy again."

The cluster of yellow lights from the barbecue were in the distance as we came out of the woods. I had my hands in my pockets, staring at the pale blue ground. Careen looped her hand through my arm and I forgot about everything.

9

*A smoking fire was started in the bottom of the tobacco
barn. The slaves fed the fire day and night with the flames
wetting their skin. Smoke flew up into the dark, curling white
out the sides of the barn. The hanging tobacco flickered
down and a haze spread over the plantation and smelled in
the trees after the fire was out. The smoking ended when the
tobacco was dry but pliable—this was called "case" by the
planters.*

After the first sugary dusting of snow on the dogwoods and
oaks, Burke was appointed to head the Herrin campaign in
Richmond. The book of articles I was keeping grew quickly
in the next three months. Even Christmas came and went with the
feeling that something bigger was going on. When I walked into his
study, Herrin pamphlets were stacked on his desk and several large
banners were propped in the corner. The bold red white and blue lettering looked out of place in the brown tones of his office. The phone
began to ring at odd hours, and many times when I went to the bathroom I saw a light on downstairs and could hear the murmur of my
father's voice.

There were many meetings where Addie would fix large pots of
coffee and men would sit around late into the night discussing strategy.
I didn't recognize a lot of these men, but Mr. Hillman was present at
every meeting. Burke allowed me to sit around and listen. Usually the

talk was about how many pamphlets and posters were needed and where the senator would be giving a speech. There were so many articles appearing that I didn't bother reading most of them and just pasted them in. I wish now I would have read the one article, but I just put it in with no idea how it would change all of our lives.

HERRIN: $1-A-DAY STATEMENT A LIE
RUMOR ATTRIBUTED TO AFL

Senator Herrin branded as a "lie" last night a purported AFL-inspired rumor that he had once said "one dollar a day is enough for any man to earn," and vigorously denounced "despicable whispering campaigns" such as that which he claimed is being waged against him.

"They are repeating an old story from years ago" he said, "that at one time I paid my apple pickers nine cents an hour. I have never paid my apple pickers by the hour, but have paid for picking by the crate at prevailing wages or better. The AFL is saying that in 1939 I permitted one-half of my apple crop to drop to the ground rather than pay more than one dollar a day. This is completely false."

It was Saturday. Cars had been coming into the drive all morning, and by one o'clock the living room was full of men. The couch had been pulled back from the fireplace and the day-room chairs brought in. Burke stood up and said he was going to read a letter he had received from the senator. There was something in his voice that made me pause outside the living room. I was in the hallway with my jacket on going to meet Clay and Jimmy. The last week of February had come and we were sure the snow would be gone with March. I sat on the bottom of the stairs as Burke read from a white paper.

"Gentlemen, as the campaign goes into its most critical stage, it is important to be alert to any false rumors that may be spread. The Political Action Committee of the AFL is expert at doing this. They have already spread it through all the unions that I stated a dollar a day is enough for anyone to earn; that

*I pay my apple pickers nine cents an hour; and that in 1939 I
let half of my apple crop drop rather than pay more than one
dollar a day. All of this, of course, is absolutely false, as I pay
more than standard wages and have always had my apples
picked by the crate. I wish you would communicate with me at
once in the event my record is misrepresented. I hope, also,
that you will use advertisements in the local newspapers and
local radio in presenting my candidacy and in answering any
charges made against me. Things look good, but we must not
relax our efforts, and it is imperative that every vote we have
be polled, as all the AFL people will be on hand. This is just
the beginning of the labor unions' fight to control our elec-
tions, and a large majority in this election would have a most
wholesome effect."*

Burke finished and placed the letter down on the table next to him.

"I'm sure everyone has read in the papers the charges made against
the senator by the Trenton people," he said slowly, placing one hand on
the table. "We will have to do our utmost to answer these charges with
facts and—"

"I say we go on the offensive against these union people!"

I stood up and saw Mr. Hillman in the middle of the room in one of
our wing chairs.

"Burke, how long are we going to let these agitators stir up the
working people of this city?" he continued, his flat eyes sweeping across
the men. "I hear they are trying to get the negroes to join the unions
and telling them they can have the white man's jobs. The unions will
do anything to win this election—we have to be willing to meet them
on their terms!"

The men in the room were already nodding. Even I felt the force of
Mr. Hillman's voice. It had the feeling of law when he spoke. My
father put his hand in his right coat pocket and nodded down to the
floor. I had seen him do that a hundred times. It meant he was tolerat-
ing something and was about to make his point.

"I think we have to ensure people do get the facts about the senator," he said quietly.

75

Mr. Hillman stoked his pipe with a wood match and looked up.

"What good will facts do, Burke, when the labor unions are spreading lies?"

My father's face was smooth.

"What do you suggest?"

The men in the room looked at Mr. Hillman. He snatched the pipe from his mouth.

"These union people spread lies—we spread lies about them! They attack the senator—we attack Trenton!"

The men murmured in agreement and I could see others nodding and looking at my father. Burke stared at the floor, his glasses down on his nose.

"I can understand your thinking," he said slowly, looking up. "But I think the temptation here is to resort to the tactics of the other party. We have to remember that we would be doing exactly what they want us to by resorting to that kind of thing. I know the senator would back me up on this if he were here. Our strategy should be to get out to the people the senator's position—and the facts that repudiate these charges."

"That won't help us, Burke," Mr. Hillman said, flatly. "I had to chase these union people out of my mill three times last week and production is beginning to fall off. Soon they won't be working, and then where will we be? It's happening to me now, but it's going to happen to all of you," he said, motioning across the room with his smoldering pipe. "These unions are parasites and once they're in you can't get rid of them. You have to stop them at the source and the source is *Trenton*! He's bringing them in; if we discredit him, we stop the unions!"

A rumbling went through the room. Burke pushed his jacket back from his vest. I could see the dull gold chain of his pocket watch.

"I'm going to have to differ with you on this," he said firmly. "I have to run this campaign as I see fit, and I'll not resort to the underhanded tactics of the other side."

Mr. Hillman leaned back against the chair with his eyes half open. His pipe smoldered two puffs. I wanted a car to go down the street, or a clock to strike, or somebody to cough, because there was a silence so heavy and ominous it gave me the chills. Burke looked around the silent room, then turned to a paper on the table.

"Now, the senator is due to speak at the courthouse...."

Clay held something in his hands that looked like a wooden book. I splattered through the slushy snow in the backyard with the late February sun on my face.

"What are you guys looking at?"

Jimmy glanced up.

"Oh, there you are! Thought maybe Careen Hillman had already dragged you away."

I ignored him and looked at the wooden book. It was Scotty's medals case.

"Clay brought Scotty's medals out and dropped them in the snow."

Jimmy and Clay were picking the bars out of the snow and putting them into the case. I knelt down and picked up the Silver Star laying face up in the sun. The smaller pins were barely visible. We picked up every medal we could find and finally it looked like we had them all.

"Don't see anymore," Jimmy said, standing up.

Clay looked at the case.

"Wait a minute—one's missing."

There was a dark spot where the medal had been.

"It's one of his bars!"

"It has to be here," I said, squinting at the watery snow.

"He'll kill me," Clay groaned.

"He's not coming back," Jimmy grumbled, kneeling down.

Clay straightened.

"What'd you say?"

"Lee—"

I turned and Careen was standing on the edge of the yard.

"Hi, Careen."

She put a hand to her mouth.

"What are you doing?"

"Clay lost something," I called over.

She looked at the slushy yard.

77

"I'd come out there, but the yard looks awful wet. Are you coming over?"

"—be there in a minute."

I hunched back down. Clay and Jimmy were examining pieces of snow.

"Find it?"

"No," Jimmy said, his eyes burning queerly.

I watched Clay pick apart pieces of wet snow and could see Careen waiting in the trees.

"Don't know if we're going to find it," I said, glancing to the woods again.

"Go on Lee, *Careen's* waiting," Jimmy said in a high voice.

"Shut up."

He waved his hand.

"That's alright—leave your friends—don't want you around anyway." Jimmy nodded with his face close to the snow. "Go on—go with your *girlfriend.*"

I glared at Jimmy, then turned and walked toward the woods.

We walked through the black - and - white forest. The snow was heavy in the trees and white tufts fell from branches with muffled thuds. The path had streaks of red clay and the sun made the tree branches like wires against the snow. Careen walked with her hands in a white muff until we came to the shrouded trees that led to the graveyard. She hooked an arm through mine.

"Let's go take a peek at Mother's grave," she whispered. "I'd like to clean the snow off."

The snow lined the iron and the smooth white had sunk lower on the grave. The HILLMAN stone had a tuft of snow washing down the face of the marble. Careen pushed open the gate and chunks of soggy ice fell to the ground. She walked to her mother's grave with her steps following her and brushed the slush off the top.

"Mother's grave looks nice in the snow," she said, her voice a glass whisper against the coated silence.

Careen knelt slowly with her coat a deeper red in front of the stone. Snow fell from the trees in the forest like small breaths as I stood next to her and stared at the cold grave. Careen reached up slowly and touched the engraved marble, then began to move her finger very slowly in the lettering. She followed each letter perfectly until she had completed the curves of her own name.

10

The tobacco leaves lay on the table running the length of the barn. The women were better than the men and stood barefoot in the hay looking down at the leaves till all the tobacco was stemmed. Wire and wood barrels were behind each slave. The slave men rolled the tobacco barrels out of the barn and used a hand press to push the leaves down. The strongest slaves muscled the wooden pole handle around, screwing the wood block down into the creaking wire and wood hogshead. Leaves were added and the slaves winched the press handle until the slats spread and the hogshead weighed almost 1,000 pounds.

A heavy white haze hung over the back woods for weeks. An unseasonably hot April had come to Richmond and popped flowers open and sprouted green leaves and grass almost overnight. People were already saying the coming summer was to be another hot one. I learned later it was during this time Fanny went to a meeting of the Second District Negro Democrats.

Fanny still helped Addie and sang with a strong voice rising up like women on the radio. Fanny said her real mother had been a singer and sang on the radio once. She never talked about her father. She would peel potatoes with her shirt tight on her body and I'd hear Nelson in the woods again, *"Ain't no secret you been sleepin' with the white men, Fanny."*

Fanny would talk and sing, then laugh for no reason, her mouth wide open with her neck moving up and down. Addie said Fanny had "strange notions" from her real parents. Sometimes Fanny's eyes became black and she would curse and talk about "shufflin' niggers" to herself like there was someone else there.

There were signs and an article I cut out announcing Eugene Trenton would be speaking to the Second District Negro Democrats. The signs were in the south part of downtown Richmond, made out of poster board with stenciled black letters. Fanny must have seen one of these, because at 7:30 she was on the bus to the colored section of town. The Southern Baptist Church had dark, soot-stained windows and a large sign saying ALL WELCOME. It wasn't a big church and the double doors were open to let the air through. By the time Fanny arrived the warm air rolling under the bare lightbulbs felt like a wall. The pews were full and the folding chairs had been taken. Fanny had to stand against the back wall.

White men in suits stood in front of the altar and Fanny noticed the well-dressed negroes who sat politely waiting. She looked down at her own clothes and pressed against the wall more. The high ceiling echo came down like a wave and a man in a black suit strode to the front in a way that made people watch.

"I would like to thank everyone for coming tonight," he said in a crisp, deep voice. "For those of you who are new tonight, my name is Silas Jackson and I am the chairman of the Second District Negro Democrats. It gives me great pleasure to introduce our speaker, the senatorial candidate for Virginia, *Eugene Trenton!"*

The clapping was loud in the church. One of the white men walked up and shook hands with Silas Jackson, then turned and waved to the people. He was thick-set, his face florid and shiny in the bare light. He wiped his brow with a handkerchief several times, running a hand back over his brown hair.

"Thank you, Mr. Jackson!"

He looked to the side and put his hands in front of him like a preacher.

"Friends, I'm mighty glad you have invited me to your meeting tonight. As you all know we have an election coming up for the senator of this great state of Virginia!" He unclasped his hands and held up one finger. "This state has been run for fifteen years by a man who has two concerns: Help the moneyed corporations and rich landowners, and keep the workingman and the negro from enjoying the benefits they are entitled to!"

There was clapping and people yelling out, *"Yes, sir! Yes, sir!"*

"I think the Second District Negro Democrats have a stake in this election! It's no news to you that Senator Herrin has not been a friend to the negro in this state!"

"Yes, sir! Yes, sir!"

"He has always represented only the rich and those who want to keep the negro and the workingman from getting their fair share!"

"Yes, sir! Yes, sir!"

"The people who want Senator Herrin are those who seek the status quo. Myself and the friends of labor want to *change* what has been in Virginia. We believe there is enough for everyone to go around! Not just for the few! I pledge to you, my friends, that if elected, I will not forget the people who put me there, and the negro can expect what's coming to him from Eugene Trenton!"

The avalanche of applause broke and people were standing and calling out. The white man smiled, his face beaded wet, holding his hand up.

"As you know, Senator Herrin has some of the largest apple orchards in the state, and you might have read in the paper that he also said *a dollar a day* is enough for any man to earn in these orchards!"

Fanny must have been alive now with the feeling that events were moving ahead and if she was to jump on the train it had to be now. She worked in the orchards and she felt this man was talking directly to her.

"DO WE WANT A MAN WHO SAYS A DOLLAR A DAY OR LESS IS ENOUGH FOR ANY MAN TO EARN?"

"No! No, sir! No, sir!"

"MAYBE SOME OF YOU EVEN WORK IN THOSE ORCHARDS!"

Fanny saw the headlight and heard the blast of the whistle as the train came down the mountain. She felt the rails shaking with thunder as she was drawn into the rumbling tide.

"YES, SIR! I DO! I WORK IN THE ORCHARDS!"

The white man squinted against the light, peering into the smoky darkness, looking for the voice he heard. The black glittering eyes turned to Fanny.

"And how much does he pay, Miss?"

Fanny heard herself with her voice clear and resonant in the church.

"SENATOR HERRIN DON"T EVEN PAY A DOLLAR TO NEGRO PICKERS! THE WHITE MAN GETS A DOLLAR AND WE GET FIFTY CENTS!"

The black faces around her shook and a buzzing anger rose.

"YOU SEE, MY FRIENDS! SENATOR HERRIN IS OUT TO *HURT* THE NEGRO! YOU HEARD IT YOURSELF! FIFTY CENTS A DAY HE PAYS HER! *THIS MUST BE STOPPED!*"

The room roared forth and people looked back at Fanny and nodded. The white man squinted at her.

"I would like to talk to you, Miss, after the meeting."

Fanny put a hand to herself as more people turned around to look at her. She felt only the wind of her ride.

The meeting ended and people hovered around the front talking. I don't know when Fanny went down and talked to Eugene Trenton exactly, but that was when she met Silas Jackson. He was the final conductor ensuring her passage. Fanny was taken with his dark suit, pressed shirt and red tie—the way his shoulder muscles broke the creases of his coat. She was taken with his brilliant smile and perfect speech and the way he never looked down.

One of the men from the union with a big-city suit and slicked-back hair suggested they give Fanny a ride home. Fanny found herself in the leather-smelling car between the Union men with Silas Jackson and Eugene Trenton in the front. Fanny had never seen negroes ride in the front with white men. The men from the union were very polite and asked questions while taking notes on pads. They all smoked and Fanny smoked too, feeling more important as they lit her cigarette for her. Silas Jackson turned around and smiled at her when she promised to help them any way she could.

At some point the car pulled over to a diner and Eugene Trenton and the labor men went in to get more cigarettes. Fanny and Silas stayed in the car, the small cardboard *"WHITES ONLY"* sign visible to them in the rainy night.

Fanny liked the sound of his voice and found out he was from the North, and this furthered her dream of the North where negroes were well-dressed and educated. Fanny turned and rolled down the window. She looked out and saw Mr. Trenton and the other men buying the cigarettes. The waitress at the counter looked past the men and could see Fanny in the car. She stared, she said later, because she was wondering what a negro was doing with well-dressed white men. Fanny met the woman's gaze, put the cigarette to her lips, and blew the smoke out in a long, white stream.

11

The hogshead rolled deadly then stopped. The sand road to the river was like the sun and salt stung their eyes. The packed tobacco barrel rolled flat dead again. Hot wood scraped their palms and turned slowly with no wobble. The slaves palmed the wood again, the sun sweat going down with the wood, and pushed with their palms again, with their arms again, with their backs again. They pushed until the rolling roads to the river could be seen a hundred years later.

Lucas came through the sunlight snapping his tie around his neck and looking more like himself than I had seen him in months. He had come back in the warming months and I think it was because of Bunny. I laid on his bed while he hobbled around and dressed, patting aftershave on his face and smoothing down his hair.

"Did I tell you she was a welder during the war, Lee?" He asked, buttoning his cuffs and looking at me in the dresser mirror.

I shook my head.

"Welded tanks during the war and loved it. Good money too—really hated to lose the job when the war ended. She supports her grandmother." He was smiling again, checking his teeth in the mirror. "But she's something. I don't think there's anything she can't do if she wants to. She'll be a great reporter one day."

He leaned back and buttoned his collar, then flipped it up and slid the tie back and forth on his neck. "It's pretty amazing—I mean with her parents being killed and all—she says they were boozers—Bunny can drink pretty good herself." Lucas had his chin up, measuring the red striped tie around his neck. "But she can hold it."

He crossed the tie, bringing it through for the knot. I sat up on the bed.

"What makes her want to be a reporter?"

He shrugged.

"Think she's always wanted to do something like that. She said she used to copy down newspaper articles when she was a kid and pretend she wrote them. She's written a lot of stories and stuff. Matter of fact she said she was going to give me one to read—I told her you're a big reader."

He slipped the knot up under his neck, snugged it and flipped his collar down.

"Told her I was a reader?"

"Sure I did—I told her I *used* to be a big reader." He grinned and winked in the mirror. "Man, I haven't read anything in a long time."

He grabbed his cane.

"C'mon, I'll pick up Bunny and we'll get a shake at Willard's."

I sat next to Bunny's long legs that slanted together to the car floor from her skirt. She looked different from dinner with her hair blowing wild in the car wind. Lucas kept his arm around her and she would hit him when his hand squeezed her side. Her lips were the deep red of the movies and when she smiled her teeth were red in the front. Lucas laughed a lot and she stayed leaning against him the whole time we were at Willard's.

"What grade are you in, Lee?"

I sucked on my chocolate shake.

"Seventh."

"Lee's smart, they ought to have him teaching the class," Lucas said, squeezing Bunny and making her jump.

"Lucas! Do you like school?"

"Like it alright—"

"*Lucas!*"

They stared at each other and kissed. I went back to my shake.

"—saying you like school, Lee," Lucas said, still looking at Bunny.

"What do you like to read, Lee?"

"*Moby Dick* is Lee's favorite."

"That's a wonderful story!"

Her slender hand was moving around Lucas's hand and then they were kissing again. I concentrated on the lump of ice cream in the bottom of my glass and determined a spoon would be required over a straw. Bunny turned and her eyes were soft and smoky and I don't think she even saw me.

"Reading is ... wonderful."

"Me too," Lucas said staring into her eyes.

Katy and Burkie had become engaged before Christmas and I had forgotten all about the wedding planned for the end of April till I saw the Dealy's car come down the drive. Mother and Mrs. Dealy had started planning right after they were engaged. On the Saturday of the first week in April, Katy, Mrs. Dealy, Bunny, and Terry Bowers were over for dinner. Katy was going to wear her mother's wedding dress and after dinner the women clustered around her in the living room to work on the dress. I had spent the time after dinner in my room searching the paper for articles about the election and found two.

NEGRO GROUP GIVES SUPPORT TO TRENTON

Silas Jackson, chairman of the Second District Negro Demo-crats, announced today his organization was supporting Eu-gene A. Trenton for the Senate. The organization probably rep-resents between 5,000 and 6,000 votes in the district, says Jack-son. "We believe in Mr. Trenton's objectives and feel a change would do everybody good." Eugene Trenton spoke to a meet-ing of the Second District Negro Democrats last Wednesday night.

HERRIN BLASTS AUTOCRATIC LABOR CONTROL
Senator J. Herrin asserted in a radio broadcast that the time has come for courageous action to control the labor unions that are destroying our way of life. Senator Herrin, whose re-election is opposed by the AFL Political Action Committee, declared that he "would prefer to be defeated a thousand times rather than to yield in the smallest degree to the autocratic labor unions, because in doing so I feel I would have betrayed the American people and particularly those in Virginia." He also challenged his opponent for the Democratic nomination, Eugene Trenton, to bring forth "proof" that he had made the statement, 'a dollar a day is enough for any man to earn.' "This is a lie and they know it, and that's why they can't bring forth any kind of evidence."

I took the newspaper and scrapbook out to the porch steps and sat down. The paper was luminous in the late evening light that bleached the gravel of the driveway and dyed the trees and grass black. A car whispered by on Hermitage Road with the motor's report lingering far behind the hum of the wheels. Bunny and Lucas were in the porch swing and Terry Bowers leaned on the porch railing. The murmur of their voices blended into the early crickets that made the night feel like summer.

"Daddy making you rich?"

I finished cutting out the last article.

"Maybe," I shrugged, picking up the jar of paste.

"Lee's become a newspaper tycoon," Lucas said. "That right, Lee?"

"Maybe."

They laughed. I pressed the articles on the blobs of glue and stood up as my father walked out.

"Lee wants his money, Daddy."

"He does, does he," he said taking the scrapbook and holding it down to see. "How many are there, Lee?"

"Two."

"Alright, if you'll leave this in my study," he said, fishing out some coins from his pants pocket.

I took the scrapbook and the two dimes and there was low laughter again from the swing.

"I'd say Lee has a racket going."

Burke took out his red pack of Viceroys.

"Lee, you tell them that what you are doing is pivotal to the election."

I glanced at them in vindication and they laughed louder. Burke cupped his cigarette, then walked over to the swing. I sat back down on the steps with the scrapbook next to me.

"Congratulations on your appointment in the Herrin campaign sir," Terry said, his face dark against his light shirt.

"Thank you, Terry. We haven't seen much of you around."

"Yes, sir, I've been meaning to stop by more, but school has been keeping me busy...." He motioned to Bunny. "Lucas has been keeping himself busy, too."

Burke's low laughter floated out.

"How's the election coming, Mr. Hartwell?" Bunny asked, sitting up.

My father turned with his cigarette just below his mouth and tilted his head.

"The unions are giving the senator quite a run." He paused. "But I think he'll win."

Addie's voice rumbled out of the hallway darkness through the screen door.

"The cloth ain't no good, Miz Hartwell, 'cause it ain't tearin' worth a damn!"

Burke grinned and crossed his arms with his watch chain peeking from his vest.

"I hope you two elope so I don't have to go through this again."

Lucas looked down.

"Don't worry about me, Daddy."

"And what lucky young lady is going to get you?"

Terry shrugged and grinned.

"All the good girls have been taken." He looked directly at Bunny. "Lucas got her first."

Bunny smiled and stretched out against Lucas with her head on his shoulder. The swing creaked in the night shadow and Burke turned back to the soft light on the lawn.

Katy hovered in the center of the living room with white billowing from her narrow waist and covering the footstool. Her neck was skinny above the lace swirling over her bare shoulders. Addie held on to the bottom of the dress with her back a flat gray table in the shaded lamplight. Mother and Mrs. Dealy surveyed the progress.

"Miz Katy, you got to stand still so I can get the pins in," Addie said from below.

"You are going to be so pretty," Mrs. Dealy murmured.

"She ain't goin' to be anything if she don't quit movin'!"

"Dear—please try and remain still."

I leaned against the wall and watched Katy's mouth pucker. Katy didn't like Addie. She had small brown mouse eyes that didn't smile when Burkie told stories about her. Burkie said she was going to make a good wife and her father owned the bank in town. Katy laughed a lot before with Scotty and Lucas, but now they just walked past each other like two strangers. Mimaw said Burkie was getting in over his head, but I knew different.

I had gone with Burkie to the hardware store the day before. The road to the store went past the cemetery and he turned into the evening-shaded trees without a word. The car lights flared the top of the headstones and burned patches on the hills of spring grass. I looked at Burkie, but he just kept his eyes straight ahead. We reached the coolness of the valley of the cemetery and started up the hill toward the back. He finally stopped the car and turned off the motor. The car heat popped beneath us.

"Be right back, Lee—gotta get something."

I stared at him.

"Where you going?"

"Have to do something for Mrs. Nettleton ... I'll be right back."

I watched him as he walked over toward the big dogwood by the Nettletons' plot. His checkered shirt and light pants floated away and vanished. I looked around nervously. The gravestones were black against the horizon light and the car didn't seem any type of protection against lingering ghosts. After a few hours, that were a few minutes, I got out of the car. The door slam was swallowed in the silence. The marble

90

stones were colored now with the faint pink of dusk; white crosses and marble slabs stretched out into the trees and down the hills. I leaned against the warm hood in the cooling damp. Blackbirds flecked across the sky.

I decided to go find Burkie and request his presence back in the car so we could get the hell out of there. I started walking, then running to the tree where Burkie had disappeared. I heard something and ducked below the branches. The leaves tickled my face as I saw him standing with his hands in his pockets. He hunched down suddenly and rested his arms on his thighs. He took a breath and looked down at the flat stone in front of him.

"Wish you were here, buddy, you'd surely laugh at all of us."

I tried to breathe quieter. Burkie picked up a blade of grass from the top of the stone. He held it between his fingers and smoothed it out with his forefinger and thumb.

"I'm going to marry Katy," he said, his mouth staying open. "I think she still loves you, but she's had a tough time of it." Fireflies floated yellow behind him. He kept moving his finger over the grass. "*Damn* ... wish I had gone with you and Lucas. I don't know what happened ... but I wish I'd been with you guys." He pulled his hand across his nose and sniffed, his eyes glistening in the dusk.

I watched him for another minute, then crept quietly back to the car and waited against the hood. By the time Burkie came back the twilight had gathered behind a line of trees in the west and the stones were black and cold. He carried a white vase and got in the car without looking at me or saying a word.

The cemetery faded and there was Katy with her hands on her waist.

"You like my wedding dress, Lee?"

I stood up from the wall and nodded.

"It's pretty."

She smiled.

"Why thank you. I think so too."

I started up the dark stairs with my scrapbook and thought that Mimaw was dead wrong about Burkie. He knew.

12

The barrels rolled hard in the winter months and the last of the tobacco was shipped just after Christmas. The land spread out flat and gray and the slaves could see others already kneeling in the seed beds. The last of the ships drew down the river until the masts were trees against the horizon. The slaves went to their cabins for the winter months. The big house trailed smoke from the two chimneys and the slaves made their fires.

I watched the afternoon light sheen dully on the back of Addie's gray uniform. Her fleshy arms wiggled. Addie set the syrup and peanut butter sandwich on the kitchen table and went back to the stove and continued peeling potatoes. She had been strangely quiet since I came home from school. The week had been full of preparations for the wedding. The reception was going to be under a tent covering the entire back yard and Addie had been grumbling all week about working too hard. But now it was the day before the wedding and she was silent.

"How's the wedding coming?"

The water plunked in front of her.

"Good."

"And Katy?"

"She good."

"Did she finally get in her dress?"

"Uh huh."

Addie dropped another potato in the water. I leaned back and touched a hole in the syrup-stained bread.

"Anything going on?"

Her arms stopped moving and her neck craned around with the brown of her eyes in the white like paint mixed by being too close.

"Nothin' goin' on."

I sat up straight.

"Concern the wedding?"

"Uh huh."

"Concern Burkie? Katy?"

Addie shook her head.

"Daddy?"

Addie wiped her hands on her apron and walked to the door. She pushed it open and peered out, then crossed back noiselessly to the table and stood above me.

"Lucas...." Addie whispered, her face close. *"He gone!"*

I stared at her.

"What do you mean—"

"Quiet, boy!"

Addie glanced at the door, lowering her voice.

"Your mother told me not to tell this to no one!"

"What do you mean he's gone?" I whispered.

"He ain't been home since yesterday morning and your mother been worried sick," Addie continued, her eyes glowing.

I shrugged.

"Maybe he just went somewhere."

Addie shook her head.

"Miz Bunny gone too an' Miz Bunny's grandmother call here this morning and say she found a note sayin' they *eloped*!"

I jerked in the seat.

"THEY ELOPED!"

Addie turned to the door like someone had grabbed her.

"Boy, you going to get us both in trouble if you don't keep quiet! Mistah Hartwell mad, an' he say Lucas is no longer a member of the family!"

I stared at Addie. She nodded solemnly.

"Threw Lucas out of the house?"

She glanced at the door again.

"Your mother call him at work, an' he say on the phone if that true an' they eloped, Lucas is out of the house! He say how can Lucas do it on the week of Burkie's weddin'. Your mother taken to her bed and talkin' about goin' to the hospital for a rest cure. Mistah Hartwell come home and call all over tryin' to find out where they is. Miz Bunny grandmother say they gone to South Carolina."

"Where's Burkie?"

"He come home from his school, an' he say that Lucas done it to him because he don't want him an' Miz Katy to get married, 'cause he goin' to marry Scotty old girl, an' he say Lucas don't like that. And Mistah Hartwell say to Burkie that Lucas thrown out of the house an' ain't goin' to the weddin'!"

Addie shook her head slowly.

"I makin' supper for your mother. Mistah Hartwell tell me to take care of her 'cause he don't want her going to the hospital with the weddin' tomorrow," she finished, going back to the stove and picking up the potatoes.

Addie took a deep breath with the back of her arms wiggling again.

"I feel these is troubled times," she said, with her head down. "I surely do."

The thunder cracked blue outside the dining room windows; a sprite of cool air smelling faintly like our garden hose flowed in on the evening breeze. The table was conspicuously empty. Mother was in bed with the beginning of the flu—at least that's what I was told. Mimaw had a real cold. Lucas's seat was empty and there wasn't even a setting. Sally and Jim had found a small apartment the week before but had come over for dinner. I knew it was because Sally wanted to hear about Lucas. My father had been silent all evening.

The kitchen door swung open.

"Takin' a tray up to Miz Hartwell."

Burke looked up at Addie as if he didn't hear her.

"—alright, Addie."

Addie groaned up the stairs, her heavy steps moving above us on the creaking boards. I moved the potatoes and ham around with my fork, jumping when the phone clattered in the hallway. Burke dabbed his mouth with the napkin and went into the living room without a word.

Sally leaned into the candlelight.

"Has anyone heard anything?"

Burkie shook his head.

"Daddy called all over South Carolina to find out if they were married by a justice of the peace."

"He really threw him out of the house?"

Burkie leaned heavily on his elbows like a judge.

"Daddy said if he's eloped, then he's banished and can't come to the wedding."

"I can't believe Lucas would do something like that."

Sally turned on Jim in a small fury.

"*Why not?* Lucas has always tried to ruin this family! And now with Burkie's wedding this weekend he's tried it again by running off with that ... that trash, Bunny!"

"Sally, I wouldn't say that—"

"I thought it was ridiculous the way he brought her over here and she gave herself airs about being a journalist." Sally turned and swept the table. "She's from no family and from what I've heard she's been around."

"I like her!"

Sally fixed me with her cold eyes.

"There are some things you are too young to understand, Lee," she said. "I think he did it—"

"Understand you never liked Lucas."

She turned back to me with her thin lips wrinkled and tight, but I heard Burkie's voice.

"Watch your mouth, boy."

Hard steps came across the hallway and Burke walked back to the

95

table and sat down. He scooted his chair up and snapped his napkin into his lap. He looked around the table and no one moved.

"That was the courthouse in Charleston," he said in a drum-tight voice, picking up his knife and fork. "Bunny and your brother Lucas were married this morning."

He cut a piece of ham and the knife snapped to the plate like a shot. Burkie's and Sally's eyes met through the candles and I looked at Lucas's empty chair. The world rumbled and darkened outside.

"Don't drop it!"

Addie handed me the food tray and her voice followed me up the steps. "She holler anyway an' I don't want to hear her screamin' about no dropped food!"

I started up the winding back steps to Mimaw's room. The steps were steep and narrow and I wondered how Addie managed to fit up and down the steps so many times a day. I balanced the tray and knocked on Mimaw's door lightly.

"Mimaw, you awake?"

"Come in!"

I opened the door into the steamy wave of medicine and old furniture. Mimaw's hair glowed against the headboard in the dim light. She turned on the propped pillows, her watery eyes snapping.

"That Addie keeps me up all night with that snoring of hers and then tries to starve me when I'm sick!" Mimaw sat up from under the blankets and comforters. "Set the tray on the bed, Lee. There's no room on the table, old people have to have their medicine ... let's see what she's trying to kill me with now."

She snatched back the napkin and squinted at the food, then sat back.

"Well, you can't ruin a ham but so much," she grumbled, spreading the napkin on the covers. "Keep me company, boy. I know everyone else thinks I'm dead already, but I'm still here, so keep the old woman company while she eats."

I sank down on the end of her bed and watched her shakily pick up a fork and spear one of the pieces of ham Addie had cut for her. She chewed on the meat and sipped her coffee. A dark spot appeared on the napkin.

"*Damn!*" She dabbed her chin. "That's the hellish thing of being old, boy—no dignity."

She set the coffee down and turned her head, staring with one glittering eye.

"Mighty quiet tonight."

I shrugged and rubbed my sneaker on the dark rug.

"Just sittin'."

"Listening to me curse." She smiled wryly. "I suppose I was quiet around old people when I was your age. But when you're young you just have to tolerate old people, Lee." Mimaw leaned back against the headboard. "Your father throw Lucas out of the house?"

I nodded. "Guess they got married in South Carolina."

Mimaw touched the napkin to her mouth and laid it on the tray.

"That boy has been troubled and I wonder anyone is surprised at what he did." She stared at me as if I should have known. "Burke is mad—I'm sure of that and I don't know how long his anger will last, but Lucas will have to fend for himself ... at least for a while." Mimaw shook her head wearily, her eyes shining like glass in the dark. "The boy was born under a dark star. He was melancholy as a child, and I don't know if that was his disposition or if it was Livvy. Lucas was the middle child and the middle child always suffers." Her hand went up. "I think Olivia was a good mother, but she and Burke were going through some times then." She smoothed the quilt, her hands moving out from the middle. "Your mother taken to her bed?"

"Addie took her a tray."

Mimaw's mouth went tight.

"That's Ramon blood—strong in a headwind, but liable to break at the mast all the same." She shook her head. "I think growing up as she did has a lot to do with the way she is now. Horrible thing when all you have is fine lineage but have to work like a dog just to feed yourself." Mimaw saw my eyes and continued. "I don't know what happened to her father. The Ramons produced a litter of drunks from what I understand and I think he was one of them—her mother worked in a department store to support them and then Livvy worked there." Mimaw pursed her lips like she was going to spit. "Those rice planters were a tough bunch, but the children and grandchildren were soft, and I don't think any of the Ramons had any money left." She paused. "I doubt she told Burke when they were courting that she worked in a department store. Of course by then I think her mother was sick, and to Livvy's credit she stayed with her and nursed her till the day she died."

Mimaw licked her lips.

"But Lucas was a tough pregnancy for Livvy and the delivery was horrible! I think it nearly killed her. She was in the hospital for weeks, and when she came out she was a different woman."

"How's that?"

She looked at me as if she had forgotten I was there.

"I think she wanted to go off and be a flapper!" Mimaw leaned her neck back on the pillow. "Burke is a good man, but I believe your mother for a time wanted a different life. Sally remembers—Livvy told that girl more than any young girl should know about her parents and I think that's why Sally is such a cold fish today. She probably thought her mother was just going to take off!"

Mimaw smiled with a gleam in her eyes.

"We all love wild men, but they make *terrible* husbands—and during all this there is this little baby Lucas—he certainly didn't look like a Hartwell with those dark eyes and hair."

Mimaw licked her lips again, the withered skin beneath her chin wiggling. I leaned back on the bed and stared up at the flowing white canopy.

"I spent a lot of time with Lucas while Livvy went off and joined clubs and did God knows what else." Mimaw let out a sharp laugh. "I can tell you, she and Burke had some arguments in those days. There were times I was sure Livvy was going to leave him. He was building his law practice and working long hours, and Livvy already had Burkie and Sally who were real attention-getters."

"They're glad Daddy threw Lucas out."

"Burkie is ornery," she said quietly. "But maybe being dumb does that to a person."

I sat up and stared at Mimaw.

"Oh, I don't mean dumb—but Burkie is not bright, school-wise, and the boy has always known it. I remember your father would have talks with his teachers and tell him to study, and Burkie would study for hours and the boy still did poorly. But Lucas was smart and did well in school and Burkie knew it. Maybe it just comes down to Lucas is smaller and looks different, but Burkie has always seemed to be jealous of the boy." She paused. "And Sally has always had sand in her craw from having to grow up too fast, and hates anyone who upsets Livvy, and Lucas has done that in his time."

She was silent and brushed something off the spread.

"But Livvy decided she wanted to be a mother again and that's when she had you, and she was very good to you, Lee."

Mimaw tilted her head back and looked down her nose.

"How old you think I am, boy?"

She didn't wait for me to answer.

"I'm eighty-six ... and I should be proud of that, and I am," she said, touching the wood table next to the bed with her fingers. She stared in the half-dark, her eyes misting.

"During the siege of Richmond there was nothing to eat and we had come into town because the Yankees had chased us off our planta- tion. I was just five years old, can you imagine that?" Mimaw put her head back. "We would have eaten anything! A dog, a cat. *Anything!*" Mimaw paused and smiled. "That's where I met your grandfather. I was just sixteen and he was older and wild, but he had left too much of himself in that war...." The light faded from her face and her skin sagged down. "Died in a duel, that's what they said, but it was probably just a bar fight."

"Daddy know him?"

Mimaw looked at me.

"No. He died when Burke was still just a baby. Burke was my last and I married Mr. Wilkins, the judge." Mimaw breathed in sharply. "He was a good man—but he was stern and God-fearing. He was a minister before he went into law and became a judge. He was a world of difference from Jesse—Burke grew up in Mr. Wilkins's world, and I know it helped him to study law and be the man he is." She paused. "But he could certainly put the fear of God into a small boy."

She looked up with the light from the door in her watery blue eyes.

"When you get everything taken away from you, you learn what is important, Lee. Mr. Wilkins saved my family from ruin and I did what

I had to do—but it was that Baptist minister who threw Lucas out of the house today."

Mimaw was quiet. Church bells rang in the distance.

"I have suffered the pain of the *damned* in my time! I just hope Burke sees through before it's too late. It's a terrible thing to split up a family."

I nodded and Mimaw shook her head, smoothing the quilt again.

"I don't like the feel of things. That Bunny is three times the woman Katy is. Katy's heart is with that dead boy and she will rule Burkie to his dying day. Burkie and Sally think that Lucas got what he deserves, but I have faith in the boy. He's got a lot of your father in him."

Mimaw closed her eyes and leaned back on the pillow with her face pale.

"Lee, take that tray for me. I'm suddenly tired."

I stood up and gently picked up the tray. She turned away and I walked to the door.

"Goodnight, boy...."

I stopped at the door. There was just the steady tick in the darkness and Mimaw's white hair by the lamp.

"Goodnight Mimaw," I whispered, closing the door quietly.

13

Black lines of snow curved into the distance on the tobacco fields. The snow was on the slave cabins and the eaves of the big house. The planter drank with his neighbors and celebrated the tobacco crop. At night, the blue-white land spread out from his window with the crackle of the fireplace at his back. He could see chimney smoke tufting from the squat cabins and a black figure passing between the moon-white houses.

The Saturday morning breeze pushed the shade from my window. I could hear people tromping up and down the steps with voices in the backyard. I pulled up the shade to the sun-bright checkerboard floating and ruffling in wind waves that snapped across the canvas like water. The tent had been set up the day before with men putting up long poles that smelled like railroad ties and spreading canvas till it covered the yard.

There had been cooking going on all week in our kitchen as well as the Nettletons' and the Masons'. I went down the back steps to the kitchen smelling already of smoked ham, fried chicken, fresh-baked biscuits, yams, cranberry sauce, grits, and thick, dark gravy.

"Fanny—get that bird out of that stove before it burn up! I told you to watch it. Sara, get those yams ready to go in an' put them rolls in—we ain't got time to cook 'em separately."

Addie rumbled into the pantry. The kitchen was full of women in gray uniforms. Addie's sister, Mary, was putting sweet potatoes in a pan, Sara from the Dealys' was stirring gravy on top of the stove, and Anna from the Hillmans' got a ham ready to go in the oven as Fanny chopped vegetables. Addie squeezed past the dull aluminum-colored warmers lined in front of the pantry door and came back into the kitchen wiping her forehead. A hot, blue haze rolled in the window light with the greasy exhaust fan above the back door running wide open.

"I told Mistah Hartwell we need more warmers to keep all this food warm. I ain't got any space left!"

Addie slammed two pans up on the counter and wiped her face again. Anna laughed by the stove.

"Mistah Hartwell havin' some kind of party."

Addie's eyes flashed up while she smeared grease on the pans.

"An' you ain't never goin' to see another one!"

Nelson came in the open back door carrying more pans.

"Got the pans from the Hillmans," he said, setting the pans down on the middle table, his work gloves sticking out of his back pocket and his cigarette ashing on the floor.

Addie stopped her greased hands.

"They ain't goin' there! Bring them pans here." She slammed her hand on the greased pan. "I ain't goin' to get all this shit done if I have to chase you for the pans!"

"Pardon me, ladies," he said, smoke puffing from the sides of his mouth, holding the pans up as a shield.

"Don't pay no attention to her, Mistah Johnson. Addie just mad 'cause she don't have no man of her own to boss around," Anna said lifting up the ham.

Addie wiped her hands and grabbed the pans from Nelson.

"I got no time for this shit."

"She is a mean one," Sara murmured, kneading dough. "Mary, how can you be so sweet an' your sister be so mean?"

Mary tilted her head down at the sweet potatoes she was arranging in a pan and smiled.

"I don't know, guess Addie just had a harder life than me."

"That right, an' it gettin' goddamn harder, too," Addie muttered, crossing to the stove and seeing me for the first time. "Lee, I ain't got no time!"

Nelson took the cigarette from his mouth.

"Where were you when I fed the goats this mornin', Lee?"

"Sorry Nelson, I forgot."

"Don't you have somethin' to do in the yard?" Addie grumbled, pushing past him.

Nelson stared at her.

"Reckon I do at that!"

He pulled the work gloves out of his pocket and went out the back door.

"—too busy to get you anything to eat now," Addie said, furiously greasing another pan.

Anna looked up at me.

"Lee, when you comin' to visit the Hillmans again? I know Careen just been pining while you ain't there."

Fanny smiled from where she was chopping vegetables.

"How come you never told me, Lee? You just breakin' all the little white girls' hearts."

"Fanny, you watch them potatoes!" Addie finished one pan and picked up another. "I ain't got time to be watchin' you every minute."

"Hello—"

A man with slicked-back hair poked his head through the kitchen door. Addie stood up, beads of sweat on her exhausted face.

"You the warmer man?"

"Sure am," he nodded. "Where do you want them? I got two more."

Addie was wiggling her arms around on the pan again.

"Put 'em in the dinin' room. I ain't got no room anywhere else."

"Will do."

Addie's voice followed me back up the steps.

"I ain't never doin' this again. Mistah Hartwell goin' to have to get somebody else. I retired from this shit!"

I don't remember a lot about the wedding itself, but the reception seemed like it went on forever. The wedding was the echoing voices of the church and a lot of tense, whisperish voices followed by a great relief when the church doors opened and Katy and Burkie were showered with rice. Then everyone was at Buckeye and I was bringing up the tail end of a long receiving line. People made their way through the house to the backyard and disappeared under the red and white tent. Food was laid out on tables with Fanny, Sara, and Anna carrying trays of drinks. Addie commanded the whole operation from the kitchen.

Cars spilled out of the driveway and lined Hermitage Road on both sides and some people had to walk four blocks to reach the house. The roar from the backyard could be heard in the front of the house. Ronny Meyer had arrived with his society band from New York and the band warmed up as the squeal of a trumpet leapt over the wave of people talking.

So many people passed through the receiving line I gave up trying to remember who anybody was. Burke greeted everyone by name and talked to them. It was Addie who pulled me out of the line.

"You slower than molasses in January," she whispered, pulling me into the kitchen. "You has a telephone call."

"Who—"

Addie shook her head and went to a big pot on the stove.

"Just go pick it up 'fore someone else does."

I picked up the phone.

"Hey boy."

"Lucas!"

"Not so loud! Daddy around?"

"No. He's still in the receiving line—where are you?"

"At a hotel, we're going to stay here till we find an apartment."

"You just got back?"

He said something, but the sound of cars took it.

"... back yesterday—but I didn't want to call ... didn't think Daddy would take it so hard."

"I know—"

Burkie blew into the kitchen and out the back door.

"—wouldn't have thought Daddy would throw me out of the house."

I talked into my hand cupped over the mouthpiece.

"I didn't either."

104

There was a buzzing on the phone.

"Got a big tent up?"

"Covers the whole backyard."

Lucas laughed.

"Wish I was there ... Lot of people?"

"Lots—Daddy says Senator Herrin is supposed to come also."

There were hard shoes on linoleum—I turned around to my father coming toward me.

"Daddy must have his hands full."

He began talking to Addie.

"Lee, you still there?"

"Daddy—"

Burke turned to me.

"Lee, who are you talking to?"

I opened my mouth.

"I told him Mistah Hartwell to quit havin' his friends callin' here!" Addie banged the ladle on the pot. "I told him that I goin' to take that old phone and throw it out if he keep talkin' all the time!"

"Lee, you better get off," Lucas said into my ear.

"Don't stay on too long, son. You don't want to miss the reception," he said, walking back out.

Addie watched him leave, then nodded to me.

"Lee—you still there?"

"Daddy left."

I stretched the phone cord into the pantry and pulled the door shut. I was in the dark with the smell of burlap potato sacks and spices.

"How's Mother?"

"Doin' alright."

There was a low buzz on the line.

"This is a bad line ... Better let you get on to the reception ... Just wanted to see how the wedding was...."

I turned into the black of the pantry.

"What are you going to do?"

"Get a job—make some kind of life...."

"I don't think Daddy will stay mad very long."

Then it got real quiet and Lucas was right there.

"Wouldn't think so either, Lee. But I've never seen him do anything like this before."

"How'd you find out?"

"Talked to Mother—"

"What'd she say?"

"You killing me, Lucas Hartwell, you killing me," Lucas mimicked in a high-pitched voice. "I thought for sure she was going to go to the hospital."

"Not yet."

"Lee, listen, thank Addie for me and don't tell anyone you talked to me."

"I won't," I promised.

Static covered him and I heard a faint "talk to you later."

I walked out into the bustling light and the wedding roared back. Addie stirred a pot on top of the stove and didn't turn around.

"How is he?"

"Alright. Said to thank you."

Addie's arm circled above the pot.

"This family ain't got no reason for splittin' up. That boy should come to his senses an' talk with your father." Addie dumped pepper into the pot, still circling with the spoon. "More trouble comes when a family split up. An' ain't no damn use to it. Mistah Hartwell should let that boy come back ... Lucas needs this family. If it was Burkie I wouldn't worry, but Lucas needs his family, an' just more hurt come from this if he don't come back."

The spoon sounded like it was going to come through the pot. Fanny came into the room balancing a tray of empty champagne glasses.

"Why do y'all look so sad?"

Addie flicked her away with her eyes, bending over and turning the flame low.

"Never you mind girl. Just get some more drinks an' keep servin'!"

Fanny stuck her tongue out at Addie's back, laughing when I smiled.

Someone rapped against the open back door and the phone rang. I picked it up and went back into the pantry to hear. Someone asked for directions. I finished giving them and looked out through the door.

There was a well-dressed man talking to Fanny in the kitchen. He was blacker than Nelson and his gray suit rippled at the shoulders and his shoes were like my tuxedo shoes. Fanny leaned back against the kitchen table with her straightened hair blowing in the fan. She laughed and I could hear his strong voice.

"I thought I might see you again." He held a white hat with a black band in front of him. "I hope you enjoyed dinner."

"I enjoyed it very much."

Fanny's eyes glowed with smoky softness. He looked down, the razor edge of hair a line across the back of his neck. Fanny moved one leg slowly while she leaned against the table.

"I didn't see you at the meeting last Thursday."

Fanny picked up some glasses.

"I was helping my aunt get ready for this wedding party."

He looked out the window and fingered the label in his hat.

"White folks do know how to have a party."

"They surely do, but you better state your business before my aunt comes back and chases you out of here."

He turned back to her.

"I was concerned where you were and the other gentlemen asked about you as well."

Fanny turned and put a hand on her chest.

"They asked about me?"

"They were very taken by your personality and—"

"And want me to get their letter for them."

He nodded slowly.

"They want their letter to win their election and so do I. They want to use the negroes, and I want to use the white man."

Fanny didn't blink.

"Uh huh, what do I get out of it?"

"Whatever you want."

"Heard that before."

A slow smile spread on his face till he was laughing loud.

"What are you laughing at?"

"*You.* You are the most outspoken black woman I know."

107

"You must not have known many, Mr. Jackson."

He was facing me and I thought of the phone cord stretched into the pantry.

"I have big plans, Fanny. I want ... *this!*" He moved his white and black hand through the air. "I want to have a large home and throw big weddings!" His eyes moved excitedly. "Fanny, our children will see a much different world ... I believe they will see the first black president!"

Fanny leaned back and shook her head.

"Mr. Jackson, you had better go back to Indiana. This is Virginia, and they'll throw you in jail for talk like that."

He laughed again.

"Fanny, that's why we need you! You're not afraid to speak your mind."

"There's a lot like me. Stay in this kitchen, you'll find the most outspoken colored women in Richmond."

He smiled, his eyes seeking hers.

"I think you had a reason for coming to the meeting." He walked to Fanny and put his hands on the table. "I think there's a lot of anger in you over what happened to your father."

Fanny shook her head.

"I should never told you about that."

He came around the table beside her.

"Why not? That's exactly the reason we should help these men and help ourselves! If a man can get lynched—"

"I have to go back to work," Fanny said, picking up her tray.

"There was another reason I came over...."

He deftly took the tray from her and it was back on the table. They were close and her head disappeared behind his. He leaned down and her fingers were just over his shoulders.

"Not here—" Fanny said, breathing fast when they came apart.

He stepped back and picked up his hat.

"You aren't just doing this so I'll come back to your meeting?"

He shook his head slowly.

"I never mix business and pleasure."

"I wonder which is which with you."

He laughed and his teeth were very white.

"For a proper black man, you sure laugh a lot."

He put on his hat, running his finger along the brim, then glanced out to the wedding. He turned back and his face was somber.

"The world will change, Fanny."

She moved to the door with her glasses, their voices fading.

"... dangerous man, Mr. Jackson."

"Will you—"

"... be at your meeting next Thursday."

He held open the back door and I watched him follow Fanny out with the buzzing phone against my stomach.

The colored lanterns swayed in the warm breezes trading places. The woods were frosty and blue behind the six-piece band as I followed Careen's shoulders with the thin blue straps leaping over her narrowing back. I had managed to get away from Clay and Jimmy who made a great deal of pointing and laughing as I stood talking to Careen. Mr. Hillman was talking to Big Jeb about the election and I heard him say he was going to introduce him to the senator and that's when we left to get a soda. Jimmy shouted something, but I didn't hear it, or didn't want to.

We slipped between a wall of people and there was a space like a clearing in the woods. Katy and Burkie were standing with my parents. Katy tapped her foot to the music and drank from her champagne glass.

"Burkie! You just spilled champagne on the sleeve of your jacket!"

He looked at his sleeve.

"You are the sloppiest man. How did you ever keep him clean, Mrs. Hartwell?"

"I have Addie," Mother said, standing in her long dress.

Katy rubbed Burkie's sleeve furiously with a napkin.

"I can see why Addie is so mean!"

Katy stood back and swayed with her pinned-up wedding dress moving like a bell. She abruptly turned.

"Keeping him clean is a full-time job!"

"You should have seen the boy when he was young."

"It's alright honey, it's just a little spot."

Katy stared at him.

"Burkie! A spot like this can *stain*!"

She started to rub again with the napkin, but it looked like she was rubbing a different spot. Fanny circled around with the drinks and everyone took one. Katy finished Burkie's sleeve and smoothed her hair down in a concentrated way. She had already finished half her champagne and sipped Burkie's.

"I'm glad you're feeling better, Mrs. Hartwell."

Mother looked at Katy and nodded slowly.

"I guess it takes a lot to keep me from seeing my son marry."

Katy nodded sympathetically.

"I think it was just *awful* for Lucas to run off and elope!" She turned wildly as if someone had yanked her around. "It was *so* nice of Senator Herrin to come to the wedding, Mr. Hartwell!"

My father held a cigarette in one hand and a frosted glass in the other. He nodded slowly.

"Yes, it was."

Katy smiled, holding her arms wide with the glass in her fingertips. I thought she might start twirling around.

"You are doing such a good job for him here in Richmond—I don't see how he could lose!"

"Why, thank you, Katy."

"I don't know a soul who would vote for that Trenton—besides maybe the nigras!"

Katy let out a long laugh while Fanny waited with the tray of drinks.

"The nigras or maybe those silly labor people—who daddy says are half black anyway!"

Katy laughed shrilly and finished the rest of her drink with some running down the side of her mouth. She wiped it away with the back of her hand. Burkie laughed shortly and reached for Katy's glass.

"Honey, maybe you better not drink anymore."

She waved her hand.

"Oh, you can have it, you can have it—it's empty!"

She laughed again and Mother grinned.

110

"Those martinis will do it."

Katy took an unsteady step and started waving again.

"Oh Burkie, I'm fine! I'm fine! It's *my wedding!*" Her arms were out and she could as easily fall as go on. She went toward my father, stopping herself with the hand he put up to steady her. "Isn't that true, Mr. Hartwell? The only people voting for Trenton are the coloreds ... and the ... the colored labor people...."

Burke smiled forgivingly.

"I'm sure there are other people voting for him."

"But the nigras and the labor people are voting for him ... *right?*"

"I would think some are," my father demurred.

"*See,* Burkie!" Katy wheeled again with both hands in the air. "I'm not so drunk...." She saw me suddenly. "Lee—am I drunk?"

Mother took her arm.

"I think they have some coffee up at the house, Katy. Why don't we go up and get some?"

She turned, falling away from Mother.

"Oh, Mrs. Hartwell, I'm fine ... fine...."

Katy's knee's buckled and Burkie had her other arm.

"*Oops!*" Katy laughed again, staring at Burkie. "Who are you?" She laughed wildly. "Oh, I know who you are—Burkie, right?"

"Come on, honey, we're all going to get some coffee."

They started moving to the house with my father leading the way.

"Oh, alright ... you know, Mr. and Mrs. Hartwell, I can't *tell* you how happy I am that you are my family ... I think it is dreadful what Lucas and Bunny did! And I don't blame you for throwing him out of the house...."

Katy stumbled again and that's when I saw Fanny staring after her.

We left the noise and light of the tent and walked toward the barn. The crickets and the tittering night animals moved through the edge of the trees. We walked through the grass and I could hear the swish of Careen's dress.

"Lee, what did Katy mean about Lucas?"

I looked up from the ground.

"She shouldn't have said that."

"You don't have to tell me, if you don't want to."

"Going to tell you—Lucas and Bunny eloped last week in South Carolina."

"They eloped!"

I nodded.

"And daddy threw Lucas out of the house."

We reached the shadowy barn. The goats thumped against their stalls as I pulled the door open to the sharp scent of fresh manure.

"That's terrible, Lee," Careen whispered.

"That's why Lucas and Bunny weren't at the wedding."

Careen stared into the barn.

"Why would they go off and elope? They could have just gotten married, couldn't they?"

"Don't know," I said, taking down the lantern from the nail in the center post. "Talked to Lucas on the phone tonight and I don't know why he did it."

I walked across the hay and felt along the wall for the cubbyhole with matches. I lit the wick, sooting the lantern glass, turning it down to an even burn. The wood stalls, rakes, bales of hay and work gloves hanging on the wall came out of the darkness. Careen walked in and I pulled the barn doors shut and hung the lantern back on the nail. The four eyes glittered in the yellow light. Careen stood beside me and rested her hands on the stall. The goats bobbed their heads.

"They like you."

"How do you know?"

"They always stomp and bob their head when they like someone."

One of the goats brayed, shaking his head like something was on it.

"See, told you they liked you."

Careen laughed and stood on her tip toes to see in. She turned slowly and I could smell a faint talcum.

"I hope your father lets Lucas come back."

I shrugged.

"Seems like Burkie and Sally are glad that Lucas got thrown out ... Addie's right—it's bad for a family to get split up."

I stared straight ahead and tried to think of something else. Lucas had sounded so far away on the phone, like he would never be back. Careen's warm hand closed over mine.

"I'm sure your daddy will let Lucas come back, Lee. He's just upset."

She squeezed my hand lightly and turned to me with the lantern light behind her. Her eyes were there and I leaned in. There was the warmth again with her soft lips. I had my eyes shut, then open and her face was right there. Then we were apart and she put her head against me and my legs were shaking. I looked over the small head of yellow light and slowly put my arms around her. The goats knocked against the wood.

PART 2

14

*The cabin cracks were filled with mud against the wind. A
fire softened the dirt floor while the door rattled and sometimes snow spouted in. The slaves stayed close to the stone
fireplace that looked like it was made of mud. The oily rags
used for light made it hard to breathe. Already the winter
had changed. Soon they would be going to the fields again.*

I watched the land roll by the car window. The magnolia trees burned
hotly against the deep country green and blasts of honeysuckle
patched the shoulders of the road. Only an occasional car came
down the two-lane highway burrowing deeper into the country. Field
rows flitted by the window in a turning arc, then a black man under a
"Drink Coca Cola" sign waved as we passed.

I laid back against the car seat. Burke had decided a week at our
place in the country would do everyone good and invited the Masons
and Nettletons. Sparta sat on fifty acres and had a pond nearby. We
usually went in late June, but May had been fierce and Mother hadn't
been feeling well since the wedding. Mimaw said that ever since she
had passed the age of her own mother's death the ailments started.
Addie fussed over her and huffed up and down the steps with her broth

and an occasional highball. Dr. Williams climbed the steps several times a week with his creased and dusty leather bag slapping his thigh. He gave her more than the usual amount of sugar pills, but the threat of a rest cure loomed larger every day.

The fields closed in to tall trees slashing the winding road with sunlight. Eventually we came to a dirt road and pulled off into the forest. Tree branches scraped along the windows and made the car dark. We bumped and dipped down the drive. Sparta emerged around a bend—a flat white two-story colonial house with a white board fence running around the side. A tar roof stretched out to two brick chimneys then rolled down to black-shuttered windows. A second roof spread over a screened porch the length of the house.

Burke pulled the car up under the magnolia tree in front. Addie helped Mother out of the car and I was out in the windy, hot silence of the country. Dragonflies swooped and glided above the willow fuzz and tall grass; across the border fence yellow fields slipped into the hazy distance.

"Lee, give me a hand with these suitcases."

Burke opened the trunk. The sun radiated dully off the black finish already too hot to touch. My father set the suitcases on the ground and lit a cigarette. He looked white and old in the harsh light. I remembered Dr. Williams' worried face the last time he reminded my father to watch his blood pressure and cut down on the Viceroys.

"I hope this helps your mother—she hasn't been well lately."

Since Lucas eloped, I thought, finishing his sentence for him.

He leaned back against the car, looking out into the countryside.

There was the small, dingy apartment with the yellowed kitchen table where Bunny explained how she had never thought my father would be so mad. Lucas stared at something on the wall with a drink in front of him. And when Bunny had asked me to speak to Burke, Lucas had jumped up and hobbled into the bedroom. Sharp voices came through the closed door as I left.

Burke finished his cigarette and picked up the suitcases. I grabbed two just as the Masons and the Nettletons came down the driveway. Jimmy and Clay came around the cars carrying suitcases and we followed our parents inside. A fine layer of pollen and dust on the porch

117

floor showed where Addie's broom had been. A swing hung down from the ceiling at the far end of the porch. The front room of Sparta was dominated by a fireplace of fire-blackened stones and a couch with its back toward the door. The room wrapped around to a dining room on the right and on the left was a hallway to the stairs and the kitchen in back. The house smelled like a musty attic.

Everyone became occupied with the mechanics of cleaning and unpacking. Addie rumbled around the house talking to herself about the "goddamn dust" and "old creaky house" as she beat rugs and threw up windows. Our parents settled down to drinks around the dining room table and I knew with the sleepy heat of midday they would retire for naps.

I went to the porch and squinted out at the bright fields. A bell clanked far off and I could hear the distant lowing of cows on the summer tide. Jimmy and Clay hurried outside in their shorts, the screen door slamming behind passing them.

"Where you going?"

Clay turned around.

"To the pond—come on!"

I ran after them across the field of goldenrod dashing bright spots of yellow as far as we could see. Cicadas wheedled like locusts and I felt the sun in my clothes. We swished through the parting weeds to a line of trees and followed a trail down through the woods; then the clearing came back, but it was a spreading green pond so still the water was like land except for a man in a boat.

"Who's that?"

I shaded my eyes. The man had on a straw hat.

"I think it's Uncle Willie."

Jimmy frowned.

"Who?"

"Uncle Willie," I nodded. "He keeps up Sparta when we're not here ... *Hey, Uncle Willie!*"

The man shaded his eyes and pointed his fishing pole to the sky.

"He's going to come over."

"I don't want to talk to some old country colored guy," Jimmy muttered.

118

I looked at him.

"Nelson's from the country and I'll bet Roy is too."

Jimmy shrugged.

"Roy's our yard man."

Uncle Willie had turned the boat and was leaning back to us. The glass became a spreading curtain. The oarlocks jumped as he rocked back and forth and came closer. He gave one last heave and slid to a halt in the soft mud by the shore. Uncle Willie stepped out into the water over his shoes and I helped him pull the sun-bleached rowboat into the grass. He took off his hat, running a handkerchief over his face. A startling white mustache stood out against his skin.

"Well, it surely is good to see y'all. Ain't seen any city folks since last year—did your whole family come out?"

"Masons and the Nettletons, too—this is Jimmy and Clay—I don't think you met them last time they were here."

He held his straw hat by his waist.

"I don't think I did meet them—nice to meet y'all." He turned back to me. "So how your parents doin'?"

"Mother's sick—that's why we came up so early."

Uncle Willie nodded and pulled on the suspenders holding his baggy canvas pants high on his stomach.

"I hope she be feelin' better. Country air make her feel good."

He put his handkerchief back in his pocket and carefully placed the straw hat on his head.

"I go an' see your father. I know he goin' to need some help 'round Sparta." He licked his lips and paused. "Anyone else come with y'all?"

I grinned.

"Addie."

His face brightened and he showed his missing teeth.

"That right? Well, I guess I say hello to her too. Been a long time since I seen Addie."

If Addie ever had a beau it was Uncle Willie. He always wanted to know when she was coming up and would hang around Sparta till she chased him away, or she went "visitin'" with him and didn't come back till late at night. Addie called him an "old fool," but we knew different.

"Y'all can try some fishin'. I ain't caught nothin' yet, but maybe you have some better luck." He nodded to Clay and Jimmy. "Nice meetin' y'all—I see you later, Lee," he called, moving off through the woods.

We pushed the boat through the water and jumped in. The wood was dried gray from the sun and the green water sliding around the bottom smelled sour. I took the oars and turned the boat. Jimmy picked up the fishing pole and a tomato can of worms and dirt.

"See—told you Uncle Willie was a good guy."

He grunted and threw out the baited hook.

"Just an old colored guy."

"You wouldn't be fishing if it wasn't for him," I said, resting the oars and letting the boat drift.

Jimmy shrugged. The bobber floated up to Clay in front of the boat.

"You ever fished before, Jimmy?"

"Of course."

"Ask him if he ever caught anything, Clay."

"Ever caught anything, Jimmy?"

"More than Lee ever has."

"Can tell you're a great fisherman by the way the bobber's going down."

Jimmy jumped the bobber.

"You wait."

Clay dipped his hand in the water.

"Scotty said he was going to teach me how to fish when he comes back."

Jimmy jerked on the line.

"He's not coming back."

"Is too. I got a letter from him."

"Right, Clay."

Clay nodded solemnly.

"Got a letter and he said everything was alright. I've heard that guys go on secret missions and tell everybody they're dead—"

"That's the stupidest thing—"

"It's true!"

120

Jimmy looked at him and shook his head in disgust. He hopped the bobber again in the water. I watched the small circles spread out into the long afternoon.

I woke early the next morning and left Jimmy and Clay sleeping in the bedroom. I sat down in one of the wicker chairs on the porch and watched the dew glistening pink on the fields and misting gold in the low parts. I didn't hear Addie till she was almost to the screen door. Her lip was swollen with tobacco and the big yellow sundress she had on rustled when she walked. She held her pie down low when she saw me.

"What you doin' up so early for?"

"Just woke up ... going to see somebody?"

Her nostrils flared.

"That ain't none of your business!"

"Don't care if you're going to see Uncle Willie."

The porch boards creaked.

"I ain't goin' to see that old fool—"

"Won't say anything."

She drew herself up.

"There ain't nothin' to say. I goin' to see Ophelia!"

"What's under the handkerchief?"

Addie's eyes went to the pie as if someone had just put it in her hand.

"Guess it's not Uncle Willie's favorite apple pie."

"They is having a pound party an' this pie is what I'm bringin'!"

"Nobody's business if you want to go see Uncle Willie."

She looked at me.

"You going to just sit out here?"

"I don't know," I said, shrugging.

"Where Jimmy and Clay?"

"Still asleep ... they like to do things with each other anyway," I said, remembering how they went off hiking together the day before.

Addie glanced at the sleeping house and then at me.

"Why don't you come and see Tip Top?"

121

I paused.

"Would be fun to see Tip Top."

Addie opened the screen door and spat a stream of tobacco juice. "Come on, then."

I jumped from the chair and touched the screen door closed.

We walked across the wet fields just starting to warm. The sun was brighter and put long shadows behind the fenceposts along the dirt road. Queen Anne lace and honeysuckle lined the fallow tobacco fields with white. Addie's dress filled with wind as she hummed and spat tobacco juice.

"Goin' to be goddamn hot today. Gettin' too damn old to be climbing these mountains," Addie said, referring to the slight elevation in the road. "This reminds me of where I was a girl. Further south than this but it look a lot like the farm my daddy had."

"Kind of farm?"

"Bad farm—can't make no livin' on sharecroppin'. He always drunk with my brothers anyway and never tended the crops."

I concentrated on walking in the red wheel path of the dirt road.

"You have a lot of brothers?"

"Too damn many. Mary and I was the only girls an' I had to do the cookin' an' cleanin' for them and you ain't cooked till you had to cook for four colored men every day."

"What was Fanny's daddy like?"

Her eyes darkened.

"Lot like Fanny ... but he could paint real nice—he painted for our church an' his paintin's are still there. But Fanny has the same crazy notions."

I kicked up some red dust and followed a grasshopper's progress till he disappeared in the high weeds.

"You think Tip Top'll be around?"

"Imagine he will."

Addie looked at me and I could see the black pigment spots under her eyes like specks of ink.

"Why ain't you gettin' along with your friends?"

I shrugged.

"They have a lot of secrets."

"Secrets! They too young to have any damn secrets."

"Jimmy tries to get Clay to side with him."

"Why he doin' that?"

"'Cause I don't hang around them as much."

Addie wiped the morning heat off her forehead, shooting a long brown stream into the grass.

"Why's that?"

"Been seeing Careen Hillman."

Addie's face lit up and I thought she was going to start laughing.

"Ain't it somethin'—they jealous, Lee!"

"Kind of what I thought."

"That ain't nothin' new, boy. You just gettin' old."

The road dipped down and rose to pink, toy houses in the trees.

"Before long you get married to Miz Careen an' have children of your own." Addie shook her head and laughed loud. "*Shit!* I ain't ready for that." She spat, wiping the back of her hand across her chin. "That too much to think about."

I looked at Addie.

"'Come you never had children?"

"I has Fanny."

"Of your own."

"Ain't none of your damn business," she muttered. "'Sides, I got you boy—an' that is enough!"

Addie spat again and nearly hit her dress.

"Goddamn tobacco!"

We started up a hill of tall weeds. Addie began to hum again as we crossed the swishing grass, her yellow dress blowing all around me.

The white houses were closer. A woman walked out holding a basket with her dress moving against the green of the country. Addie looked up.

"There's Ophelia ... *Ophelia!*"

The woman put the basket down and shaded her brow.

"Addie Jones—that you?"

"In the flesh!"

123

Addie walked faster as Ophelia came down the hill and set the basket next to the wheel ruts. They embraced and patted each other on the back. She was as big as Addie, but her face was softer and her skin lighter.

"I didn't know you was up at Sparta."

"That old Willie supposed to tell you!"

Ophelia smiled.

"Uncle Willie hasn't been round. I'm sure he would have told me if he'd seen me."

"You remember Lee."

"Why sure I do!" She stood back. "You grown since I saw you last."

"He growin' up too fast for me—Lee, take that basket for Ophelia."

"I can take it. I been carrying the wash for years," she said, picking up the apple basket the color of corn husks. "I'm glad y'all have come—we havin' our pound party."

"Willie told me that."

"An' tonight we havin' a hat rally."

"He didn't tell me that!"

"I have lots of hats you can borrow."

Ophelia set the clothes basket down by two shady dogwoods with a rope strung between.

"Lee, I know Tip Top would like to see you. Why don't you go on up to the house?"

Addie shook her head.

"He can help first."

Ophelia laughed in a slow singing way.

"I think I can hang these old sheets. I been doin' it for years by myself."

"We visitin', an' we do our part."

Addie set her pie next to the tree trunk and took the end of the sheet from Ophelia. The white sheet flapped open with the clean smell of soap. Ophelia placed two wooden pins on the sheet.

"Where Matthew John?"

"Out in the fields," Ophelia said, glancing over her shoulder to the distant rows. "This year tobacco crop goin' to be good he says on account of the wet spring we had."

Addie nodded.

"He's a good man—ain't many like him."

"Don't tell him that. We'll never get his head in the house," she laughed over the flapping sheets. "I just wish he let me buy some more things for the children from the store."

I looked over the sheets to the green tobacco plants stretched out in long lines curving out of sight. A man walked down the rows into the sun.

"I think everybody in the county comin' to the pound party, so there be lots of food for you, Lee."

Addie shook her head.

"He eatin' too much lately."

"Boys are supposed to eat a lot, Addie."

"That true, but that boy eatin' everything!"

I had never been to a pound party before, though Addie had told me of them many times. Everyone would bring a dish and there was singing and banjo playing and plenty to drink and eat. The pound party started at midday and sometimes would go straight into the night. Addie blamed the pound parties for making her big.

Addie pinned the last sheet and Ophelia picked up the empty apple basket.

"I have a nice hat for you to wear at the hat rally. Best hat wins a prize."

"That why I wish I had known. Miz Hartwell give me hats that I has won with twice!"

I followed the two swaying dresses to a house with a sagging porch and paint faded to a dirty gray. Someone stood in the blue shade of the porch and yawned. He slipped his hands into the pockets of his baggy coveralls.

"There you are, Tip Top! You just wakin' up, boy? Lee come with Addie to visit."

"I been up, Mamma."

Tip Top's name came from a bottle of hair tonic he'd swallowed. Addie said Ophelia had found the empty bottle and made him throw it up, but the name had stuck. He had the same light skin of his mother and the round softer features I associated with people from the country.

"You take Lee fishin' at the pond," Ophelia suggested from the porch.

Tip Top squinted at me.

"Been fishin' yet?"

"Yesterday, but didn't catch anything."

"Take him fishin', Tip Top," Ophelia said, shooing us away with her hand. "Addie an' I have to get ready for the pound party and the hat rally."

She held the door open.

"Mind your manners," Addie warned as the door slammed behind them and their laughter floated out with "*them boys!*"

Tip Top started toward the back of the house.

"I got somethin' more fun than fishin'."

I followed him through the cricket grass to a faded red barn with water-rotted wood showing through. We went into the morning air trapped in the barn and Tip Top walked to a tool-covered workbench. Hazy fields yawned out through a dirty window projecting a perfect square of light on the floor.

"Lot better than any fishin'," he said, looking on top of the cluttered bench.

"What are you looking for?"

He sifted through a pile of wood of various lengths and pulled out two long sticks about four feet in length and two inches in diameter.

"Here they is!"

The sticks were brown and weathered and worn shiny smooth at the top.

"What are those?"

"Tobacco sticks," he said, handing me one.

The stick was heavier than it looked and smelled of damp earth.

"What you use 'em for?"

Tip Top was looking at the workbench for something else. He turned around with his stick.

"Prop up the tobacco—tobacco leaves have to stand up in the sun or they die," he said, working the stick on an imaginary tobacco plant.

"You have to prop up *all* the plants?"

He nodded.

126

"Daddy an' I walk the tobacco rows all day long, up an' down the rows—prop up all the leaves—see how the stick all worn at the top? That from proppin' all day long."

Tip Top turned back to the bench and pulled out two pieces of tin. I looked out the window at the long field rows.

"We going to prop tobacco?"

"No, too early to be propped." He picked up a hammer and two long nails. "These old tobacco sticks—Daddy don't use 'em no more."

Tip Top picked up the piece of tin and started bending and shaping it with the hammer and his hands. He worked the dull-colored metal, using the edge of the workbench to bend it.

"There! Hand me your stick."

I gave him the stick and he laid one end on the table and fitted the tin to it. He put a nail against the back and pounded it through the tin and wood. He handed me the stick.

"What—"

"Hold on just a minute an' I show you." He started bending and hitting the other piece of tin. "We going to have fun now, Lee!"

He picked up the stick and walked to the barn door and grabbed a wagon wheel lying against the wall.

"Come on!"

Tip Top started running and disappeared around the corner of the house. I caught up with him just as he stopped in front of a tall man with a hoe in one hand. He was much darker than Tip Top. His coveralls were dusty and red clay was caked on his shoes. He set the hoe down on the ground.

"Whoa there, boy. Where you goin' with those sticks?"

Tip Top shrugged.

"Nowhere, Daddy."

"Look to me to be goin' somewhere."

Tip Top turned to me.

"This is Lee, Daddy."

"I 'member Lee," he said, nodding to me, then looking back at Tip Top.

"You still ain't told me what you doin' with them tobacco sticks, boy. Don't look like you goin' to prop any tobacco!"

127

Tip Top looked at the stick with the flashing tin and the wagon wheel.

"No sir."

"Ain't I told you not to be doin' that to tobacco sticks no more?"

Tip Top nodded.

"But you don't use these old sticks no more."

"Uh huh ... let me see your stick."

Tip Top handed the stick to him and his father held it up, examining the piece of tin.

"See, Daddy—that an *old* stick!"

His father handed it back and looked off to the tobacco rows.

"Could sure use a hand in the fields."

Tip Top shook his head.

"Looks to me like it early in the season. Tobacco don't need proppin' yet."

"Don't need no proppin'!"

Tip Top shook his head.

"None yet, not least till June."

His father ran a broad hand over his face and shook his head, his eyes glimmering.

"They do grow fast now—tellin' me how to raise the tobacco. I better hurry up an' die so you can take over the farm."

Tip Top rolled his head back and forth.

"I just know when the tobacco need proppin'."

His father laughed loud, wiping the corners of his eye with his forefinger and thumb.

"I tell you Mistah Tobacco proper, y'all can go on with them sticks, but Tip Top, they is your sticks, boy, an' I ain't goin' to see you stickin' no tin on any other sticks—you understand?"

"Yes sir."

"I'll see y'all at the house later."

His father walked off and we started running across the grass toward the road Addie and I had come down. I took off my shoes and left them in the grass. The two red paths lined the green valley and wavered on a far hill. Tip Top bent down and put the wagon wheel in one of the dirt tracks.

128

"Use the stick to hit the wheel, Lee," he said, holding the stick in the middle and picking the wagon wheel back up.

"You ready?"

He tossed the wheel down the road, swatting it with the flat piece of tin, making it hop and go faster down the hill. I ran after Tip Top with the white bottoms of his feet flying in the air.

"Come on, Lee!"

His stick flashed up and down and the wheel hummed faster down the road. I ran as fast as I could, cutting in front of him, smashing the red disc off the road and into the grass. Tip Top picked it up and shot the wheel back down the road. I was running with the stick like a bat. I hit the wheel squarely with the tin and it went spinning. Tip Top cut in front of me fast and low and his stick cracked down and the wheel left us again. I jumped in front of him, running over the grass on the side of the road. We bumped into each other and I lunged over his shoulder as he shot the wheel away. I swung wide, but the wheel scooted away again.

"Got you!" Tip Top screamed, swatting the wheel again.

"No you don't!"

I sprinted ahead of him after the wheel and lunged, just touching the edge of the black rubber. He sped past me.

"Yes I do!"

He hit the wheel with the long reach of his stick. The wheel went high in the air and jumped across the road into the field and that's when I saw Jimmy and Clay. They were standing on the road just in front of us. I went over and picked up the wheel.

"Hey ... Jimmy ... Clay." My eyes were watering and I was still laughing. "You guys ought to try this!"

Jimmy squinted with his face oddly white in the noon sun.

"Don't look like much fun to me."

I turned and walked back to the road. I could feel Jimmy's eyes on me. His voice scythed across the grass.

"Gotta play with *niggers* now, huh Lee?"

I stopped. Tip Top was looking at the ground and Jimmy was leering with his dark eyes. I took a step toward him.

"What'd you say?"

He grinned.

"Gotta play with the niggers now, huh?"

I turned away and Tip Top was still looking down, moving his stick in the dirt, then I was running straight at Jimmy. He saw me and braced himself, but he fell flat on his back. I knelt on top of him and swung wildly in the dust. He tried to crawl away on his hands and knees but I jumped on him again. He crawled away again, scrambling to his feet.

"Stop! STOP—"

I caught him in the mouth and his jaw clapped together. We fell over again into the grass and Jimmy managed to get up and run a few feet. He fell as I pounced on him. He struggled up again, breathing hard, his face blotchy red, dirt and pieces of grass on his shirt and arms. He backed away, holding his fists in front of him.

"YOU'RE CRAZY!"

I stared at him, breathing fast with my fists clenched. Jimmy brushed himself off with a shaking hand.

"Come on, Clay—let's leave crazy man alone with his *friend!*"

I watched them go down the road with only the sound of my breathing. I turned and Tip Top was standing with the stick and wheel in his hand.

"Don't pay any attention—he's a jerk!"

I glanced back to where Jimmy and Clay had gone. Their figures were small on the road. I picked up the tobacco stick and walked over to Tip Top. He had his stick down in front of him, scraping it in the red dust.

"Come on, let's do it some more."

He shrugged.

"Maybe you want to go with them."

"No...." I shook my head. "I don't want to be with those guys."

I handed him the wheel and he threw it down the road. We ran after it, but it wasn't much fun anymore. Tip Top said he had to go do chores and gave me the tobacco stick to keep. I walked slowly back to Sparta and trailed the stick all the way down the dusty road.

15

In the spring the planters rode into town in varnished carriages. The uniformed coachmen reined the horses in their silver harnesses with the women in back. Dust sparkled in the sun while people watched and men talked of the "finest tobacco in the county." The planters waved and tipped their canes, knowing the quality of their leaf and the price of their hogshead was the same as their reputation.

I ran up the noon-quiet steps clutching the newspaper that caused us to leave Sparta early. Burke had driven silently with the news paper next to him on the front seat of the car. He stared straight ahead and drove fast. He kept the paper so close I decided to get the article from the morning paper on the porch.

When we arrived I grabbed the folded paper from behind the swing and went upstairs. I tossed the paper on my bed and kneeled down next to the paper. I looked at the front page article.

AFTER DENIALS, HERRIN LETTER TO FOREMAN
SHOWS HE PAID APPLE PICKERS $1.00 A DAY!

To All Foremen:

Effective Saturday, December 31, the day wages will be re-
duced to $1.00 per working day. When we start working ten

hours again, the wages will be twelve and a half cents per hour. No one regrets more than I the necessity of this reduction, but even this wage is twenty-five to fifty cents more than the average farm wage, so far as I may ascertain. Conditions look even worse to me than they have in the past, that is to say for the next two or three years. I wish you would explain this to the men. Tell them I am exceedingly sorry that this action is necessary, and give them time enough to get a better-paying position, if possible.

Very truly yours,

Senator J. Herrin

I read the rest of the article quickly, then found some more articles and pasted them into the scrapbook. I reached the first floor as the grandfather clock struck noon through the house. There was Burke's low voice, then the squeak of his swivel chair. A breeze carried the hot, flowery scent of honeysuckle from the porch.

"... we could call a meeting tomorrow." The chair squeaked again. "I don't know what it is ... I never saw any letter like that. Yes, before we issue a statement to the press, I think we better get our facts straight ... uh huh, right..."

He breathed out heavily.

"I'd like to think the letter is a fake ... uh huh. Uh huh ... right ... if you can find out where the letter came from ... I agree ... I don't think this is the time for those tactics ... alright ... fine ... Alright, I'll see you tonight."

The phone clunked on the cradle.

"You can come in now, Lee."

I walked sheepishly through the doorway.

"Waiting till you got off the phone," I mumbled, bringing the scrapbook out from under my arm. "Cut out the articles for you—you want to see them?"

He smiled faintly.

"How many do you have?"

132

"Three."

He reached into his pants pocket and put three dimes on the corner of the desk. He looked back down to his legal pad and started writing. I took the coins off the desk and could hear the small scratching from his fountain pen. He looked up again.

"Anything else?"

I shrugged.

"Nothing, I guess."

I turned around and stopped at the door.

"Daddy?"

"Yes," he said without looking up.

I paused.

"Think Senator Herrin was lying?"

He stopped writing and put the pen down on the pad. His neck was loose in the open collar of his short-sleeve shirt. He looked at me for a moment with his lips pressed together.

"I'd like to think he isn't." He paused. "That letter could very well be a forgery—they aren't hard to do."

"What if it isn't?"

Burke's eyes were steady.

"Then we have a whole different set of problems."

"LEE! WHERE ARE YOU? I TOLD YOU TO GET THOSE SUIT-CASES FROM THE CAR! WHERE ARE YOU, BOY!?

Burke smiled, picking up his pen again.

"You better go get those suitcases, son."

It was Big Jeb's rumbling voice that brought me down to listen outside the living room. He had never attended Burke's campaign meetings before, but this meeting was different. The men had come into the house with grim expressions and the sliding doors to the living room had been pulled. I had cut out another newspaper article the day after we came home and put it in the scrapbook. The headline read, *"HERRIN DECLARES LETTER A FORGERY"* and then went on to say the AFL was behind it. I was relieved. We wouldn't have to deal with the "whole different set of problems."

133

I was struggling through a homework assignment at my desk and my eraser smudges were getting darker in the fading light. I could hear Nelson, Fanny, and Addie in the backyard, their laughter floating in the dusk with the smell of a neighbor's barbecue. That's when I heard Big Jeb's voice and went down the stairs into the tide of voices.

There was a murmuring in the crack of yellow light lining the hall floor. The blue evening squared the front door with fireflies dying softly over the lawn. I stopped next to the door and leaned in. Burke was standing in the front of the room with one hand in his suit pocket. He stood next to the curving Victorian table that was red in the buttery light.

"—I know I'm new to this meeting, but I think Mr. Hillman is right, these tactics by the labor unions can only be combatted with the same!"

"Maybe the city prosecutor can tell us if there are some charges that can be brought!"

It was Mr. Hillman.

"What about it? Can charges be brought against these people?"

Big Jeb spoke from somewhere in the room.

"That is a possibility."

"I have my people out looking and we're going to find out who's behind this letter!"

I shifted and eyed the back of the room where Mr. Hillman was sitting. The room crowded with voices again. Burke waited till the commotion subsided.

"I think we all know the letter is a forgery. I spoke to the senator and assured him we're doing everything we can to set the record straight—"

"I spoke to the senator also and he asked me to find the *son of a bitch* who put that letter in the paper!"

Mr. Hillman's voice avalanched and the other men called out with him.

"Burke, maybe it is time we fight a little fire with fire."

I turned and saw the gray-haired Mr. Woods who sat on the school board. Burke nodded slowly.

"What do you suggest, Jim?"

"Well ... maybe Buddy is right. Maybe we should adopt more aggressive tactics."

Burke made a spider on the table with his fingertips.

"Spread lies to the paper?"

Mr. Woods looked uncomfortable suddenly.

"Well, maybe not lies, but we ought to—"

"Why not? They've been spreading lies about the senator!"

I moved back and could see Mr. Hillman better. He was on the couch in his dark suit with Big Jeb next to him.

"These labor people don't think twice about it! While we sit here and discuss what we should do—they're out there spreading more lies!"

My father stood quietly, his hands just touching the table.

"I think we all feel frustrated at this point." He paused. "But as long as I am chairman of the senator's reelection campaign, I'm responsible for its conduct, and we will not engage in the spreading of lies."

The room was quiet a long time. Mr. Hillman put his pipe back in his mouth.

"I say put it to a vote."

Burke pursed his lips slightly, speaking quietly but firmly.

"I am still the head of this committee and I will not abide by those methods."

Mr. Hillman spread his arms.

"The job of the chairman is to represent the committee."

Some men nodded in agreement. Burke moved his glasses up on his nose and slipped a hand into his right jacket pocket.

"I'm responsible for the conduct of the campaign in Richmond. If you decide to act against my wishes, then I will have to tender my resignation to the senator."

The room was quiet. A bicycle clattered by the front door with playing cards in the spokes and faded into the ominous silence inside the room. I heard the short crack of a match.

"No one here wants you to resign, Burke," Mr. Hillman said, lighting his pipe. "Least of all the senator. I just think there are different ways to look at this issue." The men were nodding again. "I think it's important we find out who is responsible for this forgery."

I didn't know my heart was going fast till it started slowing. I leaned against the door with the cooling night on my forehead and under my arms. Several of the men talked about finding out who put the letter in the paper.

Mr. Hillman nodded slowly.

"I'll find out who did it."

"You will have this information soon?"

Mr. Hillman stared at my father evenly, a wisp of smoke rising from his clenched pipe.

"Very soon."

16

The Tobacco Act was passed. This was to get rid of trash tobacco and drive prices up. Barn warehouses were built on the river wharves in Virginia. The planters brought their hogsheads to the public judging and sat in shiny carriages with sleek horses. The inspectors sat at a long wood table where hogsheads were pried open with cant hooks. The tobacco was spread in the sun and the inspectors complimented the planters on the quality of their leaf. They were a long way from home.

Deep summer came to Richmond and slowed life down until only the lazy smoke from the tobacco factories seemed to be moving. We started counting the days left in school and on the last day I became friends again with Jimmy and Clay. School let out on Tuesday and we spent the next day trying to make the necessary repairs to the tree house and brought out sodas, sandwiches, and cigarettes. We returned at dusk and arranged our sleeping bags and lit the kerosene lantern for an overnight camp.

The fireflies rained yellow in the darkening forest with the sky lighter between the trees. Acorns shot down through the leaves and bounced on the wood floor. We lay in our canvas sleeping bags blowing smoke at the jeweled summer sky.

"Can you believe, summer is here?"

I lay with my hands behind my head.

"Can't believe I'll be thirteen."

"That's nothing. I've been thirteen for two months already."

"I won't be thirteen till August."

"You'll never be a teenager, Clay," Jimmy scoffed.

I watched the smoke floating off into the stars. I rolled over and stubbed out my cigarette, then stared up at the trees and listened to the breathing of the woods settling down for the night. Jimmy said something and then I fell asleep.

The woods smelled like early morning when Jimmy shook me awake. He was down a far tunnel and I snuggled deeper into my sleeping bag. He shook me so hard my head bumped against the wood floor.

"What—"

Jimmy stood in his underwear, pointing into the woods.

"Look!"

I stumbled over Clay.

"See it!"

Deep in the tree-veined dark was a yellow light.

"What is it?"

Jimmy shook his head.

"Somebody with a lantern maybe."

I rubbed my eyes and looked again.

"—time is it?"

"Gotta be at least three o'clock."

The light flickered.

"Who'd be in the woods at three o'clock in the morning?"

Jimmy moved his head back and forth slowly.

"Don't know ... where you think that lantern is?"

I looked at the glow, then where I thought Buckeye was, then back again. Tingles spidered through me and my teeth hit together.

"That's the graveyard!"

He stared at me.

"You're lying!"

"If Buckeye is where I think it is, then it's in the Hillman grave-yard."

Jimmy shivered with his arms crossed against his chest. We were both standing in our underwear. I watched the light and saw the gravestones with the caskets pried open and the bleached bones with decaying flesh peeling off.

"HEY!"

We jumped and grabbed each other.

"*Shit*, Clay! Don't yell like that!" Jimmy snapped.

Clay was sitting up in his sleeping bag.

"What—"

"There's somebody in the woods."

"Where?"

Jimmy turned around.

"Hillman graveyard—probably *grave robbers*."

"No!"

"Come look for yourself."

Clay pushed between us.

"There," Jimmy said pointing.

The light flickered again.

"What was that?" Jimmy whispered.

"Think someone just walked in front of it."

"Maybe they just got the body up," Clay whispered.

"Lantern flickered again," Jimmy nodded.

"Something's going on," I said, trying to keep my teeth from chattering.

Jimmy turned and stared at me.

"What?"

He nodded to the woods.

"Let's go find out—I'll bet it's just some kids."

"*I'm* not going!" Clay said, shaking his head. "You guys can go, but I'm not going down to that graveyard!"

Jimmy pointed to the light.

"How about it, Lee?"

"I'll go," I shrugged.

He smiled as if I was joking.

139

"You sure?"

"Yeah, I'm sure—what about you—chicken?"

"No, let's go," he said, smiling weakly.

We slipped on our clothes and told Clay to guard the tree house.

"Against what?"

"Nothing, just stay here," Jimmy said, following me down the steps.

I missed the last two pieces of wood on the tree and fell to the ground. Jimmy climbed down and we looked around at the dark woods. I wanted to climb back into the tree house.

"Still want to do this?"

Jimmy turned.

"Don't you?"

"Asked you first."

"Yeah, sure, what about you?"

"Sure."

Jimmy looked into the trees and didn't look like he wanted to go at all.

"Let's go."

"Let's...." I said, watching him closely.

He started down the dark line against the undergrowth. There was no moonlight but we were able to stay on the trail in the night glow. The lantern was no longer in sight and I cursed Jimmy and wished again for the safety of our perch in the trees. I watched his white t-shirt moving hunched over. He stopped.

"You first," he whispered. "Know the way better than I do,"

I stared at him.

"You do!"

I shook my head and went past him down the black line. The trail grew smaller and the night more luminous on the trees and bushes. Swamp mist hovered between trees and the air smelled like wet ivy.

"How much farther?"

"Trail should branch off soon," I whispered. "Probably shouldn't talk anymore." Jimmy's head bobbed again and now I was too scared to go back. "Tug on my shirt if you want me to stop."

I started again, staying low to the trail. Birds tittered and the crickets were low and sporadic. I moved slowly, trying not to step on leaves

140

or branches and wishing I had gone barefoot. The trail line curved to the left and yellow light bled through the trees. I could see the skinny iron rods of the fence. A stick snapped. I turned around and glared at Jimmy.

Tamp. Tamp.

The noise was at my back.

Tamp! Tamp! Tamp!

It was a noise Nelson made when he was planting with a shovel. I grabbed Jimmy by the shirt and he grabbed mine.

"Have to go off the trail and take our shoes off," I whispered into his ear with his eyes wide.

"Maybe we should go back—"

I stared at him in disgust. He had gotten us into this and now he was too scared to go on.

"C'mon."

I placed my feet slowly, looking for the quiet spot. The heavy breathing of a man came through the still air. The light yellowed the ruffled undergrowth outside the fence and I laid down on my stomach. We crawled in the wet leaves to the iron bars of the fence and looked through the vines.

A glass-blackened lantern hung on one of the iron points. A man in muddy overalls was shoveling dirt back into a long hole. His face was wet with black sweat and another man stood behind him and watched. He walked up out of the shadows and I heard Jimmy breathe in sharply.

"Make sure it's good and flat," he said in a heavy voice.

"Don't worry about that, Mr. Hillman," the man said in the nasally voice of the country.

I stared at Careen's father. He had on work boots and a checkered hunting jacket. His wide face changed in the lantern light as he looked down at the dirt. The man wiped a dirty hand across his face and spat. He went to the tombstone on the ground and lifted one end. His hair shook on his forehead as he grunted and cursed, dragging the stone across the ground with "CAREEN HILLMAN" sparkling in the light.

Jimmy made a noise in his throat and I put my hand over his mouth. We started to crawl backwards very slowly, watching the iron fence get smaller and getting farther away from the man with the shovel. We stayed hunched over till we reached the trail and stopped to listen. There were just the crickets and the yellow light peeking through the trees again. I started following the dark line back to the tree house with the packed dirt cold on my feet.

I stopped and hunched down to listen, looking back down the trail. Something snapped behind us and there was a shadowy outline on the path. The figure didn't move—it looked like a tree and it was a tree. I turned around and started again. I stopped suddenly and the sound of our feet went on. I turned to a black figure running toward us.

"Run, Jimmy!"

I ran down the trail and then off into the trees. Low branches scraped my face and tore at my shirt, stringing spider webs on my face. I tripped and Jimmy fell on top of me. Then his white shirt was in front and veered away. I ran into a tree and fell back stunned, but started running again anyway. The woods weren't ending and I didn't know which way I was going anymore. Someone was crashing through the woods next to me and I turned away, dodging between two black trees, seeing light and heading for it as vines tangled around me. I turned and spun to get loose, then spun again in a dive and fell out on the lawn. Jimmy rolled out and we ran for the house.

I collapsed onto the steps of the back door. Jimmy lay in the grass.

"Who ... was ... that?"

I shook my head, still breathing hard.

"Don't ... know...."

The stinging was stronger from the scrapes and briars and my head pounded from where I had hit the tree. Jimmy sat up.

"What was Mr. Hillman ... doing there?"

We both turned to the line of dark trees.

"Hope Clay will be alright."

Jimmy nodded.

"They won't find him. If you...." He swallowed." If you don't know where it is ... There's no way to see at night."

I nodded and stood up.

"We can sleep on the porch."

We started around the side of the house quickly. At the corner I looked back once just to make sure.

142

17

*Many of the inspectors had never been to a plantation
before. They rode with the planters in their carriages and
admired the planters' slaves working in the fields. They
admired the planters' manners and politeness. The inspectors worked for the English government and spoke differently. They passed the hogsheads with the planters' initials
and didn't use the cant hook on the barrels. The tobacco
brought even higher prices.*

I was in the black woods and there was the faceless figure moving
out of the darkness toward me. I tried to get through the trees, but
the branches were holding me and Mr. Hillman was coming with
the man carrying a shovel. I was trapped and the man raised the lantern
to my face and I shut my eyes tightly. The yellow blared through my
eyelids in a sea of pink and I kept my eyes closed, but the lantern was
hot on my face and I had to look.

The sun was on the porch. I shut my eyes again and curled up
tighter on the couch with the pink getting brighter and the birds strik-
ing the morning in the magnolia trees. I heard Jimmy cough and opened
my eyes again.

"Was wondering how long you'd sleep."

Jimmy was sitting up on the cot. I got up groggily.

"Just remembered last night."

"Yeah. I've been thinking ... bet I know what they were doing."

I looked at him.

"Lots of people bury jewels and stuff in graves. I figure Mr. Hillman has more money and jewels than anybody else, and you have to do it when nobody is around ... No, really, I'll bet you—"

"Wouldn't he just dig a hole?"

"People would think that he'd do that—but nobody would think of a grave."

"Who was chasing us?"

Jimmy paused.

"They didn't want anybody to know they were burying jewels— I'll bet they reburied them after we left."

I looked outside at the grass sparkling in the morning sun and tried to remember what I had seen the night before. It had the hazy quality of a nightmare.

"Maybe."

"That's why we don't say anything to *anybody* about what we saw— even Clay. They'll probably be waiting for us to come back or say something—I don't want Mr. Hillman mad at me!"

I touched the bump on my head where I hit the tree.

"You have your shoes?"

Jimmy shook his head.

"Must have dropped them in the woods—I'll look for them when I get our stuff out."

"We better not say anything to anybody. If they find our shoes, they'll know it was us!"

I shrugged.

"Won't say anything—don't know if I believe he was burying jewels though."

Jimmy looked relieved and lay back down on the cot. I sat on the couch and wondered what Mr. Hillman would bury in his wife's grave.

The day came hot and slow. I pedaled on the soft tar of Hermitage Street and decided to go see Lucas. Richmond was in deep summer with the magnolias and dogwoods clinging to the dark houses. Time was wound to the extended days and long simmering evenings. I stared into the heat and saw the shovel sliding into the dirt and the black-streaked face of the man in the lantern light dragging the tombstone across the ground. A shiver went through me. I looked around but didn't see anyone as I pedaled past the shady porches of the old Guienna Park homes.

I rode down Monument Avenue, passing the discolored statues of Jeb Stuart and Stonewall Jackson on their horses. General Lee stood ramrod straight with his hand on his sword. I slipped past the crouched row houses with crumbling steps and the dark windows of Civil War days. A sprinkler whipped silently through the heat.

I came to their apartment and creaked up the stairs, knocking on the door with the faded *2*.

"Just a minute—"

The floor vibrated up to the door and there was Lucas with a cigarette in his mouth.

"Hey, Lee!"

"—just in the neighborhood."

"Glad you came by ... place is in bad shape right now," he said, picking up newspapers and tucking in his wrinkled shirt. "I wasn't really expecting company," he said, the dark circles under his eyes harsh in the dim light. "You want a soda?"

"Sure."

Lucas picked up beer bottles from a table and hobbled into the kitchen.

"Bunny's just getting out of her bath. I'll see if she's dressed."

I sat down on a saggy couch. He went to the back of the apartment and I heard a door open and low voices. Lucas came back with a new cigarette in his hand.

"She'll be with us in a moment."

He went into the kitchen and I looked around the apartment. The curtains were pulled against the light and the furniture was sparse and old. There was a chipped brown coffee table with legs scuffed white on a colorless rug.

Lucas came back with my soda and a drink. He sat down on the couch and smoked with a trembling hand.

"How's everybody?"

"Alright. Daddy's all wrapped up in the Herrin campaign."

Bunny walked into the room with a nail file in her hand. Her hair was combed back with a loose shirt tucked into tan slacks.

"Get you something to drink, hon?"

"I'm fine," she murmured, blocking the faint light coming from the window, then going to an overstuffed chair.

Her hair hung down against her cheek as she moved the file.

"How are you, Lee?"

"Good," I nodded.

"Hey, Lee, got a birthday present for you," Lucas said, going into the kitchen and coming back with a bag. "Didn't get a chance to wrap it yet."

I held the new book.

"I knew *Moby Dick* was your favorite and Bunny saw a copy downtown."

"Thanks a lot! Thanks, Bunny."

She smiled.

"Lucas said you were a reader."

I put the book on the coffee table. Bunny glanced up from her nail file.

"How's your mother, Lee?"

"Okay. Dr. Williams still comes over and visits about once a week."

"Mother is notorious for her ailments," Lucas said, putting down his drink. "Surprised she didn't go for a rest cure."

"Is something bothering her?"

I shrugged, looking at Lucas.

"Election campaign and all...."

Bunny paused, examining her nails.

"Or is it your father threw Lucas out of the house?"

Lucas set his drink down heavily.

"Now, honey, Lee doesn't know that—"

"I don't think I'm asking anything unreasonable."

Lucas tapped his glass with his finger.

"Daddy know you came?"

"No."

"Lee, don't you think it was ridiculous to throw Lucas out of the house?"

Lucas threw his pack of cigarettes on the table.

"Leave it alone, Bunny."

"I just want to know his opinion."

"Lee came over to visit, not to hear about our problems."

I watched the bubbles rise in my soda and heard Bunny's cool voice.

"Our problems are that you don't have a job and you drink whiskey when you should be looking for one."

Lucas shook his head.

"Let's talk about it later."

"I just want to know if Lee thinks you should have been thrown out of the house for—"

"*Goddamn it, Bunny!*" Lucas was on his feet. "Forget about it! Lee can't do anything!"

A knock on the door intruded and nobody moved, then Lucas sat down slowly and stubbed out his cigarette.

"Come in, Terry," Bunny said in a different voice.

"I was on my way back from school and thought I'd see who's home—hey Lee."

Bunny became beautiful again.

"Can I get you something to drink?"

"Take a beer if you have one."

Terry put his hands in his pockets, hiking up his sport jacket. His hair was lighter from the sun and his face tan. Bunny came back with the beer and sat down. Terry looked at me.

"Seems like your daddy is going to have his work cut out for him with that letter in the paper. He think it was a forgery by the labor unions?"

Lucas scoffed.

"Senator Herrin wrote that letter."

Terry leaned back and looked at him.

147

"I believe those unions did make it up."

"It's a damn lie," Lucas said into his glass, then setting it down. "Senator Herrin would do anything to win the election and keep the unions out." He opened up his cigarettes and shook one out. "Been a crook for years and runs Virginia so he and his friends can profit."

"I don't think your father would work for a crook," Terry said quietly.

Lucas smiled.

"You don't know my father."

"I agree, I don't think your father would manage the campaign if he thought—"

Lucas laughed loud.

"You were ready to hang him a minute ago for throwing me out of the house!"

Bunny lifted her head slightly.

"That was different."

Lucas had a dark smile on his face.

"Oh y'all know him alright...." He looked up with slit eyes. "You know the side he wants you to know, Burke Hartwell—the great lawyer, the great man! I know Daddy's other side—he'd sell you out if it would do him some good."

Terry's face became wooden.

"You shouldn't talk about your father that way."

Lucas smirked with the smoke slipping between his teeth.

"Least I got one."

There was a long silence and Terry's face was like a mask. He stood up and looked at his watch.

"I've got a class in about a half hour—"

"Yeah, go," Lucas said, picking up the empty glass.

Bunny glared at him, then walked to the door with Terry.

"When he drinks—"

"When he drinks," Lucas repeated.

Terry held up a hand and nodded. He winked at me and Bunny walked down the steps with him. Lucas stared at the empty glass of whiskey.

"The great man," he muttered, shaking his head. "Like shit."

148

I ate my food thinking everyone knew where I was. Burkie, Katy, Sally, and Jim had come over and all during dinner I thought they knew I had been at Lucas's apartment. I'm not sure why I was so certain of this, but there must have been something in the air, because it all came out anyway.

"Glad to hear you're feeling better, Mrs. Hartwell," Jim said as everyone was drinking their coffee.

Mother nodded.

"I have felt better."

"Is it the flu, Mrs. Hartwell?"

"Really don't know what it is sometimes, Katy."

Burkie nodded and laughed.

"Mother just needs a week in the hospital to relax and then she'll be fine."

"Ain't what's botherin' her," Addie muttered behind me.

"Did you say something, Addie?"

Her eyes rose out of the shadows innocently.

"I didn't say nothin', Mr. Hartwell." She started walking to the kitchen door. "Just think Miz Hartwell feelin' sad 'bout things."

The slap of the kitchen door was in the silence.

"Addie is the only one who speaks the truth," Mimaw declared. "It took that old negress to say it, but you can't throw a boy out of the house and just be done with it!"

Burkie leaned into the table.

"I don't think—"

"You been after that boy ever since I can remember and I don't know if it's anything more than pure orneriness!"

"Mother Hartwell, I think you have the wrong idea of—"

"You've been on the boy too," Mimaw continued, turning back to Sally. "And now that he's down you're willing to give him the last *kicks!"*

Mimaw's shawl fell from her shoulders as she raised her small frame up in the chair.

"That boy has suffered enough! And this family has suffered enough! And it's time to stop all this foolishness!"

Mother put a hand to her forehead.

"Now look what you've done!" Sally hissed, standing up.

Mimaw shook her head.

"I'm too old to watch this family be torn apart. Nobody should be punished the way that boy has for his mistakes. Bury the hatchet for God's sake, Burke. Let the boy come back!"

Sally glared at Mimaw.

"Can't you see she's upset!"

"She's upset 'cause Lucas and Bunny are living in some lousy apartment in Richmond and—"

"Who asked you, Lee?" Burkie said ominously.

The phone rang in the hallway.

"Lee is the only one with any sense—that boy has to—"

Addie screamed and everyone stopped and turned to the dark hallway. My father was up and I heard his voice in the front hall.

"What is it, Addie?"

Addie had her hands to her mouth with the phone swinging below the table. Burke picked up the receiver.

"What happened?"

She wiped her cheeks with the back of her hands.

"They took Fanny to jail!"

"Who took her?"

Addie shook her head.

"—the police!"

Burke put the phone to his ear.

"Hello ... Mary? Calm down now and tell me what happened to Fanny ... Uh huh. Did they say what she is accused of stealing?" He nodded. "I see ... Did they have a search warrant? ...Alright... Do you know if anything is missing from the house?"

Addie dabbed her eyes with her apron.

"Did they say where they were taking her? Okay. Alright ... Mary ... alright. Let me see what I can find out ... Goodbye."

He hung up the phone slowly and paused. Mother stood next to Addie.

"What is it, Burke?"

150

He turned to her with his lips slightly pursed.

"The police have arrested Fanny and tore up Mary's house looking for some silver they said she stole."

He talked like he was sounding it out for himself. We were in the dark and I wondered why no one had turned on a light.

"*Silver!* From who?"

"From Buddy Hillman. They're saying she stole a silver tea service."

Addie stopped dabbing her face.

"She works for Mistah Hillman!"

Burke picked up the phone again.

"I knew that girl was goin' to get in trouble," Addie said, sniffing. "I knew she was headin' for trouble just like her pa."

Mother put her arm around Addie.

"Let's find out what happened first."

"Jim ... Burke Hartwell."

"Must be Jim Binford, the police chief," Burkie whispered behind me.

"Family is fine, Jim. I just talked to Mary Jones and she told me you arrested Addie's niece, Fanny." He waited. "Right ... alright. She works for me ... I understand...."

I could hear the small voice in the receiver. Burke nodded several times with his face tilted up and his hand fingering the pocket watch chain.

"Like to talk to her, Jim ... I appreciate it ... thanks."

He hung up the phone and turned slowly.

"They are charging Fanny with felony theft ... her bond won't be set till morning."

"When was she supposed to have stolen it, Daddy?" Burkie asked next to me.

"Jim Binford says he received a call this afternoon from Buddy Hillman saying a silver tea set had been stolen. Buddy said Fanny was over there cleaning and it disappeared."

"Why don't we all go back to the table so Addie can sit down," Mother suggested, taking Addie by the arm with Sally helping.

I had forgotten about Mimaw still sitting at the table.

"What happened, Burke?"

He told her and Mimaw made a hissing sound.

"Good Lord! That's ridiculous!"

My father nodded slowly.

"I'm going to the police station to see if there's anything I can do."

"Jim and I'll go with you," Burkie said, standing in the hallway door.

Mother put her hands on Addie's shoulders.

"Things will turn out alright."

"I alright, Miz Hartwell—just worried."

"You rest ... Sally, Katy, let's get this table cleared off."

"We'll be back as soon as we can," my father said, going out the front door with Burkie and Jim.

Mimaw reached over and patted Addie on the arm.

"Burke will get her out, don't you worry. I have never liked that Buddy Hillman."

Addie moved her head doubtfully.

"He a powerful man."

Mimaw looked at her with the flame points in her eyes.

"Powerful—*Bah!* He's as common as the hills! All he has is *money.*"

Mother's voice came through the kitchen door.

"Sally, for God's sake, a little soapy water won't hurt your hands!"

There was a distant rumbling. Dark clouds hovered behind Buckeye with the rubbery scent in the air. I crossed the backyard feeling the damp grass sticking to my feet. The barn light was on and glowed unnaturally against the gray woods. Nelson walked out pulling off his work gloves.

"Where you headed, Lee? Looks like it's about to rain."

"Left the sleeping bags in the tree house."

"Y'all slept in the woods last night?"

"Yup."

Nelson opened his mouth, then looked up to the sky as it rumbled again.

"Better get your bags 'fore it starts."

152

I nodded and went into the woods. It was getting dark fast and I ran down the trail not looking at the black trees, but reaching the tree house and quickly climbing up and back down with the rolled bags.

Then I stopped. The woods were perfectly still. I looked down the disappearing line to the Hillmans' and took a step toward Buckeye, then dropped the sleeping bags and took off down the trail to the graveyard. The trail veered to the left and there were the black points of iron in the trees. I squatted down and saw my shoes in the ivy.

I crept up to the graveyard and stopped outside to listen again. Beginning rain pattered the leaves. I pushed the gate and the hinge squeaked louder than I had ever heard it. The gravestones were bleached white in the radiance before dark. Mrs. Hillman's stone showed no evidence of having been moved at all. Even the grass along the edges was undisturbed.

I stepped forward, then jumped back. Something had squished under my foot. There was a black clod of dirt. I went up to Mrs. Hillman's grave and ran my fingers along the bottom of the stone and my hand came up black. Current shrilled down my spine. The darkness was in the woods and the rain began hissing in the trees. I picked up my shoes and ran.

The rain turned hard when I reached the front porch. I dropped the sleeping bags and walked around to the back. The rain misted through the sleeping porch screens and I could see Nelson's white shirt in the doorway of the barn. He just stood looking out at the storm.

I went into the kitchen. My father, Burkie, and Jim had come back and were leaning against the counters. Addie was by the oven and Mother stood next to her. Sally and Katy were seated at the kitchen table.

"Lee, you're soaked!"

I pushed back my wet hair.

"Had to get the sleeping bags."

Mother's eyes went over my wet clothes.

"Go put on some dry clothes before you catch cold!"

I turned to the stairs and looked at my father.

"What happened with Fanny?"

"We saw Fanny and she's in jail."

"Can't get her out?"

Burke shook his head slowly.

"Not till bail is set in the morning."

Katy cleared her throat.

"What exactly are they charging her with, Mr. Hartwell?"

"I imagine she will be charged with grand larceny."

"What kind of sentence does that carry?" Jim asked.

"The minimum is five years and a fine of up to a thousand dollars." Burke paused. "The maximum is twenty years."

Addie shook her head, touching her apron to her eyes. Mother held her arm and spoke firmly.

"Addie, that is not going to happen to Fanny."

Burkie stepped away from the cabinets.

"What proof do they have, Daddy?"

He raised his eyebrows.

"They say they found the top to one of the silver teapots in Mary's house."

"How could they find that so quickly?"

"I'm not sure, Jim. They claim they had a warrant to search the house. I've been trying to get hold of Big Jeb."

"Mr. Mason knows Fanny," Sally said hopefully.

Burke smiled oddly.

"Yes, he does—and he would be the one prosecuting Fanny at a trial."

"I don't believe it," Mother declared next to Addie. "Fanny didn't steal any silver from Buddy Hillman."

Addie nodded and sniffed loudly.

"She been cleanin' the Hillman silver for years, every Tuesday and Thursday she clean it at noon and then come over and help me."

"Did she come over today, Addie?"

"Yes sir—'cept she was late an' didn't come till later."

Burke raised his head slightly.

"What time does she usually come over?"

"'Round two clock—but she late a lot. That Fanny always been late."

Mother's eyes bored down on me.

"Lee, you've heard enough."

Some of the old meanness came back into Addie's bloodshot eyes. "Mind your mother an' get on upstairs!"

I started up the steps, but Burke's voice followed me in the stairwell.

"How that silver ended up in her house...."

18

The slaves rose when the sun was below the treetops. There were many slaves who had to be trained and the old slaves had never planted so many seeds. The tobacco was cut before it was ripe and shipped quickly. Sometimes the planter watched from his carriage with another man who talked differently and wore different clothes. The slaves didn't see the planter in the fields anymore. The moon was in the rows when they went back to their cabins.

The banging rattled through the house. I opened my eyes and sat up. The window curtains lifted and floated back gently with just the soft hush of night passing. I laid back down and closed my eyes again. The front door pounded up the stairs with four urgent thumps. I sat up and heard quick footsteps trailing down the stairs.

I got out of bed and peered into the hallway. The light was on, but there was nobody there. I stumbled down the stairs in my underwear to the first landing. The steps slipped into darkness on the first floor and I crouched down. A slice of light spread from the front door and Burke was in the doorway. There was a deep voice.

"... sorry to intrude on you at this time of night ... Silas Jackson ... friend of Fanny Jones."

A figure on the porch cut the street light.

"What can I do for you, Mr. Jackson?"

"Sir, I have some information about Miss Jones concerning her present situation...."

"Couldn't it wait till morning?"

"... urgent. I don't know anyone else who can help Miss Jones."

Burke stepped back from the door.

"Why don't you come into the den?"

There were hard footsteps in the hallway.

"I apologize again for the intrusion ... I know it's late—"

"Let's hear what you have to say, first, Mr. Jackson."

"Lee!"

Mother stared down in her robe.

"I heard a noise—"

My father came up the steps.

"Who is it, Burke?"

He leaned on the banister with one foot on the stairs.

"A man named Silas Jackson. He says he has some information concerning Fanny."

Mother pulled her robe tighter.

"What does he want?"

"I'm not sure ... I left him in the den." He started back up the stairs. "I have to get my glasses."

Mother watched him, still clutching her robe.

"Do you want some coffee?"

"That would be fine," he said going into the bedroom.

"Come on, Lee. Since you're up you might as well help me in the kitchen."

I started down the steps.

"But put on some clothes first!"

"Daddy, I have the coffee."

Burke took the tray and set it on his desk.

"Lee, this is Mr. Silas Jackson."

The well-dressed man I recognized from the wedding stood up and extended a large hand.

"Pleased to meet you, Lee."

He gave me a quick smile and his hand was muscled and hard. He was darker than Nelson and his shirt was bright against his neck. A gold pocket watch caught the desk light when he stood up. He sat back down in front of my father's desk.

"Tell your mother thank you, son."

I went back to the kitchen and waited to hear what Silas Jackson could be telling my father in the middle of the night.

An hour later Burke walked into the hallway and let Mr. Jackson out the front door. Mother had sat quietly drinking coffee and reading the paper while I had fallen asleep on the kitchen table. I sat up as my father walked in with his hands in the pockets of his robe.

"He told me some amazing things," he said slowly. "It seems Mr. Jackson heads up the Second District Negro Democrats."

"Who are they?" I yawned.

"A voting organization for the negroes. Apparently Fanny had joined them several months ago."

Mother clinked her spoon against her coffee cup.

"*Fanny* joined them?"

Burke nodded, but there was a hesitation as if he wasn't sure.

"Eugene Trenton has enlisted the support of the Second District Democrats."

Mother frowned and shook her head.

"What does all this have to do with Fanny?"

"According to Mr. Jackson, Mr. Trenton and some men from the unions persuaded Fanny to steal a letter from a foreman who works at one of Senator Herrin's apple orchards. Fanny worked at the orchards and had access to this letter—"

"What letter are you talking about?"

Mother's voice was approaching the exasperated level where Addie usually stepped in.

"The letter that appeared in the paper claiming Senator Herrin directed his foreman to pay a dollar a day to his apple pickers."

Mother clutched the top of her robe.

"Oh God."

"According to Mr. Jackson, the Trenton people promised certain things to the Negro Democrats if he would help persuade Fanny to get this letter."

"That's the letter Fanny was talking about," I blurted out.

Burke looked at me.

"He came over to see Fanny during the wedding and I heard him say something about the letter," I explained shakily.

"What did you hear, son?"

"Just heard Fanny talk about a letter, but I didn't know what letter they were talking about."

He nodded slowly.

"What else did he say, Burke?"

"He said that somehow Senator Herrin found out Fanny stole the letter and he claims this is the reason Fanny is in jail."

Mother stared at him.

"Buddy Hillman is framing Fanny for stealing this letter?"

"Possibly," Burke nodded. Mother was silent for a moment, then spoke in a low voice.

"What does he want from you?"

Burke smiled faintly.

"He feels he got Fanny into this. He's gone to Eugene Trenton and the labor people for help and they aren't talking to him. I told him that I was getting Fanny out of jail in the morning after bail is set."

Mother clutched her robe tighter.

"But what does he want?"

"He thinks Fanny won't get fair representation—" He paused. "He requested I represent her."

"What—"

"I said at this point that was impossible with my management of the senator's campaign. I assured him I would see she received adequate representation."

Mother put her hands shakily on the edge of the table.

"We will do everything we can for Fanny, but I think he must see that coming in the middle of the night with some preposterous story and expecting you to drop everything is ridiculous!"

She carried her dishes to the sink and began to run the water. The dishes clinked together and the water was loud on the enamel sink.

Burke scratched his cheek and stared at the tile floor. He kept his arms crossed and shifted his weight to his other foot.

Friday morning came cool and dry with the inside of the house like tree shade. Fat bacon sizzled in the kitchen and came up with the coffee smell. I dressed hurriedly and went downstairs for breakfast. Mother was already at the table. Addie flapped through the swinging door darker in the morning light.

"Just going to wake you for breakfast."

Addie plopped scrambled eggs and bacon on the table and a steamy bowl of grits. I spooned the eggs onto my plate.

"Where's Daddy?"

Mother sipped her coffee.

"He's gone down to the courthouse to see about Fanny. Isn't that the shirt you wore yesterday?"

"Just the end of the day."

Addie rumbled up behind me and filled a glass with orange juice.

"Don't have no grits on that plate."

"Don't like grits."

"You ain't been eatin' for the past week and I can't have no more trouble with Fanny in jail. You eat some of them grits."

"Don't like grits."

Mother looked over her paper.

"Haven't you been eating, Lee?"

"Yes!"

"Maybe he need some castor oil."

I gulped down the rest of my eggs and finished my orange juice. The screen door sprang and slammed. Jimmy and Clay walked into the dining room in their shorts and bare feet. Mother spoke without looking up from the paper.

"Lee has to finish his breakfast before he goes out," she said folding the paper in two.

"Where you boys' shoes? You trackin' in all the dirt an' shit from the outside!"

I spooned some grits on my plate and stuffed them into my mouth.

"Done," I said out of the side of my mouth.

The paper lowered and then went up.

"Don't be late for dinner."

I ran for the door with Addie's voice chasing me.

"Chew them grits!"

I spit the mush off the porch.

"*Damn*, I hate grits."

Jimmy and Clay got up from the porch swing.

"Ya'll hear about Fanny?"

I looked at Jimmy and remembered Burke's request to say nothing about Fanny or the visit from Silas Jackson.

"No," I shrugged.

"Stole a box of silver from Mr. Hillman and now she's in jail!"

Clay stared at him.

"Why would Fanny steal silver?"

Jimmy swelled up.

"Mr. Hillman called my daddy last night and said Fanny stole a whole silver tea set from him! My daddy is going to try her and she could go to prison for twenty years!"

"But, that's Addie's niece," Clay said, looking at me.

Jimmy shook his head.

"My daddy says it was bound to happen. He said she was uppity and that she worked for the union people and Eugene Trenton and—"

"How does he know she stole it?"

Jimmy snorted and looked at me.

"She's the last one over there and Daddy says they found it in her room."

He was nodding again with his fat stomach pushing out his t-shirt.

"She stole it alright."

We smoked the morning away and then Clay and Jimmy wanted to go swimming. I said I wanted to get some lunch and would meet them later, but I was thinking about visiting Careen that afternoon and eating was as good as any reason to leave. Addie made me a sandwich and positioned the fan to blow on her as she went to the icebox.

"Daddy come back yet with Fanny?"

Addie poured a glass of milk and shook her head.

"No and I worried they ain't goin' to let her out."

"Probably takes awhile to get someone out of jail."

"Hope so," she murmured, walking back to the icebox.

I finished my sandwich and went back outside. The noon sun was white on the grass. I walked through the garden fingering the warm, green-red tomatoes on the vines. The cicadas called out in the heat from a line of mist over the trees. I started across the lawn and stopped just before the woods to kick off my sneakers. I went past the turn in the trail without looking toward the graveyard and ran to the sunlight on the other side.

The shade came back at the top of the Hillman steps. The country-side flowed off to the horizon where the steeple of the capitol building pricked the sky. I ran my hand over my hair and rang the bell on the side of the double doors. Footsteps came up to the front door.

"Halo, Lee," Peter said in his sandy voice.

"Hi Peter—Careen here?"

He nodded and stepped back.

"Sho' she is, come on in."

I walked into the high-ceiling coolness with the rubber of my sneakers squeaking against the marble hallway. I followed his white coat down the hallway and to the left where the narrow hallway opened up into a breezy, tiled kitchen. A blackened exhaust fan fluttered the sun outside.

"Careen, Lee here to see you."

She stood up from the kitchen table.

"Hi, Lee. Like some supper?"

"Just had lunch."

Careen carried a plate to the sink with the door breeze moving her dress. Anna turned with her hands in the soapy sink water.

"You sure you ain't hungry?"

I shook my head quickly.

"Nope ... I'm fine."

Careen clasped her hands in front of her.

"Would you like to go outside?"

"Whatever you want to do."

"I'll go change."

Her steps faded down the hallway and Anna laughed as she soaped a pan in the sink.

"Careen done change her clothes every time she sees anyone. I think she wear three outfits a day."

I sat down at the table. The kitchen felt like Buckeye during a long day.

"She growin' fast. Before long she be havin' her comin' out party and she be such a pretty thing." Anna looked out the window over the sink. "Yes, sir—time surely does go fast, an' the older you gets the faster it goes." She turned around and smiled again, wrinkling the light brown scar line across her cheek. "Miz Hillman would be proud if she saw Careen now."

"You know Mrs. Hillman well?"

She looked at me.

"Know her very well." Anna took her hands out of the water and picked up a dish towel, leaning back on the sink. "Always paintin' down in that old slave house in back."

I squinted.

"What slave house?"

"The place where she paint—Mistah Hillman used to say she spent more time there than in the house." Anna walked over to the screen door and looked out with the day on her face. "You can see it from here."

I went to the door. The backyard sloped gradually down to a line of trees. Down at the bottom was a row of faded, gray cabins. One was whiter than the others.

"That one all the way over is where Miz Hillman do all her paintin'—an most of her paintin's are still there. An' all her books, too."

"Never saw that before."

"They is the old slave quarters. This house was a big plantation at one time—all of Guienna Park were the fields, an' I think this house burnt down once—but they is the old slave houses. Yard man used to stay down there too."

Anna hummed to herself and went back to the sink.

"The day Miz Hillman died—she been down there paintin' when she took sick an' they kept her down there till the doctor come, an' he say she too sick to bring to the house." Anna shook her head, her hands back in the water. "An' then she died and Careen such a sad little girl. And do you know that ever since her mamma died she won't go near the pantry."

"What pantry?"

Anna turned around and motioned to a white door at the end of the kitchen.

"That one there."

"What's in there?"

"Just cleanin' supplies for the silver." Anna looked around and leaned forward. "That where Fanny cleaned the silver. An' now they say she stole it!" Anna turned back to the sink and shook her head tiredly. "I feels sorry for that Fanny, she been headed for trouble all her life—"

"Okay, I'm ready!"

Careen came back in with a short-sleeved shirt and shorts.

"Goodbye, chile. Y'all have fun."

"Bye, Anna," Careen called as we went out the screen door into the day.

We walked around to the front and I looked at the whitewashed slave cabins down by the woods.

"Anna said your mother painted down there."

Careen glanced over and nodded.

"I haven't been down there since Mother died—it's all locked up. None of the servants will go down there either—they say it's haunted."

"Huh," I grunted, then forgot all about her mother as I watched the sun sheen run up and down her hair. "We can go to Willard's and get a milkshake, if you want."

"Oh, I'd like that!"

We slipped into the woods and Careen turned suddenly with her breath against my ear.

"Let's say hello to Mother."

She grabbed my hand and started running down the path, stopping suddenly to pick some honeysuckle.

"Ever eat the honey, Lee?"

She pulled the stem through a white flower and showed me the honey drop at the end. She sucked it off the stem and I pulled off a flower and did the same. We started walking again and reached the iron fence. Careen unlatched the gate and knelt down in front of her mother's grave. A dragonfly hovered next to the mossy blue-green edges of the gravestone.

The sun filtered down on the grass and everything smelled like dirt to me. Careen sat with her feet tucked under and her hair smooth like water down her back. I kept smelling dirt and seeing her father and the man in the lantern light.

"It's nice here, isn't it, Lee?"

"Oh yeah," I said quickly, hesitating, then sitting down next to her, running my hand through the grass.

"I came home early from school the day she died...." She turned with the forest in her eyes, then looked down at a leaf she twirled in her hand. "I can't really remember much about it—Daddy sent me to some relatives in Charleston, and then off to school. I've tried to remember, but it's almost like there's a mist and I can't see through it."

I cleared my throat.

"Maybe best you can't."

"It's so silly people die." She looked at me. "If God wanted to make people, why didn't He make them to go on forever?"

"People go on in heaven," I shrugged. "What they say, anyway."

"I know. But it seems so silly people just go away."

Her hair fell off her shoulders. The air was damp and warm and I slipped my hand over hers and put my arm around her back. Her tan legs were crossed in front of her. Careen looked at me as I leaned over, then she pecked me on the cheek and jumped up.

"I'm ready for a milkshake!"

"—sure, me too," I said, struggling up.

Careen walked to the gate. There was some dirt on the back of her shorts.

"Dirt on the back of your shorts."

"Where?" she said, trying to look.

I brushed my hand over her shorts and felt the soft curves.
"Lee!"
Her eyes were wide.
"There was some dirt there!"
She stared at me.
"There was!"

19

The slaves labored into the dusk glow when the dirt was lighter than the tobacco. The overseer walked the rows and felt the leaves and told the slaves it was ready to cut. Their eyes followed him, but their hands knew the leaves weren't ready. The planters counted on even larger crops.

I read the paper in the settling twilight with one foot hanging off the porch swing and the smell of dinner floating out the window. A dog barked down the street and our neighbor's push mower ruffled the air in the stop and start rhythm of a man walking. I turned the page and sat up suddenly.

NEGRO SERVANT WITH TIES TO TRENTON CAMPAIGN
CHARGED WITH THEFT OF HILLMAN SILVER
Fanny Jones, a negro, has been charged with grand larceny in connection with the disappearance of a $5,000 silver tea set from the residence of Buddy Hillman. Mr. Hillman was alerted to the missing silver by one of his servants and reported it to the police. Jones had worked for the Hillmans many years, and police were immediately suspicious when it was determined she was the last one to see the silver set when she cleaned

*it. A search of Jones' residence turned up pieces of the missing
set and she was subsequently arrested. Reliable sources have
reported that Fanny Jones was also a member of the Second
District Negro Democrats, who are supporting the election of
Eugene Trenton in the upcoming Senatorial Primary against
Senator Herrin. Bail was due to be set today.*

I heard Addie call for dinner and left the paper on the swing. Burke
had come back with Fanny and she was now staying on the third floor
with Addie. I had walked in while she was helping in the kitchen and
she barely lifted her eyes. It was when everyone sat down to eat that
Mimaw asked what I had been wanting to all evening.

"So you got Fanny out of jail. Did she steal the silver?"

"Mimaw!"

"Oh damn! They can't hear, Livvy, and what if they did—they
know everything that goes on around here anyway."

Burke clasped his hands together in front of him.

"I posted bail for Fanny."

Mimaw laughed wickedly.

"I'll bet Buddy Hillman was fit to be tied when he heard you bailed
her out."

My father nodded slowly.

"I did get a call from Buddy today." Burke smiled wryly. "He asked
what I thought I was doing by bailing out Fanny and risking the whole
campaign by coming to the aid of a criminal, who was also a member
of the Negro Democrats and worked for Eugene Trenton and the unions."

Mother touched a napkin to her mouth.

"What did you say, Burke?"

My father picked up his spoon and touched it to the rim of his
plate.

"I told him she was Addie's niece and I didn't want her to stay in
jail till her trial. I said it wasn't important to me what she did on her
own time—"

There were quick steps on the porch, then a rapping on the screen
door that came into the living room like someone had just walked in.
My father stood up.

"I'll get it."

He was already into the hallway when the deep voice came into the dining room.

"I'm sorry to disturb you at dinnertime ... Is Miss Jones here?"

"Yes, she is, Mr. Jackson—come in and I'll get her."

Burke crossed the hallway to the steps. I felt his eyes before I saw him standing in the slanting light. He stood with his hat in his hand and looking darker in the dusk shadows. He nodded to mother.

"Sorry to disturb your dinner, ma'am."

Mother smiled and nodded out of sync, looking like she wasn't sure what to do. Her eyes flicked to me.

"Eat your dinner, Lee!"

"He is a good-looking buck!"

"Mimaw!"

Mother picked up her coffee cup, but her hand trembled and she set it back down. I watched him out of the corner of my eye, standing there in his dark suit with the light behind him. Steps came down and Fanny crossed the hallway out to the porch. Burke walked back into the dining room and we started eating again. I could hear their low voices every now and then coming in through the open window. I had just finished when the screen door opened and Fanny ran across the hall and up the stairs. Her steps reverberated into the silence and then the screen door opened slowly. Silas Jackson walked into the hallway and faced us.

"I am sorry to disturb your dinner again, but may I have a word with you, sir?"

His voice was proper, but edged, as if something was going to tear the proper sound right off. I saw the paper I had left on the porch in his hand. Burke stood without a word and walked into his den with him following. Mother and Mimaw looked at each other, then Mother began stirring her coffee and kept stirring it. I went out to the porch swing and waited.

A half hour later Burke came out with Silas. They stood on the edge of the porch as if something had been settled.

"I don't know if they will help you, Mr. Jackson."

He still held the newspaper clenched in his hand.

"I don't either, sir, but Mr. Trenton and the union people are responsible for what is happening to Fanny right now. And I am too," he said evenly, his eyes burning through the light. "They are going to let her be a scapegoat and not do a thing to help her. I can't permit that."

Burke leaned against the porch column with his arms crossed.

"They still won't talk to you?"

"I have repeatedly tried to call them but my calls are never put through, and when I went to the campaign headquarters they refused to let me in."

"What's your next course of action?"

Silas stared at my father, his face darker in the porch shadow.

"They are reasonable men. They will have to talk to me when they realize I will not go away. I happen to know the candidates are leaving for Charlottesville tonight and Mr. Trenton is in his campaign car at the station. I have let him know I will meet him there."

Burke pulled out his pocketwatch.

"How do you intend to get there?"

"The train station is not far—I will walk till I can get a taxi," he said, looking to Hermitage Road as if he expected to see a taxi any minute.

Burke looked at me.

"Lee, tell your mother I'm going to give Mr. Jackson a ride to the train station."

"You have done enough for me, sir. I—"

"Nonsense—it's no trouble. You'll never be able to catch a taxi out here."

"I'll go with you, Daddy?"

"Just tell your mother."

I raced inside and told Addie, then ran back out and jumped in the back of the car. We headed for downtown and the train station. I leaned against the front seat between them. The tires hummed down Hermitage Road with the car lights just ahead

"Did you go to school in Indiana?"

"Yes, sir, the state university." He turned from the window and rubbed his eyes with big hands. "My father worked hard to put me through that college, Mr. Hartwell. He worked in the steel mills to the day he died." Silas held up a hand in front of him, his voice heavy. "I have tried to live up to the opportunity he gave me." He laughed suddenly, leaning his head back on the seat." He used to say the only thing holding a man back was himself." Silas turned and stared at my father. "But it's a white man's world, Mr. Hartwell."

Burke looked over, then back down the road. There was just the whoosh of the night air. Silas turned back and looked out his side window.

"I have never been to Indiana," Burke said quietly.

Silas shook his head.

"It's not beautiful like Virginia."

"How did you become involved in politics, Mr. Jackson?"

He laughed again, but it wasn't a good laugh.

"I joined the Negro Democrats in Indiana. They said they were going to form a group in Richmond and I said I'd head it. I had heard a lot about the South ... I was curious."

The train station came into sight.

"Best thing that happened to me down here was meeting Fanny." He turned to Burke like he was confessing. "She was the kind of girl I could have married."

My father pulled into the train station and parked. He opened the door and Silas put his hand on his arm. He reached into his coat pocket and pulled out a creased and dirty envelope.

"I want you to have this, sir. Please open it later."

Burke hesitated, then slipped the envelope inside his coat pocket. We went into the train station with the high, echoing ceilings. Silas asked the woman in the ticket window a question and she pointed against the glass. He walked back.

"His train is still here."

We passed through double doors at the end of the station and were outside again. The trains were puffing steam toward the cement runways lining the middle of the tracks. Silas looked at various trains, then nodded to one. We walked down the cement partition. There were two policemen standing halfway down the walkway with men in suits standing outside the train. We stopped and Silas looked at the men.

"Well, thank you again, sir."

He smiled like an old friend and put out his hand. Burke shook it, nodding to the police.

"I think you might have some trouble getting through."

Silas just kept smiling as if everything was planned out.

"Yes, sir. I'll handle it."

He put out his hand to me and it was quick and strong, then he was walking down the white runway with the steam puffing around him. He walked straight toward the police, who were still talking to each other, and didn't stop till they turned and blocked his path. His back was straight as he talked to them and pointed to the train car. The police shook their heads and pointed toward us. Silas nodded, turned, then slipped around the police and began running.

"HEY—STOP, BOY!"

"Stay here, Lee," Burke said, starting toward the police and Silas, but I could see it all happening.

Silas was running along the train car in beautiful long strides and the police were trying to catch up. He ran through the men in suits and began banging on the train door with his palms. The policemen had stopped with their hands in front of them like they were holding a hose.

"STOP WHERE YOU ARE, BOY!"

The men in suits were pointing at Silas and the voices and the hisses from the trains ran together, but I heard one voice on top of everything.

"ASSASSIN!"

Silas stepped back from the train in the middle of the runway, looking at the train, and the police were still crouched with their hands together.

"STOP, NIGGER!"

Burke was only halfway there, because all this happened at once and faster than you could see it or hear it. Cracks echoed around us like firecrackers and puffs of white smoke went up from the policemen. Silas Jackson was still motioning to the train when he jerked around like a puppet and fell down onto his stomach. He lay still in the gray light with a darkness creeping out from him.

Crack! The smoke puffed up. *Crack! Crack!* They fired again and again and Silas puppet-jumped, spurting dark on the white platform. I woke up. There was only the night purr in my bedroom and the gray of early dawn. The light streaming in from the window snowed on the furniture in my room. I lay with the dream getting further away and the cool sheet at the bottom of the bed wrapped around my feet where I had kicked it. I raised my hand in the ash dark and spread my fingers. My palm was whiter than the back of my hand.

The birds sang sporadically as if the morning had just crept up on them. I slipped out of bed and walked across the creaking floor into the blue getting brighter. I stood and looked out the window. Above the woods was a single star.

I saw Silas Jackson in the growing pool of blood while the police stood around him, looking down the way men do with dead animals. Burke was kneeling beside him while Silas looked up with the strange, faint grin on his bloody lips. Burke stood very slowly while the policemen shook their heads. Then Fanny was in the living room with Burke and I heard her out on the porch.

"*Noooo! ... No! ... Oh noooo!*" It was in every room of the house and in my head. "*Noooo!....*"

I had run into the hallway and Fanny was kneeling on the floor and holding her hands to her eyes as if she wanted to tear them out. Burke had his hand on her shoulder and when he looked up at me there was a nakedness in his eyes I had never seen before. Fanny clawed at the rug, then hit it with her flat palm.

"I ... TOLD ... HIM ... BUT ... HE ... WOULDN'T ... LISTEN...." She said each word like someone nailing a board. "...AND ... HE'S ... DEAD ... NOW ... HE'S ... DEAD!"

She hit the floor again and again, going up and down, her black hair flying behind her. Addie and Mother came in and Addie went down on her knees and put her big arms around Fanny.

"Oh Mama, it hurts so bad...."

She was crying and Addie rocked her the way she had rocked me before.

173

"Alright baby, it alright ... You going to be alright...."

We just stood there helpless, watching Addie hold Fanny in the circle of yellow light. It was the first time I had seen my father powerless to control a situation. He stood there with the naked look and even his pocket watch was dim and seemed more of a prop than a precision timepiece.

The night air came in and washed away my thoughts with tingles. I left the window and walked into the hallway toward the bathroom. The hallway was dark, but light was coming up the stairs from the living room. I turned and started down the steps. There was a lamp on and I saw the open door to Burke's study. A red line of dawn was outside.

I crossed the rug quietly and looked in the half-open door. My father was sitting at his desk with his clothes on from the night before. Dark circles were under his eyes and his bow tie was undone and limp on both sides of his open shirt. He stared at a legal pad in front of him and rubbed his eyes.

"Daddy—"

He looked up and his eyes were red and veined.

"Saw the light and thought maybe someone had left it on...."

"Come in, Lee."

I went in and sat down in the high-backed chair facing his desk. I put my feet up on the chair and hugged my knees. A bottle of bourbon was on the side of his desk. He leaned back in his chair, clasping his hands behind his head.

"Couldn't sleep?"

I nodded.

"Had a dream and woke up."

He turned in his chair to the window behind him.

"It's light already," he said, sounding surprised.

"You been up all night, Daddy?"

He stared out the window and I wasn't sure he heard me.

"I suppose I have—" He turned back around and his eyes settled on me. "That was a terrible thing that happened today, Lee. I'm sorry you had to see it."

He was quiet for a moment.

"I've been going over it in my mind, thinking about something I could have done to prevent what happened." He breathed out heavily. "It was so pointless."

He leaned back in his swivel chair and looked out to the lawn again. "I've been thinking about my stepfather," he began slowly. "He was a man who believed he was doing God's will—God's will as a minister and then as a judge." Burke squinted at something. "He had a case, a negro, who had come before him and was accused of raping a white woman...." He turned and looked at me. "During the trial there was a lot of pressure to put this man in jail. And I remember my stepfather didn't really believe this man did it, I don't know how he knew it, but he didn't think this man had raped this woman—but the town was up in arms and the jury found him guilty. He sentenced this man to fifty years in prison at hard labor." Burke paused and looked out the window again. "I thought at the time he must have changed his mind and decided the man was guilty." He took off his glasses, holding one end in his mouth. "The man hung himself in jail that first night. My stepfather found out and sat in the living room all the next day. He was never the same after that."

He put his glasses back on and picked up his pen. He tapped the pad in front of him, slowly turning the pen around in his fingers.

"Maybe it is as simple as right and wrong." He paused, looking into the air for something and held the pen just above the pad, then smiled to himself.

"At my age, Lee, you start to look for a certain symmetry that will put things into some type of order." He stopped again. "But there are people who put order above human life. And then you have to decide if you will let such things pass."

I noticed for the first time how his hand shook as he put his pen in his shirt pocket. He smiled again warmly.

"If you have any more nightmares, let me know and we can talk about them—alright?"

"Okay, Daddy."

He looked out the window at the dewy grass, pink with morning light. I knew he had made a decision, the way Silas Jackson had made a decision on the way to the train station.

"Looks like it's going to be a beautiful day, son," he said, still looking out the window.

20

A new man sat at the long wooden table wearing a govern-
ment uniform. He used a cant hook on every barrel and
wouldn't pass the bad tobacco. The inspector saw the
planters sitting in their carriages in the summer light. He
could hear wind lapping the water against the wharf and
could see the stacked hogsheads of bad tobacco. He looked
where the carriages had been and wondered if the planters
had gone back to their plantations.

July broke from June and bubbled the tar in the streets and baked
the sidewalks till even at midnight they held the heat of midday.
The day after I turned thirteen Burke said he was going to represent Fanny and would resign from managing the senator's campaign.
He said we would hear a lot of things in the press and Big Jeb would be
prosecuting for the city.

I kept cutting out articles and didn't care about getting the money
anymore when I cut out the short article about Silas Jackson.

POLICE SHOOT NEGRO RUNNING
TOWARD TRENTON CAMPAIGN CAR
A negro, Silas Jackson, was shot by police running toward
Senatorial Primary candidate Eugene Trenton's campaign car

in the train station. Jackson was reportedly the head of the recently organized Second District Negro Democrats, which had pledged support for Trenton. When reached for comment, Eugene Trenton said he had no idea why Silas Jackson was running toward his campaign car and had only met him once, briefly. Police who had been posted because of threats to Eugene Trenton called to Jackson several times to stop, and then fired, killing him.

Burke's picture was in the paper with a headline saying he resigned from managing the senator's campaign. This happened after a long meeting in the living room between him and Buddy Hillman. Mother had sat up waiting for him in the kitchen. They talked a long time and the next day at dinner he told us he had resigned. "Personal reasons" were cited in the article, but it took notice he was representing Fanny and surmised the two were connected. The article went on to say Fanny had ties to Eugene Trenton and the labor unions and was a member of the Second District Negro Democrats. The article cited "reliable sources" for the information. We knew Buddy Hillman had taken over the senator's campaign.

There was a small article in the paper that I almost missed and Burke found more interesting than the others. It said the Herrin letter was a faked copy and no original could be found. I just thought the article made things look worse for Fanny and I couldn't understand why Mr. Hillman would want to frame Fanny if the letter was a fake. Burke said the reasons he was doing it were deeper than that.

My father thought a rest cure was near and wanted to head it off. He took Mother to New York in July. The day after they left Clay came over with Scotty's golf clubs. He lugged the clubs to the side yard and dropped them down on the lawn where I was cleaning grass stain off my feet. The red leather case looked new with the tops sprouting bright tasseled socks. Clay fell to the grass and Jimmy flopped next to him. I turned off the hose and stared at the clubs.

"How'd you get those out of the house?"

Clay wiped his glasses on his shirt.

"Took 'em out the back."

"Got a bunch of balls, too," Jimmy said looking in the case. "We can take practice shots."

I knelt next to the clubs and pulled one out slowly. The club was black and shiny with wear on the grip. The case strap had marks and creases. I remembered seeing Scotty with the clubs over his shoulder. Jimmy pointed to a zipper on the side of the case.

"What's in there, Clay?"

"Think that's where more balls are."

Clay unzipped the pouch with a small tearing sound and brought out some yellowed golf balls and a brown leather glove.

"It's his golfing glove," Clay whispered, seeing the residue of perspiration in the leather from the muscles of Scottie's palm and fingers.

"Put it on, Clay," Jimmy whispered.

Clay held the gnarled leather and slowly slipped it on. The clawed hand came to life.

"What are ya'll doing with Scotty's clubs?"

Clay flung the glove off into the grass as Lucas hobbled across the front lawn.

"Hey Lucas!" I stepped back. "You're all dressed up!"

He rested on his cane in a short-sleeved white shirt and tie.

"Yeah—got a job yesterday—selling paintbrushes in a hardware store." He looked toward the house. "Daddy and Mother gone to New York?"

"For the weekend."

"Thought so, just wanted to pick up a few things." He looked at Jimmy and Clay standing behind me. "Y'all looking bigger every time I see you." Lucas pointed with his cane. "What do you have them laying in the grass for? Scotty would throw a fit."

Clay picked up the clubs.

"He was going to teach me to play golf. Thought I might practice a little."

Lucas shifted his weight to his good foot and looked at Clay.

"Well, he told me the same thing, Clay."

Clay looked up.

"He did?"

"Sure he did, told everyone that he was going to teach Clay to be a great golfer like he was."

"Really!"

"Matter of fact," Lucas continued, "he asked me to help you out. Come on, let's go in back and we'll hit a few balls."

Clay hoisted the clubs onto his shoulder and followed Lucas with the case just scraping the grass tips.

Lucas took us for some milkshakes after we had taken a turn at golf. He had a dusty black Dodge. We put Scotty's clubs in the trunk and opened the doors to the worn seats and the rubbery smell old cars have when they get hot. I sat in front and touched a crack on the dashboard.

"When did you get this?"

He started the engine.

"Picked it up downtown—she's been through some hard miles, but I think there's some more in her."

He put the car in gear and we lurched down the driveway with spinning wheels until he jammed on the brakes as a car drove past on Hermitage Avenue. Lucas screeched onto the street and turned on the radio. Band music filled the car.

"How's Bunny?"

Lucas nodded, lighting a cigarette.

"Alright—happy I got a job."

"That's good."

"I suppose." The smoke from his cigarette whipped out the window. "She thinks I have another woman because I go out drinking at night." He shook his head, driving with his elbow out the window. "Sometimes I just go drink by myself at Scotty's grave."

I stared at him.

"Hey, Daddy's going to represent Fanny?"

"Yup."

Lucas shook his head, flicking his cigarette ash out the window.

"Surprised the hell out of me when I saw in the paper that he had resigned from the Herrin campaign ... but I suppose he had to."

I leaned back against the seat and let the motion of the car carry me. Lucas glanced over.

"Y'all saw that negro get shot?"

I nodded slowly.

"That must have been something."

I looked at Clay and Jimmy to see if they were listening, but the music and wind was loud.

"Daddy is a bastard," he said evenly. "Going off and eloping isn't the worst thing in the world."

"Why do you think he threw you out of the house?"

He smirked.

"'Cause other people's kids run off and elope—not his." He threw his cigarette out the window. "I don't know if you know anything about his daddy, but disrespect was second only to blasphemy."

"Mimaw told me some."

"Honor and respect have always been high on Daddy's list." Some of the anger left his face and he shook his head slowly. "But he's taken on a lot this time with Fanny. From what I have read in the papers, it sounds like Fanny had something to do with those labor fellows and Trenton. I don't know what, but it's a hell of a coincidence, this thing with the silver and Buddy Hillman and that letter appearing in the paper. One thing's for sure, Buddy Hillman wants Fanny locked up and Daddy is going against him." Lucas raised his eyebrows. "Buddy Hillman is probably the most powerful man in the state—more powerful than the senator. You don't do anything without consulting Richmond Steel first and Richmond Steel is Buddy Hillman." He nodded. "He'll make life hell for Daddy for standing up to him. He sits on all sorts of councils and gives money to lots of organizations. Nobody is going to want to have that money cut off and Daddy's in all those organizations."

I was watching the road in front of us and feeling sick to my stomach.

"But the first thing going to happen is his law firm is going to lose all of Richmond Steel's business." Lucas pulled into the parking lot in front of Willard's Drug Store. "Bet they have lost it already."

"But if Daddy knows all this is going to happen...."

He turned off the engine rumble and the radio was gone. He looked at me with a strange smile on his face.

"He must think she's innocent." He reached back for his cane. "Come on, y'all, let's get a milkshake."

I got out of the car slowly. The summer day was startlingly bright as we walked to the door. I walked slow and almost didn't see the group of men coming out of the drugstore in front of us. They wore canvas pants and work boots and were dark with sun under dusty hats. They climbed into the bed of a pickup truck. One man came out of the drugstore after the rest.

"Come on, Pete, we ain't got all day!"

The man spat on the sidewalk and I stopped moving. The dirt-grimed face in the lantern light passed by. I grabbed Jimmy's arm as the man swung up into the truck.

"Ow!"

"*Jimmy*, that's the guy we saw in the Hillman graveyard!"

"Where?"

"In the truck!"

Lucas came up behind us.

"What are y'all looking at?"

I stared at the truck as it pulled out of the parking lot.

"Thought I knew someone...."

Lucas's eyes darkened.

"One of those men?"

"Guess it wasn't who I thought it was."

Lucas stared at the road where the truck had gone.

"Those men are foremen down at the orchards." He walked in front of us, pulling the door open to Willard's. "Good thing you didn't know them."

"Why's that?"

"Richmond doesn't have any Klan that I know of," he said, nodding to the road. "But those boys are damn close."

We had our milkshakes and Lucas dropped us off at Buckeye. Jimmy and Clay stayed for dinner and Addie gave us each a slice of watermelon for desert. The pines were dark against the sky and a white cat slipped along the tree line stealthily. We sat on the back steps, holding the slices out and spitting the seeds into the grass.

The back door of our neighbor's house opened. Old Mr. Preston came out and walked toward the back of his yard with his light checkered shirt glowing. I bit into the gushing sweet melon and juice darkened the cement steps.

Thip! Jimmy's seeds went into the lawn.

"How come your daddy is defending Fanny?"

"Why do you think, stupid, she's Addie's niece."

He shook his head.

"My daddy says that your daddy is crazy to do it and that she's guilty."

"Thip!"

I looked at him with his face white under his black hair and there was Fanny who used to laugh and sing with the craziness in her eyes and the crazy laugh. Her eyes didn't glint anymore and her whole body sagged like a weight was on her. I wondered about the craziness Addie said she got from her mother and father and where it had gone. But here was Jimmy's fat face with watermelon slobbering down. I forgot my promise to silence.

"We don't think she did it!"

"Thip!"

"Daddy says they found the silver in her house and that she was the one who cleaned it and the last one there." He bit again, water running out both sides of his mouth. "And he says that your daddy is going to ruin the standing of your family in the community!"

"Thip! Thip!"

"Maybe Buddy Hillman is framing her. Ever think of that?"

He looked at me.

"Why would he do that?"

"Thip!"

"He might have his reasons."

"Thip!"

"Daddy says she works for the labor unions and is a troublemaker."

Jimmy spit out a piece full of seeds.

"You don't know all there is to know!"

"Thip!"

"Mr. Hillman thinks she did it and he talks to my father almost every day now and we're going to be rich when my daddy gets a job at Richmond Steel."

"Thip!"

"Who said that?"

"Thip!"

"My daddy—*Thip!*—says Mr. Hillman and Senator Herrin even tried to talk your daddy out of representing Fanny—*Thip!*—but your daddy wouldn't listen—*Thip!*—and now y'all aren't going to be able to hold your head up in town."

Jimmy didn't finish because I knocked the watermelon clear out of his hand into the grass. He looked up.

"What'd you do that for?"

I stood over him.

"You shut your mouth!"

"My daddy said Mr. Hartwell is courageous."

I looked at Clay, then back at Jimmy.

"There!"

Jimmy shrugged and got his watermelon, brushing the grass off it. I sat back down and began eating again. Blackbirds skimmed across the faint pink between the trees.

"Did I tell you I saw Jackie? I'm gonna meet her in my parents' garage—she said she's going to take her clothes off for me."

Clay turned.

"Really?"

Jimmy's eyes glinted.

"Yup—she'll probably do more."

"You aren't going to do anything," I said, cleaning the rind with my teeth.

He grinned and raised his black eyebrows.

"You and Careen doing anything?"

"Maybe."

"She's a nice girl—you won't get anything."

"How you know?"

"Nice girls don't show their tits."

"What about Jackie?"

He shrugged.

"She's a bad girl."

Clay stood up.

"I better get home and sneak Scottie's clubs back into the house."

He walked off and we finished what was left of the watermelon. The heavy dusk was giving way to night over the trees.

"Hey, Jimmy."

He paused from cleaning his watermelon.

"You know that man I saw today in the pickup truck?"

"Yeah."

I looked at the black woods.

"He was the one we saw in the Hillman graveyard."

Jimmy shrugged.

"Didn't see him."

"It was him, I know it!"

"So?"

"So, Lucas says they're foremen at the orchards and probably do the night riding in the country!"

Jimmy stopped chewing on the rind. We had all seen the occasional article in the paper where a cross was burned or a negro beaten and left tied up. It was blamed on men from the country who drove in dusty old cars and worked in the fields.

"How's he know that?"

"That's what he heard."

Jimmy turned back to his watermelon.

"Even if they are, I didn't see the guy, and you could have been mistaken."

"Told you it was *him!*"

Jimmy sucked on his watermelon with a loud noise. I turned away and looked at the line of trees again.

"Wonder what they were doing down there?"

Jimmy stood up and yawned.

"Don't know—none of our business. I'm gonna go. I'll eat the rest of this on the way home."

I watched him walk around the side of the house. His steps became faint and the quiet came back. I stared at the dark woods and saw the man again getting into the pickup. I kept staring till the stars burned over the trees.

21

The slaves watched the planter from the ground as they worked bent over. They watched him walk between the tobacco rows with the foreman and the overseer. The tobacco flicked his shiny boots by their eyes. The planter crushed leaves between his hands and cursed at the foreman and overseer. He moved down the rows with the tobacco spreading around him. The slaves stayed bent over and didn't say a word.

Burke leaned against one of the columns next to a square of moonlight. I saw a match flare and a luminous web ghost through the light. I could see his wingtip on the top step as he leaned against the porch column and smoked quietly. I watched him and wondered if he was thinking about the newspaper article that said Fanny was "a pawn of the labor unions," or the article announcing Richmond Steel was with a different law firm. I considered he might be thinking of his resignation from the school board and the Richmond Chamber of Commerce with the hints in the paper he worked for the labor unions and was asked to leave. Maybe it was the empty classroom on Sunday when he went to teach the men's bible class that preoccupied him, or his decision to take a leave of absence from work.

But I knew it was probably his conversation with Buddy Hillman and Senator Herrin that brought him to the porch. They had come before dark and the door to his study was closed for several hours. The trial was set for the first week of August and the primary was the third week. The papers said the trial would affect the election and the labor unions would try to make it into a spectacle. Mr. Hillman had been quoted in the paper as saying, "It is unfortunate when one of Virginia's own turns his back on the state."

They came out later with grim faces and disappeared into their dark cars. I had watched them leave from the shadows on the stairs and was sure they tried to dissuade him from representing Fanny. That's when I saw him come out of his study and walk onto the porch.

He finished his cigarette and rested against the column. I watched him and stayed in my shadows with him in the loud quiet.

It was Saturday and there had been a storm the night before that drained the humidity from the air. The sheets were crisp like early fall and I jumped out of bed thinking about going swimming with Careen at noon.

"I didn't think he'd say that, Burkie...."

I looked over to the window.

"Your family is going to be destroyed because of this!"

I got out of bed and crept over to the window. I could see Katy's dress through the gray of the porch screens.

"Keep your voice down! God! What will I say to Daddy!"

"I didn't think he would print it—."

"I knew I shouldn't have talked to him—I knew it!"

"I just wanted somebody to tell our side of it ... look at all the horrible things they've been saying in the paper!"

"But it sounds like we're against him, Katy!"

There was a silence.

"But what if she's guilty? Then what? Your father has thrown away his career—"

Burkie's voice came low.

"Daddy doesn't believe she—"

"Have you been reading the papers? It sounds like she's mixed up with those nigras that work for the unions—"

"Just because it's in the paper...."

"—found the silver in her house and she was the last one to be seen with it."

Burkie came to the screen and looked out. I could see his head moving.

"What will I say to Daddy? I've got to explain...."

"Why would a powerful man like Buddy Hillman go to the trouble to frame...."

"Katy—"

" ... Ridiculous—"

" ... isn't that bad, our side of it—"

" ... thinks she might have somehow gotten mixed up in some way in this election."

Katy was by the screen.

"She's working for those damned unions, Burkie!"

"—your voice down!"

"Ridiculous for your father to try to defend her ... destroy everything he has worked for ... Hillman is framing her. Let someone else defend her ... it's not going to change anything...."

Burkie's voice rumbled up, but I couldn't understand what he was saying.

"... the only thing that is going to happen is your family will be hurt."

"What will I say to Daddy?"

Katy moved away from the screen and I leaned back in and began to get dressed. I had a bad feeling in my stomach. Katy and Burkie had done something and were afraid. I tried to think what they could have done, because I had never heard Burkie sound so scared before.

I rode downtown with my father to get my hair cut before I went swimming with Careen. Burke was bringing some things home from his office and the barber was in the basement of the building. Addie and her shears were my barber till I turned ten and Burke introduced me to Sonny Tyler. He was an older man with slicked-back hair and a thin mustache that was a perfect line over his lip. He talked a lot and told me jokes in the smell of tobacco and hair tonic.

The trees and lawns of Guienna Park fell away for the quick beat of the downtown buildings. Richmond looked like a cluster of building blocks on hills. The streets dropped down suddenly, then climbed back to the sky. We went past the park with the old men on the benches and parked in front of a ten-story building.

A little man in uniform held the door.

"Mornin', Mistah Hartwell."

"Hello, Thomas, you remember my son, Lee."

"Oh yes, I surely do."

We walked into the wood-paneled lobby and down the steps to the shops that were closed and dark behind the glass doors. A red and white spindle whirred slowly in the hallway. Sonny Tyler was reading the paper in his chair.

"I have a customer for you, Sonny."

He put the paper down and got out of the chair. Sonny nodded to Burke and patted the seat for me to sit down.

"I'll be back down before you're done, Lee," Burke said, lingering a moment longer.

Sonny nodded in the mirror as the white apron flung out in front of me and tightened around my neck. He bumped me higher in the chair.

"How you doin', Sonny?"

I watched him in the mirror, but he turned back to the counter with his slicked gray hair longer in back. Sonny's face was pale and I thought he might be sick. He started with scissors, clipping around my head, breathing loudly through his nose. Hair tufts tickled my ears and face like feathers and didn't look like my hair on the white floor. He tilted my head forward, then pulled it back up. He just kept breathing and clipping.

I looked at the table where he had thrown the newspaper and there was my father's picture on the corner of the page.

HERRIN CITES BETRAYAL OF CAMPAIGN MANAGER
HINTS AT LABOR INFLUENCE
Son and Daughter-in-Law "Regret" Representation of Union Negro

"Ow!"

Sonny had clipped my ear and bright red showed in the mirror on my earlobe. He pressed a tissue to the cut, then stung it closed with a styptic pencil. Sonny continued cutting with the shears. My face was burning and it came up warm into my eyes. I knew why Sonny was acting strange now. He had read the paper and he hated us. He didn't care if he cut my ear or not. I kept my eyes toward the floor the rest of the time and watched my hair fall around me.

Around noon I headed over to Careen's in my bathing suit. I jogged down the path and saw Jimmy looking up to the tree house. Jackie was halfway up the tree with her long legs white against the bark. She waved as I walked up.

"Hi, Lee, haven't seen you in a long time."

"He's been busy," Jimmy grinned.

"You coming up with us, Lee?"

"No, he's not—get on up before you fall off." He leaned over. "Jackie's going to take her shirt off."

"I'm up!"

Jimmy looked up and waved.

"Okay."

He turned back to me, raising his eyebrows and grabbing the first piece of wood.

"Might even take off the rest of her clothes." He hoisted himself up onto the tree and looked down. "I'll do a lot more than you will with Miss Priss over there."

I waved him away and went on down the trail. Just before I went around the bend I looked back and didn't see Jimmy or Jackie. I walked back slowly and reached the tree. The cover was pulled over the bottom of the tree house. I started up quietly and stopped just below. There were giggles and I looked through a crack in the wood and saw Jimmy wrestling around on top of Jackie. Jimmy's white blubber kept bouncing around and Jackie was chewing gum with her brown legs on both sides of him.

"You done yet?"

191

Jimmy grunted something and she knocked him off.

"I told you you could just lay on top of me, not put it in!"

I climbed back down and crept away till I was safely in the trees. Then I ran for Careen's house.

I pulled on the two ends of the towel around my neck and listened to the doorbell. I assured myself Mr. Hillman wouldn't be around and I would wait for Careen outside. Footsteps came up to the door and it was Peter.

"Come on in."

"I can wait here."

He stopped and turned with his white jacket in the shadows.

"No reason for that. Come on back and wait in the den, you can sit down there."

I walked in reluctantly and felt naked in my swim shorts in the dark house. I followed him past the kitchen and into the den.

"You wait here, an' I get Careen."

I nodded and sat down on the couch. The room was the same as before with the plaques and the large desk in the corner. There was the slightly sweet scent of pipe tobacco and burnt wood from the fireplace. I saw the same black piece of steel on the hearth. A clock measured out the slowed time of midday.

A soft breeze blew in behind me and I stretched out my legs as the doorway became dark. Mr. Hillman held his pipe in front of him. I didn't move or breathe as he walked to his desk and took a file out of a drawer. He looked at me, then walked over and sat down in the chair across from the couch.

"How you doing, Lee?"

"Fine," I said, a drummer beginning in my chest.

He put the pipe in his mouth.

"How's your daddy?"

"He's fine."

"Your mother?"

"She's fine."

He cleared his throat loudly and leaned back in his chair.

192

"Why you think your daddy is representing that colored girl, Lee?"

His dark eyes were almost friendly. I pulled on the ends of my towel and wished the drummer would slow down.

"Guess he thinks she didn't do it."

A puff went up from his pipe, then he smiled.

"Lee, I don't know if your daddy is fully aware of what he's doing. That negress works for the labor unions and Eugene Trenton and is a thief to boot. She's trying to stir up all sorts of trouble!"

He leaned forward.

"I know that she is ya'll's maid's niece and I can understand your feelings. Forget about my silver—this girl is connected with these unions and other nigras who are trying to destroy our way of life."

I glanced at him nervously and noticed how small his eyes were. The drummer was doing double time now and I thought my neck would break from pulling on the towel so hard.

"I just hate to see your daddy throw everything away on a colored girl." He nodded to me. "Maybe you can tell him that, Lee," he said, winking with his left eye.

Now the drummer was doing a drum roll and sweat was breaking out on my face.

"Sir?"

"I said, maybe you can tell him."

I concentrated on the tip of my sneaker and hoped my chest wouldn't just explode.

"—no, sir."

He leaned forward.

"What's that?"

Everything went hot to cold and back again while I kept my eyes on my sneaker.

"Can't do that."

"I don't think I heard you right, son—"

"Ready!"

I jumped up. Careen had her swimsuit on and a towel in her hand.

"Bye, Daddy."

I walked by him, keeping my eyes straight, and then I felt a vise on my arm that stopped me dead. His voice came low.

"You remember what I said." His black eyes bored into me and I knew he could crush my arm like a stick. "You remember and tell your daddy before it's too late, boy."

"Come on, Lee," Careen called from down the hall.

I stood frozen, concentrating on putting one foot in front of the other.

"LEE!"

He leaned back in his chair and the vise let go of my arm. He tapped the ashes out of his pipe.

"Go on now."

I began walking, then running out of the house.

We swam for a few hours, then walked back through the woods. Pale beams fell through the trees and black insects buzzed slowly through the hot light. Careen walked slowly with her hair combed back and her wet suit coming through her shorts.

"Were you and Daddy talking earlier?"

"Little," I shrugged.

Careen walked in front of me.

"I hope he didn't say anything about Fanny."

"Nah," I said quickly, glancing at her. "Your daddy talk much to you?"

"I talk to Anna mostly—since Mother died it's been different."

"How so?"

Careen paused.

"I've never told anyone this before."

"I won't tell anyone, I swear!"

"It's just that ... well, sometimes when I get close to Daddy, I feel ill."

"Sick?"

Careen nodded.

"Just when he gets too close ... I really don't know why—" Careen looked at me. "You're the only one I've ever told that too."

"I won't say anything."

Careen smiled and walked closer. Our hands brushed together as we passed under the tree fort. The board was off the entrance.

194

"Haven't shown you the tree fort."

Careen stopped and squinted up into the tree.

"How do we get up there?"

"I'll go first," I said, taking hold of the first board.

I climbed up the tree and turned around.

"Come on—I'll help you when you get to the top."

"Alright," she nodded hesitantly.

She came up slowly and I helped her through the entrance. We stood on the plywood floor covered with sticks and bark dust. There was a brown blanket laid out in the corner that hadn't been there before. She peered down the opening, smoothing her hair back behind her ears.

"That's quite a climb."

We looked out into the forest. Sun rays shot down through the trees and lit small fires on the flowing lawn of second growth below. I stood next to her and could feel Jimmy and Jackie had done something. Her clean straight hair was touching my arm as I held her hand and she squeezed my palm back. I could see the rumpled brown blanket as she turned and there was that moment between things and I knew we would kiss again. Her lips were clean like pool water and I felt her wet hair against my arm. Then she turned around in my arms. The back of her shorts were wet and I could feel her pushing out as I leaned against the back of her. She whirled and my cheek blazed with pain. Careen was across the floor.

"Maybe your daddy defends negroes, but don't expect me to act like one!"

I stared at her.

"What'd I do?"

She glared at me.

"You know what you did! Pushing up against me with your ... your ...." she finished with a look, then her eyes just flooded over.

"I'm sorry, Careen."

She wiped her cheeks with the back of her hand, pushing me away as I tried to help her down. I climbed down and ran after her on the trail.

"I'm sorry, Careen, I really am!"

She walked with her eyes straight ahead.

"I don't ever want to see you again, Lee Hartwell!"

She didn't look at me once, but went straight toward her home. I followed her and kept apologizing, but she reached the end of the woods and started up the hill. I watched her till I heard the front door slam like a distant shot, then I turned and walked slowly back home.

The night breeze floated the white curtain and rustled the trees outside my bedroom window. The curtain fell back and I could hear the house creaking. I tossed on top of my sheets in the humid air looking for a cool spot. Thunder rumbled distantly.

I flipped my pillow to the coolness on the other side and tried to clear my mind. After dinner the evening had grown dark with rain that never fell. Burkie came over and went directly into my father's study and closed the door. I could see a strip of light under the door as I stood in the hallway listening to the rise and fall of Burkie's voice.

He came out later and didn't look at me when he crossed the porch and got in his car. I thought about that light under the door because if I didn't there was Sonny Tyler cutting my ear, then Careen in the tree fort—"*Maybe your daddy defends negroes, but don't expect me to act like one*"—then Jimmy—"*Your daddy is going to ruin your family*"— then Katy—"*Your family is going to be destroyed because of this!*"

Glass shattered around me. I sprang up, staring into the darkness. I was surprised there was no glass on the floor. I heard a car door slam and tires screeching on the street. A door opened and quick footsteps went down the stairs. I was on the floor and out of my room into the ache of light. Mother came out wrapping her robe around her and I followed her down the steps to the landing.

"Where's Daddy?" I whispered.

She looked into the darkness of the first floor.

"Burke—"

The lights in the front hall came on.

"Stay where you are!"

He was at the bottom of the steps in his light blue pajamas. Addie and Fanny stood on the second floor staring at us. I realized I didn't

196

have anything on except my underwear. Burke turned to the living room.

"Someone threw something through the window."

Mother touched her mouth like her lips were on fire.

I started down the steps slowly.

"What'd they throw, Daddy?"

He looked at me, the dark circles under his eyes.

"A brick."

I peered into the living room. The floor-to-ceiling front window was slices of jagged glass. Shards gleamed on the floor like water. The wind was inside the room and a bush tapped against the glass left in the window. A dark brick lay among the glittering pieces like something from another world. There was a white glow that became letters when I stepped into the room. The letters went across one side, sloppily painted and dripping, but the word was clear—NIGGER.

Burke walked carefully into the room and looked out the window. I picked my way across as a single car went slowly down Hermitage Street. The lights flared, then disappeared behind red taillights.

"My God!"

We turned. Mother was in the hallway, staring at the brick. The shadows wavered over the glass from the wind outside. I didn't realize it but my teeth were chattering.

"Heard a car door and a screech, Daddy."

He nodded slowly.

"Whoever it was had to get pretty close to throw that brick."

The rustling trees were loud in the room again. A single shard of glass fell and I jumped. Burke walked across the room, glass crackling under the slippers he had somehow managed to get on before coming downstairs.

"Mistah Hartwell—"

"Lee, you go on up the stairs and keep Addie and Fanny up there till I do something with this brick ... And you better put something on, son."

I picked my way back to the stairs and turned.

"Who do you think did it, daddy?"

197

He looked at the brick and shook his head slowly.

"I'm not sure."

"Who would do such a thing?" Mother whispered.

Burke stood among the glass and looked at her.

"Someone who doesn't think I should represent Fanny."

Her eyes saw something terrible to come.

"Why would they care so much? She didn't do anything."

She looked at Burke, wanting him to explain, but he was staring at the brick with the white word.

22

The cropmaster walked his rows. His wide hat floated white among the green leaves turning brown. He pushed the leaves up with his tobacco stick and talked to the few slaves in the field. The tobacco smelled sweet and he knew without touching the leaves when he would cut. He worked the stick against the callouses of his hand and when he looked up he saw the large planters coming.

Sunday came and was sunny for the workmen putting the glass in the living room window. But Monday brought a steady rain and dark skies turning Buckeye into a soggy black and white world. I sat on the porch and watched the rain. The yellow honeysuckle on the edge of the lawn and the pink magnolia trees were just a dim gray. Even the postman's light blue suit was part of a world alternating between dark and light.

By noon the rain had subsided to a drizzle. I rode through sky-colored circles on Hermitage Street and lifted my feet against the spray. I thought Lucas might be working and pedaled toward downtown to tell him about the brick.

The hardware store was on Ninth Street. I parked my bike and walked into the store with the faint smell of sawdust and oil. A man with a pencil behind his ear tipped his glasses down.

"May I help you?"

"Looking for Lucas Hartwell."

The man tipped his head up.

"Is there something I can help you with?"

"I'm his brother."

The man took a quick breath, then pushed his glasses back onto his nose.

"He no longer works here."

I stared at the man.

"But I just talked to him, and—"

"He didn't come to work for two days."

"Oh."

The man clicked his tongue, then disappeared back into the aisles. I walked slowly back out to my bike and wondered what had happened. I started to ride home, then turned down the street to his apartment. The sky rumbled in the distance.

I was soaked by the time I reached his building. I went inside and ran up the musty stairwell, pausing at the door to shake off some of the rain.

"Just a minute...."

The door swung open and Bunny smiled, then didn't, then smiled again.

"Hi Bunny, Lucas around?"

"He's at the hardware store," she said, looking behind me. "Why don't you come in?"

She shut the door with a wind of perfume. She looked like she was going somewhere with her high heels and perfect hair.

"I can come back later—"

"Oh heavens no, Lee! ... can I get you something, we're all out of soda — "

"Water's fine."

She walked into the kitchen, jingling her earrings. I sat down on the edge of the couch and looked around the apartment. Thunder rumbled in the open window and the room grew darker.

She came back with my glass of water.

"I hope you didn't get too wet," she said, smoothing her dress with a slender motion.

"Not bad."

Bunny sat down in a chair and crossed her legs, moving one foot up and down.

"How's your family? Your daddy certainly has been in the paper a lot."

"I cut out the articles for him."

"Oh, that's right," she nodded, tilting her head so her hair hung down. "Well—your father must have his hands full representing poor Fanny. It sounds like the papers have already tried her." The rain hushed in the window and her foot moved quicker. "Did Lucas tell you about the hardware store job?"

"No—I mean, yes. Saw him when he came over last weekend to pick up some things," I mumbled.

She nodded, spreading her red nails above her knee.

"I think he really likes it—"

There was a soft knock on the door. She looked at me oddly.

"I wonder who this is."

She walked to the door and opened it. Terry Bowers stood there, grinning.

"Hey, sugar—"

"Terry! What a surprise! *Lee* is here, Terry."

Terry's face fell, then the smile came back.

"—Lee."

I stood up.

"Hey, Terry."

"—just thought I'd stop and see if Lucas was around," he said quickly.

The tips of his loafers were dark from the rain and it glistened on the shoulders of his sport coat.

"Didn't Lucas tell you?" Bunny said, facing him, then looking at me. "He's working at the hardware store now."

Terry clapped his forehead.

"That's right," he said, turning to me. "I forgot."

"Can I get you something to drink, Terry?"

"I'm fine. You know, I just saw Lucas at the store yesterday and he told me all about the job."

Bunny called from the kitchen.

"He worked through the whole weekend, he said the job is going well."

I stood up as Bunny came back in with a beer.

"Can I use your bathroom?"

"Why certainly, Lee—it's down the hall."

I walked down the short hallway into the bathroom and shut the door. I stood in front of the toilet and the door creaked open from the breeze. I walked over to shut it and heard Terry's voice.

"When did he get here?"

"Shhhh—he'll hear you—"

There was a rustling sound.

"Damn—it's a good thing I didn't kiss you."

"Terry, don't ... he'll be coming back—"

My face warmed and I shut the door quietly. I waited a few minutes, then flushed the toilet and opened the door loudly.

"Better be going," I said coming into the room, not looking at anybody.

"You aren't leaving, Lee?"

"I just got here," Terry said weakly.

"You have to stay and visit, Lee—we never get to see you!"

I looked down at my sneakers.

"Have to go."

"Well, I'll tell Lucas you stopped by," Bunny said brightly.

"I'll go out with you, Lee."

Terry followed me out of the apartment and down the steps onto the porch. I picked up my bike and he stood with his hands in his pockets.

"Looks like the rain has stopped some."

The rain splotched on the sidewalk sporadically. I knew he wanted to say something, but I just wanted to get far away.

"Say hello to your family."

I nodded and pedaled away quickly down Monument Avenue. A mist had pushed the rain away and I passed through the white grayness going faster and faster. I didn't want to go back to Buckeye. I wanted things to be normal somewhere and saw Clay's house and dropped the bike on the front lawn. I ran up the steps to the front porch and went inside feeling the rain cool on my skin. The house was dark and smelled damp.

"Anybody home?"

"Back here!"

I walked through the darkness toward the kitchen and the rain began again like a faucet turning up. Mary was in the warm kitchen by the stove.

"Hi, Mary—Clay around?"

"He's upstairs, I get him for you."

She walked into the hallway and called up the stairs. From somewhere above came Clay's faint voice. She waddled back to the stove.

"He's comin' down."

The kitchen was warm and the food smelled reassuring. Thunder shook the room like a weight hitting the ground.

"Angels are bowlin' today," Mary said, humming to herself.

"It's been raining all day," I said, wanting to talk and not think about the small gray apartment with Bunny and Terry and the fake smiles.

"I know it—but we need the rain. Miz Adalia's flowers been dyin' from the dry summer. She should be comin' back from the store soon—went to get Scotty's picture framed."

I sat down at the small kitchen table and began tapping the edge with my fingers.

"What picture?"

"They had a paintin' done of him in his uniform," Mary said, smiling. "They goin' to hang it in the livin' room above the fireplace."

Mary stirred the rice slowly with one hand resting on her hip.

"Yes. I think it'll console Miz Adalia havin' that picture in the livin' room 'cause she been havin' some hard days." She adjusted the flame below the pot. "Seems every time August come near, she get sad."

"Why's that?"

"August was when Scotty was killed."

"Oh, yeah."

I began tapping again.

"Yes sir. I was the only one here when the soldier come to the door." Mary nodded. "I was cleanin', an' then I heard a knock an' I remember thinkin', now who knocks like that, 'cause it was a hard knockin', an' most folks just walk on in."

She stirred slower.

"I went to the front door an' there this man is all dressed up in a soldier's outfit, an' he have medals, an' he just standin' out there." Mary banged the metal spoon against the pot. "He ask for Mr. Nettleton, an' I told him that Mr. Nettleton at work. Then he ask for Miz Nettleton, an' I say she at the hospital."

Mary smiled and nodded to me.

"She was visitin' your mamma when she on her rest cure." Mary scratched her brow. "Then he looks at me an' says, 'I regret to inform you, Private Scotty Nettleton been killed.' I just 'bout faint right there, an' then he hands me a yellow telegram."

Mary paused, dabbing her eyes with a dish towel.

"I didn't know what to do—I try to call Mr. Nettleton, but can't find him, an' then I call the hospital an' they say Miz Nettleton left already. So I just sat in the livin' room, cryin' an' starin' at the telegram until I hear Miz Adalia come up the drive. She walk in an' she had these groceries in her arms, an' I stand up an' walk into the hallway."

Mary opened up the oven, squinting at the ham. She picked up the spoon again.

"I couldn't talk, 'cause I couldn't stop cryin'. Miz Adalia kept sayin' 'what's wrong,' but I couldn't say anything. Finally, I point to this little picture of Scotty on the wall when he a boy, an' I just kept pointin' an' Miz Nettleton stare for a moment, then she drop the groceries on the floor an' grabs onto the wall. She look at me an' the picture an' she just starts to fall an' I had to hold her up. An' she just cryin', 'Oh Mary, Oh Mary,' an' I ain't never seen anyone with such grief."

She shook her head and looked at me with wet eyes.

"That was one sad day."

I nodded, remembering Addie coming out to the backyard and telling Clay he had to go home immediately, then Clay running through the yards with Jimmy and me behind him all the way to his front porch. Clay went in and we heard his mother's cry out on the porch and no one told me, but I knew Scotty had been killed.

"I don't know where that boy is."

Mary went out as the front door slammed. Clay's mother came into the kitchen and set her groceries on the counter. The phone rang.

"He on his way down," Mary said, coming back into the kitchen.

His mother turned to me with the phone in her hand.

"Yes, Addie, he's here."

She put her hand to her mouth and it was the look Mother had when she saw the brick. Clay came into the kitchen.

"Hey Lee."

"I will, Addie. How's Olivia? Alright, I'll be over."

She hung up the phone and turned to me.

"Lee—you have to go right home."

"Why? He just got here!"

Mary had stopped and her eyes met Miz Adalia's, and I knew there was something bad. She walked over to me and spoke softer.

"You have to go home, Lee—your father is ill."

I stared at her, then ran from the kitchen and out the front door. I ran across the lawns in the rain and saw Dr. Williams' car in the driveway. I slammed the screen door open and went up the steps three at a time. Mother, Addie, Sally, Katy and Burkie were in the hallway outside my father's room with death in their eyes. Addie's head was bowed and Mother was red-eyed.

My mother said my name but I didn't hear her because I was running to the closed door of my father's room. Burkie stepped in front of my path. I slammed into him and he held my arms.

"LET GO!"

"Calm down, Lee!"

"LET ME GO—I WANT TO SEE DADDY!"

Burkie shook his big head above me holding onto my arms.

"You can't, Lee, the doctor's in there—"

Every time I got one arm free he grabbed the other. I tried to bite him, but he got me in a bear hug and I couldn't move.

"LET ME GO, LET GO!"

Addie was next to me.

"He's goin' to be alright, honey."

"NO!" I shook my head. "He's dying! THEY'RE KILLING HIM!"

"He's not dying, Lee!" Mother's voice was next to me. "Your father had a stroke."

Then Addie's big arms were around me and I smelled the cloth of her uniform and the large warmth of her body.

"It's alright, Lee. It's alright, honey, don't you cry now, you goin' to be alright."

Dust gossamers floated down through the still evening light on the landing of the second floor. Sally leaned against the wall holding the little cross off her chest and moving her lips. Burkie walked back and forth pulling his hands apart and clasping them again. Mother waited stiffly until Dr. Williams came out of the room and said he wanted to talk to her. He put a hand on Burkie's shoulder and winked at me, then went downstairs with Mother.

I sat back down on the steps leading to the third floor and stared at the dirt on my bare feet. I heard the front door slam and footsteps cross the hallway irregularly then up the stairs a step at a time. I looked over the banister and Lucas came around the corner.

Burkie moved so fast I didn't see him till he was blocking Lucas at the top of the steps.

"What are you doing here?"

Lucas looked as if he had not shaved for several days and I could smell hard liquor. Sally stood by Burkie with smoldering eyes. Lucas stopped on the stairs.

"How's Daddy?"

"What's it to *you*?" Sally snapped. "You're one of the reasons he had a stroke!"

Burkie's face was red and the veins in his neck swelled.

"You aren't supposed to be here!"

"—wanted to see how Daddy was."

Burkie took a step down the stairs.

"You can't. He's sleeping—and he doesn't want to see you. Now get out of here!"

Sally's voice cut icily.

"Go back to your *wife*!"

Lucas put a hand up and seemed to shrink back. I pushed through them and went next to Lucas on the steps. Burkie's eyes narrowed.

"Get over here, Lee."

Sally was almost spitting.

"Get away from him!"

I glared at them evenly.

"Leave him alone, *you bastards*!"

Burkie's face turned crimson.

"Don't you talk that way, boy—"

He reached forward and I felt a clamp crushing my arm. Burkie drew a hand back and I put my arm up to my face, waiting for the blow that would kill me, but then there was a short smack and Burkie was lying on the steps with blood coming from his nose. Lucas was standing over him breathing hard, his cane on the steps.

"GET OUT OF HERE!"

Sally advanced on him, pushing him down the steps just as Mother and Dr. Williams came up.

"What happened!"

Dr. Williams knelt to examine Burkie's nose.

"It was Lucas," Sally said, glaring at him.

"I don't think it's broken," he said, tilting Burkie's head back.

I pointed at Burkie and Sally.

"They ganged up on Lucas!"

"We ganged up on him!"

"They did! They wouldn't let him come up and—"

Mother grabbed onto the banister.

"I can't take this!"

"Lee Hartwell, you wait—"

"QUIET!"

Dr. Williams stood, his iron-gray eyes stopping everyone. He smoothed his beard, drawing himself up in his loose black suit that always looked dusty.

"This is no time for fighting! Your father just had a serious stroke and he needs support, not a lot of trouble! Now help me get Burkie up."

Everyone started moving again. I looked down the steps to the first floor for Lucas, but he was gone again.

23

*The crop master went to the fields with the planters. He
poked the leaves with his tobacco stick, crushing leaves
between his forefinger and thumb. The planters watched him
run the sandy dirt through his fingers. They stood under the
curing barns while the crop master went up into the hanging
tobacco. He climbed down from the dark and walked on. The
planters followed him silently.*

Night in the woods under a moonless sky. That's how it was for
my father now. Burke went to the hospital for five days and
came back home. His illness had left one effect Dr. Williams
explained to the family in the living room. The blood had been squeezed
off from his eyes during the stroke and left him blind. After Dr. Williams said this he walked from the fireplace to the middle of the room.
He said we should be thankful his condition wasn't worse given my
father's history of high blood pressure.

Burke came home from the hospital with dark glasses and spent
most of the time in bed. I tried to imagine how it was for him now. I
walked down the stairs with my eyes closed and then got in a closet
and shut my eyes very tight. I tried to write, but couldn't keep the
letters on the lines. I knocked my glass over when I ate, then felt my

209

way around the side of Buckeye and across the backyard till I hit the hanging sheets.

Everyone came over the night my father felt well enough to come down to dinner, except Mimaw, who had a cold and stayed in her room. Mother helped Burke to the table and Addie even managed to not get teary. She had been crying on and off ever since he came home. The first time she saw him being led by Mother she ran into the pantry and cried for an hour.

Burke ate slowly with his dark glasses making his face pale. He had his coat off and his red bow tie was slightly crooked. I watched him from the corner of my eye. He ate much better than I had with my eyes closed.

The phone rang and Addie called me. Mother looked at her because she usually told people to call back when we were eating.

I picked up the phone.

"Lee!" Bunny was breathing fast. "I didn't know who to call...." She took a deep breath. "Lucas left."

"... Good thing I didn't kiss you...."

"I told him I wanted a divorce and he just went crazy—he's been drinking so much ... I don't know where he's been at night. Lee—" She breathed in loudly. "Lee ... he has a gun."

I leaned back against the counter and felt my legs weaken.

"Where—"

"He always kept a gun in his dresser ... I ... I saw him load it and I tried to stop him, but he just pushed me away and took it with him."

I couldn't think, then I was thinking too quickly.

"Where'd he go, Bunny?"

"I don't know! ... I don't know where he goes!"

I must have hung up on her, because I was suddenly in the dining room with everyone staring at me. Mother put a hand to her throat and she knew even though I couldn't speak. There was nothing in my throat. Burke turned.

"What is it?"

I swallowed with my breath coming in queer spasms.

"—a gun!" I swallowed again. *"Lucas has a gun!"*

Everyone began talking at once. Mother's hands closed on the table-cloth and she stood up with it still in her hands.

"Come here, Lee," my father said, putting his hand on my shoulder. "Tell me what happened."

Everything began pouring out of me and I felt a great relief just to say it.

"Lucas lost his job—Bunny is leaving him for Terry Bowers ... he came here the other night after you got sick to see you, but Burkie and Sally ganged up on him and made him leave—"

"Now, just a minute—"

"What else, Lee?"

"—lost his job he had in a hardware store ... and, and, I think Terry and Bunny are together because Bunny told him she wants a divorce ... that's when he took his gun with him—Bunny just called—said she doesn't know where he's gone—"

My father sat for a moment, then his hand squeezed down hard on my shoulder.

"Burkie, get the car."

"Daddy, he—"

"Get the car, Burkie!"

Burkie threw his napkin on the table and left the room.

"Nobody told me Lucas came to the house when I was sick."

Mother spoke quietly.

"I was waiting till you were stronger, Burke."

Sally cleared her throat.

"Daddy, I didn't think it was important—"

"It was *goddamn* important!" He felt for the table, shaking his head slowly. "Olivia...."

Mother came and put her arms around him. Burke patted her shoulder.

"Don't worry—we'll get him back."

Addie came in with his suit coat and held it for him.

"Here your coat, Mr. Hartwell."

"I'll go with you, sir," Jim said, standing up and ignoring Sally's stare.

Burke nodded, slipping on his coat.

"Alright, Jim. Come on, Lee, lead me to the car."

"Burke—are you sure you're strong enough?"

He nodded, looking fine in his suit.

"I'll be alright."

We got in the car and started down Hermitage Street with Burkie driving. The night was warm and the wind whipped in the open windows.

"Lee, do you have any idea where he might have gone?"

I leaned over the top of the front seat.

"Goes down to a pool hall and a bar—"

"Alright. We'll go to the pool hall first. Let's go faster, Burkie."

We went into the smoky pool hall and asked if anyone had seen Lucas, then we went to the Supper Club bar and asked around. We drove to a second bar, but we were met with the same blank faces. I rode in the back seat thinking about Lucas taking us for milkshakes. I leaned up against the seat.

"Daddy, there might be one place."

We reached Hollywood cemetery and drove down the hill toward the back where Scotty's grave was. Tombstones flared up in the car lights with the etched names vanishing as we passed. I saw the black shape of Lucas's car first.

"There's his car!"

"Pull up behind it, Burkie."

We came to a stop and the car lights faded to black. I got out and my father took my arm. The car doors slammed in succession, echoing off the hovering stones. A slight balmy wind stirred the air.

Burkie took the lead.

"It's this way."

We started toward the Nettleton plot. Our feet swished in the damp grass as we passed between ghostly shapes and black trees. A pale moon cast blue shadows. Burkie's voice came out of the darkness.

"Over here."

My father held tightly to my arm and walked steadily. I squinted and "NETTLETON" floated up on a long rectangular stone.

"There it is!"

The stone blinked.

"Lucas!"

"Where is he, Lee?"

"By the stone," I said, pointing stupidly.

The dark figure became clear and something glinted in his hand.

"Daddy—" I stopped. *"He has the gun!"*

"Everybody stop!"

Jim and Burkie's walking ceased. There was stillness and I could hear my father breathing.

"Lucas!"

Only the wind answered. The black outline was still against the pale stone. I could see the faint glow of his checkered shirt.

"Take me closer, Lee."

We started walking again and I could see the shiny black metal.

"Stop, Daddy!"

The voice came from the stone and the shiny metal was raised up. Burke's grip closed on my arm.

"We're here to take you home, son."

"No, you're not."

"He still has the gun, Daddy—"

"Lucas," Burke said in a calm voice. "Put down the gun."

The wind moved the trees slightly.

"Doesn't matter now...."

We took another step toward him.

"Stay where you are!"

Lucas held the gun up again and I felt a sudden coolness on my upper lip and forehead.

"He's holding the gun up," I said trying to whisper, but my voice sounded like a shriek.

"Lucas—come home with us."

"Can't come home ... being punished for what I did."

His head bent to the ground. We were way out in front of Jim and Burkie and I felt something bad was going to happen.

"You didn't do anything, Lucas," Burke said in the same steady voice.

Lucas waved the gun.

"Don't understand—I killed him."

"You didn't kill anybody, son."

Lucas moved the gun across his face.

"—I killed Scotty."

There was a train whistle far off followed by the rumble and clacking of cars. We took another step.

"You weren't responsible for Scotty's death, Lucas."

We were close now—almost just talking. The "NETTLETON" stone was big.

"—wanted to get the souvenirs, Daddy ... I did—not Scotty."

We walked again.

"What souvenirs, son?" ·

We took another small step and Lucas floated the gun toward us. The gun made two metallic clicks.

"Daddy—"

He waved me silent as the gun floated around again.

"What did Scotty want to do, Lucas?"

He shook his head and the gun disappeared and reappeared in the darkness.

"—wanted to go on with the platoon...." Lucas looked at Burke for the first time and I could see his shiny eyes. "He knew, Daddy—"

"What's that, son?"

We took another step. Lucas was staring at us and I was outside and inside myself, hearing everything and seeing everything.

"He knew they were alive!"

Lucas's face was wet.

"Who was alive, Lucas?"

The train whistle blasted again and it was louder. Lucas wavered, opened his mouth, then put his hand to his forehead.

"Don't you see? He *knew* we shouldn't have gone near them!"

"Why not, son?"

We walked again, the rolling, clicking train cars rumbling up behind us.

"Because ... *they—weren't—all—dead!"*

He choked, his head moving crazily. His hand went up, then fell. The train blasted us with its long, wailing horn and stretched out and passed in some distant field.

"The grenade ... it just rolled out and I saw the pin was gone and I screamed for him to get away, but Scotty ... he ... he fell on it!"

He was crying so hard it sounded like he was throwing up. The gun was on the grass and he was down on his hands and knees.

"*I killed him!* ... I killed him...." he sobbed, his voice getting smaller.

Burke let go of my arm and walked toward him unsteadily. He knelt down and put his arms around him.

"I'm sorry, Daddy," he said, grabbing his coat.

Burke held him and patted his back.

"I am too, son."

Jim and Burkie walked up quietly. Lucas was small in his checkered shirt against my father, and we stood around them with that train whistle just fading away behind us.

24

The crop master had the slaves bring hogsheads of tobacco to the fields. The tobacco burned with a crackly roar, sweating their skin as they threw more hogsheads into the flames. The tobacco burned all day and into the night. The fire lit the trees and the glow could be seen from the slave cabins. The slaves watched the crop master standing against the fire with his tobacco stick and wide hat. He smelled the bad tobacco as it burned into morning.

The white heat of August came to Richmond and I became my father's eyes. The sun blazed outside his quiet study while I recited cases out of dusty black law books. He told me what cases to look for in what sections and I read them till long after dark. I kept cutting out the articles and read these out of my scrapbook while he listened behind his desk.

The week before the trial the papers speculated Burke would give the case up because of his stroke. One paper suggested the labor unions had staged everything and my father wasn't even blind. The election was in two weeks. The headlines were predicting the largest voter turnout in Virginia history with the trial as the first test of the labor unions versus Senator Herrin.

216

The trial started on a Monday. On the Thursday before, my father asked if I would assist him in the courtroom. He said he would need someone to lead him around and read things. I wondered why he hadn't asked Burkie, but he must have thought it simpler for everyone if I did it. Burkie hadn't been around Buckeye much after Lucas came back. Ever since the night at Scotty's grave he'd had a peculiar look on his face. It was the same look when he came out of Burke's study after the article appeared about him and Katy.

I knew that my father still blamed himself for not understanding Lucas more, but I think he and Lucas had made their peace. Lucas took him on long walks during the evenings. When I saw them walking up the drive, Lucas with his cane and Burke holding on to his arm, I thought they were more alike than not.

But I don't think Burkie and Lucas really cleared the air till one night on the porch. I was on the swing and Lucas was leaning against one of the columns when Katy and Burkie came out. They stood looking out from the top of the steps and Lucas just kept smoking his cigarette. Katy swished her skirt back and forth.

"Well," she said brightly, glancing at Lucas. "You wouldn't guess who I saw downtown. This might be of interest to you. I was walking out of Miller & Rhodes, and who do I see, but Terry Bowers with Bunny—"

"Katy!"

She looked at Burkie with her mouth still open.

"I would think he'd want to know—"

"Just forget it, Katy."

"All I was saying—"

"*Drop* it!"

She glared at him, then walked into the house and slammed the screen door. Burkie took a long breath and shook his head.

"Sorry about that."

Lucas dropped his cigarette down on the step.

"She didn't mean anything."

Burkie stood for a moment. He crossed his arms, then scratched his forehead.

"I ..." He cleared his throat. "I've been on the wrong side of the fence on a lot of things, Lucas."

Burkie jammed his hands in his pockets and looked down. I came to a stop on the porch swing.

"I know I haven't been too good of a brother at times ... probably a real bad one," he said, letting out a quick laugh. "I wish I had been with you over there—with you and Scotty." His face darkened. "What I'm trying to say is ... well, I'm sorry...."

Lucas stared into the light mist settling on the lawn. He took out a cigarette and struck a match with a trembling hand. He inhaled deeply, the white trailing as he spoke.

"You were a rotten brother."

Burkie didn't move. Lucas turned back to the yard and then sat down slowly on the porch steps. Burkie stood awkwardly, then he sat down.

I moved the swing with my foot. Burkie breathed loud and rested his hands on his knees. Lucas flicked the ash of his cigarette.

"Going to be a nice night."

Burkie turned like a rifle had just gone off, then squinted up at the sky.

"Yeah, it is ... going to be a nice night."

Burkie breathed, glanced at Lucas, then looked down again. I moved the swing a little faster. He put his hands on his knees, took one loud breath, then grinned.

"It's kind of like the night we shot that old .22 through Miz Tucker's house and she thought an assassin was trying to get her." He looked at Lucas. "You remember that?"

Lucas shook his head.

"Wasn't that you and Scotty?"

Burkie's grin faded like a candle dying.

"That's right...."

He looked down and I let the swing squeak to a halt. Lucas finished his cigarette and I thought he was going to stand up, but he leaned back on his hands and tilted his head.

"Aren't you going to tell me the story?"

Burkie turned and looked at him, a grin spreading across his face. He held his big hands out in front of him.

"We had police *all over* this neighborhood!"

Lucas shook his head.

"I don't remember this at all—you making this up, Burkie?"

Burkie held a solemn hand up.

"God's truth, Lucas! Scotty and I, we took this old .22 and...."

I started to swing again, listening to the sound of my brothers' voices in the evening.

The Nettletons were over a lot helping out before the trial and I wondered where the Masons were. Big Jeb had called right after Burke got sick, but he never came over. I called once to ask for Jimmy and his mother answered the phone. There was a hesitation on the line and then she told me, "He's not here now, Lee. I'll tell him you called."

"What did you expect?" Mimaw's eyes had a hard gleam. "Jeb Mason is showing his true colors and they aren't very pretty." She smoothed down her covers, looking at me on the end of her bed. "His father worked in Buddy Hillman's mills till the day he died and he left owing more than he ever made. I'm sure Jeb remembers that."

"So—"

"So, this is his big chance! Burke has always outshined Jeb. I told you, Jeb tried to go with the same firm and they wouldn't offer him a job, but gave it to Burke."

"You told me."

"Well, Jeb Mason has been waiting for Burke to stumble. Now Burke is down and he thinks it's time to kick him!"

"But it's his job to prosecute Fanny."

"Bah!" Mimaw wiped away the whole trial with the tissue in her fist. "Jeb's working for Buddy Hillman and that Senator Herrin to win the election—you can bet they've promised all sorts of things if he helps them frame Fanny and make it look like she's working for the unions and that other boy that's running...."

"Eugene Trenton."

"That's it—they'll make it look like she was mixed up with that young negro you saw get shot down like a dog at the train station. They'll say she's a troublemaker and trying to stir up the negroes and in the process make your father look bad as well."

There was silence in the shaded room and then Mimaw spoke quietly.

"You can see for miles on a sunny day, but it's just before the storm you see how things really are. You watch," Mimaw nodded. "Jeb's going to lose the one true friend he has."

Sunday came. Burke said he didn't need me for the day and wanted to talk with Fanny alone about the trial. I was lying on my bed when someone knocked on the door. Sally walked in and stopped in the middle of the room. Just the night before Jim had announced he had been offered a foreman job in a factory in Atlanta and they would be moving.

She looked around the room quickly, then thrust a book in front of her.

"I know you already have a couple of copies," she said quickly. "But you've always liked this edition, so ... here."

I took the copy of *Moby Dick*.

"Thanks, Sally."

She stood a moment, then looked at me, her eyes not as pale.

"Are you still seeing Careen Hillman?"

I sat down on the bed and shrugged.

"—not really."

She nodded, crossing her thin arms.

"I would think with everything that's going on it would be hard."

She stood for a few more moments then left. I sat on my bed and thought about what she said. I heard the clock downstairs and realized it was time to meet Careen.

The sun pressed down on the back of my neck as I walked toward Willard's. The silent houses looked like pictures under the noon heat that bent shingles up and cracked paint. A door slammed and I looked up at a dark house, but there was only the windy silence.

Willard's Drugstore was cool after the heat. A sign in front announced the new air conditioner whirring silently in a window. I sat on the stool with my feet on the metal railing, tapping the counter and looking at the door every time the bell jingled. The bell rang again and Careen waved as she shut the door. I watched her come to the counter looking older in her white gloves and dress.

"I'm glad you came," she said, sitting down on a stool. "Anna's coming to pick me up, so I just have a moment, but I wanted to see you."

We ordered two milkshakes. Careen looked around, her eyes flicking over the mirrored soda fountain with the gleaming mixers and long-handled soda faucets. The milkshakes came and I drank mine slowly with a tightness in my stomach.

"So, how's your daddy?"

"Good," I shrugged. "Still blind, but Dr. Williams says he's getting stronger. He doesn't want him to work, but Daddy's going to do it."

Careen sipped from the glass in her gloved hands.

"It's too bad he has to work when he should just be resting and getting stronger." She stirred her milkshake with the straw. "It's too bad someone else couldn't—"

"Addie's niece," I said, feeling strangely angry.

She put her hand on mine.

"Oh, I know!"

Careen took her hand away and I could still feel the cloth of her glove. She stirred her milkshake slowly.

"I did want to tell you one thing." She paused. "I'm going away to school. Daddy doesn't think the public schools are good enough to get into the universities."

I looked at her.

"Probably go away myself," I said nonchalantly. "Maybe to Woodbury," I continued, thinking of Mother's campaign that had resulted in the application I never seriously considered.

She smiled and put her hand back on mine.

"We'll both be going off to school then! We could write to each other."

"Sure."

"Oh—there's Anna. I have to go, Lee," she said, getting up.

I stood up with her.

"Guess I'll see you around."

She smoothed her dress and smiled.

"Call me, if you like. I leave for school in two weeks, so I have a lot of things to do."

She was quiet.

"Careen—"

She looked up, her eyes the color of the trees for a moment.

"You really want to go away to school?"

She blinked, her smile fading, then returning suddenly.

"Of course! Daddy thinks it's best...." She looked to the door. "Well, I have to go. Goodbye, Lee."

She waved a white glove, then disappeared into the sun just outside.

25

*The crop master came back just before the New Year and
went to the seed beds with the planters and the slaves. Early
white mist rose from the ground as he felt the furrowed soil.
He dug into the black dirt with his fingers and planted a
seed, carefully putting the dirt back and pressing the soil
flat. He had the slaves plant the same way and then cover
the seed bed with branches for the frost. He didn't come
back till the spring.*

The old courthouse in the heart of downtown Richmond was
where I heard Senator Herrin speak so long ago. We walked up
the front steps under the shady oak to the first floor, past the
city offices, and up to the courtrooms on the second floor. Voices echoed up and down the marble hallways that smelled of old wood, dust,
and brittle yellow paper. We had arrived early to get settled, but even at
eight o'clock there were people in the second floor hallway. Reporters
shouted questions.

"*Mr. Hartwell, did you resign from Senator Herrin's campaign
because Fanny Jones worked for the labor unions?*"

"*Do you see the trial as a test of Senator Herrin's power?*"

"*Fanny, did you steal the silver from Buddy Hillman on orders
from the labor unions?*"

223

"Mr. Hartwell, how do you react to the charge that you have turned against the senator and Virginia?"

A flashbulb popped and I hesitated.

"Just go on through, Lee," Burke said in a low voice with Fanny holding onto his other arm.

We continued into the courtroom, facing a high, walnut-colored desk with two long tables on the right and left. To the right of the judge's bench was the witness stand and a drooping American flag in the far corner. On the wall behind the bench were slightly crooked pictures of George Washington and Thomas Jefferson. The floor-to-ceiling windows near the flag were wide open and offered the jurors a view of the city.

The floor creaked and snapped as we walked in. The room was already stuffy from the unusual number of people crowding in for the trial. I saw Big Jeb bent over the table on the right and my father must have felt him there, because just when I was going to say something he spoke.

"Hello, Jeb."

He looked up surprised.

"—Hello, Burke."

My father sat in the middle of the long table. I felt better now that we were settled. I hadn't been able to eat any breakfast and my mouth was dry. I tugged my tie loose. Fanny sat quietly with her hands in her lap. She wore a dark blue dress and kept her eyes focused on the table. If she was worried about spending twenty years in jail she didn't show it.

Burke leaned over and whispered something that made her smile. He turned to me.

"Lee, take the papers out of my briefcase and put them in front of you to read."

He brought his briefcase up to the table unsteadily. I opened it and took out the papers clipped neatly together.

"Do you have them, son?"

"Right in front of me, Daddy."

"Good."

I looked at him.

"Your tie is crooked."

His hands clutched at the tie, trying to straighten the ends.

"How is it now?"

I pulled on one end.

"Better."

Burkie and Lucas came in from parking the car.

"Need anything, Daddy?"

"No, I'm fine," he said turning to Lucas.

They looked around at the courtroom filling quickly. Burkie cleared his throat.

"Better get a seat. Good luck, Daddy."

"Thank you, son," he said tilting his head slightly.

They went back to the visitors' gallery behind the wooden banister. The courtroom was full and hot. I picked out the Nettletons sitting in the middle. The back rows were dark with well-dressed black people who Burke said were from the Negro Democrats. I looked to the judge's bench and the witness stand next to it, then at Big Jeb. He was still writing. I thought he looked larger in his gray pin-striped suit with his hair slicked-back neat. He looked up and our eyes met. I looked quickly to the desk top with its layer of worn veneer. When I looked up he was writing again.

My nervousness was soon replaced by boredom. Burke and Big Jeb went through the jury selection process for three long days. These were long, warm, sleepy days with the lulling drone of a black fan in the corner behind the judge and the crackling of people fanning themselves. At one point Big Jeb came over to the table and shook my father's hand. A glistening line formed on his lip while he stood in front of the table making a joke.

Finally, late on Wednesday, the opening statements began. The jurors sat in the twelve varnished chairs. I counted three women and nine men. Most of the men wore suits, but a few wore checkered shirts and tan work pants. Judge Clemmings looked down upon the courtroom with a sharp gleam in his lazy gray eyes. Burke said he was one of the better judges in the state with a reputation for running a tight court and being tough on offenders. He said we needed a stern judge for a trial of this sort. Judge Clemmings looked as I thought a judge should: large patriarchal eyes, wrinkles running to his gray temples, and jowls that wiggled when he moved his head too fast.

Big Jeb walked to the front of the room and faced the jury. His low voice grew louder as he talked about how the worst thing that can happen is for someone to breach the trust put in them by their employer and what a "heinous crime" it is when this trust is abused. He talked about what an asset Buddy Hillman had been to the community and made several references to the election by saying "Richmond is under siege by outside influences," and there were people who put ideas into the heads of others to stir up trouble. While he was talking, he took long steps and gestured with his hands, poking the air to make a point. Finally, he was resting his hands on the banister in front of the jury.

"We intend to prove that Fanny Jones did willfully commit grand larceny against Mr. Hillman by stealing a priceless silver tea set, a family heirloom, that is valued at five thousand dollars. And we contend that she stole this so her boyfriend—a Mr. Silas Jackson from Indiana, who came to Richmond to organize the Second District Negro Democrats—could sell the silver for money and marry her."

There was a stir in the courtroom and Fanny looked up.

"The commonwealth will prove that Miss Jones did have in her possession part of this silver set the night of the larceny, and this, coupled with other inculpatory circumstances, will sustain our contention of her guilt."

Big Jeb leaned toward the jury, his hands wide on the rail.

"We believe that if Fanny Jones is found guilty of this form of embezzlement, this violation of trust, where a man is no longer safe in his own home, a maximum sentence of twenty years should be imposed."

There was a slight murmur again and Judge Clemmings looked at our table.

"Mr. Hartwell."

My palms were wet and I felt the eyes of the courtroom as I guided my father out from the table to where the jury was sitting. Burke put a hand on the banister.

"Alright, Lee, thank you," he whispered.

I hesitated and he nodded for me to go on. I crossed the creaky floor and sat down.

Burke slipped his right hand in his coat pocket and turned to the jury. Someone coughed in the back.

"You'll forgive me if I speak from here, it's much easier than running about looking for the best view."

There was some laughter, then just the slight whip and snap of paper.

"It's been proven," he began in a low voice, "that when you get a group of people together and have them all watch the same event, and then you ask those same people what happened afterwards, they will all give you a different version."

He shifted his weight and tapped the banister with his left hand.

"But in the courtroom, we try to determine, as closely as we can, what happened at a particular time and place and then we all have to reach the same conclusion." He took a step. "Because if we all come to different conclusions, then there is doubt—and in law and justice, there can be no doubt." He turned slightly to Big Jeb. "The burden on the commonwealth is to prove beyond the shadow of a doubt that Fanny Jones did steal the silver tea set." He took a few steps along the banister. "It's not good enough for the prosecution to tell us what they *think* happened—they have to prove what happened." He paused again. "The law in Virginia is well-established—that the possession of stolen goods is of itself not even *prima facie* evidence of larceny." He stopped and brought his hand off the banister into the air. "But the fact of possession is a most material circumstance to be considered by the jury when other inculpatory circumstances are proved and such proof will warrant a conviction. The law is very clear on this."

He turned and faced the jury, gripping the railing with both hands.

"I will show that the commonwealth can only paint a picture, if you will, of what they *think* happened—but that painting is only an impression and does not have the proof of a photograph! And without that hard proof there can be no guilt and no conviction." His dark glasses reflected the outside light. "The commonwealth is presenting, for the conviction of grand larceny, possession and inculpatory circumstances—

227

but they are deficient in both, and therefore Fanny Jones must be found not guilty."

The courtroom was quiet and I sat waiting. Burke turned.

"Lee—"

I jumped up and walked quickly across the courtroom. He turned to the jurors and spectators.

"It's his first day in court."

There was the gentle laughter again.

Thursday morning came hot, still, and humid.

I looked around the courtroom. Mr. Hillman was sitting in the front row of the visitors' section not bothered by the heat. Two men sitting next to him fanned themselves. One of the men leaned over and Mr. Hillman nodded slowly. He had a hat pulled down over his face and his head was tilted back, but I recognized the dirt-streaked face I'd seen in the glow of a lantern.

"And what time did you receive this call, Chief Binford?"

Big Jeb's voice brought my attention back to the police chief sitting in the witness stand. The light from the windows danced on the brim of his hat and dabbed gold on the buttons running up both sides of his coat. He looked too large for the witness box and his boots thudded against the front several times. His face was dark from sun and a toothpick hovered in his right hand. I wanted to listen, but I felt the man from the graveyard behind me.

"Well, Jeb—I mean Counselor," he began in a voice heavy with the country, "must have been around five o'clock."

"And what day was this?"

"Ju-ly the tenth."

"Who called you, Chief?"

"Dispatch took it—they gave the call to me and it was Mr. Buddy Hillman."

"Is it unusual for dispatch to give you a call like that?"

Chief Binford's bushy eyebrows went up.

"No. They don't give it to me all the time ... but then Mr. Hillman is not just anybody, either."

Big Jeb smiled and clasped his hands together.

"What did Mr. Hillman say to you, Chief?"

He held the toothpick straight up in his hand.

"He said that an expensive silver tea set had been stolen from his house."

"And what did you do then?"

"Well, Jim and I—I mean Officer Marks—we took the squad car and drove out to see Mr. Hillman and get a description of the missing item."

"Go on."

"Mr. Hillman told us what the silver looked like and who would have seen it last."

Big Jeb crossed his arms.

"And who was that?"

"Colored woman he had working for him named Fanny Jones."

Chief Binford popped the toothpick into his mouth and moved it from one side to the other. Big Jeb started a slow trek across the courtroom.

"Why did Mr. Hillman single out this person, Chief?"

"He said it was her job to clean the tea set."

"What did you do then?"

"Secured a warrant, went to this colored girl's house and searched it."

"And what did you find in her house?"

Chief Binford looked up to the ceiling as if many things had been found in Fanny's house.

"Found the top to the silver tea set under the bed."

Big Jeb paused in front of the jury.

"Whose bed, Chief?"

"Fanny Jones's bed."

"And where was that bed?"

The chief grinned.

"In her bedroom."

Judge Clemmings brought his gavel down, squelching the light laughter. Big Jeb looked across the room at the chief.

"Is this piece of silver you found under Fanny Jones's bed in the courtroom?"

Chief Binford nodded.

"Yes, sir. Sitting on that table there."

I leaned forward and saw on Big Jeb's table a gleaming teapot lid with a piece of wire and a tag attached to it. He crossed the room to the table and turned to Judge Clemmings.

"At this time I would like to enter this silver teapot lid as evidence."

The uniformed bailiff picked up the lid and brought it to Judge Clemmings whose sleepy expression didn't change. Big Jeb was back by the witness stand.

"What happened after you found the silver teapot lid?"

"Waited for Fanny Jones to come home and then we arrested her."

Big Jeb walked toward us.

"Is the woman you arrested in the courtroom, Chief?"

"Yes sir."

"Could you point her out and identify her please?"

Chief Binford nodded, extending his arm.

"That's her—Fanny Jones."

Big Jeb nodded.

"What did you charge her with, Chief?"

"Grand larceny," he said, drawing out the word.

"Could you please tell the court the definition of grand larceny?"

"Theft of anything more than two hundred dollars."

"Thank you, Chief."

Big Jeb walked over to his table and picked up some papers.

"At this time I would like to enter into evidence the report of a jeweler who has appraised the silver lid as being worth in excess of two hundred dollars."

The bailiff took the papers and gave them to Judge Clemmings.

"I have no further questions, your honor."

Judge Clemmings' droopy eyes were on us.

"Your witness, Mr. Hartwell."

Burke stood up.

"Thank you, judge. I just have a few questions for Chief Binford, and with the court's permission I'll ask them from here."

Judge Clemmings leaned on his arms and nodded.

"That's fine."

"Chief Binford?"

"Yes, sir."

Burke smiled and turned toward him, putting his fingertips on the table.

"There you are ... Chief, you say you got the call from Mr. Hillman at five o'clock?"

"That's right."

"When did you get the search warrant?"

He squinted with the toothpick in the corner of his mouth.

"Oh, reckon 'bout quarter to six ... maybe six o'clock."

Burke hesitated, his fingers bending as he pressed down on the table.

"That's fast work, Chief. How were you able to get a warrant on such short notice?"

"Judge gave me one," he drawled, eyeing Burke coolly.

"What judge, Chief?"

"Judge Hicks."

Burke nodded slowly, his voice becoming flinty.

"And who did you serve this warrant to?"

Chief Binford shifted in the chair and grinned.

"There was no one there ... can't give it to no one, if no one is there."

"Maybe we can get Judge Hicks to tell us how he was able to give you a warrant so quickly."

The chief shrugged and his boots clunked against the witness box.

"If you can find him."

"Beg your pardon."

"I say, if you can find him. He's gone fishing in Fredericksburg for two weeks. I don't think he'd want to spoil his vacation for this trial."

Judge Clemmings' steel-gray eyebrows went up and he watched the witness closer.

231

"So you went to Miss Jones's home, went into the bedroom, and found the piece of silver. Is that how it went, Chief?"

"Close enough ... had to look around a bit. You know, they don't keep their places so straight—"

Judge Clemmings turned to him.

"Just answer the questions, Chief."

Burke tapped his middle finger against the table top in a steady rhythm.

"How long did you look around?"

"Probably 'bout an hour or so."

"About an hour," Burke repeated slowly. The flinty tone came back. "The police report says you arrested Fanny Jones at six thirty. And let's see, you got there at six—how did you fit an hour into a half hour, Chief?"

"Maybe it was a half hour."

"Well, which was it Chief?"

"Half hour."

"I see, and then you went into the bedroom and found this small piece of silver?"

"About right."

"How did you know this was from the same set?"

"Mr. Hillman described it."

"This expensive tea set is gone—and you find one small teapot lid?"

He nodded, the toothpick shooting across his mouth.

"Yep, all we found."

"Did you ever wonder, Chief, where the rest of the silver was?"

"I did."

"And what did you do about it?"

He moved and his boots scraped the wood.

"Well, like I say, we looked around a bit, but couldn't find it anywhere ... and we figured we had found a piece of it."

"Didn't it seem odd to you that Miss Jones had just enough time to hide a teapot lid under her bed and then, what—hid the rest somewhere else?"

232

The chief's boots clunked again.

"You never know how they think. Maybe that's what she did."

Burke straightened up and slipped his hand into his right pocket.

"Or do you think it's easier to carry in a small piece of silver and put it under someone's bed, than to bring in a whole set that people will see?"

Big Jeb was on his feet.

"*Objection!* Counsel is implying the silver was planted!"

Judge Clemmings nodded.

"Sustained."

The room stirred and Chief Binford was leaning back, his eyes glinting at Burke.

"Just one more question, Chief ... you went out to Mr. Hillman's house. Had you ever been there before?"

He considered this with his eyes up under the brim of his hat.

"Been out there before," he answered slowly.

"Business?"

"Suppose you could say that."

"Objection—this has no relevance to this trial."

Judge Clemmings tilted his head, his gray eyes looking more dull.

"I'll allow it."

Burke touched the rim of his dark glasses.

"Well, which was it, business or pleasure?"

"Business."

"Do you work for Buddy Hillman, Chief?"

"No, sir."

"Did you ever work for him?"

The chief paused and leaned back.

"Used to do security work at his mills."

Burke nodded, touching the table top again with his fingers.

"I see—and doesn't your son work for Mr. Hillman in the mills, now?"

"Yes."

Burke leaned forward on his fingertips.

"Would you say that you and Mr. Hillman are friends?"

"Objection, your honor!"

Judge Clemmings hesitated and looked at Big Jeb.

"I'll allow it," he said, but slower.

"I'll repeat the question, would you say you and Mr. Hillman are friends of a sort?"

The fan whirred in the corner.

"Maybe."

Burke paused, then spoke so quickly it was like he slid one sentence behind another.

"—might even say you're indebted to Buddy Hillman, Chief."

"Objection!"

"Sustained."

Burke tapped the table once, then tilted his head toward the judge.

"I have no more questions, your honor."

"You may step down, Chief Binford."

The police chief got up heavily from the stand and crossed the courtroom. He glanced at our table when he passed and I was glad my father couldn't see at that moment.

"Peter Thomas!"

I looked up. The small, wrinkly, grizzled man who answered the door at the Hillmans' was making his way to the front of the courtroom in the same hunched-over gait, but looking different in a dark baggy suit. Peter's slow journey to the front of the courtroom made the heat seem worse and I expected someone to get up and hurry him along.

After he had raised the white palm of his dark hand and sworn to tell the truth and nothing but the truth, he sat down. Big Jeb crossed the creaky floor.

"State your name and occupation."

Peter licked his lips and cleared his throat.

"Peter Thomas, an' I'm the butler for the Hillmans."

"And how long have you been working for the Hillmans in that capacity?"

He licked his lips again, showing a few teeth.

"Must be 'bout twenty-five—no ... just a minute." He spread his hand out in front of him and moved his lips.

"Approximately."

"Just a minute, now—"

Peter went on counting on his fingers, then looked up triumphantly.

"Twenty-eight an' a half years."

Mr. Mason nodded.

"Needless to say, you've been working for the Hillmans a long time—almost thirty years."

Peter nodded.

"Just about."

"How would you term Mr. Hillman as an employer?"

Peter leaned over, cupping his ear.

"How's that?"

"How would you say it's been working for Mr. Hillman?"

Peter licked his lips again.

"Been fine, been fine."

"Would you say Mr. Hillman's a fair man to work for?"

"Yes sir."

"Have you ever had any reason to think about working anywhere else?"

"No sir, I haven't. Mr. Hillman always been good to me."

Big Jeb stood to the side of the witness stand, his voice echoing slightly off the back wall.

"And have the other servants seemed satisfied with working for Mr. Hillman?"

Peter's lower lip protruded.

"Reckon so."

"He pays decently?"

"Yes sir."

"Provides room and board, if needed?"

"Yes sir."

Big Jeb put a hand on the witness box like he was just leaning against a neighbor's fence.

"Peter, do you know Miss Fanny Jones?"

He bobbed his head.

"Yes sir."

"What was her job at the Hillmans—to your knowledge?"

I noticed for the first time how tightly clasped Peter's hands were.

With each of the questions, the muscles in his hands flexed. Peter licked his lips and moved his jaw around.

"Fanny's job was to clean the silver."

"And where was this silver located, Peter?"

"Dinin' room."

"Was this a lot of silver?"

Peter pursed his lips.

"Yes sir, suppose it was. All the place settin's an' all the servin' sets."

Big Jeb leaned closer.

"What days did she clean the silver, Peter?"

"Tuesday an' Thursday."

"What time did she usually start cleaning and when would she finish?"

Peter's eyes looked at something in front of him, his hands still clasped together.

"Reckon Fanny come 'bout twelve o'clock, an' she finish cleanin' by two."

"How would you know she was finished by two o'clock, Peter?"

"I set Mr. Hillman's place for him. Sometime he come home for early dinner."

"You knew that Fanny was done with cleaning the silver then?"

"Yes sir," Peter nodded. "'Cause she bring it back from the pantry by then."

"The pantry?"

Peter licked his lips twice.

"Yes sir. The pantry is where she clean it, an' when she done, she bring it back in to the dinin' room."

Big Jeb moved one hand in front of him in a slow circle.

"So when the silver came back out of the pantry by two o'clock, it was done?"

Peter nodded.

"About right."

"Did it ever take Fanny longer to clean the silver—past two o'clock?"

Peter scratched the bald front of his head.

"Not that I can recollect."

Big Jeb took a step to the stand.

"I have one more question for you, Peter."

He sat up straighter.

"Yes sir."

"Were you familiar with the missing tea set?"

Peter's eyes glazed.

"Sir?"

"Had you seen this silver tea set before?"

"Oh yes," Peter nodded.

Big Jeb put his hand on the banister

"Was it part of Fanny Jones's duties to clean this silver tea set as well?"

Peter looked down, his hands flexing and knuckles turning white.

"Yes sir."

"And on the day this set was reported missing—was the other silver finished by two o'clock?"

Peter looked for a moment as if he hadn't heard the question.

"Yes sir."

"Do you remember seeing the tea set after two o'clock, Peter?"

Peter shook his head.

"No sir."

"I have no other questions."

Judge Clemmings yawned, then looked at us.

"Your witness, Mr. Hartwell."

"Take me over to him, Lee," Burke said, standing up.

We walked across the floorboards, stopping in front of the witness box. Burke put a hand on the railing. I walked back and sat down. He was looking just past Peter, and suddenly looked very old with his harsh black glasses.

"I just have a few questions for you, Peter."

"Yes sir, Mr. Hartwell."

"Now you say you set an early dinner for Mr. Hillman at two o'clock?"

Peter bobbed his head.

"Yes sir."

"What kind of silver did you use—knives, forks?"

"Knives and forks."

Burke paused, taking a step away from Peter.

"Did you ever put out the silver tea set for Mr. Hillman's dinners?"

Peter blinked, then shook his head quickly.

"Oh, no, sir—that for special occasions."

Burke slid his hand down the rail as he walked.

"Special occasions—was this tea set kept in the same place as the other silver?"

"No sir—it kept in the chest at the end of the dinin' room table. The place settin's is in the chest at the other end."

Burke nodded and stopped at the corner of the witness stand.

"So on the day the tea set disappeared, you wouldn't have known if it was there or not?"

Peter paused, then smiled suddenly.

"I reckon that's right."

"The silver tea set could have been there at two o'clock when all the other silver was done?"

Big Jeb's chair scraped back.

"Objection, your honor, counsel is leading the witness!"

Judge Clemmings flicked something off his desk and looked up.

"I'll rephrase the question, your honor."

Burke turned back to Peter.

"Do you have any reason to look in the cabinet where the silver tea set is kept when you set Mr. Hillman's dinner?"

"No sir."

"Now, Peter, you would set an early dinner for Mr. Hillman at two o'clock, is that right?"

He clasped his hands in front of him again.

"That's right."

"Did Mr. Hillman make a habit of coming home early for dinner?"

Peter's hands pulled.

"Seems like sometimes he did."

"About what time would he eat on these days?"

Peter's eyes flicked to the ceiling.

"Bout three o'clock."

238

"Would he ever come home earlier?"

Peter hesitated, pushing his lips out.

"Think sometimes he come in at two—just when I was settin' the table."

"And on the day that the silver tea set disappeared...." His right hand came off the banister rail and slipped into his pocket. "Did Mr. Hillman come home early that day?"

Peter looked suddenly miserable and I hoped he would bring out his hand and start figuring again, but there was only the whirring fan in the silence.

"Would you like me to repeat the question?"

"No sir, I heard you." He shook his head slowly. "I can't remember, Mr. Hartwell."

Burke nodded slowly.

"You're right, Peter—that was awhile ago ... Let me just ask you this. If you had to pick, would you say Mr. Hillman came home early more on Tuesdays and Thursdays, or on Mondays, Wednesdays and Fridays?"

The courtroom was silent. Peter looked down and I thought his hands would tear apart. He glanced up and licked his lips twice.

"Tuesday an' Thursday."

Burke nodded slowly.

"Thank you. No more questions, your honor."

The bailiff's voice rang through the room again.

"Pete Hastings."

Somewhere a clock ticked off the hour with a solemn march of bongs; I counted eleven strikes of the distant bell in some gray church tower. The air had become heavy, swollen with rain, and the flag, crooked pictures, and the people were tired, still, and waiting. The yellow-lit courtroom was unnaturally bright as the heavy work boots trudged across the wood floor. When I looked up spiders began running up and down my back. The face in the lantern light was now in the witness chair. I wasn't sure before, but now I knew it was him as he put his right hand up and muttered about the truth.

His face was like a field worker's with creases under his eyes and a

239

white hat line across his forehead. His eyes were sleepy and unmoving above a stubbled jaw. He could have been going to work in the fields with his checkered work shirt and dungarees. The only thing it looked like he had done to get ready for court was put water on his hair and slick it back, but long strands kept falling onto his forehead, destroying even that small effort.

Big Jeb walked to the witness box, dabbing his forehead with a folded handkerchief.

"Please state your name and occupation for the court."

The man shifted in the chair, his head rolling to one side, clutching a dusty hat in his lap.

"Pete Hastings—foreman at the Herrin orchard outside town."

Big Jeb nodded, still dabbing his face.

"How long have you been at your present position?"

"'Bout three years."

"What exactly are your responsibilities at the orchard, Mr. Hastings?"

He looked up from his hat.

"Watch the pickers."

"Supervise the pickers," Big Jeb said, putting away his handker-chief. "Then you are their manager?"

He nodded with a dead glaze in his eyes. Judge Clemmings leaned toward him.

"Speak up, Mr. Hastings."

His sleepy face didn't flicker.

"Reckon I'm the manager."

Big Jeb had his hands together like someone praying as he crossed in front of the witness stand.

"Mr. Hastings, was Fanny Jones one of your pickers?"

"Yep."

"Yes or no, Mr. Hastings," Judge Clemmings said, leaning toward the witness chair.

"Yes."

"And do you see the same person in the court?"

"Yep ... Yes."

"Could you point her out, please, and state her name?"

He raised a heavy hand toward our table, and I felt the dark woods.
"Fanny Jones."

Big Jeb turned toward him.

"What type of employee was Fanny Jones, Mr. Hastings?"

He shifted in the chair and leaned his head back.

"Alright for a while, but about last year she started to go bad."

Big Jeb turned on one foot, his shoe squeaking.

"What exactly do you mean?"

"Wouldn't show up for work—come late, slow pickin'."

"So in general, her work conduct was unsatisfactory."

"Could say that."

Big Jeb started his slow walk out from the witness stand.

"Now, you say this started about a year ago. Do you have any idea why her conduct changed? Did anything happen?"

"Seems to me it was 'bout the time she started runnin' with that fancy nigger."

Judge Clemmings' eyes narrowed, his voice crashing down.

"Mr. Hastings, in this courtroom you will use the term 'negro' or 'colored person' or I will hold you in contempt—is that understood?"

The man's eyebrows went up and he grinned at the courtroom, showing tobacco-stained teeth.

"To whom do you refer, Mr. Hastings?"

A wry grin slipped across his face.

"The one in the paper that got killed and worked with them labor unions ... Silas Jackson."

The courtroom came alive and Burke was on his feet.

"Objection, your honor—this testimony is hearsay and not relevant to the case before the court."

Judge Clemmings nodded to Big Jeb.

"Let's get to the point, counselor."

Burke sat down and spoke to Fanny. She shook her head.

"Did you ever see Fanny Jones with Mr. Jackson?"

"Objection, your honor! Who Miss Jones chooses to see has no relevance to this case," Burke said, staying seated.

Judge Clemmings' eyes followed Big Jeb.

"Your honor, this testimony is relevant to establishing a motive."

241

The judge nodded for him to proceed.

"I'll ask the question again—did you ever see Fanny Jones with Silas Jackson?"

The man nodded.

"Sure I did, he'd come an' pick her up and drop her off at the orchards."

"How did you know this man was Silas Jackson?"

"Someone might have told me ... Not every day you see a nig—negro in suits like he wore," he finished, glancing lazily up at the judge.

"But how did you know for sure that this man who picked her up and dropped her off was Silas Jackson?"

"Knew it was that colored boy when I read 'bout him and Fanny in the paper."

Big Jeb walked to his table and went back to the witness stand. He held up a small picture.

"Is this the man you saw with Fanny Jones at the apple orchards?"

"Yes, sir, that's the ... ne-gro."

"Let it be noted that the witness has identified Silas Jackson with Fanny Jones," Big Jeb said, handing the picture to the bailiff. "Mr. Hastings, did Silas Jackson come to the orchards often?"

"'Bout everyday."

"Would you say he was Miss Jones's boyfriend?"

"Objection, your honor."

"Sustained."

Big Jeb turned, looked like he was going to speak, then nodded.

"I have no other questions, your honor."

The man started to get up.

"Not so fast, Mr. Hastings," Judge Clemmings said, sitting him back down with his hand. "Mr. Hartwell, do you have some questions for the witness?"

"Yes, your honor, just a few, and I'll ask them from here."

Burke stood up and scratched the front of his head absently.

"Mr. Hastings, you say you worked as foreman at the orchards for three years?"

"Tha's right."

"How long has Miss Jones been working at the orchards?"

The man sat still like something not alive.

"Been there every season."

"And her performance fell off last year?"

"'Bout then."

Burke touched the top of the table with his hand.

"You are Miss Jones's foreman?"

"That's what I said," he answered, yawning.

"What did you do about it, Mr. Hastings?"

He ran his tongue over his teeth.

"Don't get your meanin'."

Burke put his other hand down on the table.

"Did you say anything to Miss Jones about her poor performance?"

He leaned back in his chair.

"Think I did."

"You *think* you did?"

"I did."

"What happened then—did she improve?"

The sullen dead look was there.

"Nope."

Burke's forefinger tapped the table top.

"So why didn't you fire her, Mr. Hastings?"

"How's that?"

"You were her foreman. She was not doing well. You warned her and she didn't improve. Why didn't you fire her?"

"Objection, your honor, Mr. Hastings' skill as a manager is not on trial here!"

Judge Clemmings paused.

"I'll allow it for now."

Burke tapped the table again.

"So what was stopping you, Mr. Hastings? If Miss Jones was not doing her job, you could certainly fire a negro."

The man's eyes smoldered like a fire coming to life from ashes.

"Figured to give her some time."

The still air shook for the first time with distant thunder.

"Give her some time, that's very generous, Mr. Hastings. Then she must not have been such a bad worker?"

"Like I said, weren't till that nigg—I mean, ne-gro, started comin' round that she started to slip."

A smugness crept over his dark face. Burke stood up straight, slipping his right hand into his coat pocket.

"Now you say this well-dressed black man dropped off Miss Jones at the apple orchards?"

"Yep."

"When did you first see this, Mr. Hastings?"

"Last summer."

"And this well-dressed black man drove a car. What kind of car was it, Mr. Hastings?"

He grinned brown teeth.

"Black car."

"A black car ... was it his?"

"Reckon." He leaned back, his eyes closed halfway. "Maybe it belonged to one of them union people."

There was the murmuring again and Burke waited for it to subside.

"Silas Jackson owned no car, Mr. Hastings—but for the sake of your story we'll assume it was borrowed. Now, how did you know that this man who came in well-dressed suits to the apple orchards in a black car was Silas Jackson?"

"Somebody might have told me."

"Somebody at the orchard?"

"Must have been."

"But you don't know who?"

"Can't recollect." He breathed loudly. "But I read the paper about those Nigra Democrats and knew it was him."

"So it was the newspaper that you read much later that made you put a name to the face."

"Right."

"How far did you go in school, Mr. Hastings?"

"*Objection, your honor!*"

Burke turned toward Judge Clemmings.

"I will show relevance, your honor."

Judge Clemmings had been leaning on his arm and his mouth barely moved when he said "proceed."

"Thank you. I'll repeat the question—"

"I heard you, cap'n," he said, sitting up, his hard eyes almost eager. "About eighth grade."

"Can you read?"

"Sure can."

"Do you read the paper?"

"I said I did, didn't I?"

Burke tilted his head down toward the table.

"Would you say you're more educated than the rest of the foremen at the apple orchards?"

He coughed once.

"Probably more."

"I wonder if you would do me a favor, Mr. Hastings?" He put his hand on the morning newspaper and slid it to me. "I wonder if you would read the headline off the paper for the court?"

The spectators' murmuring came in like a catching fire and Judge Clemmings stamped it out with his gavel. Big Jeb was up again.

"Objection! Mr. Hastings' literacy is not on trial here!"

Judge Clemmings' eyes went to the witness, then Burke, then Big Jeb. I held my breath until his gray head dipped in our favor.

"Proceed, Mr. Hartwell."

The bailiff walked over and took the paper from me and handed it to the witness. He held it like he was going to drop it and was glaring so hard at Burke that he couldn't do two things at once. He opened it slowly, still looking toward us.

"Just the headline please, Mr. Hastings."

The air shook again with closer thunder as the man licked his lips and held the paper in his lap. The bailiff's loud steps faded into the silence. Boards creaked, paper moved, the fan hummed in the background, then it all stopped and he was just looking down at the white paper with his face dark. He looked and looked, then there was a sound different from his voice, but a sound I remembered from class when the slow readers read.

"—The ... Pre ... Pre-si-dunt ... gura...." The paper cracked in his hand. "Guara ... guar ... an ...." He licked his lips and began again. "The Presidunt guar ... guarrrr ... guar...."

Burke spoke quietly.

"That's enough, Mr. Hastings."

"Guara, guarrr...."

"That'll do, Mr. Hastings," Judge Clemmings said louder.

The paper slapped shut and his face was darker than the sun could ever make it and his eyes were glittering slits. Current flowed in the silence and I thought he was going to jump out of the witness stand. Burke's voice was like flint against steel.

"I don't see how you could have identified Mr. Jackson from the newspaper, Mr. Hastings, when, obviously, you don't read newspapers. I have no more questions, your honor."

"I—"

"Does the prosecution wish to cross-examine?"

Big Jeb shook his head miserably.

"No, your honor."

"I say I read—"

"You may step down, Mr. Hastings."

He was glaring out at the courtroom like a trapped animal.

"Damn lawyer tricks—"

"You may step down, Mr. Hastings!"

He snapped the paper out of his lap and stomped loudly across the floor, carrying the paper wadded in his closed fist. Judge Clemmings paused, letting the echo of his work boots die before he announced the court was recessing for lunch.

26

The rain came in the spring. The crop master went to the seed beds with the planters and the slaves. He kneeled down into the splattering mud and pulled up a tobacco plant, then walked to the field rows and put the plant on one of the small mounds and molded the dirt around the stem. He talked to the slaves with water dribbling off the brim of his hat. They went back to the seed beds and worked in the hissing ground.

A little man named Stanley Wright was in the witness box. He was bald and a bushy mustache made his mouth look small. Big Jeb stood in front of him.

"What exactly do you do, Mr. Wright?"

He cleared his throat.

"I run a resale establishment downtown. We specialize in items of a definite value."

"Please tell the court who came into your resale shop on June tenth?"

"A man did—a colored man."

"Did you know who this man was?"

"At the time I didn't, but later—with everything going on and the articles appearing in the paper—I became suspicious."

"Why were you suspicious, Mr. Wright?"

"Because this man asked what I would give for an unspecified amount of silver and when I asked him what kind and how much, he acted strange and left."

"Then what happened?"

"He never came back. I read about the stolen silver at Mr. Hillman's and began to put the two together."

Big Jeb swung around to the side of the man.

"And you did what every good citizen would do?"

Mr. Wright showed his teeth under his mustache.

"Yes, sir. I went to the police and told them of this incident."

Big Jeb came back from his table holding a picture in front of him.

"Was this the man who asked about the silver?"

He eyed the small square of paper.

"Yes, that was him."

"Could you name this man?"

"Silas Jackson."

The spectators behind me were talking and Judge Clemmings brought quiet again.

"No more questions, your honor."

Big Jeb walked to his table and sat down.

"Questions for the witness, Mr. Hartwell?"

"I'll be brief, your honor," Burke said, standing up. "Mr. Wright— you said that a colored man came in and asked you about selling some silver?"

"Yes, sir."

"Then you went to the police because you were suspicious?"

"Yes, after I had read in the paper about the theft of silver, I—well, naturally, I thought there might be a connection."

Burke nodded slowly.

"What if a white man came in, Mr. Wright? Would you have been suspicious?"

The man opened his mouth.

"If he asked about silver I would be suspicious."

Burke tapped the table slowly with his index finger.

"But the fact he was a colored man asking about selling silver made you more suspicious?"

Big Jeb prevented an answer, saying he was leading the witness, and Judge Clemmings, after his customary pause, agreed. Burke began again.

"Mr. Wright, how many people come into your pawnshop and inquire about selling an item?"

"In a single day?"

"Roughly?"

He raised his eyebrows.

"That's hard to say. I do a heavy volume of business, and that's really hard to say—"

"Approximately, Mr. Wright?"

"Well, approximately—I would say, in a day—maybe ten or fifteen."

"And how much silver do you buy and sell, Mr. Wright, on a daily basis?"

He showed his teeth again.

"We specialize in jewelry, silver, and metal, so we do a good bit of volume."

"So people come in and inquire about the price of gold or silver quite a bit?"

"Well ... yes, but—"

"So really what this man did was not that unusual?"

"I see what you're getting at, and—"

"Was inquiring about the price of silver that unusual in your shop, Mr. Wright?"

"—no."

"But he was a colored man."

"Objection, your honor—counsel is not letting the witness answer the questions."

Judge Clemmings looked at Big Jeb wearily and nodded.

"Sustained."

"Mr. Wright ... what would you have given for a pair of silver candle holders, some various silver settings—say a silver salt and pepper shaker?"

The man squirmed in the chair.

"That's hard to say. I'd have to know the amount—whether they

249

were silver plated or sterling—and you would have to bring them in so I could evaluate the pieces."

"Then I could not adequately describe the silver for you to give me a price?"

"I would have to see them."

"If I came in and asked you at your shop about these items, would you tell me to bring the silver in?"

"Well, yes, but—"

"And sometimes as many as fifteen people a day come in and ask about the price of items?"

"On certain days—"

"How many of those fifteen people who come into your shop are negroes, Mr. Wright?"

"I don't really know."

"Where is your pawnshop located?"

The man stopped with his mouth open.

"I beg your pardon?"

"What is the street address of your business, sir?"

"Three thousand Broadway."

"Is that a white or a black section of town?"

"Objection, your honor! I fail to see the relevance of where Mr. Wright's business is located."

Judge Clemmings rolled his eyes to our side.

"I'll allow it."

Big Jeb sat down slowly.

"Now, Mr. Wright, is your business in a predominantly black section of town, or a predominantly white section?"

"Well, I suppose you could say it's in a colored section, but I have quite a few white customers."

"Then the majority of your customers are negroes?"

He looked in his lap and didn't say anything till Judge Clemmings leaned toward him.

"Answer the question, Mr. Wright."

He kept his eyes in his lap.

"Yes."

"So asking the price of an unspecified amount of silver is a normal practice in your business, negroes coming into your pawnshop is a normal occurrence. My question, Mr. Wright, is—what made you suspicious of a black man coming in to ask what the price of silver was?"

"Because I knew it was him!"

Burke paused, his finger tapping his belt.

"How?"

His face was getting so dark I thought he was going to burst.

"I just knew! I said I did! *It was him!*"

"Out of all the black men coming into your establishment?"

"It was from the paper ... when I read about the theft—"

"Could you have been mistaken?"

"No! It was him."

Burke took a loud breath and shook his head slowly.

"I have no more questions, your honor."

"You may step down."

Mr. Wright left the witness stand and walked out of the courtroom. I hadn't realized what a short man he was.

Then came a waitress who claimed to have seen Fanny with Silas Jackson and men from the labor unions. Burke objected and said her testimony was irrelevant, but Judge Clemmings allowed Big Jeb to question her. She was a large blond woman with a tight-fitting dress. She said she saw Fanny through the window of a diner and Burke asked her how she could be sure it was Fanny if it was raining and she was looking out through a window. But the waitress said she knew it was her from the "uppity look" she gave her. Burke let her go after that.

"Mr. Buddy Hillman!"

Careen's father walked across the courtroom in his dark blue suit, was sworn, then watched Big Jeb approach the witness stand. I couldn't decide if he looked bored or amused. His presence seemed so much larger than the courtroom.

"Please state your name and occupation for the court."

"Buddy Hillman," he said in a clear voice. "I am the owner of Richmond Steel."

The impact of his voice came from the back wall and I noticed the jurors and spectators sitting up.

"How long have you been the owner of Richmond Steel?"

"Since my father died—about twenty years."

"Your father owned it before you?"

"And his father before him."

"Where do you live, Mr. Hillman?"

"At 105 Old Magnolia Lane." He smiled faintly. "On top of a large hill."

There was some tittering in the courtroom.

"Do you employ many servants?"

"Suppose I do."

"Is one of the people who was in your employment in the courtroom?"

"Yes," he said, looking faintly amused.

Big Jeb turned.

"Could you please point the person out and state their name?"

He raised his hand in front of him, jabbing his index finger to Fanny.

"Fanny Jones."

The lights in the courtroom became brighter as the world outside the window became low and dark again.

It was then established Fanny's job was to clean the silver, and that she worked on Tuesdays and Thursdays at twelve o'clock, and it usually took her two hours to finish cleaning.

"I'd like to go back to the day of June thirteenth. Could you please explain to the court what happened that day?"

Mr. Hillman rested his arm on the banister.

"I came home from work about four-thirty or so and went into the dining room and noticed the chest at the end of the table was open."

"What was kept there?"

"Silver service—coffee servers, teapots."

"Go on," Jeb said, beginning his slow trek across the courtroom.

"I went to shut the chest and saw the wood case was missing—"

"That's what the teapots are kept in?"

Mr. Hillman nodded.

"So I looked around a bit, thinking it might have just been misplaced. I knew it was Thursday and that Fanny had come over and cleaned the silver. I checked around some more and called Peter in. He said he didn't know anything, so I asked if Fanny had come to clean the silver and he said she had."

Big Jeb nodded.

"What did you do then?"

"Called Jim—Chief Binford. He and his men came over and I told them exactly what I told you. They left and called up later and said they found part of my silver teapot in Fanny's house. I had hoped it would all be there—been in the family a long time."

Big Jeb nodded solemnly.

"Thank you for your time, Mr. Hillman, I have no other questions."

Judge Clemmings' gaze went out to some spot on the opposite wall.

"Your witness, Mr. Hartwell."

"Take me up to the witness stand, Lee," Burke whispered, standing up.

I took my father's arm and led him past my chair when he suddenly fell into me. I hadn't pushed my chair in.

"I'm sorry, Daddy—"

"It's alright, son," he nodded. "Just get me up to the front."

We started again toward Mr. Hillman. He had an amused expression on his face and I knew he was laughing at all of us. We reached the witness box and Burke grasped the corner of the railing. I went back to the table and could hear a soft patter beginning outside the window. Burke's coat was open and his watch chain had hooked on one of the buttons of his vest. The smooth arc I had seen for so many years was broken.

"I think we have covered the basics, so why don't we get to the heart of the matter."

"Alright, Burke," he said softly, almost friendly.

"Have you ever had any trouble with Miss Jones during the time she has worked for you?"

"No real trouble."

Burke nodded, still holding onto the corner of the witness stand.

"Then up to this point, you had no reason to think Miss Jones was capable of stealing?"

"I suppose not."

"On the day you came home and found the silver tea set was missing—what time would you say that was?"

He tilted his head slightly.

"Four-thirty—around there."

Burke nodded.

"About four-thirty then and you came home and went into the dining room?"

"I wouldn't say it was the first thing I did."

Burke was farther from the stand, his hand just touching the corner.

"But you made your way into the dining room at some point and saw the open door to the chest at the end of the table?"

"Yes."

"When you come home from work, you don't usually look in this chest?"

"I wouldn't say that." The shining eyes were flickering now, a beginning rumble high up on the mountain. "I might go into the chest for something else."

"Such as?"

"Objection! This is immaterial."

"I'll allow it."

Mr. Hillman kept his eyes on Burke.

"Such as a drink when I come home—the liquor is kept in the chest."

"I see ... now, did you use the silver tea set often, Mr. Hillman?"

"Not often. It's more of an heirloom."

Burke took a step away from the witness box.

"How did you know the tea set was stolen that day?"

Mr. Hillman grinned.

"Assumed it was stolen that day, because that's when I saw it missing."

"But you couldn't be sure."

"I suppose the tea set could have been stolen on another day ... but the teapot lid would have to be found in somebody else's house then."

The laughter blended with the flowing hush of rain and then Judge Clemmings' gavel. Burke paused.

"Mr. Hillman, you come home occasionally for early dinners."

"That's right."

"And these days you came home were mostly Tuesdays and Thursdays?"

For the first time he leaned forward.

"I don't know that, but if Peter thinks I came home early more on Tuesday and Thursday than other days, I guess I did."

"Did you come home early this particular Thursday?"

"Some would say four-thirty is early."

"You called the police station at five o'clock?"

"That's right."

"Mr. Hillman, when you walk into your home is the dining room near the entrance?"

His face flicked with a smile.

"You've seen my house, Burke. It's off on the other side of the living room."

"Then there is no reason to walk through the dining room?"

"Unless I have a drink."

"Did you have a drink on that Thursday, Mr. Hillman?"

"I think I did."

"You employ quite a few servants. Do you usually make your own drinks?"

A chair clunked back.

"Objection, your honor! Mr. Hillman's drinking habits have no relevance here!"

"Usually Peter makes my drinks, but I will make my own if he's not around."

Big Jeb sat back down slowly as if he had missed his cue. The rain came inside the courtroom with a wet breeze and a tapping on the window sills. Burke paused.

"Mr. Hillman, are you a contributor to Senator Herrin's reelection campaign?"

"I am a contributor," he said, his eyes hard as chestnuts.

Burke took a step toward him, resting his right hand in his coat pocket.

"A large contributor?"

The amused expression played through his eyes.

"You know I am, Burke."

"Are there unions in your steel mills, Mr. Hillman?"

"No."

"Are you against the unions?"

"In some instances."

"You are aware the man running against Senator Herrin in the senatorial primary is for the labor unions?"

"Yes."

"Then you would have a lot to lose if Senator Herrin lost this election. The unions would come into your mills, meaning higher wages, possibly shorter working hours—is that a fair statement, Mr. Hillman?"

"Objection your honor, this—"

"That's a fair statement."

Big Jeb sat back down slowly again. Mr. Hillman stared straight at Burke with two points burning far behind his eyes.

"How would you feel about someone who worked for you and supported those unions?"

A quick flame flicked through his eyes, then they were dull again.

"That would be their business, Mr. Hartwell."

Burke nodded slowly. I waited for him to finish, but he merely tapped his belt, then turned to the judge.

"I have no more questions."

27

The sun hazed over the green-brown rows and the planters could see the white hat floating and dipping toward the ground. The crop master picked a leaf and crushed it between his fingers. The heat rose around him as he walked down the rows and stayed in the fields till the heat of the day was only in the dirt.

The day tilted toward evening. The rain sounded like the ocean with the shhhhhh wavering near then far in the open windows of the courtroom. The prosecution rested after Mr. Hillman testified and Judge Clemmings declared a brief recess. When we came back he nodded to Burke.

"Would you like to call your first witness, Mr. Hartwell?"

"Just one today, your honor."

"That's all we'll have time for today."

"I'd like to call Fanny Jones."

Fanny stood up and straightened her blue dress. She clasped her hands together to keep them from shaking as she walked across the courtroom. She swore to tell the whole truth and sat down without her back touching the chair. I led Burke up to the witness stand, then heard him ask her to state her name and occupation.

"Fanny Jones, and I do housework and work in the apple orchards in the pickin' season."

"In what capacity did you work for Mr. Buddy Hillman?"

Fanny's knuckles were white gripping the arms of the chair.

"Clean silver."

"What type of silver?"

"Settings and large pieces."

"How long have you been cleaning the silver for Mr. Hillman?"

"'Bout four years."

Fanny's eyes were on Burke as he took a step away from the witness stand.

"Did Mr. Hillman ever tell you he was dissatisfied with your work?"

Fanny hesitated, then shook her head.

"No one ever said the silver weren't clean enough."

"In the four years you were performing this job for the Hillmans, was there ever any type of problem?"

"No, sir."

Burke rested his hands on his suit vest.

"How long would it usually take you to clean the silver?"

"'Bout two hours."

"Two hours ... Would it ever take longer than two hours?"

Fanny hesitated.

"Sometimes, but that was usually if they was entertainin' an' wanted it extra shined."

"What days did you work for the Hillmans, Miss Jones?"

"Tuesdays and Thursdays."

Burke turned to Fanny.

"Let's go back to the day of June thirteenth—a Thursday, you went to clean the silver at the Hillmans'?"

"Yes, sir."

"Could you describe what happened that day?"

"Yes sir ... I went to the dining room to clean the silver and the tea set weren't there."

The courtroom was quiet. Burke took a step back and placed his hand on the varnished wood.

"Do the Hillmans have more than one silver tea set?"

Fanny swallowed again, holding her back off the chair.

"That's the only one I clean."

"Does the tea set have a case?"

"It's in a wooden case, an' Mr. Hillman's initials are on top."

"What was the practice in cleaning the silver?"

"I take it to the pantry."

"In the pantry—and where is that?"

"The kitchen."

Burke moved closer, one foot on the ledge of the witness stand.

"Why would you take the silver to the pantry to clean it?"

Fanny's eyes flickered over to Burke.

"'Cause the cleanin' supplies are there."

"And this is the only place you ever took the silver—to the pantry?"

"Yes, sir."

"What would you do after the silver was cleaned?"

"Put it back in the dinin' room."

Burke stepped to the corner of the witness box.

"Miss Jones, have you ever taken any of the silver that you were charged with cleaning out of the Hillman residence?"

"No, sir."

"What did you think when you saw that the silver tea set was not where it should have been?"

Fanny hesitated, blinking several times.

"I know Mister Hillman entertains sometime, an' I thought maybe he'd taken it out and not put it back."

Burke nodded.

"Did you look around for it?"

"Yes, sir, but I couldn't find it anywhere."

"Did you clean the rest of the silver on this day?"

"Yes, sir."

Burke pivoted toward the jury.

"After working at the Hillmans—what was it your custom to do then?"

"Go over an' help my aunt clean," Fanny said, her voice quivering slightly.

"What time did you usually do this?"

"'Bout three-thirty."

"Three-thirty ... let's see, that leaves a gap of an hour and a half. What would you do between that time, Miss Jones?"

Fanny pulled on her fingers, her face taut.

"Sleep."

"Where would you sleep?"

Fanny's expression hardened like wax cooling.

"In the pantry."

"In the pantry," Burke repeated slowly. "Did you do this much?"

"Yes, sir." Her eyes flickered down. "There's a couch in there."

The rain drumming on the roof mixed with the whirring fan in the corner.

"How long do you think you slept on this day, Miss Jones?"

Fanny's hands were moving in her lap.

"'Bout an' hour."

"Then you walked over to help your aunt?"

"Yes, sir."

"How long does it take you to get from the Hillmans' to where your aunt works?"

"'Bout a half hour."

"So you finished the silver at two o'clock, fell asleep for an hour, and then walked over to help your aunt at three-thirty."

"Yes, sir."

Burke stepped closer to her.

"Miss Jones, have you ever been arrested for anything?"

"No, sir."

"Have you ever been fired from a job?"

She shook her head mechanically.

"No, sir."

Burke patted the banister rail.

"Thank you."

I went around the table and led my father back. Big Jeb was already by Fanny when we reached the table.

"Miss Jones, you say the silver tea set was missing when you came to clean?"

Fanny was watching him out of the corner of her eye, her long fingers knotted in her lap.

"Yes, sir."

He turned and faced her directly.

"Did you think this odd?"

Fanny tilted her head back.

"Sir?"

"Did you ask anyone where the silver was?"

Fanny shook her head slightly.

"No, sir."

Big Jeb walked to the jury with his hands out.

"So the tea set is gone and you start cleaning...." He wheeled around. "But what were you cleaning without the tea set?"

"Other silver."

"The other silver ... the settings?"

Fanny's chin dipped slightly.

"Yes, sir."

"It took you *two hours* to clean the settings?"

"Yes, sir."

Big Jeb started back toward her.

"On what day would you clean the tea set, Miss Jones, Tuesday or Thursday?"

Fanny hesitated.

"Depends."

Her eyes grew as he came to her.

"Depends on what?"

Fanny looked like she was going to jump out of the chair.

"What I do first."

"On this Thursday, June thirteenth, what were you planning to clean?"

"Silver tea set."

"The tea set ... Well, then, I ask the question—without the tea set, what did you do for two hours?"

Big Jeb's voice reverberated behind me in the silence.

"... cleaned the other silver," Fanny mumbled.

"But hadn't you just cleaned the settings the previous Tuesday?"

261

"Yes, sir," Fanny said, her mouth barely opening.

Big Jeb took a few steps away from her, shaking his head.

"That must have been mighty clean silver!"

Fanny's eyes were down in her lap.

"Miss Jones, what was your relationship to the late Mr. Silas Jackson?"

Burke was standing.

"Objection, your honor, this has no bearing on the case before the court."

"I will show relevance."

Judge Clemmings' eyes cleared.

"I'll allow it."

Big Jeb turned back to the witness stand.

"I'll repeat the question. What was your relationship to the late Mr. Jackson?"

Fanny's eyes were darting from side to side.

"Sir?"

"Did you two date?"

"Yes," she said, looking down.

"Where did you meet Mr. Jackson?"

"At a meeting."

"A *meeting,* Miss Jones?" He repeated, louder, turning to the jury. "What type of meeting?"

"—Political meeting."

Judge Clemmings leaned over.

"Please speak up, Miss Jones."

"What type of political meeting?"

Fanny took a deep breath and looked up.

"Second District Negro Democrats."

"The Second District Negro Democrats," Big Jeb almost sang. "And what was Mr. Jackson's role in this meeting?"

Fanny looked at him.

"What did Mr. Jackson do at this meeting, Miss Jones?"

"He was the chairman."

Big Jeb was close to the side of the witness stand where he could see Fanny and the jury.

"When did you first attend this meeting of the Second District Negro Democrats?"

I heard my father's voice next to me.

"Objection your honor, when or why Miss Jones went to this meeting has no relevance."

Judge Clemmings nodded this time. Big Jeb smiled and swung around to the front of Fanny, speaking in a softer voice.

"Were you and Silas Jackson planning to get married?"

Fanny sat very still.

"Please answer, Miss Jones."

"Yes," she said in a whisper, her eyes fixed straight ahead.

"But you needed money to get married, didn't you?"

Burke's chair went back.

"This questioning has no bearing on this case, your honor!"

"If the court will permit me to continue I will show relevance," Big Jeb said, walking before the judge.

"Proceed."

"I repeat the question, you needed money to get married, didn't you, Fanny?"

"Yes, sir."

"Was Mr. Jackson paid for his work for the Negro Democrats?"

"I don't know," Fanny said in a low voice.

"Did he ever receive money from Eugene Trenton or the labor unions?"

"Objection!"

"Sustained."

Big Jeb began a slow trek across the room.

"Now on the day the silver had disappeared, you took two hours to clean a very small portion of silver and then you then went ... to sleep?"

"Yes, sir."

He turned around.

"You went to sleep in a pantry?"

"Yes, sir," Fanny nodded.

His hands were out as if to catch rain.

"Did anyone see you asleep in this pantry?"

263

"Don't know, sir. I was asleep."

There was tittering in the courtroom behind me and Big Jeb smiled.

"Did you tell anyone you were going to sleep in this pantry, Miss Jones?"

"No, sir."

Big Jeb walked quickly back to Fanny.

"Miss Jones, how did a teapot lid from the Hillmans' silver tea set end up under your bed?"

Fanny met his stare and a spark flickered in her eyes.

"I don't know."

"*You don't know!*" His voice came off the walls. "An expensive silver tea set disappears from your possession and part of it appears in your house hidden under your bed and you *don't know*?"

Fanny's eyes were dull again and her back touched the chair. Big Jeb moved in closer.

"I think this is how it happened, Miss Jones. You stayed till two o'clock, then you left and took with you the silver tea set and met Silas Jackson. He hid the tea set and you put that top under your bed to find out what the pawnshop would give you for such a piece. Then you went over to help your aunt at three-thirty with the story that you had just been at the Hillmans' and had been asleep. You and Mr. Jackson needed money to get married, so you stole from your employer, Mr. Hillman—"

Burke was on his feet again.

"Objection, your honor! This is pure conjecture."

Judge Clemmings agreed, but Big Jeb was done.

"I have no other questions."

He returned to his table. Judge Clemmings asked Burke if he was finished, then banged his gavel once and court recessed for the day.

28

The summer passed. The planters waited to begin cutting the tobacco. They followed the crop master's dull hat, walking over the dark holes his stick made in the dirt. His legs flicked the brown leaves as he passed. He stopped to crack one between his thumb and forefinger, then walked on in the shallow air between the plants. This went on into September.

The storm broke during the night. The rain drummed on the roof and night flicked into day. Thunder cracks shook Buckeye with the wind sweeping curtains of rain across the back lawn. I lay awake smelling the soggy yard and remembering the relief when Judge Clemmings said court would be adjourned. The ride home was like the gloomy rain. Burke rode with his mouth set and Fanny kept her head down in the back seat not looking at anyone. There was only the slap of the windshield wipers above the splattering tires.

Burke went into the den with Fanny after dinner and shut the door. Lucas and I sat in the wet air on the porch. He said Big Jeb made Fanny look like a troublemaker working with Silas Jackson for the labor unions.

"The only evidence Big Jeb has is the teapot lid under Fanny's bed." His cigarette streaked into the wet grass. "Problem is, Fanny doesn't have a good alibi. She claims she was asleep, but nobody saw her. Who the hell's going to believe that? The thing is, even if Daddy

265

shows Buddy Hillman framed her, the jury already thinks she's a trouble-maker connected to the labor unions." He shook his head slowly, staring out at the glassy lawn. "She couldn't get a fair trial now if her life depended on it."

On my way to bed I stopped in Burke's study.

"Daddy?"

"Hello, Lee," he said, smiling tiredly.

The cool air picked at the curtains behind his desk; the quiet order of his study descending on me like a warm nap. I sat down in the chair facing his desk.

"I should turn in," he said yawning. "There's nothing I can do tonight."

"How do you think the trial went?"

He tilted his head and frowned.

"Hard to say."

"Seems like you showed most of the witnesses were lying."

He smiled, his cheeks going against the black frames.

"I showed inconsistencies in their stories, but I haven't shown why Buddy Hillman would have framed Fanny and I can't go calling him a liar. We don't have the silver tea set and we can't account for Fanny's whereabouts. That gap from two to three-thirty is very damning in the jury's eyes."

A beginning rain came in through the window behind him.

"What about tomorrow?"

"Tomorrow is the battle of the jewelers ... I'll try to show that top isn't worth two hundred dollars and get the grand larceny charge dismissed." The rain turned hard and streaked black on the window. Burke shook his head slowly. "It would be helpful if that tea set would turn up."

I heard his voice again as I turned in my bed and looked at the square of night glow. I crossed to the window and knelt down. Drops clung to the screen from the drizzle. I leaned on the damp windowsill and stared at the dark woods against the gray. I watched till the rain stopped in the early dawn.

"Can't remember last time you was sick!"

Addie brought the tray of fruit into my room and I slid further under the covers.

"An' your father needin' you in the courtroom an' all."

She kept grumbling as she set the tray down on the table next to my bed.

"Burkie and Lucas can help him."

Addie's brow was lined with worry.

"I know, I just hope they let Fanny go. That old jury is going to decide an' I been prayin' so hard."

She looked at me with a sharp eye and I groaned.

"You ain't too sick to eat, is you?"

I groaned again, shaking my head.

"I leave this tray here for you an' you call if you need anything. I be down in the kitchen—your mother is barely standin' up to all this an' she likely goin' to collapse any time, so I goin' to make her a good breakfast," she continued, picking up my suit coat off the floor and putting it over a chair.

"Alright," I croaked.

"Bad times is what we have now ... bad times," she muttered, going out and down the back steps.

I waited till a pot clanged in the kitchen before throwing the covers back and jumping over to my dresser. I slipped on my shorts and t-shirt, listening again, then went down the front stairs. I held the screen door so it wouldn't slam and hopped off the front porch into the grass.

Wet blades of grass stuck to my ankles with the sun already hot on my face as I ran along the hedge bordering the side lawn. I went into the woods and stayed just behind the line of trees till I reached the barn. The damp hay was strong like fertilizer and hissed around under the goats' hooves. I glanced up to the second floor where Nelson slept.

"Hey Nelson!"

I waited, then grabbed a rusted brown shovel with dried manure caked on the blade and ran out of the barn into the woods. I ducked down the trail to the Hillman graveyard, getting wet from twanging branches and slipping on the black mud. Beads of rain fell from the iron gate as it squeaked open. I went to Mrs. Hillman's grave and put the shovel blade into the earth.

Everything was racing inside me. I bent down and ran my hands under the edge of the stone. The dirt moved into it and fell away. I ran my hand around the marble, feeling more of a ridge on the far side. I levered the shovel lip under the stone and bent the handle, leaning my weight on the shovel and bending it more. There was a sucking noise and the stone moved up from the earth. I dug the ridge away and wobbled the slab with my hands.

The rut was dark. I stood up and listened. Crows cawed in the trees and flapped darkly across the graveyard. My heart thudded as I picked up the shovel and stabbed into the grass in front of the rut. The shovel slid into the wet dirt up to the middle of the blade and I brought up the earth wondering how the man had replaced the grass so perfectly. I laid the black dirt carefully next to the stone.

I dug quicker with the dirt pile growing. Sweat streamed down my face and stung my eyes. At two feet the mound of earth was large. My feet kept sinking into the soft dirt as I dug down another foot. I sat down by the edge of the hole to rest.

A twig snapped, then there was the steady crush of underbrush. I looked at the trail from the edge of the hole, hearing the man rushing toward me with blood thudding in my ears. They were coming down the trail and they would see me sitting on the edge of the grave. The footsteps were near and I wanted to scream, but nothing came out of my mouth but dry spit. Through the green foliage came a black Labrador plodding clumsily toward me.

"Beat it!"

He paused and went into a hunting point, sniffing the air. I picked up a clod of dirt and threw it. He loped off through the woods. I picked up the shovel and began to dig furiously, getting down another foot and stopping.

"That's it—no more!"

I climbed out and threw the shovel down into the hole. The dirt clunked. I stared down at the shovel in the black earth, then slipped back in cautiously and picked it up. I began tapping the dirt with the blade, then brushing the dirt away.

A brown slash caught the sun as I scraped away more dirt. The wood ended and there was an edge and then another edge. I cleared more dirt away from the top with my fingers and stopped. Down in the hole a shiny rectangle held the sun. I brushed the dirt off with my index finger, hearing my breathing till the two engraved initials appeared— *"B.H."*

I dug the box out the rest of the way and slid it up the side of the hole by its brass handles. I climbed out and bent down, unhooking the latch with trembling fingers. The heavy lid swung back and I saw red first, then the two gleaming teapots nestled against the velvet lining. The lid of one teapot was missing.

I shut the box and started shoveling the dirt back into the hole, replacing the grass and tamping it down so the edges of the sod were concealed. I maneuvered the stone back in place, packing in dirt on the bottom. Except for some dirt in the grass the graveyard looked undisturbed. I picked up the wooden box and started out of the forest.

In the side yard I set the heavy case down at the corner of the house and wiped my face. My t-shirt was black across the front and I tried to brush some caked mud off my knees. I began wondering what would happen if the trial ended before I got there. I grabbed up the case and ran to my bicycle under the magnolia tree in the front yard. I propped the bike up, hoisted the box onto the handlebars, and began pedaling just as Addie came out onto the porch.

"WHAT YOU DOIN' HERE?"

I bumped across the lawn, balancing the box with one hand on the handlebars. Addie bellowed behind me.

"WHERE YOU GOIN'? AN' WHAT HAS YOU GOT?"

I came to the end of the driveway and started toward downtown. The houses slipped by faster and I kept thinking the trial might end and pedaled harder. The box nearly slipped off as I bumped across some railroad tracks. The downtown buildings loomed in the haze and the streets were filling with cars. I pedaled in and out of people and cars breathing exhaust, riding across Main Street toward a hill. I pushed my legs down, but with only one arm I came to a wobbly stop. I dropped the bike on the side of the road and started running.

My arms burned as though the case were filled with lead. I wheezed up the hill, sweat falling onto the varnished wood, running weakly for the courthouse at the top. My feet were heavy when the split tree came into view.

Then I was under the tree and staggering across the lawn to the wide steps when the ground rose up and the box fell open on the grass. The teapots tumbled end over end. I lay flat on the lawn, gasping, seeing the gleaming teapots laying in the grass. I wanted to just lay there, but I struggled up, scooped the teapots back into the box, and began lugging it up the courthouse steps.

A guard with sun in his face stopped everything with a large, white palm.

"Hold on there!"

I could see my sweaty, dirty, ripped, exhausted self in his eyes.

"I have to ... get to the courtroom!"

His lined, caramel eyes went to the dirt and the varnished box, then slowly up to me.

"You can't go into the courtroom like that," he said, shaking his grizzled head. "I can't let no one in without no shoes and all dirty like you are!"

I felt the case slipping in my aching arms.

"I have ... something ... *very* important—"

He looked at the dirty case again and shook his head.

"Ain't nobody can go into the courtroom all dirty and sweaty. Go on home an' get yourself cleaned up."

"Trial will be over then!"

He took a step back and stood squarely in my way.

"They are the rules, an' I might lose my job letting you in." He shook his head. "No, sir!"

I stared at him, then turned slowly.

"Alright."

"That's right, go on home an' get cleaned up, an' you can come in anytime," he said turning to the door.

I bolted past his back.

"Hey!"

He grabbed at my shirt, but it slipped out of his hand and I was running down the echoing marble hallway to the second floor courtroom. There was another guard by the steps. He was old like the first one and stood in front of the stairs with his arms wide.

"Where you goin'—"

I crashed into his arm and stumbled up the steps till I straightened up. Footsteps were right behind me when I reached the top and started running down the hallway with the weight of the box carrying me forward. People on the hall benches stood as I passed and one woman put her hand to her mouth. Another guard was coming down the hallway from the other end.

He reached the courtroom doors first and I veered, falling toward the double doors, putting the weight of the box and my exhausted body into the soft stomach in front of me as we went through the doors together. There was the floor, the woody courtroom air, then the case floated out of my hands. I watched the wood box go farther than either of us down the aisle. It bounced once and opened. The silver teapots clattered on the wood floor, rolling jerkily and coming to a stop in the middle of the courtroom.

The world righted itself and I was on the floor looking at shiny work shoes and dark blue pants. There was a hushed quiet, then someone picked me up under my arms. Burke was standing in front of the witness stand with a bewildered look and Big Jeb was staring at the teapots. The bailiff had me by my arms and I shouted at my father.

"DADDY, I GOT THE TEAPOTS ... MR. HILLMAN BURIED THEM IN MRS. HILLMAN'S GRAVE!"

The courtroom erupted.

29

Blackbirds dipped through the open doors of the curing barns. The crop master watched the slaves climb up into the darkness and hang the heavy tobacco over cross-beams. He had old hogsheads placed at the bottom in a pile. At dusk the hogsheads were lit and the smoking fire yellowed the barn. Slaves dashed water on the walls. The crop master watched the sparks fly into the darkness.

I remember Judge Clemmings banging his gavel until I thought he would break it. Everyone was on their feet. Burke was standing by the bench while a bailiff picked up the teapots and held them. Big Jeb looked at Mr. Hillman several times, then started talking fast to Judge Clemmings. It finally ended with the judge calling a recess and telling my father and Big Jeb he wanted to meet with them. I was taken by a bailiff to a room off the courtroom.

I sat and waited until Burke came in with Lucas. I told him everything that had happened. I told him about camping out, then seeing Mr. Hillman in the graveyard with Pete Hastings, then being chased through the woods. I wondered why he didn't look happy.

"Why didn't you tell me about this before, Lee?"

I looked down at my dirty feet and shrugged.

"—was going to, Daddy, but Jimmy said people bury jewels in people's graves and guess I was scared."

272

Burke was quiet.

"Lee—"

I looked up.

"It took a lot of courage to do what you did today, son. I'm proud of you."

He held out his hand and pulled me to him—the same smell of pencils and papers was in his suit. Lucas winked at me over his shoulder.

"There's a washroom down the hall—you better try to clean yourself up. I'm going to have to put you on the stand along with Jimmy—that is, if Judge Clemmings doesn't declare a mistrial."

I stopped at the door and turned.

"You think we'll win, Daddy?"

He tilted his head.

"I think it's a whole new shooting match."

I sat at the table and tried to brush some more dirt off myself while Burke and Big Jeb talked to the judge. My father came back with Lucas and said they would continue with the trial.

"Lee Hartwell."

My name sounded different when the bailiff said it.

I stood up and walked across the floor. The sneakers Lucas had gotten for me squeaked on the planks. I raised my dirt-streaked arm to the bailiff and looked around. Only Judge Clemmings was higher and I could see the faces of the jurors and spectators. The witness stand was surprisingly tight. I touched the toes of my sneakers against the front.

Burke questioned me from the table. I told him about the night we camped out, seeing the light, then seeing Mr. Hillman and Pete Hastings. He had me point to Mr. Hillman, and when I did there was a murmur in the courtroom. Mr. Hillman just stared at me with his black eyes.

My father then questioned me about digging up the silver and how I knew it was Mrs. Hillman's grave. I explained that I had been there with Careen. He had me identify the silver teapots as the ones I found buried in the grave. He then had the teapots entered into evidence as the missing silver tea set.

Big Jeb approached the stand with a big smile.

"Hello, Lee, looks like you got a little dirt on yourself."

I looked down at my clothes and nodded.

"Yes, sir."

He laughed and put a big hand on the rail.

"This is quite a story you have, Lee ... camped out, saw a light in the woods, went down to the Hillman graveyard and saw Mr. Hillman burying his own silver in his wife's grave ... yes sir, quite a story."

The pleasant expression vanished from his face and his eyes narrowed.

"What did you really see that night, Lee?"

I leaned back.

"Sir?"

He leaned closer.

"You say you saw a light in the woods. Who did you really see in that graveyard?"

My calf muscles were twitching and I wanted to reach down and stop them.

"I saw Mr. Hillman and Pete—"

"Are you saying Mr. Hillman *buried his own silver* in his *wife's grave!*"

I hesitated.

"—saw them burying something."

"And you saw this how long ago?"

He waited.

"June."

The smile was an even line across his face.

"And you just now decided to tell someone about it?"

I nodded mechanically.

"Yes, sir."

He took a step back, keeping his eyes on me with his hands out to his sides.

"Why?"

I could see none of the Big Jeb I knew. There was just this man staring at me with unfriendly eyes.

"Do you have an answer, Lee?"

"Why...."

"Why did you wait to mention this till now?"

I shrugged, feeling my face warm up.

"Wasn't sure what Mr. Hillman was doing ... Jimmy thought he might be burying jewels or something...."

"IN HIS WIFE'S GRAVE?"

I heard his voice off the ceiling and hunched down.

"That's what Jimmy said," I said, hearing how I sounded to everyone else.

A funny expression went across Big Jeb's face and he rubbed his eyebrows.

"For the sake of your story, Lee, we'll assume that you saw Mr. Hillman on this night burying something." He quit rubbing his eyebrows and turned. "What made you think it was the missing silver?"

My mind wasn't cooperating with my mouth and all I managed was, "Sir?"

"All this time passes and suddenly—you go and desecrate Mrs. Hillman's grave and dig up a box of silver. What made you think the missing teapots were there?"

A steady burn went up my neck.

"Just guessed."

"You guessed?" He came back to the witness stand and I could feel his breath. "Alright, enough stories, Lee. Who did you really see that night at the graveyard?"

"Sir—"

He pointed at me.

"Who did you really see in the graveyard that night?"

I thought he was forgetting himself, he had already asked the question.

"Mr. Hillman and—"

The hard eyes came closer.

"Do you know what the penalty is for lying under oath, Lee?"

"Objection, your honor. Counsel is intimidating the witness."

Judge Clemmings nodded down to me.

"I agree. Counsel will refrain from intimidating the witness."

Big Jeb moved back and winked at me, then turned to the judge.

"I have no more questions."

I was free.

"I have a few questions, your honor," Burke said, standing.

"Proceed."

I settled back into the chair.

"Lee, are you friends with Mr. Hillman's daughter, Careen Hillman?"

"Yes, sir," I nodded feeling the heat in my face again.

"If you had come forth and said you thought Mr. Hillman had buried something in his wife's grave, how would that have affected your friendship?"

I stared at my father.

"Don't know."

"Would you still have been friends, Lee?"

I looked down at the floor, feeling the whole world was watching.

"No."

"And that would have bothered you?"

"Yes, sir."

"So you didn't tell anybody?"

"No, sir."

"Thank you, Lee."

I walked back to our table as the bailiff called Jimmy to the stand. He walked through the courtroom looking stiff in a coat and tie. He didn't look over when he was being sworn in. I had seen him come in during the recess, but he had been off with his father since that time.

Burke went to the front of our table.

"Jimmy, we might as well get to the point here and the reason you have been called to the witness stand."

"Yes, sir," he nodded.

"The night of June twelfth, you, Lee, and Clay Nettleton all slept out in the tree house in the woods behind the Hillmans'?"

Jimmy nodded.

"Yes, sir."

"Could you tell the court what happened that night?"

Jimmy shifted his weight and grabbed the arms of the witness chair.

"Uh, we had fallen asleep and I woke up in the middle of the night and, I, uh, saw a light in the woods."

The back of my father's head moved up and down slowly.

"Which way was the light?"

His eyes darted around the courtroom.

"It was toward the Hillmans' ... the graveyard."

"How did you know that?"

Jimmy licked his lips and put a hand to his tie.

"We had been down to the Hillman graveyard before." He stopped for a moment, his eyebrows going straight up. "Just to look around— we never did anything down there," he said quickly.

"I'm sure you didn't. Go on."

"We decided—Lee and I—to, uh, go down and look and see what the light was ... So we went down through the woods and toward the light—"

"And what did you see, Jimmy?"

He shifted in his chair again.

"Uh—well, we saw the light in the graveyard." Jimmy's hard shoes clunked against the wood of the witness stand. "We, um, saw a man by a lantern."

"Did you say you saw one man by lantern light?"

Jimmy's head bobbed mechanically.

"Yes ... yes, sir."

I felt sick to my stomach.

"And what was this man doing?"

Jimmy was moving all over the witness stand, turning, fidgeting, licking his lips, wiping his face.

"He was, uh, digging, and I could see that he, uh, had moved a gravestone."

"He was digging in the grave?"

Jimmy nodded crazily.

"Yes, sir, he was digging in the grave ... I didn't know exactly what he was doing, but I figured he must be burying something."

Burke paused, speaking in the quiet.

"This man digging—did you recognize him?"

Jimmy moved more and licked his lips again.

"Uh—not at first ... but later I did."

A train was roaring in my ears.

"And could you say now who this man was digging in the Hillman graveyard?"

All the people in the courtroom were leaning forward and Jimmy was nodding like a puppet. I heard the fan distantly.

"Yes, sir, he was a negro ... Silas Jackson."

The courtroom erupted. I felt a needle jab into my stomach and I jumped to my feet, shouting, pointing at Jimmy.

"*HE'S LYING!* THAT'S NOT TRUE—HE'S LYING!"

Jimmy sat back in the witness stand open-mouthed. Burke turned to me.

"Lee—sit down!"

"BUT HE'S LYING, DADDY! IT WAS MR. HILLMAN! I SAW HIM—" I kept pointing at Jimmy. "YOU'RE A DIRTY LIAR!"

"Sit down, Lee!

"HE'S LYING, DADDY!"

"SIT DOWN, LEE!"

Judge Clemmings' gavel hit the wood block endlessly.

30

The crop master held the tobacco leaf, feeling for the stems and dropping thin sticks to the dust. The tobacco lay over his brown hands when he was finished. The slaves followed and lay the leaves into the empty hogsheads, then pressed the tobacco into the swelling barrel. The planters watched from the red and gold-turning trees.

Evening came to Buckeye and the earth cooled under a simmering twilight. Crickets and grasshoppers jumped away through the yard as I walked through the damp grass toward the barn. Nelson sat in the doorway on a chair with his white shirt and straw hat holding the late light.

He held a piece of wood in front of him with one hand and ran a knife across it. A wood shaving fell to the ground. I plopped down in the grass.

"Making something?"

He held the piece of wood up in his wrinkled hand.

"Don't rightly know yet—I just whittle till I come up with something." He looked down and shucked off another piece of wood.

"Nice part of the day. Mamma always said the Lord, He come out just before dark. An' if you real still you can see Him."

He laughed and showed his missing teeth.

Shuck! The wood fell like carrot peels. I picked a blade of grass and chewed on the end.

"That was how she kept us children quiet. We all be settin' on that porch watchin' for the Lord."

The goats thumped the sides of the stall. White flared in the corner of his eyes as he turned back from the barn.

"They always get upset just before dark."

Shuck!

"How that trial goin'?"

"Going to end on Monday."

Nelson's tongue circled his lips.

"Fanny, she in trouble now just like her pa."

"Knew her father?"

"Yes, sir. I work with him before."

"Where'd he work?"

"For Mistah Hillman, I work for him too," he nodded, leaning back into the darkness of the barn.

"Didn't know that."

Shuck!

"He done the same thing I do and tend the grounds. 'Course in those times we was a lot younger an' did a lot more. He a lot like Fanny—always talkin' 'bout things, an' all that talkin' what got him in trouble." He stuck out his lower lip and brushed some wood shavings off his pants. "Talkin' and Miz Hillman."

I looked at him.

"Mrs. Hillman?"

The knife scraped the wood and caught.

"Yes sir—he just always talkin' 'bout how colored man don't have to take what white man say. He was a artist, too. That what got him in trouble with Miz Hillman."

Shuck!

"How's that?"

Nelson looked down at his stick.

"Miz Hillman want to learn paintin'—an' one thing Fanny's pa good at and that was paintin'. In those times we slept down in the ol' slave cabins, an' Miz Hillman start comin' down an' askin' him to show her how to paint. She seen his paintin's an' like 'em. Old Luke, he show her, an' then she start spendin' more an' more time down in the slave cabin."

Shuck! The white shavings fell around his shoes.

"You know how people talk 'bout white lady like Miz Hillman spendin' time with a colored man—an' Mistah Hillman don't like it none. Luke—he start talkin' 'bout how Miz Hillman don't think herself any different than colored folk and he says she say we all the same." Nelson's head swiveled on his neck. "I told him to not talk like that—but he just keep on, an' everybody talkin' 'bout Miz Hillman an' Luke."

Shuck!

"Where was Luke's wife?"

"She done run off before to O'leans an' left Luke with Fanny."

Shuck! Shuck!

"One night Miz Hillman stay down at Luke's cabin late. An' Mistah Hillman don't know where she is, an' they call police. And they come and find her down with Luke."

Nelson looked one way then the other.

Shuck!

"They took him to jail an' he never come back!"

Shuck!

Nelson pulled the silver blade across the inside of his pants, then ran it lightly over the long stick.

"Police say they take him down an' then they let him go home. But Luke never come home ... An' they find him in the country next mornin'—lynched."

I remembered the conversation long before with Burke.

"Who did it?"

Shuck!

"Don't know, night riders, some say. That why I say Fanny just like her pa."

I threw away the soggy blade of grass.

"Thought we would have gotten her off after I found the teapots."

Nelson looked up from his stick.

"Teapots?"

281

I nodded.

"Silver teapots they say Fanny stole."

"Where you find 'em?"

"Back in the woods, in the Hillman graveyard."

Nelson's eyes grew.

"Mr. Hillman buried them there the night we camped out. We saw a lantern in the graveyard and Mr. Hillman and another man burying something." I looked at Nelson. "That's why I dug up the grave."

Nelson's eyes were gleaming.

"Dug up a grave!"

"I just dug up the box of silver—it was in Mrs. Hillman's grave. It wasn't in her coffin or anything."

His head wobbled back and forth.

"Ain't that somethin'!" He looked at me. "They going to let Fanny go?"

I shook my head.

"Jimmy lied and said he saw Silas Jackson burying the silver teapots that night."

Nelson scratched his forehead with his knife hand and pushed his hat up.

"Why he lie like that?"

I slapped at a mosquito on my leg.

"Don't know. Wants his dad to win, I guess."

Nelson shook his head slowly.

"They shouldn't believe him—that weren't him."

Shuck!

I stared at the blood splotch on my leg, then looked up slowly at Nelson.

"How you know?"

Shuck!

"What's that?"

Shuck!

"How you know that wasn't Silas Jackson?"

"Ain't nothin'."

Shuck! Shuck! The blade flashed across the wood.

"You see something, Nelson?"

Shuck!

He kept his eyes on the stick.

"I told that girl." *Shuck!* "I told her she be gettin' in trouble with her ways!"

I sat straight up.

"Nelson! Did you see Mr. Hillman in the graveyard?"

A sliver of wood flipped onto my foot.

"What's it matter, Lee? If they ain't goin' to believe you, they ain't goin' to believe some ol' yard nigger."

Shuck!

"But if you were there, they have to believe you!"

His knife flashed over the stick.

Shuck!

"I seen 'em."

Shuck! Shuck!

"I seen 'em down there."

"You were in the woods that night!"

He nodded his head slowly, flipping the stick around in his hand.

"Yes sir—I seen the light and Mistah' Hillman and that other man buryin' somethin'."

"Why didn't you say anything, Nelson?"

He shook his old head.

"Colored man don't go 'round sayin' he sees white men doin' things."

I jumped up.

"It was *you,* Nelson! You were behind us that night!"

There was a snap and the wood fell in two pieces. Nelson looked down and held the open knife.

"I didn't know it was y'all. But I heard Jimmy on the trail when y'all run away," he said, letting his long hands hang between his knees.

"Nelson! You can testify!"

Nelson shook his head doubtfully.

"Ain't goin' to believe a nigger over a white man, Lee."

"But they might—let's go talk to Daddy—he'll know."

Nelson paused, then clicked his knife shut and stood up slowly, dipping his chin to the ground.

"I talk to Mistah' Hartwell."

We went up to Buckeye and found Burke in his study. He sat behind his desk and listened till Nelson finished telling what he had seen. Nelson was rigid in the high-backed chair facing my father. Burke tapped a pen in front of him slowly.

"This could be very helpful, Nelson."

"Yes sir," he nodded.

Burke paused.

"Would you repeat in court what you have told me?"

Nelson blinked several times, blacker in the dim light of my father's study. The mantle clock was loud as he sniffed, then cleared his throat.

"I ain't never said anything against a white man before, Mistah Hartwell," he said, keeping his long hands on his knees. "And I is afraid of Mistah Hillman, 'cause I know he goin' to be mad as a hornet."

Burke raised his hand.

"Nobody is going to force you to do anything."

Nelson licked his lips and cleared his throat again.

"But if you think it goin' to help Fanny." He nodded once. "I do it!"

Saturday morning I sat at the kitchen table while Addie broke eggs into a clear bowl. I read the article describing how I'd found the silver in the Hillman graveyard buried by Silas Jackson and Fanny. The article went on to say Big Jeb had established a connection between the labor unions and Fanny and that she was working for them.

"What you doin' up so early?"

"Just woke up and felt restless," I muttered, letting the paper drop.

"I bet you ain't restless enough to clean up your room."

"It's clean."

"You make your bed?"

Addie glanced up.

"I didn't think so. You get your restless self up there and make your bed," she said, thumping into the pantry.

"It's made!"

Addie came back with a sack of oranges.

"If I climb up them stairs and your bed ain't made, you ain't goin' to be restless no more."

"Time is breakfast?"

"Same time it always is."

I slid off the stool and stood in the open back door. A breeze came across the dew-tipped lawn. I watched the trees sway slowly against the cold blue.

"Anybody call for me?"

Addie began feeding orange halves to the humming cone of the orange juice machine.

"No, who you 'spectin'?"

"No one, just thought somebody might have called."

Addie threw the pulpy oranges into the trash.

"Well, ain't nobody called and I tell you if they do while you makin' your bed."

I went upstairs and threw the sheets up, then mooned around Buckeye till Addie chased me out after breakfast. I picked up my bicycle from the yard and began pedaling down Hermitage Street. I pedaled fast, watching the tar run beneath me till I was almost to Clay's house. I looked up and Jimmy and Clay were on the sidewalk. I slowed to a stop.

Clay crossed into the street.

"Going to Willard's?"

I shrugged, squinting down the street, then at Jimmy as he became interested in something on the sidewalk.

"I got a lot of things to do."

"Alright, see you later then."

I watched them walk down the empty street and I heard Jimmy lying again in the courtroom.

"I would go, but I don't like the company!"

They kept walking.

"I SAID, I DON'T LIKE THE COMPANY, MASON!"

Jimmy wheeled around, his face red in the sun, his mouth open.

"NOT MY FAULT YOUR DADDY'S DEFENDING SOME LABOR UNION NIGGER!"

I let my bike drop and Jimmy tried to brace himself, but I cracked

285

into him and we went through a hedge. The bushes sprang back and I drove Jimmy's face into the warm yard grass.

"You're a goddamned liar!"

Jimmy rolled away with his hands on his face. I grabbed him by his white t-shirt and felt his shirt rip.

"YOU LYING—"

His fist blew the air out of me and I went to my knees gasping. Clay knelt down next to me.

"You o.k., Lee?"

I just kept holding my stomach, looking at the grass blades.

"That's what you get for starting fights," Jimmy said somewhere over me.

There were red marks on his face and arms and he was trying to piece his shirt together. I managed to get some air in my lungs.

"Everyone is going to know you ... lied." Jimmy kept piecing his shirt together as I struggled to my feet. "Nelson ... was ... there."

Jimmy looked at me.

"You're lying."

"He's going to testify on Monday ... you *asshole!"*

I smiled, still holding the pain in my stomach and now Jimmy looked like he got punched in the stomach. I went back to the street and slowly pedaled home with Jimmy staring after me. When I reached Buckeye he was still there in the middle of the street.

There was only a dull ache when I breathed. Buckeye was quiet with the stillness the hot part of the day brought. I wandered to the backyard and saw Nelson's yellow hat bobbing up and down among the red-spotted vines. He sat up on his knees.

"They needs lots of work," he said, picking up a blue tin watering can and darkening the dirt. "Mistah Hartwell's tomatoes is gettin' cooked by this old August sun."

"Time to pick 'em?"

Nelson wiped his brow.

"No, they ain't quite ready. Mr. Hartwell, he says, 'Nelson you know just when to pick the tomatoes, 'cause we have the best tomatoes in Richmond,' and he ask me how I know when to pick 'em." Nelson smiled suddenly. "I say, 'when the late August rain come, then I pick 'em'. Yes sir, just after the rains."

He bent over another vine and started working his spade.

"When do the rains come?"

"Comin' soon."

I listened to the spade sliding.

"How you know it's the August rains and not just some storm?"

"'Cause they the first storms of the season change, an' they come at the end of the days, an' always after the hottest days."

The back door slammed and Fanny walked out with the wash in a wicker basket. She had on a loose white shirt and a blue scarf tied up in her hair. Nelson's spade moved quicker in the garden as she set the basket down.

"That old Nelson down there in the dirt?"

Nelson kept on working. Fanny looked out at the yard, then at me.

"What's he doin' down there?"

"I's tendin' the garden," he said with a sharpness I hadn't heard before.

Fanny shaded her eyes and moved some dirt around with her shoe.

"Hear you testifyin'."

Nelson's spade hit a small rock. He brushed dirt away from one of the vines, then started digging again. Fanny bent over and picked up the clothes basket. She looked down at Nelson for a moment.

"Just wanted to thank you."

Nelson stayed bent over the dirt, a dark line of sweat down the middle of his shirt. Fanny hesitated, then walked down into the yard to the clotheslines. Nelson's spade clinked against a rock.

Blackbirds crossed the horizon, dipping through the lines connecting the telephone poles on Hermitage Street. Burke leaned back on the swing, the glow of his cigarette hovering between his fingers as he considered my question.

"It takes a lot for Nelson to say he is going to testify. He's never gone against a white man before and now he's going against one of the most powerful men in the state." He paused. "I think Nelson has always looked out for Fanny, but I'm not sure he's approved of her much lately."

I watched Addie pass by the window.

"How come?"

"Fanny is too outspoken for Nelson. I'm sure he thinks that's what got her in all this trouble in the first place."

A car passed through the twilight with a low roar that faded to nothing. Burke leaned back and smiled.

"It's nice during this time. I can feel the evenings."

I nodded, watching the first stars emerge over the houses across the street.

"You think Fanny will get off now, Daddy?"

"I think she'll be found not guilty if the jury believes Nelson." He moved the swing with his foot just enough to make it wobble. "Do you talk to Careen Hillman anymore?"

"Nope."

Burke nodded slowly.

"Well, I'm sorry. She'll be as pretty as her mother was one day."

"You remember her mother?"

"Oh yes, she was a very refined lady."

"Careen talked about her a lot."

"Very cultured."

I paused, seeing something white moving across the lawn. The rabbit stopped.

"Remember the day she died?"

Burke nodded slowly.

"I do."

"I guess Careen was home that day from school," I said, hearing Anna say it again. "You know that pantry Fanny cleaned the silver in?"

"Yes."

"I was over at the Hillmans' and Anna told me Careen's never gone near the pantry since her mother died."

Burke nodded slowly.

"Did she say why?"

"No, just she won't go near it."

Burke pursed his lips and rocked his body enough for acknowledgment. I turned back to look for the rabbit, but it had vanished.

It was past midnight when symbols of glass shattered in my dreams. I opened my eyes. The white curtains breezed in before a short, muffled *"woof!"* lit the yard with a *"whoooooosssssh!"* that painted yellow on the walls of my bedroom. I jumped up, seeing a spitting blaze of yellow fire making the grass and trees pale. I ran into the hallway.

"THE BARN'S ON FIRE!"

Lucas was out of his room in his t-shirt and pants going down the back stairs three steps at a time. I ran after him and somehow got through the dark kitchen to the outside, following his white t-shirt to the roaring pyre. It was daylight in the backyard. Crackling wood exploded against the howl of the blaze. Lucas held his hand up against the heat. The barn doors lay smoldering on the ground and inside the barn were layers of flame. I came up next to him with the sear on my face.

"NELSON!"

Lucas yelled again.

"NELSON!"

The fire was so hot I couldn't look at it and turned to the side of the yard. There was a smoldering figure walking out of the trees. I tried to say something, but no sound came out of my mouth. I grabbed Lucas's arm and pointed to the smoky man coming closer. The man was coated in white soot with only his pants and suspenders on. Burn holes in his pants were still smoldering.

Lucas grabbed Nelson by the arm.

"Are you alright?"

He shook his head up and down, his eyes watering, leaning on Lucas. We backed away from the fire as my parents came into the yard with Addie and Fanny.

"Nelson!" Burke called.

Nelson shook his head and licked his lips, speaking for the first time.

"I still here, Mistah Hartwell" he croaked, leaning against Fanny.

My father reached out and Nelson put his hand up.

289

"Let me just make sure you're all there," he said, holding Nelson's arm and hand.

He smiled, showing his few teeth.

"I all here, Mistah Hartwell. Not by much, but I here."

Addie hugged Nelson, tears shining on her cheeks.

"We thought you done burnt up, you old nigger."

"Do you know what happened, Nelson?"

He shook his head and moved his long feet in the grass.

"Don't know, Mistah Hartwell. I was sleepin', an' next thing I hear is voices outside the barn, an' they sayin', 'This what happens to niggers goes against white men,' an' I got up and put on my pants to go out the back window ... I think maybe I can get in the woods." Nelson shook his head, his face shiny wet. "Then I hears somethin' come in the barn, an' then just feel somethin' hot an' I knocked out the back window' an' everythin' blow up an' I was in the woods. I run in the woods till I hear Lucas an' come back."

Burke didn't have on his dark glasses and his eyes were colorless and vacant.

"How could anyone know you were going to testify?"

"Don't know, Mistah Hartwell—didn't tell nobody."

The licking fire sounded like someone rolling logs on the street. Fire truck sirens were in the distance.

"Let's get everyone up to the house, before something else happens," Mother said, moving with Nelson toward the house.

Lucas stood next to my father, staring at the licking flames.

"Buddy Hillman sent them—you can be sure of that."

Burke pulled his robe sash absently and shook his head.

"I don't know how he would have known."

The crackling heat was on my cheeks and Jimmy's red face was in the flames and he was laughing. I bent over the grass. The world swam from under me and I gagged. Then my father's hand was on my back and the fire was blurry and long.

"I told Jimmy," I burst out. "I'm sorry, Daddy ... I told Jimmy—"

Burke's white eyes were uncertain, but his hand wasn't. His checkered robe was against my face as I watched the barn collapse into a pile of exploding flames.

31

*The hogsheads ground the sand flat on the rolling roads.
Slaves guided the packed tobacco with their backs wet. The
brown barrels rumbled down to the river and were shipped.
The crop master stood apart from the planters and watched
the ships go down into the trees.*

"Fanny Jones!"
I sat next to Burke and watched her cross the floor to the
witness chair, remembering the stale, burnt-wood smell in the
air and Burke saying heavily in the amber light of his den that Nelson
couldn't testify. He wouldn't put Nelson's life in danger, and for him
to testify would do just that. I knew he was thinking of Silas Jackson
and couldn't accept someone else getting hurt. The fire bomb had done
its job.

Fanny and Burke spent hours in the den that night, then I sat up
with him. I sat in one of the high-backed chairs and listened to the
steady ticking of the clock that lulled me to sleep against the deep
upholstery. I woke in the pink morning. Burke was still in his chair and
his vacant eyes were unmoving. I wondered later if he had developed
the powers blind people are supposed to have. Maybe that allowed him
to see so clearly.

"I do," Fanny swore, holding up her hand.

She settled into her chair and the bailiff crossed a beam of light one way and Burke the other as I led him to her.

On Sunday I had seen another slanting beam of light in Mimaw's window. I had come upstairs to see her. She was the oldest. Buckeye was brooding and silent. The late afternoon sun passed through the translucent curtains on the landings as I climbed to her room. I had done nothing all day except wander around rooms, listening to the hot wind boom doors shut but never seeing it. "Just try and do the right thing sometime," Mimaw said with a small fist above the covers. "They'll kill you for it."

Burke stood in front of Fanny as he asked if she was in the pantry from two o'clock to three o'clock.

"Yes, sir," Fanny answered steadily, her chin barely dipping.

"Then you went to go help your aunt, Addie Jones?"

"Yes, sir."

Fanny sat rigid and straight like a soldier. Burke turned to the jury.

"You said you were asleep?"

Fanny's head dipped more and her neck moved as she swallowed.

"Did you always stay in the pantry from two o'clock to three on Tuesdays and Thursdays?"

She nodded and looked at the floor.

"Yes, sir."

"How old were you when you started staying in the pantry?"

"Fifteen."

My father was leaving the house with Lucas on Sunday. I was sitting on the porch.

"Lee—I'm going over to the hospital to get some records. When I come back, I want to talk to you."

"What are you looking for, Daddy?"

"I'll let you know if I find it."

Burke turned to Fanny.

"Is there anyone who saw you in the pantry from two o'clock to three o'clock on the day the silver disappeared?"

"Yes, sir."

Judge Clemmings dipped his head and cupped a hand to hear better.

"Who?"

Fanny was a statue again. Only her mouth moved and the words came mechanically.

"Mr. Hillman."

The room came alive. I turned to Mr. Hillman, but his face was smooth and unchanging.

"Mr. Hillman could confirm you were in the pantry from two to three o'clock?"

Fanny's head moved up and down once.

"Yes."

Big Jeb snorted and threw his pen down on his table. Burke paused, then turned to the judge.

"I have no further questions, your honor."

Big Jeb was almost running toward Fanny. He stood close to her with a strange grin on his face.

"Well, Fanny, this is the best story yet. First Mr. Hillman is burying the silver in his own wife's grave and now he visits you in pantries!" He walked away from the witness chair and shook his head. "Alright, Fanny, how could Mr. Hillman know you were asleep in the pantry?"

"He come to see me."

He leaned forward.

"What?"

"He come to see me," she said steadily.

"To see you!"

"Yes, sir," Fanny nodded.

He walked up and leaned in close.

"You are saying Mr. Hillman just came in to see you?"

"Yes, sir," Fanny said, her back not touching the chair and her eyes straight ahead.

Burke's face was grim when he came back from the hospital on Sunday.

"Lee, we had better talk," he had said. "I think I might have one chance tomorrow to keep Fanny from going to jail." He held a yellow file in front of him.

"Why don't you admit you are lying?"

"Objection," Burke said, standing up.

"Sustained."

Big Jeb leaned back and walked away from the witness stand, then turned on her again.

"Why in the world would Mr. Hillman come into the pantry to see you?"

Fanny's eyes wandered out in the room, looking right through Big Jeb. She shook her head like she wanted to get rid of something. He walked forward.

"Why would Mr. Hillman come into the pantry while you were in there?"

Fanny put a hand up to her face and said something into her hand.

"I didn't hear that, Miss Jones."

Fanny looked up, her wet eyes sparkling with hate, but her voice cool like steel.

"So he could lay with me."

Her voice echoed off the back wall and Big Jeb didn't move.

The courtroom cracked quiet, then loud.

So he could lay with me like Jimmy and Jackie, except with smells of ammonia, cleaner, chemicals mingled with heavy breath in the small room at the end of the kitchen.

Big Jeb took several steps back. Judge Clemmings' gavel banged on and on till the room quieted. Big Jeb stood directly in front of Fanny with a blank look on his face.

"YOU ARE ACCUSING MR. HILLMAN OF HAVING RELATIONS WITH YOU?"

Fanny sat unmoving in the echo of Big Jeb's voice.

"Please answer the question, Miss Jones," Judge Clemmings said, watching the courtroom closely.

Fanny's eyes stayed on Big Jeb, her head moving before she spoke. "Yes."

The courtroom came apart again. I looked at Burke, but saw none of the surprise on his face I was feeling. Big Jeb looked like he wasn't quite sure how to proceed. Judge Clemmings banged away at the courtroom noise till almost all of it was his.

"Miss Jones—this is the most preposterous lie you have come up with yet!" He stopped, staring at her like she was some kind of animal. "And how long have these *alleged relations* been going on?"

Fanny was like a statue.

"Miss Jones, please answer the question," Judge Clemmings said, leaning toward her.

"Three years."

The courtroom was talking again. Big Jeb looked at her slack-jawed. Mr. Hillman whispered something to a man seated next to him. Judge Clemmings banged his gavel.

Big Jeb was animated now.

"I'm afraid to ask you any more questions, the story gets wilder as we go!"

I looked at Burke. He was listening quietly. I remembered his rule about juries from long ago; they always believe the other lawyer when he brings out information from your witness.

Big Jeb stared at Fanny, then walked away from the stand and turned around.

"How much did the labor unions promise you to say this?"

"Objection," Burke said, still sitting.

Big Jeb stared and Fanny looked back evenly, looking more like herself than she had in months.

"I'm not going to dignify this ridiculous testimony with any further questions, your honor."

He walked back to his table and Judge Clemmings called a brief recess. The doors were opened for a cooling breeze to pass through the courtroom. Fanny sat quiet next to Burke. He patted her arm and people were talking in the courtroom, but no one was saying anything. I thought of the pantry and Fanny's feet touching a cold floor and Mr. Hillman on top of her.

The recess ended and the courtroom was full of people. Everyone was waiting when Judge Clemmings reentered. I was back in the den with my father.

"I'm going to have to do something, Lee, and I want you to know about it beforehand."

"You have a witness, Mr. Hartwell?"

"A subpoena has been issued."

295

He stood up in the courtroom and leaned forward as my stomach tightened.

"Who for, Daddy?"

"I call Careen Hillman to the stand."

I turned and watched Careen come down the middle aisle of the courtroom. Her white dress and gloves glowed against the dark wood. She must have come in during the recess. My throat was tight and my stomach a drum as I watched her sit and raise a gloved hand.

"Take me up to the witness chair, Lee."

I crossed the sunlit boards with my father to where Careen was staring straight ahead. I went back to the table and was far away. No one moved or coughed.

"Hello, Careen," Burke said in a gentle voice.

Careen tilted her head toward him.

"Mr. Hartwell."

He put a hand into his left coat pocket and paused for an instant.

"I'd like to go back to the day your mother died—"

Big Jeb was on his feet.

"Objection, your honor! This has no relevance to the case!"

Judge Clemmings' gray eyes were on Burke, then on the small blonde head to the left of him.

"I'll allow it for now."

Big Jeb sat down slowly.

"Fanny Jones was working for your family on the day your mother died. It was Tuesday, the ninth of September, 1944."

Her eyes were glassy and Big Jeb was out from behind his table.

"It is cruel and unheard of to put a young girl through this!"

"I'll watch closely, counselor."

Burke continued, "Careen, where was your mother on that day, do you remember?"

Her hand flitted under her eye.

"In her painting studio behind the house."

"On the ninth of September 1944, you went to school?"

"Yes sir."

"What happened at school, Careen?"

Her gaze fell and Burke took a step toward her.

"Was it a normal day?"

"It was a normal day ... except—" She looked down at her gloved hands. "I went home early."

"Why did you go home early, Careen?"

Burke's right hand slid down into his coat pocket.

"I was sick."

"And what time did you get sick, Careen, and leave school?"

... there's a mist....

"I don't quite remember."

"Your honor, this is ridiculous, I—"

"I'll decide what is ridiculous in my courtroom, counselor."

Burke turned to her with the chain of his pocket watch glinting.

"It was a long time ago, Careen—was it before or after lunch?"

Careen stared at the back wall.

"It was after lunch," she said slowly.

"Do you remember how you got home, Careen?"

Careen shook her head.

"I don't remember."

"Did someone give you a ride?"

"Wait ... Mrs. Merriam took me home I think."

"Mrs. Merriam took you home and dropped you off at the house," Burke repeated, standing close to her. "Did you go in the front of the house or the back?"

Careen's gaze faltered.

"I, I can't really remember," she said, shaking her head again. "I think ... no, maybe I went in the back."

"Why would you go to the back door? Was the front door locked?"

"No...." She paused. "No, mother liked me to use the back door."

I was aware of Mr. Hillman moving and talking to a man next to him. The man leaned forward and said something to Big Jeb. He stood up.

"Your honor, I must request this be stopped. I have been told that Careen Hillman has been under a doctor's care and bringing her mother's death up could cause a nervous collapse."

Judge Clemmings let out a loud breath and looked at Careen.

"I will take that into consideration and watch the witness closely."

"Your honor, I—"

"That will be all, counselor."

I looked at Mr. Hillman again and his eyes had come alive.

"So you went in the back, Careen. Where does the back door lead?"

"The kitchen."

The man leaned up again and Big Jeb's chair scuffed loudly.

"I request an immediate recess!"

"Sit down or I will hold you in contempt!"

Big Jeb sat down slowly, his face red and shiny.

Careen's eyes stayed on Burke.

"Was anyone in the kitchen?"

She shook her head.

"I don't think so—"

"You were in the kitchen and what did you do, Careen?"

Tears came from her eyes and she put a hand to her face.

Big Jeb was on his feet again.

"This is barbaric!"

"Mr. Hartwell, I'm afraid this questioning is going to have to stop, unless—"

"No!"

Burke turned to her and Big Jeb was in the middle of the courtroom.

"OBJECTION!"

"Quiet!" Judge Clemmings commanded.

"I won't tolerate this anymore!"

Mr. Hillman was on his feet. His face was red and he pointed at Judge Clemmings.

"I demand this be stopped!"

Judge Clemmings stared at him for a moment and I thought for a moment he was going to obey. Then his voice crashed down.

"Sit down, Mr. Hillman!"

"YOU CAN'T DO THIS TO MY DAUGHTER!"

The judge stood up.

"SIT DOWN, MR. HILLMAN!"

Burke was still by the witness stand.

"What happened, Careen?"

"There's a noise," she sobbed.

"Where did you hear a noise?"

"STOP THIS!" Mr. Hillman roared.

"You are in contempt of this court, sir!"

Careen grabbed her head.

"Where, Careen?"

She had her hands on her ears and she shut her eyes.

"In the pantry!"

Mr. Hillman and Big Jeb were in the middle of the courtroom and Judge Clemmings was on his feet, but nobody moved.

"And you went to the pantry and opened the door and what did you see, Careen?"

"Oh...." She was choking. Tears streamed down her face. She was staring at her father. *"Daddy...."*

"Who did you see?"

Mr. Hillman held his hand out.

"Careen—"

"Who, Careen?"

"Daddy what are you doing?"

"Who is in the pantry, Careen?"

She stood up suddenly and raised her arm across the room and pointed directly at our table.

"DADDY—IS—ON—TOP—OF—HER!"

Burke put his hand on her arm in the absolute quiet that followed.

"And then you went and told your mother down where she painted, didn't you, Careen?"

"Mother...." she whispered, crumpling slowly back to the chair till she was crying on the rail.

32

The snow lined the rows of the fields. Slaves looked out from the cabins curling gray to the sky. Spirit voices sang from inside their doors and died in the fast wind. The crop master walked through their voices with his stick leaving tunnel holes in the snow behind him. Then he was gone. And soon the holes were gone too.

The rest of the trial went fast. Burke and Big Jeb talked for a long time during a recess and the yellow file never came out of my father's briefcase. The bleeding suicide in the slave cabin was never examined—the suicide that found Mrs. Hillman's wrists cut down to the bone—too deep for the small razor found next to her. It was the suicide, Burke said later, that proved to him more than anything else Mr. Hillman had killed his wife. That case had been closed long ago, but Burke had to understand why he had done it. Mr. Hillman, who had averted disaster before by having Fanny's father lynched, did it again by nearly cutting off his wife's hands.

I sat for a long time during the recess, seeing the dimly lit pantry with Fanny lying on her back on an old couch with Mr. Hillman—seeing it as Careen must have seen it, the same scene being played out for years, behind the small doorway off a colorless kitchen. Somewhere in the corner of her mind there had been an uneasy yearning for the knowledge behind that doorway shut to the morning light. Maybe her mind was able to stay with her soul and leave her mother's grave still white like her dress on that first day in the woods. But the truth was there—like the glimpse of something that is gone when looked at directly—till one day the mind is quicker than the eye.

The courtroom filled again. Mr. Hillman and Careen were gone. The closing statements sounded hollow to me. Burke's summation was brief and I remember the jury was gone for a very short time. Then the verdict came in and Fanny hugged my father. She was crying and laughing at the same time. Burke smiled, but he was pale and his hands trembled as he picked up his papers. Burkie and Lucas came up and Big Jeb stood by his table and let us pass into the aisle. He kept his head down and clutched his briefcase by his side as my father passed.

The August rains came the next week with long downpours that swept twigs and acorns from gutters and made a hollow tinny sound in the drainpipes. I sat on the sleeping porch and read about Senator Herrin's reelection. The paper was damp and the pages stuck together as I looked for articles on the trial. I was sure Mr. Hillman had been able to keep that courtroom scene from making print. He had been able to keep the details of his wife's death a secret for years, known only to the hospital and possibly the police, and I didn't doubt his ability to control the papers now. There had been only a small article after the trial saying Fanny was found not guilty. I pasted it on the last page of my scrapbook.

Burke had to stay in bed. Dr. Williams said it was exhaustion and was worried about his heart. I read to him a lot during the last weeks of August. His chest was small and white above his red pajamas. It rained hard, sizzling in the window while I sat on the end of his bed, struggling through Shakespeare, Keats, and Conrad. He listened, nodding every now and then, many times asleep before I left the room.

At some point I was accepted to Woodbury Forest. I had finally decided to go away to school. I'm not exactly sure why I changed my mind. Maybe it was the feeling that the summer had ended with the first cool days and the new quiet of the neighborhood.

Scotty came back the week before I was to leave. The Nettletons had finally gotten his body and were having a burial service. Burke went to the service in a wheelchair. He said that he didn't need the wheelchair, but it was the only way Dr. Williams would allow him to go. My father didn't leave his bedroom again.

The week went by with my preparations for school and then it was the day before I was to leave. I wandered around Buckeye and took out the tobacco stick with the piece of tin nailed on the end. It had been sitting in a dark corner of my closet since we returned from Sparta. I carried it outside into the steamy grass of the backyard with the tin flashing in the sun as I swung it over my head. I walked toward the trees and the black charred wood of the barn. The walls had collapsed and the barn was just the burned wood of a large bonfire. I flipped several pieces of wood in the air with the tin stirring up the ash. I flipped another stick and saw something red. I scooped out the floating ash and there was a wagon wheel from an old wagon Nelson used to haul his garden tools in. It was black and the rubber was melted on one side.

The sun was in the top of the woods and only half on the lawn. I picked up the wheel and rolled it out of the shade and hit it with the stick. The wheel hop-jumped and I cracked it again with the twanging tin and it went up into the air and rolled. I ran across the hot grass with the wheel running away from me until I hit the wheel so hard it shot across the yard and disappeared in the woods.

I left the wagon wheel and followed the narrow, packed-dirt trail. There was the tree with boards nailed on. Up in the cradle of the tree the wood was dark from rain and some of the boards had pulled away from the nails. A twig fell onto the plywood roof and somersaulted down next to me on the path. I stared at the summer passed.

I continued down the dark line into the woods. I turned off the path when I saw the black iron poking through the trees. Brown leaves lay on top of the Hillman stone. Mrs. Hillman's grave was in shadow, but then it was white and Careen was putting flowers on it. I was watching

302

in the vines and Jimmy and Clay were hitting each other to get a better look.

The sun left the way a movie house darkens and the grass was dull and the stones gray. I gripped the black iron and shook it till the gate clanged and clanged.

Nelson's yellow hat hovered just below the vines as I came out of the woods. I walked up and sat down in the grass with the stick next to me. Nelson pulled a fat red tomato off the vine and put it in the straw-colored basket.

"Rains came?"

Nelson leaned back on his haunches.

"They surely did, an' now these tomatoes is perfect for pickin', an' I think they goin' to help Mistah Hartwell feel bettah."

"Look pretty ripe."

Nelson looked at me.

"You leavin' tomorrow for school?"

I nodded and put a blade of grass in my mouth.

"You an' Fanny both leavin'—ain't goin' to be the same 'round here."

"Where's Fanny going?"

"North. She goin' up there to work." He licked his lips. "Might be best thing for old Fanny." His eyes came to me. "Richmond too small for her now."

I nodded slowly and Nelson's head was back in the vines.

"But it ain't goin' to be the same without you 'round."

"I'll be back. Semesters don't last long," I said, wondering how long a semester did run.

"I won't worry then," Nelson said reaching for a fat tomato on his knees. "Long as you comin' back."

I saw Dr. Williams' dusty Buick in the drive. He came down from my father's room with his eyes hard and his creased leather bag low by his side. He talked to Mother in the living room, pulling on his iron-gray beard. He nodded once, then left.

Dinner was quiet. Burke's chair stayed empty and Mother kept her eyes on the table. After dinner I went out and sat on the porch swing and pushed it slowly, running my fingers up and down the chain links. The door opened and Lucas came out. He nodded, leaning against a porch column, pulling a cigarette from his top pocket. The match hissed yellow into the lawn.

"Daddy's real sick, Lee."

I stopped the swing with my foot.

"Dr. Williams says his blood pressure is way too high."

His cigarette flared orange.

"I think that damn trial took the life right out of him," he muttered with his face in the shadows. He turned from the lawn."Looks like you're going to be the one to go to college."

"Burkie's in college."

"He quit—took a job with Parsons' construction company."

Lucas was quiet, then he laughed.

"Maybe I'll go back someday."

He flicked his cigarette to the lawn, then hobbled across the porch with his cane.

"Don't get too smart on us, Lee."

"I won't."

The screen door slammed behind him. I looked out to the lawn where a single white curl of smoke drifted away.

I wandered into the living room and saw the yellow light on in my father's study. I looked in, hoping to see him at his desk, but I knew he wouldn't be. There was the same smell of pulpy old books and stale tobacco. The clock ticked in the quiet. I walked in and stood in front of the desk, running my hand along the top of the smooth wood, feeling the graininess that had come through the finish. I went behind the desk and pulled the swivel chair back.

I sat with the two dark armchairs facing me. A sliver of paper stuck out from under his legal pad. I pulled on it and held up a dirty envelope and turned it around slowly, seeing Silas Jackson's dark hand pulling it out of his coat and handing it to my father in the car. I listened for footsteps, then flipped open the envelope and took out a letter that was badly creased.

To All Foremen:

Effective Saturday, December 31, the day wages will be reduced to one dollar per working day. When we start working ten hours again, the wages will be twelve and a half cents per hour. No one regrets more than I the necessity of making this reduction, but even this wage is twenty-five to fifty cents more than the average farm wage....

I skipped down to the bottom, to the blue-ink signature of Senator J. Herrin. I folded the letter and put it into the envelope and back under the legal pad. I stood up and saw a black book on the corner of the desk with "Burke Andrew Hartwell" embossed in gold across the front. There were paper markers in places where he had used quotes in his Bible class. I opened the first page to black handwriting.

Presented with heartfelt gratitude to our teacher,
Burke Andrew Hartwell,
whose masterful interpretations of the Bible
are a liberal education.
From the St. Thomas Episcopal Men's Bible Class
December 25, 1937

I closed the Bible and put it down next to the letter on his desk and turned off the lamp. I crossed the hallway into the dining room and pushed open the swinging door into the kitchen. Addie glanced up from the table.

"There you is. I just goin' to call you to take up some tomatoes to your father." Addie lifted a tray with a plate of freshly sliced tomatoes on it. "Don't spill any o' these now," she said, wiping the corners of her eyes with her fingers. "Take Miz Mimaw her cup of coffee, too." She put the coffee on the tray and her wet brown eyes didn't look away. "I's worried 'bout your father," she said, looking sadder than I'd ever seen her. She dabbed her eyes with her apron. "I hope the Lord takes care of Mistah Hartwell." She crossed heavily to the stove. "Things just goin' too fast 'round here. You is off to school tomorrow, an' Fanny leavin', an' Mistah Hartwell so sick," she said, stirring the spoon in the pot on the stove.

I noticed the flecks of silver in her grizzled hair up under the cloth. Wrinkles pulled at the corner of her eyes and her body didn't seem as big and comforting.

"I'll be back ... school isn't that long."

Addie dabbed her eyes, walking back to the stove.

"Just don't come back too damn soon—just when I done got rid of you—now take them tomatoes up to your daddy an' don't be spillin' 'em!"

I went all the way up to Mimaw's room and gave her the coffee. She was knitting, her room dark except for her bedside light. I picked up the tray of tomatoes off the foot of her bed.

"Taking those to Burke?"

I nodded. Mimaw touched a tissue to her nose, her gaze faltering. She looked down and moved her needles faster.

"You better get them to him, Lee."

I shut the door quietly and went down the steps. I passed my room, seeing the suitcases at the foot of the bed with the tobacco stick on top. I crossed to my father's room and knocked on the door. There was no sound and I pushed the door open slowly. A shadowy twilight was in the room and there were only dark shapes against the autumnal pale. The large bed emerged from the light.

"Daddy?" I whispered.

He moved his head as I walked into the darkened room.

"Brought you some tomatoes."

He coughed and sat up.

"Thank you," he said weakly.

I came over to the bed and held the plate. His face was pale against the backboard.

"Nelson just picked these today, Daddy."

He smiled and turned his head toward me.

"Put them here, Lee," he said, motioning to the table next to the bed. "Sit down, son."

I sat gently on the edge of the bed.

"What time is it?"

"About eight."

"Must have slipped off to sleep after that dinner your mother served me."

He felt the covers with his hands, smoothing them.

"So, you're off tomorrow."

"Yes, sir."

"Woodbury is a good school—it was when I went there all those years ago," he said smiling, then he winced. I stood up.

"You alright, Daddy?"

He nodded and took a deep breath.

"Yes ... I'm fine."

I sat back down on the bed.

"Does it hurt a lot?"

"Sometimes," he said after a moment.

He was quiet and I heard a dog barking far down the street.

"You've seen a lot of things, Lee," he said slowly. "I hope you don't judge people too harshly because of it." He turned his face to me. "People are capable of bad things, but very good things too."

I looked at the floor and nodded.

He smiled.

"I know right now that might be hard for you to believe." He coughed several times and then settled back into the pillows. "I'm tired son, but I did want to speak to you before you left."

I looked down at my sneakers quickly and moved my toes against the hole in the tip of them. The shoes became fuzzy. My father held his arms out from the covers and I was hugging his pajama shirt and his small body. He just patted my back while I cried on his shirt.

"That's alright son," he said. "I'll always love you very much."

I nodded, wiping my eyes.

"Try to help your mother when you can."

Tears dropped off my face in little spots on the light bedspread.

"Now, let's have some of those tomatoes, Lee."

I handed him the plate and he felt for the edges, but his fingers trembled as he set it on the bed. He felt for the fork and then dropped it.

"I seem to be losing my coordination," he said in a low voice.

I slipped my hand into his and he grabbed onto it tightly. His grip was strong and then it grew steadily softer.

"Let me do it, Daddy," I whispered.

I sat down on the bed and picked up one of the tomato slices with the fork. I fed it to him, still holding his hand in mine. My father nodded and chewed the tomato slowly. I fed him another slice.

"Oh God, Lee," he said, shaking his head with his vacant eyes to me. "I do love the taste of fresh tomatoes."

His hand squeezed mine very tightly.

"I know you do, Daddy."

I fed my father that whole plate of tomatoes before the dusk.